PRAISE FOR PARTY PLANNING CAN BE MURDER: ADDY WINTERS BOOK ONE

"A marvel of a book—original, funny, suspenseful, and with a murder mystery at its heart. The characters are so real, you will want to drive to their houses and demand to hang out with them. I've read this book twice now, and I'm thinking of reading it once again tomorrow. It's a master class in writing a book that is wonderfully unique."

— **MADDIE DAWSON, AUTHOR OF** *LET'S PRETEND THIS WILL WORK*

"Darkly hilarious and utterly unputdownable, *Party Planning Can Be Murder* delivers a fresh, sharp-witted mystery with a twist no one saw coming. Addy Winters is a firecracker of a protagonist—equal parts savvy, stubborn, and snarky—as she juggles party planning, nosy small-town drama, and a suspiciously premature death. The banter crackles, the mystery keeps you guessing, and the sizzling chemistry with Leno's broodingly handsome brother? Chef's kiss. If you love a mystery that's as clever as it is thrilling, with a side of humor and heart, clear your schedule—this one's a must-read! 5 Stars!!!

— **JENNIFER MOORMAN, BESTSELLING AUTHOR OF** *THE VANISHING OF JOSEPHINE REYNOLDS*

"With an indelible protagonist, vivid cast of suspects, and humor galore, *Party Planning Can Be Murder* is pure cozy fun."

"PARTY PLANNING CAN BE MURDER is a charming, hilarious mystery with tons of heart. It's a great read for fans of THE THURSDAY MURDER CLUB."

"Humor sets the stage in this wonderful new page turner about Addy, an event planner in a small town and the mystery she is compelled to solve when a rock star who hires her to execute his final bash dies unexpectedly. *Party Planning Can Be Murder* is mysteriously great fun."

ALSO BY KERRY SCHAFER & KERRY ANNE KING

A PARTY TO DIE FOR

KERRY SCHAFER
KERRY ANNE KING

WRITE AT THE EDGE

Copyright © 2025 by Kerry Schafer

Published by Write at the Edge publishing, Colville, Washington

Book cover design by Steven Novak

Paperback ISBN 979-8-9922807-7-7

For my Viking, always and forever.

A PARTY TO DIE FOR

SATURDAY
DECEMBER 21

CHAPTER 1

"PLEASE HELP ME. I'm dying and I need... Oh God, I can't do this."

The woman's voice on the recording is panicked, half-strangled, as if she can't catch her breath. There's the sound of a suppressed sob, and then—nothing. Message ended.

Britt stares at me, wide-eyed, across the table. "Play it again," she says.

I do, turning up the volume, both of us crowding the phone to try to hear over the noise of the café, hoping we somehow got it wrong.

"That's not good," Britt says.

"You think?"

It's her fault that I didn't pick up in the first place. I always answer my calls, even when they're from unknown numbers. Sure, sometimes I have to brush off telemarketers, but about half the time I get to chat with a new client wanting me to plan a party or a wedding or some other event.

Today I didn't pick up, and now there are consequences.

In Britt's defense, it's Saturday morning, the week before Christmas. When the call came in, we were luxuriating in late morning coffee at *Grounded,* Fox Valley's one and only café. Or at least, *I* was luxuriating in coffee—my signature frozen caramel macchiato, never mind that it's twenty degrees outside and blowing snow. Britt, as usual, was drinking green tea, hot, no sugar. Not so much as a dollop of honey to add a little sweetness.

"Besides all of that sugar forcing your poor little cells to exist in an acidic environment, aren't you already freezing? We're in the middle of a blizzard," Britt said, just before the phone rang. She shivered, snuggling deeper into her oversized sweater.

"Maybe if you added sugar to your tea, your poor little cells would grow some fat around themselves and not be shivering their way into hypothermia. Besides, who wants to live to be old if you're forced to subsist on twigs and seeds and bitter green water anyway?"

And that's when the phone started up, playing Toyah's *It's a Mystery* in a key and tempo that clashed horribly with the rendition of *Jingle Bells* blasting out of the speakers.

"God, you do pick the most bizarre ringtones," Britt said. "Send it to voicemail. Rapido."

She grabbed my phone and turned off the ringer.

"That's my new client ringtone," I objected. "I need to get that."

"It's not your new client ringtone, it's your unknown caller ringtone. Whoever it is can leave a message. We're planning a party for ourselves for once."

She had a point. I'm moving into my new condo tomorrow, and three days after that it's Christmas, so we're planning a housewarming-slash-Christmas party to celebrate. Which is pushing it. It means I'll actually have to unpack right away instead of dragging the process out over the course of a year like I did when I moved into my first (and last) apartment. I've taken the week off work to move, get settled, and throw my own party, something that I'm finding unreasonably stressful. I like planning parties for other people. For myself, not so much.

All of this led to Britt grabbing my phone, and me letting her, and the call going to voicemail.

Fortunately, I'm afflicted with the sort of curiosity that supposedly kills cats (my cat Bruno, while certainly curious, appears to be immune to danger). What if this call is from a total dream client and they go looking for another planner? What if I magically won a million dollars without playing the lottery, or a secret wealthy uncle died and left me his entire estate?

So obviously I have to listen to the message and now here we are, bent over my phone so we can both hear over the clamor of voices competing with an absolutely awful cover of *Last Christmas*, performed by some pseudo rap group. It's my least favorite seasonal song to begin with, and this is the worst version of it ever, especially paired with the message on my voicemail.

"Please help me. I'm dying and I need... Oh God, I can't do this." The ragged breath. The sob. And then, the nothing.

"Call her back," Britt says.

I feel like one of those tiny little flies trapped in amber, unable to move. All of my logic and motion circuits have gone offline. My heart is attempting a new world record for speed.

Britt, a doctor's daughter who grew up in a house where her father was always being called out on emergencies, grabs the phone and taps the call back option. Nobody answers. The phone rings and rings and finally goes to voicemail.

"This is Johanna. I can't imagine how I missed your call, but you know I'll call you back." Same voice that left the message, minus the breathlessness and panic.

"That's not good," Britt says, again.

"Do you think she's dead already? Maybe a murderer was actually in her house and she just dialed a random number and then we didn't help her." My mouth has figured out how to work again, although my brain is still mostly offline.

"If that were the case, surely she would have called 911. I'll do that now." Britt taps at the phone again, waits, then says, "Yes, hello. I got a voicemail from a woman who says she's dying and is asking for help. Can you send somebody to check on her?"

I drag my chair over next to her and press my head up against hers so I can hear too.

"This person's name and address please," a professional voice says.

"All I've got is a first name and a phone number."

The dispatcher takes the name and number, and then Britt supplies my name and cell number when asked.

She hangs up and sips meditatively at her tea. "How strange. I wonder how she came to call your number?"

I suck up a freezing mouthful of macchiato and feel a little bit better. A lick of whipped cream and a bite of my blueberry scone further aid my recovery. "I think what you mean is how terrifying and unsettling. Strange is like—when the internet password stops working for no reason. Or Bruno steals the neighbor's Playboy tie."

"No, that truly is terrifying. Really, Addy. Think. You're sure you don't know a Johanna? Why would a total stranger call you in the middle of some sort of crisis?"

"If I'd answered the call, maybe we'd know." This is totally snarky and probably not even fair. But my adrenaline rush has to go somewhere and Britt is the only person I can vent it on.

"Maybe we can find her address." Britt digs her laptop out of the backpack she always carries with her and starts tapping away at the keyboard. It only takes her a minute to locate our caller. I shouldn't be surprised.

Britt is all the things I am not. She's got a dancer's body, long and lean, wavy black hair cascading down to the middle of her back, big brown eyes, skin that looks sun-kissed winter and summer, and cheek bones to die for. Worse, this exterior, about as far as you can get from the stereotypical tech geek, houses a brain as sharp as her cheekbones.

Last year, when her dad got diagnosed with leukemia, Britt walked away from a high profile, six-figure salary position in Silicon Valley to come home and be nearer her parents. Now she has a remote, part-time gig that allows her to help her mother with housework and meals and with getting her dad to doctor's appointments and chemo. She's bored, although she'll never admit it, which is unfortunate for her but makes it easier for me to persuade her to set aside logic and caution and join me in my harebrained schemes.

"You're brilliant," I tell her now, reading the info on her

screen. "Every time I try reverse caller ID I get asked for a credit card and it all looks super sketchy."

Her expression goes blank, her go-to expression when she's trying to hide something, which raises questions about her reverse caller ID site. Despite being generally law-abiding, at least on the surface, Britt is not above a little computer hacking under the right circumstances.

"That address is like five minutes from here," I say. "We could—"

"No. We couldn't. I'm calling 911 back, in case they didn't find the address yet. And then we'll finish our breakfast and let the emergency responders do their job."

By the time she's done relaying information, I've packed up my own belongings, stacked our cups on a tray, and am on my feet.

"No, Addy. We're not doing that." Britt reaches for her cup.

I yank the tray out of her reach.

"Addy, we are not going to that woman's house!"

I head for the door, carrying tray and cup with me and dropping them off in the designated space. There's no need to look to see if Britt is following, because of course we are going to Johanna's house. She's right behind me when I open the door and step out into the swirling snow. She shivers, pulling up the hood of her parka.

"I don't see why we couldn't just let the police and EMTs do their jobs while we stay cozy and warm," she complains, but she still helps brush the snow off of Jezebel, my battered old harridan of a Crown Vic. "I also don't understand why you persist in driving this wreck when you could be driving the Maserati."

"Shh. She'll hear you. Plus, Hannibal isn't a snow car."

"Jezebel isn't a snow car, either. She's not an any season car. Also, she can't hear, doesn't have feelings, and won't be jealous if you drive the Maserati."

Which just proves that after years of explanations—and demonstrations—Britt still doesn't understand thing one about Jezebel. I pat the steering wheel to mollify her (the car, not Britt) before she (still Jezebel) gets her feelings hurt and decides to play dead.

"I love you and only you," I tell her, and when I turn the key I'm rewarded by a cough, a shudder, and then the asthmatic sound of a long-suffering engine that would like me to know it doesn't appreciate the cold.

"You didn't drive the Maserati in the summer, either," Britt says, shivering dramatically as she struggles with a recalcitrant seatbelt. "I bet Hannibal has seat warmers."

"How do we get there?" I ask.

Britt sighs and relays directions while I focus on navigating the snowy streets.

Once we turn onto Shady Grove Way the house is easy to locate. A police car and an ambulance are already parked in the second driveway on the left. Neighbors in snow boots and parkas are clumped together on the sidewalk across the street, staring and chattering.

I pull up to the curb and park, then wrestle open the door and brace myself against the wind and blowing snow. Someone in the little cluster of bystanders will surely know something, and by unspoken agreement, Britt and I walk over to join them.

"What's happening with Johanna?" I ask, as if I know the woman and have the right to an answer. "Is she all right?"

Animated faces instantly turn guarded. After a long,

uncomfortable silence and a complicated series of exchanged glances, an elderly woman with close cropped gray hair and skin two shades darker than Britt's takes one step forward. "I don't know whether you're reporters or some of those influencer people, but Johanna is none of your business."

A reedy, pale little man wearing a Santa hat steps up to stand beside her. He looks much more like the Grinch than St. Nick. He's beardless, snaggle-toothed, and there's not a pinch of fat anywhere on him. He takes a drag on a cigarette held between two nicotine-stained fingers, blows the smoke in our faces, and says, "You've never been here before even the once. So if you heard about this from one of them police scanners and you're here to sniff out a story, you can just sniff some place else."

"Johanna called me and asked for help," I protest, finding myself at a highly unusual loss for words.

Britt shifts her position a little to get out of the direct path of the smoke. "We're the ones who called 911," she says. "We wanted to make sure she was okay."

"What would she call you for?" the spokeswoman demands.

I consider a story, something like 'I'm Johanna's niece from out of town,' but probably they will have seen pictures of all of Johanna's relatives. They'll know her family members' names and where they live and what they do for a living. I judge this to be one of those occasions where it's best to go with the truth.

"Honestly? I have no idea. Wrong number?"

"There, you see? You didn't even talk to her," Mutant Santa says.

"She left me a voicemail that said she was dying and asked for help."

Again, a complex exchange of coded glances.

A young woman balancing a toddler on one hip adjusts a woolen hat down over the kid's forehead. "If Johanna is dead in there they'll have to knock down a wall to get her out."

"Reckon they'll bring her out through the door like anybody else," Mutant Santa says.

The kid, now half blinded by the hat, squirms in her mother's arms and pulls it off, flinging it into the snow.

"Ashley, I swear to God." The young mother fishes the hat out of the snow and tries, unsuccessfully, to brush it off. "You ever seen Johanna come in or out of that house? Only reason for somebody never leaving the house is she's too big to walk through the door. Like that show *Supersized*. With the guy who weighed like a thousand pounds and couldn't get out of bed?"

She tugs the still snowy hat down over the kid's head, and the little girl starts to howl.

The spokeswoman raises her voice to be heard over the noise. "Johanna doesn't weigh a thousand pounds."

"How do you know, Serena? You ever seen her? Has anybody here ever seen her?"

"I have," Mutant Santa says. "We exchange books on the regular."

"Tell us another one, why doncha Ralph," a woman in a puffer jacket says. Between the jacket and a matching knitted hat and scarf, the only part of her that's visible is her eyes. "Like what, you just waltz into her house for coffee and cake and book club?"

"Well, not exactly. She stands in the door," Ralph says. "But I seen her. Talked to her yesterday."

"If Johanna wants to stay inside and keep to herself, that's her business," Serena says.

"Surely she must go out sometimes," I say, inspecting Johanna's house. There's a small gap between the curtains, where someone on the inside could peer out without being seen. Her sidewalks have been shoveled in the recent past. Christmas lights festoon the eaves and the neatly trimmed shrubs. A tall privacy fence conceals the back yard.

"How does she eat?" Britt asks. "Who shovels the snow? Who put up the lights?"

"Gets her groceries delivered," Serena says. "Once a week, on Mondays. She hired somebody to do the Christmas stuff. And she pays Nat from down the street to shovel snow and feed her birds in the backyard. She gets Amazon deliveries on the regular."

"Bet she's one of those hoarder types," Puffer Jacket says. "I watched that *Hoarders* show —some of those people let their dogs shit in the house, did you know? Surprised the ambulance people aren't wearing gas masks."

"She hasn't got a dog," Serena says.

"How do you know that?"

"You ever heard a dog in there? It would bark."

"Maybe she keeps it muzzled. Or, I know, she puts one of those bark shock collar things on it and zaps it whenever it tries to make noise."

"She has a cat," Mutant Santa says. "Black."

"Maybe she's a witch."

The door to the house opens and I brace myself for the sight of a woman being wheeled out on a stretcher—maybe with an oxygen mask and an IV. Maybe dead, with her face covered by a sheet. But there's no stretcher, and the emergency response people come sauntering out like they're just returning from brunch.

First out the door is a compact Black woman in police uniform. I know who she is—Officer Michelle McCarty—but only because I saw a write up in the Fox Valley Times. She's an import to town, so she hasn't got a clue who I am and there's no point trying to get information from her. The EMT who emerges next is another Fox Valley import. But the last one out is an old classmate, Perch. We're far from friends, but he's approachable, at least from a distance.

"Show's over, folks," Serena says. "Johanna's fine, or they'd have done something. You'll be leaving now." Obviously she's talking to me and Britt, not the neighbors.

But as far as I'm concerned, this is the opening act. Maybe Perch will be my backstage pass. I shuffle and slide through the snow after him, shouting, "Perch, wait up!"

He turns, puts his hands up to ward me off, and takes a step backward. "Whoa, Addy. Don't be mad."

Perch is six-foot-three and built like a linebacker. He's got a shaved head and skull-and-crossbones tattoos and I've always suspected there's a swastika etched into his skin somewhere. Him looking scared of little old me is every bit as unexpected as Johanna's voicemail, and it takes me a minute to figure out that he might think I blame him for the bar brawl he and Dad got mixed up in.

"It's not about Dad," I say. "He told me what happened."

"Wasn't sure he'd remember what happened and blame me," Perch says. "Alvin clocked him pretty good and then someone threw a chair. I'd have given him a ride to the ER but the chair hit me. I was out cold."

"Dad's fine. No hard feelings." Truth is, even if Perch had

beat up my father, I wouldn't be mad at him for it. There have been plenty of times in my life I've wanted to do it myself.

He slowly lowers his hands, but still looks wary. "So, if it's not your old man, what then?

"Johanna Meyers. She called me and said she was dying. Is she okay?"

His partner is brushing snow off the windshield. Perch glances at him, then back at me.

"So is she?" I ask. "Okay?"

Surely they wouldn't leave her there if she was dead or dying. But what do I know about dead-on-arrival procedures? Maybe Johanna has advance arrangements with *Ever After*, Fox Valley's one and only funeral home, and they'll come and get her. Maybe she refused treatment.

But the panic in that message didn't sound like someone who has been making funeral arrangements. It sounded like somebody in need of help.

"I can't tell you anything about her, Addy. You know that. Confidentiality."

"You gonna help out or what?" his partner shouts.

"Coming!" Perch holds up a hand to indicate his forthcoming compliance, then turns back to me. "Theoretically speaking, people are allowed to refuse treatment. But if someone was, say, unconscious, then we'd never leave them alone. Unless, of course, they had one of those death with dignity things like your boyfriend Leno had."

"He wasn't my boyfriend. And you've told me absolutely nothing I couldn't have figured out for myself. Either she's dead, or she's well enough to refuse treatment, or she's unconscious but the law says you can't interfere with her dying. Which is it?"

"Sorry, Addy. I gotta go."

He turns away and starts brushing snow off his side of the ambulance windows. I trudge back over to Britt. The bystanders have vanished, presumably all into their own houses, not one of them making a beeline to check on Johanna.

"That's weird, don't you think?" I ask.

"Which part? Some random lady calling you to say she's dying, Perch being scared of you, the creepy guy in the Santa hat? I mean, *why* would he wear that?"

"If the ambulance and the cops were at my mother's house, everybody within a ten block radius would be knocking at the door with one pretext or another, trying to find out what happened. Not one of these people have checked in on Johanna."

Britt frowns, surveying the deserted street. "Point. Same at my house. An ambulance came for Dad one time when he had a bleeding episode, and neighbors we'd never spoken to were in and out for the next three days trying to get the inside story."

"Exactly."

Decision made, I head up the sidewalk toward Johanna's house.

"I'm sure she's fine," Britt calls after me.

"Did she sound fine to you?"

"Well, no, but. Listen. Maybe she'd done this sort of thing before. Maybe she cries wolf all the time. Maybe she's a psychopath. Or a serial killer, even."

"You can wait in the car if you'd rather." Holding onto the snowy railing, I carefully make my way up the four slippery steps onto the front porch.

I ring the doorbell. Nobody answers so I use my knuckles,

already stinging from the cold, and rap three times. There's no answer. But I know Johanna is in there.

I knock again. Still nothing.

"Come on, let's go," Britt says, from the bottom of the steps.

But then I hear the sound of approaching footsteps. They stop on the other side of the door, and again there is silence.

"Johanna, it's me. Addy Winters," I call out.

"Go away."

"I want to make sure you're okay."

"Fine as I'm going to be."

Britt, who has climbed up beside me, tugs at my jacket sleeve. "Come on. Let's go."

I lean in closer to the door and raise my voice. "You left me a voicemail. You asked for my help."

There's the sound of a bolt sliding back. The door opens, only a crack, revealing a narrow strip of pale face and one hazel eye.

"You," she says, accusingly. "You're the reason the ambulance came. And the cops."

"You said you were dying," I retort. "What did you expect me to do?"

"Oh, damn it. It was that message, wasn't it? I hate voicemail," she says. "Never know what to say."

"I hate it too, but don't usually leave random strangers a message that says I'm dying."

"It wasn't exactly random. And I *am* dying." She bites her lip, then adjusts the crack in the door so she can see us better. "I called because I thought you might throw me one of those death parties. Like you did for that rockstar."

"Could we maybe come in and talk about it?" I ask.

14

Her eyes widen and the crack in the door narrows.

"Or you could come out. I usually meet my clients at *Grounded*."

She laughs, then, a rusty, awkward sound as if it's not something that happens often. "I don't come out," she says. "Surely they told you that, the neighbors? I haven't walked through this door in seventeen years."

CHAPTER 2

My curiosity is now at an all time high. If Johanna isn't coming out, then I'm definitely finding a way to get in.

"If you want me to throw a party, we're going to need to talk," I say to the one eye and the sliver of pale face still visible through the barely cracked open door. "How are we going to do that? I mean, I suppose we could zoom or phone but it would be awkward."

"Don't try to make me come out. I won't. Not until they carry me out of here. Dead." But the door opens infinitesimally wider. Progress.

"Understood. You don't want to come out in any case. It's cold. We're freezing our asses off."

A moment of silence.

"I don't suppose we could possibly come in? Britt over here is turning into a popsicle."

Another moment of hesitation, but then the door opens wider and she steps aside. I squeeze through the narrow opening, Britt hard on my heels. The instant we're through the door Johanna slams it shut and deadbolts it.

The neighbors were wrong. Johanna is certainly not too fat to leave her house. She's thin and fragile, her skin so pale I can see the tracery of blue veins in her cheeks, on the backs of her hands. Despite that, she's beautiful. Luminous green eyes, too large in her thin face, Angela Jolie lips, a dimple in her right cheek.

She is also not a hoarder.

The house is an open floor plan that looks like the love child of Martha Stewart and Architectural Digest. It's all high ceilings, tiled floors, and comfortable but stylish furniture organized around earth-toned squares of carpet. A floating staircase rises gracefully to an equally airy second floor, edged by a wooden railing. A built-in breakfast bar divides the kitchen from the living area.

Tasteful paintings and tapestries decorate the walls. Minimal window treatments invite in natural light, with the exception of the big living room window that looks out onto the street, which is concealed by a full panel of drapes. And yet, despite its airiness, the high ceilings, the light—the house feels suffocating and heavy, as if the air is thicker than it ought to be.

"What did they tell you, the neighbors?" Johanna inquires, gesturing us toward a grouping of furniture next to the fireplace, in which crackles a cozy fire. "That I'm a witch?"

"The conjecture is that you are either a hoarder or that you weigh six hundred pounds. Or both," I tell her. "Also yes, that you might be a witch."

Again the awkward, unpracticed laughter. "I'd wondered what they were thinking. Go ahead, have a seat."

I settle down onto the couch, Britt beside me. Johanna takes an overstuffed armchair, perched stiffly on the edge as if prepared to leap up at one wrongly chosen word or gesture. I wait for her to begin, looking around the room and taking in the polished mantlepiece adorned with an oversized ceramic nativity set. I'd bet a caramel macchiato that each piece has been uniquely crafted and glazed by hand and the set is easily worth a couple thousand bucks. The roughly tree shaped white object on the coffee table, on the other hand, looks like it came from the dollar store and bears as much resemblance to a real tree as powdered instant granules resemble real coffee.

Johanna's gaze must have followed mine because she smiles, softly, and says, "Tasteless, I suppose, but last year I attempted a full-size tree and the cat broke half the ornaments before he toppled it completely."

A black cat pads in right on cue, pausing to look us over with indifferent green eyes before leaping lightly into Johanna's lap. "By all means, make yourself at home," she says. He sits upright, staring at us unblinking, the tip of his tail barely twitching.

Johanna's thin hand alights on the cat's head, tentative, as if asking permission to touch him. "Funny thing. I don't even like cats. I love dogs, but it wouldn't be right to have a dog, since the poor thing would never get walks."

"Well, he's a beautiful cat," Britt says. "Not like some others I could mention."

Of course she means Bruno, my lug of a cat, who is beautiful only to me.

"What's his name?" I ask, not because I want to know so much as that it seems awkward to dive right into the important questions like, 'So when are you dying, and why, and what kind of party were you looking for after you're dead?'

"I call him Bagheera," Johanna says. "I don't know what he calls himself."

"Well, it's good that you have a cat," Britt says. "For company."

"Oh, he's not mine." Johanna skims her palm down the cat's back. "I imagine that he belongs to himself, though he probably has a home and another official name. He comes in to keep an eye on me. He kills birds in my backyard."

There's really nothing to say after that, so that is exactly what we say.

The cat sits and stares. Johanna strokes him.

After what seems like about a decade but is probably no more than a minute, I ask, "About this party. Can you tell me a little more about what you were thinking?"

"Oh, certainly. I apologize. I'm unused to conversation or company. Probably I should have offered you something. Tea, maybe?"

"I'm good," Britt says, a touch too rapidly. I hate the insipid stuff myself—tea is just hot water with delusions of grandeur—but Britt loves it. If she's turning down a cup of tea, it's because she doesn't trust Johanna not to poison us.

"We've just had coffee and breakfast," I say. "So, about the party?"

"Right. That. Well, here's the thing. As I mentioned, I am actually going to die. Soon. Sorry about this morning. I was all prepared to tell you calmly about my situation and what I want, and then the voicemail came on, and I just..."

"Panicked," I say, when she doesn't finish the sentence. "I'm not fond of voicemail myself. Well, I have put together a

19

few after-death parties. My fee depends on the scope of the event, number of guests, that sort of thing. Do you know what it is that you want?"

"What I want," she says, with a sudden ferocious intensity that makes the hair stand up on the back of my neck, "What I want are all the things I've been blocked from for years. I want this house filled with people and music and laughter. I want a Christmas party. Also, I want to be there. At the party."

Britt gives me a *here comes the crazy* look.

I clear my throat. "I'd thought we were planning this party for after you're, um, dead?"

"Of course, after. If I could manage a party now, I'd hardly need you, would I? I've planned out where my coffin should be. I'll show you in a minute. You could drape it with a garland and some of those battery operated Christmas lights. Guests can all pop in to say hello—or goodbye, I suppose—grab some food and a drink. Maybe sing some Christmas carols, don't you think?"

Britt gives me an 'I told you so' glance. Not without reason.

"Christmas is only four days away," I say, very gently. "And you are still very much alive. Were you thinking about... pretending to be dead, in the coffin?"

She smiles, but there's no joy in it.

"No, as I've told you, I will be very much dead in the coffin."

That's about it for me. Obviously this woman is not wrapped quite right. Time to extricate ourselves without setting her off by attacking her delusions.

"I'm terribly sorry," I say, getting to my feet. "But I need more time to plan a party. Particularly so close to Christmas. I have other clients and things to take care of—"

"I'll pay you enough to put the other things on hold," she

interrupts. "Also, you'll be giving away the house to one of the guests, which should be incentive for a good attendance."

"You want to give away the house," I repeat, feeling like I've fallen down a rabbit hole into an alternate reality. Which, I suppose, I have. Johanna's reality. Which is maybe not a world I want to hang out and throw a party in.

"Is that a problem?" she asks. "It seems straightforward to me."

"Probate of an estate can take years," I protest. "Even if you've written an actual person into the will. Giving your house to somebody whose name we draw out of a hat after you're dead is a whole new layer of legal complexity."

"Especially since you're not actually dead," Britt chimes in.

Johanna waves away this concern, as if it's a bothersome fly. "I will be dead. And I'll deed the house over to you before I die. And then you can give it to whomever you wish."

"Um, question?" Britt actually raises her hand, as if she's in school, and I recognize the tone as the one that used to get her sent to detention for making a teacher feel stupid. "What's to stop Addy from, you know—keeping the house? Or selling it and keeping the money? If you were actually dead. Which you're not."

Johanna leans toward me and lowers her voice as if sharing something in confidence. "Your friend secretly believes that I really am a witch. She's afraid I'll curse you. Or haunt you. Or, you know, both."

The cat flattens its ears and hisses at me, as if I'm the one at fault. A little chill runs up my spine and I remind myself that I don't believe in witches, and that I have no fear of the dead.

"Would you do that to me, Addy? Keep the house? I don't think you are a woman to break a promise," Johanna says.

"Of course I wouldn't. If I agreed to this plan in the first place. Which I don't. I'm sorry, Johanna, but this falls outside the scope of what I'm able to do as a party planner."

What I mean is that it's so far beyond the pale as to be insane. We need to get out of here. Then we need to call 911 again and request a mental health check.

Britt asks the question that I've been avoiding. "Are you... thinking about ending your own life?"

"Of course not. Why would I do that? I don't want to die. I've barely even lived." Her voice cracks and she pauses to take a deep breath and regain her composure. Then, she adds with great dignity, "If I must die—then I want to be certain that my last wishes are clear and carried out."

Britt is walking toward the door. Slowly. Like the videos say you're supposed to if there's a wild animal thinking about attacking you. Don't run. Don't show fear. I follow. If Johanna snaps and starts waving around a knife or a gun and we make a run for it, Britt already has a head start. She is definitely going to leave my clumsier, slower self in the proverbial dust.

Johanna doesn't show any signs of violence. "Look, I was going to offer you ten grand up front," she says, still in her chair with the cat in her lap. "But I do see that I'm not giving you very much time to put things together, so let's make it fifteen. Your costs should be moderate. The food doesn't need to be fancy. I've got an extensive sound system installed that will connect to Bluetooth, so no need to hire a band. I've already chosen my coffin and paid for it in advance. Ricky at *Ever After* will be expecting your call. He's promised to make sure I'm ready, and to deliver me for the party and then take me back again for burial."

I stop walking and turn back to look at her. She's so calm.

So matter of fact about all of this. So certain. Also, I don't know a lot about mental illness but aren't psychotic people supposed to be disorganized in their thinking? Johanna has planned everything.

"Addy," Britt says, from the safety of the door. "You're not actually considering this. Even if Johanna died today, you don't have time to put this thing together. You can't let her give you the house. Use your brain. There might be debts. A lien on the house."

"There are no debts," Johanna says. "And I own the house free and clear."

"No offense," Britt says, "but we only have your word for that."

"Easy enough to check, isn't it?"

I shake my head to clear it. Pinch my arm to ground myself back in reality. "I still don't understand. If you're not planning to end your own life, how do you know you're going to be dead in time for the party?"

"Indigo told me."

Here we go. Actual evidence of psychosis. She's hearing voices. My survival instinct kicks in way too late with some very good advice. *Don't ask questions. Run for the door and don't look back.*

"And Indigo is?" my mouth asks.

"Indigo is my online psychic."

"Of course she is," Britt says. "Addy. That's it. We're out." She opens the door and steps outside.

Johanna stops me from following with the three little words I'm never able to resist.

"I need you." Her voice breaks. Tears track silently down

her cheeks. "Please. You're the only one who can help me make this happen."

My heart turns over in my chest. Maybe she's crazy, but she's also frightened and sad and alone.

"Fine. I'll start working on your party," I hear my voice saying. "I need to go now, but if you could text me any favorite foods, favorite Christmas songs, that sort of thing. I'll get everything put together. Okay?"

"Wait. Let me write you a check."

"Leaving," Britt says.

I take a step toward the door. "You can pay me later."

"There won't be a later. I want to be sure you get paid. My check book is right here."

Britt closes the door behind her, giving it a little slam for emphasis. I wait.

Johanna walks to the kitchen, opens a drawer, then carries a checkbook and pen to the breakfast counter. "Do I make it out to you?"

"*Next Level Events* is better," I say. Of course it doesn't matter. I have no intention of cashing the check or taking money for a party that is obviously never going to happen, so she could make it out to Donald Duck and it would make no difference.

"Here you go. I'll text you the things you've asked for." She wipes away tears with the back of her hand and tries to smile. "Thank you," she says. "I know I can trust my last wishes with you. I've got an attorney coming over to make my will. I'll have him draw up a deed for the house and you will come and sign it when we're ready, yes?"

"Are you sure?" I ask. "About dying, I mean. Maybe you should see a doctor. Surely something can be done."

She shakes her head. "Indigo has been right about everything. I'm sure she's right about this too. You'd better go let your friend know you're safe before she calls in the SWAT team."

We both laugh a little at that.

"I'll be in touch as soon as I can line things up," she says, as I open the door.

I have no intention of cashing the check and I'm certainly not letting her give me her house, but I nod and smile before stepping out into the cold.

The door closes behind me. I hear the sound of the deadbolt shooting home.

Britt has cleared Jezebel's windshield and is waiting for me, snowy and shivering. "You can't actually be planning to do this! What is wrong with you? The woman is psychotic!"

"Delusional, maybe," I say, drawing on extensive psychological knowledge gleaned from watching reruns of *Criminal Minds* and reading mystery and thriller novels. "It's not like she's hearing voices and thinks we're demons or something. She's pretty normal, considering."

"Except for the fact that she believes she's going to die before Christmas because a psychic told her. An 'online psychic.'" Britt emphasizes those two words with air quotes, just in case I've missed her point.

I open my door. "That's only natural, don't you think? That the woman might believe a psychic? She's so horribly alone. Can you imagine being in your own head all the time, instead of getting your thoughts tuned up by the reality consensus?"

"I agree it's sad. But it's not your job to try to fix her," Britt lectures, climbing into the passenger seat. "She needs a real mental health person."

"Probably. But what she has is me. So I'm going to spend a few hours planning a small Christmas party. And then, when she's still alive on Christmas Day, maybe we show up and sing a few carols in her backyard, persuade her the psychic is full of shit, and get her to see a counselor. I'm not going to cash the check."

"*You*," Britt says. "You can do those things. There is no *we* in this. Delusional people can get violent. Obsessive."

"So can non-delusional people. Come on, Britt. She's harmless."

"I wouldn't be so sure about that," she mutters.

One thing to be said about Jezebel—she may be an old rust heap, but she does have very expressive and satisfying door slams. I close mine a little more gently, just to keep on good terms. Jezebel allows her engine to be started, and the windshield wipers and heater actually work.

Britt sits in rigid silence, arms firmly clamped across her chest, face turned away from me.

"Want to tell me what's really up with you?" I ask.

"With me trying to stop you from doing something stupid, you mean?"

"With you being outright rude and confrontational with a sad and lonely woman who may or may not be dying."

Silence stretches out long enough that I think she's not going to answer. When she finally does, her words are clipped and hard-edged. "There's nothing wrong with her. Maybe she made up the psychic, even. She's pretending she's dying just to get attention. An ambulance today. A morbid viewing party for Christmas. Meanwhile, good people who want to live really are dying..." She breaks off on a gasp and sits there, looking out the window, breathing raggedly.

"How is your dad?" I ask, understanding dawning way too late.

"He's *living*. As long and as well as he can," she snaps. "And I plan to spend Christmas with my family. It could be the last one, Addy."

Britt's dad—and therefore Britt and her mother—are coping with blood transfusions and chemo infusions and a brutal medication regime. He had to retire early from his medical practice. He spends way too much time at doctor's appointments. But he's still busy living the best life he can. I imagine he's made arrangements for his death, but quietly and competently, the way he does everything. No ambulances. Certainly no outrageous parties. But then, he's a well-adjusted man who has lived a full life already. He has people who love him. He's not imprisoned by his own house.

"I'm so sorry, Britt. Of course you need to focus on your family. I can fake plan a party on my own. You're off the hook."

I drop her off at her car in the *Grounded* parking lot, and about five minutes later I get a call from Vic, my ever perfect twin. Obviously, and expectedly, Britt has filled him in.

"Are you out of your ever-loving mind right now?"

"I wouldn't know, would I? I mean, if I thought I was out of my mind I'd probably still be in it, right?" I ask, barely navigating a turn. Jezebel is a two-hands-on-the-wheel kind of car at the best of times and she is not equipped with a hands-free phone system.

"You can't raffle off somebody's house."

"Why not?" I ask, as if I'm actually planning on doing it. As usual, Vic has managed to activate my contrary streak.

"Because it's not legal," he says. "Raffles have all kinds of official rules and regulations."

"It's not a raffle, it's a door prize."

His answering silence is deafening, and I relent. "Vic. It's a moot point, because Johanna's not really dying and none of it is going to happen. I'm fake planning a small Christmas party. When she's still alive on Christmas Day, obviously we'll call it off."

"Maybe you could ask for a mental health evaluation," he says.

"She's isolated and scared. Not psychotic. I don't think."

"I meant for you," he says.

"You'll help me, right Vic? We can get a few people and go sing her some carols on Christmas Day. Mom, maybe. The church ladies."

There's no answer. He's hung up on me already. Obviously, though, he'll come around. He always does.

CHAPTER 3

BY THE TIME I make it home, my hands ache from a death grip on the steering wheel and my body is vibrating with adrenaline from three near death experiences caused by drivers who have forgotten how to navigate in the snow. All I want is to get into my apartment, warm up in a hot bath, and maybe have a drink. Or two.

But of course it's not that easy.

Technically, I don't have an officially designated parking space—my apartment complex is not nearly so hoity and toity as all that—but by unspoken mutual agreement we all have our unofficial spots and nobody messes with the natural order of things.

Now, on this day of all chaotic days, somebody is parked in my spot.

I can either commandeer Nancy Henderson's spot, which happens to be empty, or find one at the very far edge of the lot where parking is a free-for-all. That means a long walk in blowing snow when I'm already tired and soggy and cold. But Nancy Henderson is eighty-two and uses a walker, so there isn't really a choice to be made.

I wrangle Jezebel into a snowbank and slog through the dark lot to my apartment. I pause with my hand on the knob. I know I locked my door when I left, but it isn't locked now. Maybe my neighbor, Carmen, has popped in to look for something. Maybe I'm being robbed. I crack the door open, slowly, cautiously, ready to scream or run or whack an intruder in the head with my bag.

Unfortunately, the intruder is not a thief or a squatter. It's worse than that.

My father, comfortably ensconced in my one and only armchair, looks up and says, "There you are." His tone indicates that I've been missing for days, and that my absence has profoundly inconvenienced him.

"Dad. How did you get in?"

"Your neighbor. Candace, is it?"

"Carmen." I make a mental note to give Carmen a list of people it's okay to let into my apartment, my father definitely not being one of them.

Bruno rubs against my legs and I pick him up and cuddle him. He's got a sticky patch on his belly. God only knows what he's gotten into this time, but a least he's warm.

"And you're here because?" I ask.

"Can't I just be visiting my favorite daughter? It's Christmas."

I set Bruno on the floor and start the process of removing my boots and jacket.

"Try again," I say.

Dad left us when Vic and I were twelve, and in the years

following he has never once dropped in for a visit. Occasionally we get phone calls on our birthday, but in-person appearances are few and far between. He is definitely not a part of the Christmas tradition.

"I was in town and I needed a place to stay," he explains, as if his behavior is perfectly logical. "Your mother wouldn't let me stay with her for some reason—"

"Possibly because you cheated on her repeatedly and have been divorced for a gazillion years?" I bend down to pick Bruno up again and rub him under his chin. He purrs and snuggles in, warm and comforting. "Local motels all booked up, were they?"

"I don't want to stay in a motel. I'm planning a more extensive visit. I've lost touch with my kids, and nothing is more important than family, right?" He gets up and takes a couple of steps toward me, arms spread wide for a hug.

"How extensive?" I hold my ground, my arms full of cat, staring him down.

Dad's hands drop to his sides. His shoulders droop theatrically. "I thought you'd be excited to see me. Spend some father-daughter time."

I *want* to believe him. There's an emptiness at the center of me that I've never quite managed to fill, thanks to Dad's abandoning me, and I'd love nothing more than quality father-daughter time.

But. I know him. Something is up.

"You're working an angle," I say. "You always are. Just cut to the chase and tell me. Should I be expecting a bounty hunter at the door? A vengeful husband? The FBI?"

He puts a hand over his heart and gazes at me sorrowfully.

"You are devoid of filial respect and affection. Where did I go wrong?"

"Really, Dad? Let me count the ways."

Bruno, who is every bit as dramatically inclined as Dad, struggles to get free. As soon as I set him on the floor he meows piteously, as if he's been starved for days, and I cross to my tiny kitchen to open a can of cat food.

"Just skip the storifying and give me the facts. Why you're here. What you want."

Dad retreats to the chair and settles in. "Let's have a drink and I'll tell you. I know you've got some of Vic's Raven Brew hanging around here. I prefer the—"

"No, Dad. I'm not going to sit down and have a beer with you while you spin this out."

"Were you raised by wolves?" he proclaims. "Have you no empathy?"

"I was raised by a single mother with a chip on her shoulder. As for empathy—let me check. Hmmm... nope. Tell me why you're really here, or don't. Sit there all afternoon if you like." I spoon food into Bruno's bowl.

Dad sighs. "You want the truth? I'm... getting older, all right? I hate to admit it, but it's true. Good roles are harder to come by and my retirement account is kind of thin. I had to give the house to your mother—"

"Because you cheated on her and she was raising two kids."

"Can I never be forgiven for my sins of twenty years ago?"

I roll my eyes. "Forgiveness has nothing to do with it. You did what you did. There were consequences. And there are consequences now. You've never expressed any interest in being involved in my life before. And this is not a good time for you to begin."

I sweep a hand expressively around the room to indicate the cramped bachelor suite layout, with the twin bed in one corner, the worn old sofa, the sagging armchair he's occupying, the tiny kitchenette with its one square foot of counter space. Not to mention the collection of packing boxes—a few taped and labeled and neatly stacked, the others still open, waiting for last minute additions.

"I can help you move. The new place must be bigger than this one. In any case, one of us can sleep on the couch."

"It would be you. Theoretically. If you were moving with me, but you're not. And since you won't come clean and tell me why you're here, let me guess. You are overextended and underemployed. Can't pay your bills and the rent is due, so you decided to come and mooch off of me. Close?"

"Family is supposed to help each other out, I always thought. Did I teach you nothing?"

He's taught me things, all right. How to manipulate people. How to work an angle. Never to fully trust a man or allow myself to fall all the way in love. I should be immune to this bullshit from Dad by now but apparently I'm not. It's amazing how much it still hurts.

"Shouldn't you be in LA?" I ask. "Looking for work so you can pay your bills and afford your own rent?"

"My agent is conducting the search. It's not like I need to be out pounding the pavement."

"I think I saw a help wanted sign at Safeway."

"Come on, Addy. Wouldn't it be fun to be roomies?"

"No. It would not be fun. And I don't have room for you, even in the new place."

"Oh, come on. I got the rundown from Candace. Lovely girl. You're moving into that rockstar's condo. The one I helped throw the party for. I'm sure it has at least two bedrooms."

This is a low blow. Dad did actually help out with Leno's party. And he helped with investigating the murder and got beat up in the process. For purely self serving reasons, and he deserved the beating, but still.

"Her name is Carmen. And I'm using the second bedroom for an office. You keep telling me I need to grow my business. Step one, I need an office. Step two, I need a living space fit to bring clients into. That means no roommate, you or anybody else."

Dad smiles, a toothpaste commercial smile, all white teeth and phony good will. "Step three, you need a business partner. And here I am, ready to partner up."

"No."

"Why not? I have connections; I'm good with people. Born salesman, that's me. I did a great job for you with the media on that Leno Masterson bash." He gets up and wanders over to my fridge. "I'm hungry. You got anything to eat?"

I sigh, knowing what he's going to find, and how the rest of the day is going to play out, as clearly as if the two of us are following a script. I even count down in my head. *Three, two, one, roll tape.*

"Hey, you've got a bottle of champagne in here," he calls out, right on cue. "Nothing else, though. Are you on some obscure celebrity diet?"

"I'm moving, remember? I don't want to relocate a bunch of groceries."

"And the bubbly is for celebrating the move. I get you. Good idea. Only you should have bought a charcuterie board.

Maybe some strawberries. Champagne is only half of a celebration."

"I'm ordering a pizza. That's the other half of the celebration."

Dad gives me the sort of look generally reserved for circus
oddities and extreme reality TV. He opens his mouth, closes it
again, and shakes his head, making it clear what he thinks of
my menu.

"What? Pizza pairs perfectly with champagne."

My phone rings. It's all the way across the room, closer to
Dad than it is to me.

I launch myself toward the phone as I see him reach for it,
but he gets there first.

"Hello, Rich speaking. Addy's in a meeting right now, can I
take a message?"

I mime grizzly bear claws raking down his face. And then
stabbing him repeatedly with a knife. He just grins and turns
slightly away from me.

"Absolutely, I understand," he says. "We can head over
right away. Addy has your address? Perfect. Yes, you can count
on it."

He hangs up and beams at me as if he's done something
profoundly professional and helpful. I snatch the phone out of
his hand and check the call history.

"Oh my God. Johanna? What did she say?"

"She said she knows that you just left, and apologizes, but
is sure you'll understand that time is of the essence. Her words.
Her lawyer and the notary are on their way and she needs you
to come and sign the documents. What? Did I do something
wrong?"

"Wrong doesn't even begin to encompass this." I hit redial. The phone rings and rings and goes to voicemail.

"No answer?" Dad asks, helpfully.

"We aren't... we can't..." Words fail me. I cross the room and smack my forehead deliberately into the wall. For about five seconds it feels good, and then the pain kicks in.

"Don't do that, it will leave a mark. Perhaps you could use your words instead of resorting to self harm tactics? See, look at you. Now you have an unattractive red splotch in the middle of your forehead."

"I'll explain and use small words. Johanna wants to give me her house so I can give it to somebody else at the after-death party that I'm pretending to plan because she isn't really dying."

"Why would you pretend?" Dad asks, as if I'm the one in the wrong. "If you don't want to do it, why didn't you say no?"

"Because... oh, never mind. It's a long story."

"Give me the short version."

"She hasn't left her house in years. She's isolated and lonely and a psychic told her she was going to die. I figured I'd play along for a bit, provide her some company. But obviously there won't be a party because she isn't really going to die."

"I get that." Dad nods his understanding, which is terrifying in itself. Somehow, I've done a thing that Vic and Britt think is insane, but which makes sense to the most self-centered and manipulative man I know. "You have a good heart, Addy, but you didn't think this through."

"I had everything under control," I say, defensively.

"Until now," he says, cheerfully. "Well, let's go on over and explain, then. Best to get it over with."

"There is no we."

"There is now."

"No. You stay here and…" I look around the apartment. The TV is packed and the cable disconnected. Even the WiFi has been discontinued. I've been pirating off of Carmen's, with her permission, of course, but I'm not about to trust Dad with her password.

"And what?" he says, sensing me weakening and moving in for the kill. "There's nothing for me to do here."

"Read a book?" I suggest. "Take a nap?"

"I suppose I could repack some of your boxes so they are more efficient. Maybe your mother would come over and lend a hand."

"You wouldn't."

He smiles.

I feel my resistance crumbling. Partly because he's worn me down, but also, what if he really does want to be part of my life, and this is my chance to get closer to him? Britt's dad is dying. Mine is—suddenly and unexpectedly and maybe even miraculously—here.

"Oh, all right," I say. "You can come with me. But let's be clear. I am not signing anything. We are not cashing the check she gave me. And we're only fake planning her party until after Christmas. Then we fess up."

"That's my girl," Dad says. "I promise, you won't regret this."

CHAPTER 4

I DO REGRET IT, before we've even pulled out of the parking lot. I regret it even more when we get to Johanna's.

She meets us at the door this time, and opens it before I have a chance to knock. "Thank you so much for coming back, Addy. Everybody was surprisingly available now, so it seemed like the best time."

Before she can turn to lead the way, Dad goes for the intercept.

"Johanna, right?" He reaches out his hand for hers. "I'm Rich. Addison's father—and business partner."

Johanna casts an uncertain glance at me.

Before I can open my mouth to explain that he is just visiting and is not, in fact, connected with my business in any way, shape, or form, he raises her hand to his lips and kisses it.

"I've been a largely silent partner up until now. But when Addy told me about you and your plan, I could stay silent no longer."

There's a dazed expression on Johanna's face, the sort of expression I imagine Alice was wearing when she found herself on the other side of the looking glass. As for Dad, he clasps her hand in both of his and holds it, oozing sympathy, respect, and attraction.

"I'm so terribly sorry to hear of the impending death of one so luminous, so beautiful," he murmurs. "Is there nothing that can be done?"

"Not much of a loss, I fear," she says, her voice tremulous. Her gaze is locked with his. "But no. Nothing can be done."

Because you're not really dying, I want to shout. But it's a little late for that. Also, I should have listened to my inner self telling me not to bring Dad. I should have seen this coming. She's a beautiful, vulnerable woman. He can no more resist taking advantage of that than a hungry bee can resist a flower.

"You let me think she was some little old spinster," Dad whispers, in a tone meant to carry to Johanna's ears. "How could you not mention how young and lovely she is?"

I didn't think it was possible to underestimate the scope of the disaster that is my father, but clearly I have. It's too late now. I'll have to ride this out and minimize the damage as much as I can.

The two of them are off in their own little world, gazing into each other's eyes. I elbow Dad in the ribs. Hard. With the pointiest possible part of my elbow.

He yelps.

Johanna startles and turns toward me. "Forgive me, Addy. Thank you again. Mr. Fitzwilliam can explain everything and answer all of your questions. Come."

Dad is still gazing at her like a lovesick puppy. She smiles tentatively, her pale cheeks flushed, then gently tugs her hand free and turns to lead us toward a gleaming antique table that would easily seat a dinner party of twelve. Two people are seated side by side, watching us.

The woman, Charlene Belgrave, is my high school nemesis, now a paralegal, apparently here to serve as Notary Public. Process of elimination says the stranger sitting beside her must be Johanna's attorney, but he looks more like a pirate. Swap out his suit for leather breeches and a tunic, slap an eye patch and a hat on him, and he could be part of the cast of *Pirates of the Caribbean.*

A gold hoop gleams in one ear. His wavy black hair falls to his shoulders. One side of his face is smooth-skinned, clean-shaven and sun-bronzed, with a strong jaw and firm, well-shaped lips. The other is a network of scars that tug the corner of the eye downward and the lip upward. Desperately trying not to stare at the scars I gaze into his eyes instead, and wish I hadn't. They are hazel, more green than brown, with little amber flecks. There is something hot and dangerous in their intensity, a tightly leashed rage, an ability to see what most people would miss.

"Miss Winters," he says, in a deep, smooth voice that sends a little shiver up my spine, "I'm Chip Fitzwilliam, Ms. Meyers' attorney."

My mouth has gone dry, and my brain has apparently forgotten how to send words in that direction anyway. I feel my lips moving but nothing comes out. I swallow and try again. "Mr. Fitzwilliam, I fear there may be a mistake—"

"Call me Chip."

That can't be right. He doesn't look at all like a Chip. *Cujo. Magnus. Alucard...*

"Miss Winters? At my client's request, I've drawn up a gift

deed to sign the house over to you, effective immediately. If you'd like to sit down? I'll go through the terms with you. Fortunately, my assistant was able to join us as our Notary, and we can be swiftly done and return you to your holiday celebrations within the hour."

Charlene does not look happy to be here, not that she ever looks happy to be anywhere. She scowls at me and glances pointedly at her watch, making it clear that she would like to get this show on the road.

Johanna takes a seat on the other side of Mr. Fitzwilliam. Dad sits down across from her. All eyes are on me, waiting for me to sit down and sign paperwork which obviously I'm not going to sign. Not that I care about putting Charlene out, but I hate to disappoint Johanna, and the attorney has already done a ton of work, which Johanna will have to pay him for, whether I do what she wants or not.

It's a hell of a lot of pressure, but it's time to end the charade. This is what I get for not being honest in the first place. Maybe there's still wiggle room, though.

I sit down beside Dad. Smile at Johanna. "The house would be mine after Johanna's um... death, though, wouldn't it? I mean, we don't know exactly when that will happen, so this seems premature to me."

"We discussed that option," Fitzwilliam says. "But Ms. Meyers has been quite insistent that she wants the house to be yours effective immediately."

"You must see that it's the most expedient option," Johanna explains. "Otherwise it won't be yours in time to give it away at the party. Mr. Fitzwilliam has insisted on writing in a clause that mandates I will continue to live here until the time of my death, which will hopefully not be a problem for you."

"All of this is a problem for me," I say.

"What Addison means," Dad says, smoothly, "is that I'm the representative of the company best suited to deal with this sort of unconventional request. I'm Addison's father. Richard Winters. Perhaps you've heard of me?"

He tilts his head slightly to better show off his profile. When nobody gasps, "Oh my God! Not *that* Richard Winters!" he changes tactics, covering one of Johanna's hands gently with his own, gazing soulfully into her eyes. "We want to make this process as easy as possible for you. Please trust that we hold your last wishes in the highest regard, as if they were our own. Do not spend a moment worrying."

I can see her falling under his spell. Even Charlene's spiteful expression has softened. Mr. Fitzwilliam at least must see that this is insane, but he says nothing.

"Don't listen to him," I blurt out. "He's full of shit."

"You want Johanna to worry?" Dad asks. "Addison. I'm disappointed. I raised you better."

"Oh my God. That's not what I mean at all." But I can see by their faces that they are all buying into his story.

"What Addison is really concerned about is the risk to the company," Dad says, looking into Johanna's eyes and patting her hand. "While we all would wish her to be a little more understanding and compassionate, as the owner of the business it's reasonable that she might be concerned about any complications. Unsuspected liens on the house—unknown to you, Johanna, of course, I'm sure a woman with eyes like yours could never be anything less than honest—especially as you are an angel destined to leave this earth far too soon. But should there be, as Addison's own attorney has rightly advised, any liens or other encumbrances on the house, then it would be best for her business, and for her, as well, not to be involved. So were you to make the gift deed out in my name, Richard L. Winters, that would resolve the issue."

"That's not what I'm concerned about at all! I mean, I am. But I really don't think—" I say, desperately, but this time it's Johanna who cuts me off.

"This is the perfect solution. You would do this, Richard?"

"Rich, please," he says. "I would do anything for Addy. And to make your last days peaceful, of course."

I make a gagging sound, like I'm an adolescent instead of a grown woman and the owner of my own business. This doesn't help my case.

"And for you, Johanna." Dad's eyes are full of tears, his voice choked with emotion. "Are you certain nothing can be done? It breaks my heart that we've only just met, too late, too late..."

The delivery is way overdone, Dad flashing back to his blessedly short-lived soap opera days, but Johanna appears to be drinking in every melodramatic word, her lips parted, eyes glistening. Charlene, legendary mean girl, is wiping away tears.

I turn to Mr. Fitzwilliam, hoping to find at least one rational person in this room who isn't falling for Dad's theatrics. He's watching Johanna and Dad with a wolfish, hungry expression that makes me feel shivery. But then he turns to me and smiles and I think maybe I've been imagining things. The scarring on his face is disorienting, making him look sinister when probably he's just a little impatient.

"Surely you can see this is not in her best interests," I say.

"Let me be clear. It is not my intention to have her sign the house over to me or to my father."

"I agree," the attorney says. "Think carefully, Johanna. You don't know these people. They could be grifters."

While I resent being included in the grifter designation, I keep my mouth shut in hopes that Johanna will listen to her attorney.

"What does it matter?" she says. "I'll be dead. I've got no one to provide for." She turns back to Dad. "But you won't fail me will you, Rich? You'll give away the house as a door prize at my party?"

"We'll have everyone who attends put their name in a hat and I will draw the winner myself. I promise. Scout's honor."

"No." I say. "Johanna. Listen to me. You can't give away your house."

"Why not?"

"Because you're not really dying."

"You don't know that," she says.

"Oh, come on. Some online psychic told you you're going to die. You haven't even seen a doctor. You'll be living here for years to come." I turn back to the attorney. "You can't do this. Surely it's unethical."

Johanna, still holding Dad's hand, frowns. "Indigo has never been wrong. In any case, it's my property, and I'm of sound mind. I can give the house to whomever I wish. Also, as I've already explained, there is a clause that makes it clear I will live here until I die. Mr. Fitzwilliam, could we redo the deed in Richard's name? You can print it on my printer, can't you? Then we'll get everything all signed so our lovely notary can get home to her family."

"It's fine." Charlene dabs at her eyes. "I can take all the time you need. Just so sad, you know?"

"Oh my God, you are all insane. Char, you should know what Rich is like." I turn to my father, drop my voice, and make it as menacing as I can. Which, admittedly, isn't very. Still, I mean what I say and he knows I mean it. "You do this, and I never want to see your face again. Not at my apartment, definitely not at the condo. Understood?"

"Addy. I know you don't mean that. I'm trying to do a good thing here."

"It's not a good thing. And you know it. I'm leaving. Are you coming or not?"

"I am not," he says, with quiet conviction. "I'm so sorry that you feel that way, but I can't abandon Johanna in her time of need."

"Mr. Fitzwilliam. Chip. Surely you aren't really going to—"

"I work for Johanna. Whether I agree with her or not," he says.

"Listen to me." I turn to Johanna. "You are not dying."

"You took my check. You said you would plan my party."

"I didn't cash it. I was humoring you! But this? This is going too far. I'm not planning the party because you're not going to die. Here, I brought the check back. Take it."

I dig the check out of my bag and hold it out to her, but she doesn't lift a hand to accept it.

"It's my last wish. You promised."

"Well. I'm breaking my promise. I'm not taking your money. I'm not planning the party, and I go on record as being absolutely one-hundred-percent opposed to you gifting your house to this man. Clear?" I tear the check in half and drop the pieces on the table before I let my anger and frustration carry me out the door.

It's not until I've brushed the snow off of Jezebel and climbed into the driver's seat that I remember I'm Dad's ride. Well, whatever. He can con Charlene or Johanna's bogus attorney into giving him a lift back to his car. I'm not coming back for him. And he is not, under any circumstances, going to be staying with me.

SUNDAY

DECEMBER 22

CHAPTER 5

"I CAN'T BELIEVE you were going to let Richard move in with you," Vic says, as I stop to rest my end of the sofa on the stairs and catch my breath. My twin is not remotely winded and hasn't broken a sweat, another evidence of the manifest injustice in the DNA distribution between us. Well, all right, maybe it has to do with eating habits and exercise—he eats a healthy diet and works out at the gym, while I lean toward whatever tastes good and rely on walking from my car to the coffee shop for cardio. But it's still mostly DNA, just like he got slightly wavy and effortlessly perfect dark hair while I got copper-colored frizz, currently in an awkward growing out stage following an involuntary pixie cut. (The hair cut is not DNA's fault, but still. The whole nearly-getting-scalped incident would never have happened to Vic.)

"I wasn't going to *let* him do anything," I gasp, as soon as I have enough breath to get the words out. "I said no. You know how Dad is."

"So instead you let him manipulate your mentally ill client into giving him her house?"

"Spare me the lecture. I tried to stop it."

"I don't understand why you would have taken him over there in the first place."

"He said..." but I can't actually repeat what Dad said. Voiced out loud, especially to Vic, it sounds too stupid for belief.

Vic doesn't need me to actually tell him. He knows both me and Dad too well. "What yarn did he spin this time? Something about wanting to make up for the past, or get closer to his daughter? Don't tell me—he's a changed man."

"People change," I say, defensively.

"Not Richard. Speaking of which, where is the old man?"

I feel a twinge of unease. His rental car is still in my parking lot. He hasn't called or texted. Which is exactly what I wanted. And what I told him I wanted. Still. It's not like him to comply with my wishes and you'd think he'd come fetch his car. Unless, of course, he followed all the way through with Johanna. Sweet talked her into bed.

The unease shifts to guilt, which morphs into anger. I hate it when Vic is right. "I know how he is, Vic. And you're right. I should never believe a word that comes out of his mouth. It's just ... Look at what's happening with Britt's dad, you know? What if Dad died, and we never had a chance to know him any better than we do now?"

"Fine with me," Vic says. "I made peace with not having a father years ago. You deserved better, Addles. But you didn't get it, and if you keep hoping to get what you missed out on from Dad, you're going to keep getting screwed over. It sucks, but it's the way things are. Now, I'd like to get this couch moved before Christmas arrives."

I pick up my end and we go back to dragging the couch up the stairs, then down the hallway, and finally into my new condo.

Mom is in the kitchen, opening and closing cupboards with the tips of her fingers, as if all surfaces should be considered contaminated until proven otherwise. "I'll just scrub down the kitchen cupboards for you. And the floor. Where are your cleaning supplies?"

"In a box," I say, flopping down on the sofa to rest, even though it's barely inside the door. It looks ratty and mangy and doesn't belong in this space any more than I do. Already, I want to go home. Back to my tiny little box with its unofficial parking and Carmen next door in case I need brownies, help, or someone to talk to, not necessarily in that order of importance.

"Which box?" Mom asks.

"One of those marked KITCHEN, probably?"

"Addison, for heaven's sake. When you move, always make sure that the things you'll need first are properly labeled and immediately available. You were going to scrub down the cabinets and drawers before you put your eating utensils and glassware away, weren't you?"

"I'm sure it's fine."

"In a place like this?" She sounds utterly aghast and I can't help laughing, now that I've recovered enough breath for it.

"Mom, it's not like this is a crack house. It was Leno's—"

"Precisely." She looks meaningfully over at the mural on the wall, a life-size depiction of the rock-and-roll band Leno and the Lonely, with Leno in full rock god mode. "Drugs and sex. Who knows what kinds of people he had in here, pawing all over everything? Orgies and body fluids everywhere most likely."

The mural was supposed to be painted over before I moved in, but something has gone wrong. I don't like it any better than Mom does, not that I'm about to admit it.

"Mom. First, eww. Second, Owen had the cleaners come in. I'm sure they've scrubbed the kitchen surfaces."

"And you're going to trust that? People cut corners all the time. They're just like you, probably. Take a look, decide it appears clean and doesn't need scrubbing. Even if they did clean it—did they use bleach? Germs are invisible. And the AIDS virus? Covid?" She shudders.

"Dies on surfaces in a matter of hours, I'm pretty sure."

"Well. You should paint over that," Mom says. "It's... practically idolatrous."

I text Owen a picture of the wall, without comment. He replies instantly.

> Owen: WHAT? Gene said he painted everything!

> Addy: clearly not everything everything

> Owen: Hang on. Calling him.

A few minutes later another text rolls in.

> Owen: Bad news

> Addy: Let me guess. Gene didn't actually paint over the mural?

> Owen: He says "he refuses to desecrate the creation of a fellow artist."

Addy: Like it's a Michelangelo fresco or something?

Owen: Sistine chapel, from his tone. I'm so sorry Addy. I'll get it fixed

Addy: Maybe you wanted to keep it?

Owen: 😔 Loved my brother, don't need a monument to his ego. We could paint it together? I'm in town over Christmas.

My heart dances a little at the thought of Owen. Maybe painting will lead to something... more. Owen is coming to town for Christmas, despite the fact that his mother no longer lives here. I know he's coming to look in on his nephew, Jackson, who is practically an orphan, but I'm still hoping he'll have some time for me.

Vic jolts me out of my happy little daydream. "Are you planning to leave the sofa here? Convenient, right inside the door like this, I suppose. You can set things on it. Any visitors with mobility problems won't have to walk across the room."

I stick my tongue out at him, then give him the middle finger salute for good measure, before rolling off the sofa and helping him carry it all the way into the room.

"Tell me again why we didn't just haul this monstrosity out to the parking lot and put a free sign on it?"

"Because it's mine and I like it. So does Bruno."

Bruno howls, most likely protesting his confinement in a cat carrier, but possibly in agreement. Who really knows the mind of a cat?

"See? He disapproves of you maligning his couch," I say.

"Out of my way," Britt gasps, tugging an overloaded wheeled cart through the door. "I thought maybe somebody was going to come down and help me with these boxes. But no. Leave me to do the hard work all by myself."

I run over to help her. "I don't suppose the cleaning supply box is in this lot. Mom wants to sterilize the kitchen."

"I think I brought up an Alexandria Library worth of books. I don't know about cleaning supplies."

"How about if I just go buy what we need?" Mom suggests. "That will be easiest. You probably don't have the right products anyway." She heads for the door. "Do not put anything away in the kitchen or the bathroom until I clean them, understood?"

She stops to give Britt a hug. "Hello, Brittany. Please forgive Addison's thoughtlessness. You know how she is. It's not intentional. It's so good of you to be willing to help." And with that she's out the door.

"What's with the mural?" Britt asks. "I thought it was getting painted over."

"Gene didn't want to sully the work of a fellow artist."

"Gene as in the wall-painter guy? He fancies himself as an artist now?"

"Apparently."

A loud knock interrupts us. Vic, closest to the door, flings it open. The woman standing there is maybe fifty, but it's hard to tell for sure given the smooth, glowing skin that only comes from being on a first name basis with a dermatologist. Gleaming chestnut hair with henna highlights is pulled back in a chignon so tight it's got to be painful, and her smile is even tighter.

"I'm Debbie Osterlyn, your neighbor across the hall." She holds out a small basket. "Also president of the homeowners' association. Which one of you is Addison?"

"That's me," I say. "Thank you so much."

I take the basket and look into it. "Oh, lovely! Chocolates and a... book." I'm trying to sound enthusiastic, but there are exactly five chocolates, meaning that in current company I only get three, and the book does not look like a fun and relaxing read to look forward to after a hard day of moving.

Debbie's mouth puckers as though she's just sucked on a lemon. "That's the Echo Ridge Homeowners' Association manual. Perhaps you weren't given one before you moved in, or you'd have noted on page seven, item fifteen, that propping the door to the lobby open is against the Association rules."

"I've always thought door propping was acceptable when somebody is moving," Vic says, holding out his hand and offering up his most ravishing smile. "I'm Victor, Addison's brother."

Debbie is the rare woman who is unmoved by Vic's charm. Her nostrils pinch together as she looks at his outstretched hand, and when she deigns to shake it only the tips of her fingers are involved.

"I trust that you will abide by the regulations as they are set out, in future. No exceptions."

Bruno howls and swears, probably wondering how he's going to be able to roam the neighborhood and steal things if the door is never propped. Debbie shifts her glare to the cat carrier. I think she frowns, but her skin is so tight it's hard to tell for sure. "Cats are tolerated, but he is to stay in your condo. No wandering the hallways. No prowling around outside, yowling and raiding the dumptser."

"Of course," I say. "Bruno is absolutely an inside cat."

This is a huge lie. I've tried keeping him in before. He will yowl nonstop until I give in. And then he will conduct regular raids on people's belongings.

"Also, that... painting... on the wall is not in accordance with our decorating polices," Debbie says.

"Haven't read the handbook yet," Vic says, in his lawyer voice. "But I'm pretty sure it's not legal for you to dictate the interior décor. Especially since there appears to have been an exception made for the previous owner."

Debbie attempts to toss hair that would stand up to a seventy-five mile-per-hour wind gust. "Leno, of course, was an exception, given his... well..."

"Money?" I ask. "Fame?"

Debbie looks down her nose at me and huffs. "It would be lovely if I could collect your association dues while I'm here."

"Right, of course. Let me get my checkbook." My bag is on the bookcase beside Bruno's carrier. "How much is it? Three hundred, right?"

"Three hundred and ten, due on the first Monday of every month."

I jerk upright to stare at her. "Wait, three hundred and ten a month? I thought that was, like, for the whole year."

Again that sour pruning of her mouth. "We've discussed raising it even higher as a deterrent to riffraff moving in."

I smile at her, brightly. "Well obviously. We don't want riffraff."

At this less than opportune moment, there's an authoritative knock on the door, which is not strictly necessary since it's already open.

It's Alex, aka Detective Gardner, aka my former boyfriend.

"What are *you* doing here?" I ask.

Not so long ago, Alex would have been part of the moving

crew, but it's been months since he showed up at my place uninvited. Or invited, for that matter. As usual, he's dressed in civvies so he can pretend he's doing his detecting thing under the radar, even though everybody in Fox Valley knows exactly who he is. Including Debbie of the HOA, who will think I'm a criminal element in addition to being riffraff, because Alex isn't here on a social call.

I can tell by his posture, the way he's knocked on the door but hasn't yet come in, and even more because he's got his cop face on.

"We need to talk," he says, and my alarm bells turn up the volume to deafening.

My knees go wobbly and threaten to drop me. "What's happened?"

Vic and Britt are here, and safe, but Owen is flying into Spokane today. And Mom is out buying cleaning supplies because I didn't bother to label my boxes. What if she was in a car accident, or shot down by some gun-toting idiot melting down in the Safeway parking lot? It would be my fault.

"Addy," Alex says, jolting me out of my imaginings of blood and doom and disaster.

"What?"

"Can I come in?"

If this was a social call he wouldn't wait for permission. But if Mom or even Owen were dead or dying his approach would have at least a little bit of compassion and sensitivity. This is something different.

"Of course," I say, for the benefit of Debbie the HOA rep. "So long as you're going to tell me what this is about."

He brushes past me and stops to stare at the mural of Leno.

"Couldn't bring yourself to paint over him?"

"Pretty sure you're not here about either a dead guy or that painting," I say. Work of art or not, I'm going to take a paintbrush to the mural myself in the very near future.

"When was the last time you saw your father?" Alex demands, shifting gears with a rapidity that makes the room spin.

I stare at him with my mouth open. It didn't even occur to me to worry about Dad. But his rental is in the parking lot. He hasn't tried to talk me into letting him stay. A flurry of images flashes through my brain. Dad, shot dead by a jealous husband. Dad, dead behind the wheel of a car wrapped around a light post. Dad, stabbed or poisoned by a woman scorned.

Debbie the HOAR needs a bag of popcorn so she has something to pop into her open mouth.

"Addy," Alex repeats. "When did you last see your father?"

I take a breath and my heart starts to settle down. This isn't the tone of an officer breaking bad news. This is an interrogation.

"Aren't you missing something?" I quip. "Flashlight? Cattle prod? Bucket of water and a tilt table?"

"What I'm missing is your answer to a very simple question."

He's deadly serious. Whatever this is, it isn't going to be as simple as Dad getting into a fistfight with a jealous husband.

"Yesterday afternoon. Why?"

"I heard he was staying with you. Planning to move in here."

"We talked about it. Last I checked that's not a crime."

"Maybe not, but it is against the HOA regulations," Debbie volunteers. "Page twenty-five. Article fifty-seven. Primary

57

owner needs to file notice with the HOA when subletting or bringing in a roommate."

"Well, he didn't move in. And he isn't here now."

Vic comes over to stand beside me. I'm grateful. I can feel the twin solidarity. Plus, Vic did go to law school even though he changed his mind and switched over to small batch brewing.

"Where is he?" Alex asks.

"Last I saw him, he was ingratiating himself with my client. Technically, I guess, my former client."

"Would that be Johanna Meyers?" Alex asks.

"How would you know that?"

"Because Johanna is dead," Alex says. He skewers me with a meaningful look and I lean against Vic for support as my knees go wobbly.

"She's actually dead?" I whisper. "I can't believe this."

"If you won't tell me where Richard is," Alex says, "maybe you'll tell me where you were last night."

CHAPTER 6

VIC SLIDES an arm around my shoulders. "This isn't funny, Alex," he says.

"Do I look like I'm laughing? Addy, you were at Johanna's house twice yesterday. Once with Britt, once with your father. So yes. I'd like to know where you were last night. You too, Brittany."

"Are you saying she was *murdered*?"

Of course that's what he's saying. If Johanna had died due to natural causes she wouldn't even be on his radar. And if she'd quietly committed suicide, he wouldn't be asking about Dad, or wondering if I have an alibi.

My knees have gone beyond unwieldy to absolutely unreliable. I want nothing more than to fling myself onto the couch and retreat from consciousness, like a Victorian woman with the vapors. Vic steadies me, tightening his arm and pulling me in closer.

"That poor woman," Britt says. "She sounded suicidal to

me. No wonder, either. I can't imagine living like that. And then with a psychic planting ideas in her head."

"Just tell me where you were last night, Brittany." Alex actually has his notebook and a pen out now, ready to write down answers.

"Home. Dad can attest that I spent most of the night emptying vomit bowls and bringing him ginger-ale." Britt's tone is ice, and I know Alex well enough to see that the hit goes home. Dr. Dalisay is an icon in the community and Alex knows perfectly well that Britt would never kill anyone.

Apparently he's not quite so sure of me.

"Addy?" he asks.

"I was here. By myself."

"Did anybody see you?"

I think that through and shake my head, wishing I'd stayed in the old apartment. Carmen would have popped in. Hannah Ames would have been spying out her window. Not that anyone would have watched all night, but still.

"And can anybody else back that up?"

"No. I was here alone."

He looks around at the chaos and evidence of moving. "What did you do, sleep on the floor?"

"As a matter of fact, yes. You'll find a sleeping bag and a pillow in the bedroom if you look. The bed is still out in the U-Haul. Maybe you could help bring it up."

"I'll pass on dragging furniture up the stairs, but I'd love to look around." Alex walks through the living area and into the master bedroom. I hear the closet doors sliding open, followed by the cabinets in the ensuite bathroom.

"Is he actually searching your bedroom?" Britt asks. "I mean, officially?"

"We invited him in," Vic says. "Addy gave him carte blanche to look around. So yes, he can. Legally. Anything he finds is admissible in court."

"That's not so much what I meant," Britt says. She giggles. "It's just ironic. Given what he used to do in the bedroom. And like he thinks you'd actually shelter a possible murderer."

Alex emerges from the bedroom and proceeds to the kitchen. "So why did you spend the night here last night when you still have a bed at the old apartment?" he asks, opening and closing cupboards.

"How do you know I still have a bed in the old apartment?"

"Still have a key."

"You were in my apartment?"

"It's not like you were there," he says, defensively. "I knocked first."

"That's still entering without permission," Vic says. "You two broke up like a year ago."

He shrugs. "Addy never asked for the key back. Technicality, but I think I'm on reasonably solid ground. Doesn't matter, since I didn't find any evidence."

He moves to the fridge and stands staring into its depths, letting the cold air out. Probably driving up my electric bill by the minute.

Irritation and annoyance are a great antidote to fear and guilt and shock. "Not that it's anybody's business, but I wanted to celebrate moving into the new condo. Thus the remains of a pizza and half a bottle of champagne in the fridge. And I didn't want to drive after drinking, thus the sleeping bag on the bedroom floor. Are you happy now? And no, you can't eat my leftover pizza."

"I'm not happy, no," Alex says. "What would make me happier is you having an alibi."

"I can attest that she arrived here at 7:10 pm," Debbie the HOAR says. "The pizza delivery guy showed up at 7:45. Her car was here when I woke up this morning but I can't guarantee that it was there all night. Did you want to see the security footage?"

For half a moment I think I've misjudged her, but then I register the tone of her voice and the way that she's looking at Alex and realize her helpfulness has nothing to do with any goodwill towards me and everything to do with the fact that Alex is, much as I hate to admit it, pretty hot.

"I'd love to see the security footage," he says, smiling at her. "Can you get me access?"

I roll my eyes and try not to make gagging noises. If Alex wants to look at security footage, all he has to do is ask the security guard on duty.

"Let's watch it together," he says. "You can point out anybody who doesn't belong here. Do you have time for that?"

"Yes! I'll go ask the security guard for it now." She simpers and lays a manicured hand on his arm. He returns the smile with one that suggests he'd be happy to watch the footage in dim lighting over a bottle of wine.

As soon as she's gone, Vic says, "Tell me you don't already have that footage."

"She was eager to help," he says. "And it gets her out of our hair. One moment please."

He grabs his cell and dials a number.

"Jenn. There's an HOA rep on her way to talk to you... Yes. Debbie. Do me a favor, and don't tell her you already gave me access to the security feed? Go ahead and give her a flash drive or... I don't care how you do it, Jenn, just do it. You're a smart woman. Be creative." He shoves the phone back into its holster.

"Now. One last time. None of you has any idea where Richard is right now?"

"Did you check the hospital? Maybe he was in an accident or something," Britt says. A little niggle of guilt sets in at her words. The last words I said to Dad were that I didn't want to ever see him again. What if he is actually hurt or dead and those are the last words I say to him ever?

"I suspect he's just run off, as one does after committing murder," Alex says.

I test a wobbly laugh. The expression on his face stops me cold. "You're actually serious. Come on, Alex. Being at her house doesn't make him a suspect. What's the motive? Maybe one of the neighbors did it. That Ralph guy is pretty sketchy."

"If it looks like a chicken and squawks like a chicken, it's probably a chicken."

"Duck," Britt says.

I fold over and cover my head with my hands, my heart kicking up into overdrive. Is somebody trying to murder us now?

"What are you doing?" Vic inquires.

"Ducking?" I've realized too late that everybody else, including Britt is still upright. This is what comes of being in adrenaline mode.

Britt sighs. "It's duck. Looks like a duck and quacks like a duck. Leave the chickens out of it."

"Maybe you could at least tell me how long Richard has been in town," Alex says.

"He showed up yesterday. Out of the blue."

"And why is he here?"

"To visit his kids?"

"Get real, Addy. Why is he really here?"

This is the problem with small towns and everybody knowing everybody's business. Alex knows as well as we do that Dad doesn't pop in for visits.

"We can do this here, civilly like the friends I thought we were," Alex says, "or you can come down to the station and make it official."

I glance at Vic. "Do I have to tell him anything?"

"You don't have to, but you might as well get it over with," Vic says. "Then we can get on with the moving process. It's not like you have anything to hide."

"Oh, all right. Like I said, Dad showed up out of the blue. Said he wanted to stay with me and help me with my business. It sounded, to be honest, like his finances aren't in great shape. And then Johanna called and we went over there and... things took an unexpected turn."

"What did she want?" Alex asks. "That you'd need to go back there. Twice in one day."

"She wanted me to plan a party."

"Christmas? Birthday? Wedding?"

"She said she was dying and she wanted a send-off party. Like I did for Leno. Are you sure she was murdered?"

He just looks at me, pen poised over his notepad.

"He's playing with you," Vic says. "He already knows all of this. He's hoping you'll give something away."

"How well did your father know Johanna Meyers?" Alex asks. "How well did you know her?"

"I just met her yesterday. Dad just met her yesterday."

"I know you think I'm stupid, Addison, but surely you don't really expect me to believe this," Alex says, with a real edge to his voice now. "That she'd gift her house to a man she didn't know. And then, apparently sleep with him and wind up dead a few hours later? And you can drop the shocked act. It's not like this is news to you."

"Look, here's what I know. She wanted me to plan an after-death party for Christmas Day."

"Pretty specific timing for somebody still alive and breathing," he says.

"Precisely. I felt bad for her so I pretended I was going to go along, but said a hard no when she wanted to sign over the house. The reason for that, by the way, is because she wanted me to give it away as a door prize at the party. I said no to the house. I said no to the party. So then Dad talked her into gifting him the house and I told everybody involved in no uncertain terms that it was a terrible idea and I left. That's the last time I saw him Alex. And that's all I know. Swear to God."

"You didn't know that you're the executor of Johanna Meyer's estate. And that she left everything to Richard in her will."

"Wait, she did what? Why would she do that?" That's it. I have to sit down. Fortunately the couch is handy.

"You can see now why it would be good for you to have an alibi," Alex says.

"But I don't know anything about her will. I mean, I knew she was making one, but that's all. Wouldn't I have to sign some sort of agreement? Like they wanted me to do for the house?"

Vic shakes his head. "Anybody can name you executor without getting your consent. You can refuse, if you want."

"Call your father," Alex says. "Tell him you need to talk to him about the will. Set up a meeting."

"I don't want to talk to him. You call him."

"Oh, trust me. I've tried that. But a man on the run isn't going to be inclined to pick up a call from either an unknown caller or the local PD. He might from his beloved daughter, though. Especially if the two of them were... let's just say, collaborating."

"What the hell, Alex? You really think I'm capable of that?"

He shifts his gaze pointedly to the mural of Leno. "You do seem to be in the habit of accumulating real estate acquired from dead people. A Maserati. A condo. Why not a house, to sweeten the deal? The opportunity to play fast and loose with the estate of a friendless dead woman?"

"Fuck you, Alex. And I mean that with all my heart."

He smiles his most annoying smile.

Vic picks up my phone and dials Dad's number. It goes directly to voicemail. "Turned off. Or his phone's out of battery."

"Where's your mother?" Alex asks. "Went by the house but she was out."

"At Safeway. Can't you leave Mom out of this?"

"I can't leave anybody out, Addy. This is a murder investigation. There's a warrant out for Richard's arrest. So if any of you know where he is, you call me, or you'll be charged with harboring a fugitive."

"Get out."

"What she said." Vic gestures toward the still open door. "You're not arresting her and you're here on sufferance."

"I was done, anyway." Alex strides to the door. Turns, and says, "Don't leave town. And don't call and warn your mother, either, or I'll charge you with obstruction."

He leaves, like any old cop who has just warned a suspect.

No apology. Not so much as a regretful look. He doesn't even bother to close the door.

I get up and slam it, which is satisfying but not quite satisfying enough. So I open it and slam it again. Childish, yes. But I do feel marginally better.

Then I sink back down onto the couch and ask the question that has been bubbling around inside me ever since Alex spilled the bad news. "Do you think Dad actually did it?"

"Addy, listen," Vic says.

I put my hands over my ears. "Don't want to hear it."

He sits down beside me and gently tugs my hands away. "If there's anything Richard's good at, it's looking out for himself."

"So you really think he did it?"

He shakes his head. "He's a self-centered, morally ambiguous prick, but murder's not his style."

"Then where is he? What if somebody killed him too?"

"He's scored the deed to a house. He's the beneficiary in her will. I'd guess that he knows what happened and is lying low until the murderer is caught so he can cash in."

"That's just so...reprehensible," I say.

Vic shrugs. "Agreed. Not surprising though, is it?"

A lump swells in my throat. Tears prick at my eyelids. Of course it's not surprising. It's precisely the sort of thing Dad would do. Once again, I've fallen for his shit, stupid enough to believe that he really did want a relationship with me. But he didn't. He never has. Believing that he ever will is imbecilic.

"Look at the bright side." Britt flops down onto the sofa on the other side of me. "You don't have to try to plan a party in... two and a half days. Or give away a house. You can just enjoy Christmas."

I appreciate what she's trying to do, but it doesn't help. All of this is my fault. If I hadn't been stupid enough to believe Dad really wanted to spend time with me, I never would have taken him to Johanna's, and he wouldn't have conned her. I don't really think he killed her, but if he did, then that, too, is on me.

Swallowing a sob and blinking back tears, I get to my feet and physically brush myself off, as if I'm covered in dirt. Wallowing won't change anything. It won't bring Johanna back, find Dad, or plan a party.

"Here's what I'm going to do. I'm going to find Dad. I'm going to make him give the house away and I'm throwing the best after-death Christmas party ever. Who is with me?"

"You don't have money to plan this party," Vic says, in his most rational and also most annoying tone. "Dad now owns the house and he's missing. Even if you did know where he was and could make him do the right thing, you can't possibly pull everything together by Christmas."

"That's why I'll need you both to help." I try on a smile, but neither one of them returns it.

"Come on, we can do this," I say. "How many after-death Christmas parties do we get to plan in a lifetime?"

"You're crazy, you know that?" Britt says. Which is a yes.

Vic sighs. "Fine. I'm in. But if we find him, I might just kill him myself."

MONDAY
DECEMBER 23

CHAPTER 7

A BRAND new sign that reads FITZWILLIAM, ABRAHAM AND GILLARDI LAW OFFICES has replaced the old, weathered one for DLS DAWLISH, ATTORNEY AT LAW. Dawlish had been a fixture in Fox Valley for thirty-some years before a series of unfortunate events mandated his departure. I can't help but wonder what could possibly induce an entire firm to relocate here. Especially an obviously driven man like Chip Fitzwilliam. It's not like town is a hub of criminal activity. Johanna's murder will top the news for weeks, especially with Dad as a suspect.

Charlene is not happy to see me. "Do you have an appointment?"

Each word is sharply bitten off. She looks half-feral this morning, a female Tarzan who somebody has washed and dressed and put makeup on.

"Just let Chip know I'm here, will you? Or shall I go on back? Is he in Draco's old office? I can't imagine where you've managed to stash three attorneys. Not a lot of room."

Charlene stabs at a button on her phone with a crimson fingernail. "Addison Winters just walked in *demanding* to see you," she says, into her headset. A pause. She sits up straighter. Her eyes dart furtively in my direction and then away. "Yes sir. Absolutely sir."

"He'll be right out," she says to me, sounding like she's got a mouthful of broken glass. "If you'd like to have a seat? Could I offer you an iced drink, or maybe a coffee?"

I glance at the Keurig in the corner and decide to hold out for one of Kathy's perfect macchiatos after I'm done here. I don't really need a drink, and if I did I'd be perfectly happy to fill a paper cup from the water cooler in corner, but I want to make Charlene do something for me. Yes, I can be petty. Bite me.

"A bottle of water would be fabulous. Sparkling, if you have it."

Charlene gets up from her chair and stomps into a small room behind her desk. I've got to give her credit— successfully stomping in high heels takes both skill and a high tolerance for pain. I settle into a chair to wait, checking out the selection of glossy magazines on a glass-topped coffee table. Just in case Charlene is responsible for cleaning it, I make a point of pressing my entire sweaty palm against the glass as I lean forward to select a magazine.

When Charlene flounces over with a bottle of water, the expression on her face is a warning I'd be stupid to ignore.

"Thank you so much, I hope it wasn't too much trouble."

I smile up at her, then set the bottle on the coffee table with zero intention of drinking it, not with Char mad enough to spit. Who knows what she's done to it? I've just begun paging through an Oprah magazine when a door opens and footsteps approach.

It's Chip Fitzwilliam, come to fetch me himself. Pretending to be deeply absorbed in my magazine I make a point of checking him out in my peripheral vision. He's wearing a tailored three-piece suit and looks like he should be on the cover of a particularly spicy romance novel. One of those with the word 'shades' or 'millionaire' in the title.

"Addy Winters. What can I do for you?" he asks.

Looking up with my best imitation of being startled, I say, "I thought you'd be expecting me, given what's happened."

"I'm afraid I'm not plugged into the gossip mill," he says. "Something I should know?"

"Johanna Meyers is dead."

"Murdered," Charlene says. "Addy's father killed her."

"You have some evidence to put where your mouth is?" I snap.

"Richard is missing and the cops are looking for him. Looks pretty suspicious to me. Especially given that shady business with the house and the will and—"

"Gossiping about legal matters is not one of your duties as a receptionist, Miss Porter," Fitzwilliam says. "Addy? If you'd come this way? Miss Porter, please hold my calls." His voice is even, carefully modulated, but there's a dangerous undercurrent in it that quells even Charlene.

The office he leads me to, where I once sat and had a most interesting conversation with Draco Dawlish, has been redecorated. A framed diploma from Harvard declaring one Chip F. Fitzwilliam a Doctor of Jurisprudence takes center stage on the wall behind the desk. A smaller framed certificate of his admission to the Bar hangs next to it. A bookcase is full of heavy hardcover books that are probably legal tomes.

He sits down in the chair behind the desk, and I take one of the two visitor chairs and immediately confront him on his lie.

"You knew that Johanna was dead. The police already talked to you. Alex knows about both the deed for the house and the will."

He shrugs. "It's best to discourage my assistant from gossiping."

"Good luck with that." I keep my eyes moving, anywhere and everywhere, trying not to stare at his scars. Michelangelo might have used the two sides of that face for before and after studies, Lucifer the angel of light, and then Satan. Or he could be a model for a story, a modern day Dorian Gray...

"Take a good long look," he says. "Let's get the staring out of the way."

"I'm sorry. I didn't mean to—"

"But you just can't help yourself. I'd prefer not to be encountering surreptitious glances as we go along, so just get it out of your system. And while you're at it, what is it that you'd like me to do for you?"

"I'm here to find out if it's true I'm somehow the executor or trix or whatever of Johanna's estate, because I did not sign up for that."

"It's true. Johanna was adamant, although I did advise that she should get your consent. She said, and I quote, 'It's easier to ask forgiveness than permission.' When I asked what exactly she meant by that, she said, and again I quote, 'Addy doesn't believe I'm dying. She'll say no if I ask her, but she'll follow through once I'm already dead.'"

"And now she is actually dead," I say. A little shiver runs up and down my spine. Partly because Johanna's death occurred as predicted, but even more so that she'd read me so accurately during our very brief acquaintance.

"And now she is actually dead. God rest her soul. And we all know who we have to blame for that."

"And who would that be?"

"You know perfectly well. Whether you're in on it with him or not, you brought that man into her home—"

"And you deeded the house over to him! I made it perfectly clear that it was a bad idea."

"You know what I think? I think you're an excellent actress. Between the two of you, it was the perfect scam, wasn't it? You all innocent, trying to help her out. Him, taking advantage of her loneliness and vulnerability. Both of you making off like—"

"We haven't made off like anything, Chip."

The tone of his voice and that hot, hungry expression in his eyes makes me want to run for the door, but instead I paste on the smile I perfected in high school when I first learned to sharpen my claws against the mean girls.

"My father is innocent until proven guilty. And, while the police are looking for him and hopefully also for whoever really did kill Johanna, I'm going to throw that party for her that she wanted."

"You're going to—what? Even if you could give away the house, which you can't, as it belongs to your father, you won't be able to have her body there for a viewing, as she'd requested. And the house is still a crime scene."

I wave this all away. "Details, details. If you think those small obstacles are going to stop me, you clearly don't know me at all."

"This whole situation is irregular," he says, "Although possibly not out of the ordinary for you."

I don't even twitch at this accusation, keeping my smile in place. "Would you care to elaborate your meaning?"

He sits back a little in his chair, scrutinizing me as if we're in a high-stakes poker game and he's trying to figure out what I hold in my hand.

"I understand that you have recently acquired a condominium. And a Maserati. Willed to you by one of your clients. I don't know much about the party planning business so I'm willing to be enlightened. Is this a usual thing?"

"Party Planning 101," I say, lightly. "Anything can and will happen. I'm not the enemy here, Mr. Fitzwilliam. I didn't ask to be Johanna's executrix. I was opposed to the house being deeded to anybody. And, as you witnessed yourself, I tore up the check."

"But you're still going to throw a party. Unpaid. Out of the goodness of your heart."

I feel like an insect under a magnifying glass, with the sun being focused onto me. I can smell the smoke, very nearly feel the sizzle of my skin. Maybe he'll lunge across the desk and strangle me.

"Exactly," I say. "Unpaid. Out of the goodness of my heart."

"Or, you're in this together with your father, who has surely cashed the fifteen thousand dollar check she wrote to him."

I stare at him, letting this sink in. "I'm going to kill him as soon as I find him," I say. "Regarding the party, consider it my Christmas gift to a woman who had no family or friends. Now, could you possibly take me through the terms of the will?"

He leans back in his leather chair, looking exactly like what he is—a guy on a power trip—for long enough that I think about consulting an attorney of my own. Just as I'm ready to tell him what he can do with himself and his attitude, he relents.

"The will is simple and straightforward. I've made you a copy." He slides a document across the desk. Clearly, he's been expecting to have this conversation and was even prepared for it. He's just been messing with me for some reason. Escalating a power struggle at this point won't get me what I want, so I swallow my pride and look through the document.

Last Will and Testament of Johanna Leona Meyers is written across the top in fancy font. There are only a couple of pages, as compared to the small tome that was Leno's will.

"Everything she owns goes to Dad once any debts are paid," I say, working my way through the legalese.

"That's the gist of it," he says.

And then I reach the end. Read the very last Article. Stop. Read it again:

Contingent Beneficiary: In the event that Richard Winters predeceases me or is otherwise unable or unwilling to accept this bequest, I direct that my entire estate be distributed to Addison Winters.

"Ah, you've found it," Chip says. "Not to worry. It's not relevant, given that your father is still alive."

"But it says 'otherwise unable.' If he's missing, then—"

"Trust me. He'll have to be missing for quite some time before anything falls to you. However, if he is convicted of murder, he is barred by law from profiting from his crime."

"What about the executor bit? Can she just... do that? Assign me that job without asking?"

"She can."

The weight of responsibility makes me want to lie flat on the floor of the office. I'm good with being responsible for myself, my cat, and the events I plan. That's it. That's as far as I'm to be trusted. I think about Johanna's museum of a house and wonder where would I even begin? Also, what if Britt was right and there are debts or liens?

"Listen," Chip says, softly. "She wasn't quite right in her mind, I believe."

"And yet you helped her create a will that says she was of sound mind."

"Sound enough," he says. "It would have been difficult to prove otherwise. But. She was frightened and didn't have a lot of time. She met you and made a rash decision. You do not have to agree to the executor's duties. You can decline."

"What happens then?"

"I'm happy to take over."

"You're expecting me to believe you would do that for free?"

"No, I would pay myself out of her estate. Just enough to compensate me for my time. Your father—or you, if it comes to that—will still get the bulk of her assets."

Usually I'm good at reading people, one of the dubious talents I inherited from Dad, but Chip is like a foreign language. Something about the contrast between the two sides of his face, the way neither of them matches his eyes or his tone of voice or even his body posture, keeps me totally off balance. I'm unsure whether I believe him. I know I don't trust him.

KERRY SCHAFER & KERRY ANNE KING

"I need to talk to my attorney before I make a decision," I say. "This is my copy?"

"It is." He scribbles on a sticky note and slaps that on top of the will. "My cell number. Call me when you've made your decision. Night or day."

He rests his hand on top of mine, looking deep into my eyes. "I know you feel responsible for her. Because of your father. But you're not. I'd advise you to leave the legalities to me."

His gaze is mesmerizing. His hand on mine is warm. Strong.

But. I've been bamboozled by the best and a small part of me manages to shake itself free. I smile, still holding his gaze, as I slide my hand out from under his and pick up my copy of the will.

"I'll let you know."

I can feel his eyes on my back as I walk out of his office. Charlene looks up from her computer as I fast walk past her, and I don't even bother with a smart-ass remark. I need to get away from Chip Fitzwilliam and his compelling personality so I can think.

CHAPTER 8

THINKING WILL HAVE TO WAIT.

Owen is waiting in the parking lot, leaned up against Jezebel like they're on a first name basis. He's wearing blue jeans and a black leather jacket, and against the background of my snow dusted car and the grey winter sky, he looks like he's stepped out of a black and white rock-and-roll album cover from the '60s.

Next to him is a gangly kid in a fleece lined jean jacket and a stocking cap. Owen's nephew, Jackson.

My heart skips a beat or two, my pulse surging with the memory of the last time Owen kissed me. That was our second kiss, steamy enough that if there is a follow up kiss, the third in series, we might want to get a room. The condo is a mess and I'm not taking him back to the old apartment in the state it's in.

Also, there's the kid, who is glaring at me as if he is holding a massive grudge.

Thanks to my own overthinking and the hostility radiating from Jackson, instead of running over to fling my arms around Owen's neck I freeze in place without even saying hello.

As for Owen, he doesn't rush over to ravish me right out in public the way I've played it out in my imagination, or even to give me a hug. "Addy. I think you've met Jackson," he says.

"Not officially. Hey, Jackson. How's it going?" I flash a tentative smile at the kid. It is not returned.

"Your hair grew," he says, but not like this is a good thing.

"So did you."

He's done more than grow. He looks years older than he did when I saw him last spring. His curls have been cut short. A wary, sullen expression ages him more than the passage of a few months can account for.

"Come over here and we can take a selfie," Jackson snipes, and I realize that I've been staring.

"Jackson," Owen warns.

The kid continues to glare his insolence and defiance. But I read something else in his blue eyes, so much like his father's, that reminds me what it was like to be his age and to feel all alone against the world. And Jackson has much more reason to feel that way than I ever did. I've always had Vic. Jackson's got Owen now, but they hardly know each other.

"How did you know I'd be here?" I ask, moving towards them with the same slow, cautious steps I might take when approaching a frightened animal.

Owen stands up straight and takes three steps toward me, then stops. "Went up to the condo first. You weren't there, so I called your brother. He checked in with Britt, and here we are." His keen gray eyes search mine. "How is the new lawyer? Anything like old Draco?"

"Not in the slightest. But, seriously. I could have met you somewhere. You didn't have to freeze your butts off out here in the cold."

"We're not on a socializing mission. We're your painting crew, ready to work."

I search his face for how to take that. Does he not want to socialize? Maybe he regrets kissing me.

"Both of you?" I ask, hoping I'm coming across casual.

"I was involuntarily volunteered," Jackson says.

"If you'd rather I tell them to send you to a group home, just say the word. I can be on a plane and back to Chicago by day's end." Owen's tone is indifferent, but the intensity in his eyes betrays him.

I know that Jackson has been staying with his maternal grandparents and that there have been issues. His grandfather has dementia and his grandmother doesn't have the time and energy to deal with an angry, grieving adolescent. This is the first I've heard of a group home, which means some new development Owen hasn't mentioned.

"Well?" Owen asks. "What's it going to be?"

"Whatever," Jackson mutters.

"Pardon? I didn't quite catch that."

"Fine. I'll perform slave labor for you and your girlfriend."

Owen's jaw tightens and I foresee disaster. He's about to demand respect and politeness. Which will backfire and everything will blow up. This kid has a right to be pissed. Chances are good he's actually pissed at me. What's happened to his mother is not my fault, but he's thirteen years old and not likely to see it that way.

"Perfect," I say, a little too brightly and definitely too loudly, before Owen can attempt to assert dominance. "What do you want to do first? Take a look at the worksite or go buy supplies? Also, I should warn you that I have a complicated party to plan by Christmas Day, so my time is kind of premium. Could we maybe wait and paint after the party? How long are you in town?"

"Until sometime after New Years," Owen says. "Everything with Jackson is up in the air until after family court, and the court system is pretty much shut down until after the holidays. Could we go look at the scope of the disaster and decide from there? Hey, maybe we can help plan your party."

"I have limits," Jackson says. "I'm not helping plan any stupid party."

"Suit yourself," I say, determined not to get sucked in. "Let's go look at the painting then. Did you want to ride with me?"

Owen laughs. "Much as I hate to miss out on the opportunity to ride in this monstros... lovely car of yours... it's probably most expedient if we have our own wheels. I'll meet you up there."

Jezebel consents to start and I lead the way, Owen's rental behind me. The roads have been plowed and sanded, but even so, when I approach Suicide Corner I slow almost to a crawl. Even when the roads are dry, my palms get sweaty on this bend. Owen and I nearly died here. It seems like years and also like only two minutes since that terrifying moment when the car skidded out of control and I seriously believed it was the end of everything.

After the corner it's straightforward driving until I reach the manned—or more accurately, wo-manned—gate that is supposed to keep riffraff out of the condo. Jenn waves me to a stop.

"Somebody waiting for you, Addy," she says.

"Who? I wasn't expecting anybody."

"Skye," she supplies cheerfully. "And Daffodil."

"I don't know anybody named Skye. And I certainly don't know any Daffodils."

"Well, that might be because they're really here looking for your dad." She leans out through her window and lowers her voice, as if there's somebody besides me in the car. "He didn't really kill that woman, did he?"

I ignore the question and ask one of my own. "So you let two strangers in because they were looking for Dad. Who doesn't live here. Where are they, exactly?"

Associates of Dad could mean anybody. Movie stars, musicians. Debt collectors. Mafia. Most likely movie stars, or hookers even, which sounds most likely. It's hard to picture kneecap breakers named Skye and Daffodil.

"They're waiting in the lobby," Jenn says.

"How? Why?"

"It's cold, Addison. And they were dropped off, so they didn't have a car to wait in. I didn't know how long you were going to be."

"Isn't the whole point of a gated community to keep strangers on the other side of the gate? And like, not actually let them into the building? What would Debbie say?"

"Well pardon me for living," Jenn snipes, then makes a sudden about face. "You won't tell Debbie, will you?"

"I won't tell on you. But maybe you could use the security gate for security."

"Thank you for sharing your concerns and teaching me my job," she says. "Whatever would I do without you and your wisdom and experience?"

The trouble with the security guard being somebody I went to school with is that she's somebody I went to school with. Funny thing how all of those old dynamics have carried into our thirties.

But the gate opens, and I maneuver Jezebel into my officially designated parking space, get out, and look around for Owen.

His car is still idling behind the security gate. Which is still closed. My phone rings. It's Owen.

"What's happening?"

"Your friend Jenn the security guard says you told her not to let anybody through."

"I told her not to let strangers through. More strangers. Because apparently there are two in the lobby already waiting."

"Well, if you want me on that side of the gate, you're going to have to talk to her."

I watch him hand his phone out the window to Jenn.

"Can I help you?" her voice says.

"Oh for Pete's sake, Jenn. Let Owen through."

"I believe you wanted me to use the gate for security."

"You know Owen. You know perfectly well that he technically owns the condo."

"Make up your mind, Addy. You can't have everything both ways."

But the gate opens, and Owen's car drives through and parks next to Jezebel.

"You might want to have a word with her supervisor," Owen suggests.

Of course he has a point, but high school loyalty and the

ingrained reluctance to be a tattle tale are also surprisingly enduring, and I won't be complaining to anybody about Jenn.

"Just a minute," I say. I plunk my bag up on Jezebel's hood and root around for the can of bear spray I lug around with me. Vic has pointed out multiple times that I could be tortured, raped, and slowly slaughtered in the time it would take me to locate my protection. He's unfortunately not wrong. When I finally emerge with the small black canister and a pair of scissors, all three of us are shivering.

Jackson stares at me and my weapons with the expression of weary disdain that is the trademark of teenagers the world over. "What is that?"

"Protection."

"From what?"

"My client has been murdered and my father has gone missing and apparently two strangers named Skye and Daffodil have come looking for him and are sitting inside my lobby waiting for me."

"A gun would be better," Jackson says. "Mom had a gun." He apparently realizes that this isn't helping his case and reverts to sarcasm. "So you're going to stab them with scissors?"

"Or spray them with bear spray."

"What if *they* have guns?"

"They won't have guns," Owen says.

"How do you know?"

He sighs and gives me the sort of look I'm used to getting from Vic. "It's cold out here. How about we go on in and meet the dangerous criminal element known as Skye and Daffodil."

"Whatever. I'll wait here." Jackson lounges against the car, looking exactly like exactly the riffraff element Debbie the HOAR would call the cops to report.

"You'll come with us," Owen says. "So you can see the work we're going to do."

Jackson shrugs. "Suit yourself. You can be my human shields."

Owen's jaw tightens. So does the rest of him. I can tell he's about to get sucked in to Jackson's goading and I don't have time for the two of them to hash this out right now. I grab his hand and drag him toward the building. Jackson slouches along behind us.

I scan my keycard, enter the code, and open the door, scissors and bear spray at the ready.

At first glance, the visitors don't look particularly threatening, at least not in a physical danger sort of a way. A young woman sits in one of the armchairs in the lobby, wide-eyed, on full alert. Honey-colored hair, artfully disheveled, tumbles over her shoulders. She's wearing a button up shirt but apparently considers buttons optional, given the amount of cleavage she's chosen to display. Her face is pretty, her expression halfway between sulky and frightened, and I guess her age at somewhere between sixteen and twenty.

I have no guesses about the age of the baby, sound asleep in her lap. I'm not a baby person. Never did the babysitting thing. Never even played with dolls.

"Addy?" the woman asks. "You are Addy, right?"

"Yes, that would be me. And this is Owen and Jackson. Can I... help you with something?"

"I'm looking for Rich."

"Aren't we all."

"He's not here, then?" Her voice wobbles and her eyes get

shiny, like she's about to dissolve into tears. "I don't know what we're going to do."

The baby yawns and stirs and opens her eyes. She sits up on the woman's lap, puts a thumb in her mouth, and looks us over with drowsy curiosity. Her dark curls, big brown eyes, and even the expression on her face are alarmingly familiar, and the bad feeling I've had ever since Alex showed up this morning takes a dramatic turn for the worse.

"If you're looking for Dad, there have been been some alarming developments," I say. "He's wanted for murder and he's gone missing. We're all looking for him. Including the cops."

"Rich killed someone?"

"I don't think that he did, but the police want to talk to him."

"And you really don't know where he is?"

"I haven't the foggiest."

Her face sort of crumples in on itself in slow motion and she dissolves into a flood of weeping. Not the silent kind, either, but the kind that comes with giant gut-wrenching sobs. The baby screws up its chubby face and adds pathetic wailing to the noise.

Owen, who has always seemed to know exactly what to do in an emergency, appears to be in a state of shock. Jackson, too, just stands there staring, like he's been struck motionless and dumb by some bolt out of the heavens, with his mouth slightly open and his eyes practically bugging out of his head.

One of the downstairs condo owners, an elderly gentleman I've seen but haven't had a chance to talk to, sticks his head out through his door. "What's going on out here? I knew you'd be trouble when you moved in. This is an adult community. No kids."

"They're just visiting," I tell him. "Sorry to disturb you, but she's just gotten some really unfortunate news."

His face softens a little. "Well, all right. At least it's not that caterwauling music we had to put up with off and on when that rock star lived upstairs." He goes back into his place and closes the door.

"We need to help her," Jackson breathes. "Them, I mean. We can't just..." He turns to Owen. "Don't you know who this *is*?"

"No?" Owen says. "Should I?"

"It's Skye," Jackson says, his voice awestruck. "Wait until I tell Tony I met her. In person."

This solves one small quandary. I now know who is who. The weeping girl is Skye. Which makes the dark-haired baby Daffodil. Because, of course.

"You have to help her," Jackson says, directly addressing me for the first time with anything other than insolence.

I've already come to that conclusion on my own. Obviously I need to know what she wants with Rich, but the last thing I need is for Debbie the HOAR to get involved.

"Come on, let's go to my place." I stow my bear spray and my scissors in my bag and start down the hallway to the elevator.

"Nobody's going to hurt you, Skye," Jackson says, in a protective voice. "We'll totally help you find Rich."

"Thank you," she says, in a small voice. "You're very sweet. It's not like we have anywhere else to go."

CHAPTER 9

WE DO THE ELEVATOR THING, all of us standing in a row, staring straight ahead. Fortunately there are only three floors and it's a short trip. I lead the way down the hall, Skye and Daffodil behind me, Jackson following them and Owen bringing up the rear.

When we walk into the condo Skye gasps and takes a quick step forward, face lighting up with wonder as she gazes upon the Leno mural. Her eyes aren't swollen; her nose isn't red. Either she was faking the crying or she's mastered the magical art of crying pretty, which would be manifestly unfair given the other physical assets she's also been blessed with.

"Oh, my God. That's so cool. I loved Leno and the Lonely. It was so sad what happened to him!"

"He was my dad," Jackson says.

Skye turns to him. "For real? And your mother... Oh, wow. She's *that* Lisa."

"I think we need to go back to the beginning," I suggest

"Jackson appears to know who you are, but other than the fact that your name is Skye, I'm afraid I have no idea.

"He didn't mention us, then? Rich?"

"Not a word."

"She's Skye," Jackson says, in the tone of zombie adoration.

"I'd gathered that part. What I don't know is who Skye is, or why she's looking for Dad."

"She does films," Jackson says. "On the internet, not the big screen. I've seen them all, Skye. You're just... you're a goddess."

"You're um, maybe a little young for those, aren't you?" Skye says.

"I'm sixteen."

"Try thirteen," Owen says, drily.

"Maybe you should put some parental controls on what your kid is watching online," Skye says, haughtily.

"He's not my kid, but I will definitely take that under advisement."

"None of this explains what you are doing here, or why you're looking for Rich," I say, trying to get the conversation back on track.

"Can I take a picture with you to show the guys?" Jackson begs. "They will never believe this."

Skye flashes him a smile. "Why not? Here. Hold Daffodil, will you?"

She shoves the baby at me and I'm too taken off guard to resist. The kid is heavier than I'd expected. She smells like sour milk and pee and her butt feels suspiciously soggy. But she looks up at me with an expression of hope, as if finally here is somebody who might do something about her condition, and clenches her little fists into my shirt.

"Okay, I've got you," I murmur, in the tone usually reserved for Bruno. Her bottom lip trembles and I add, "Please don't cry," and jiggle her a bit, the way I've seen people do with babies. It works for some reason. She pops her thumb back into her mouth, still clinging to me with the other hand.

"Jackson," Owen commands. "Do not..."

But Jackson has already scooched over right next to Skye. She bites her lips and runs her tongue over them to wet them. Dishevels her hair. Then she puts an arm around Jackson's shoulders and leans her head up against his.

Bruno, who has apparently been hiding under the couch, sticks his head out experimentally and then pulls it back.

Jackson holds up his phone to snap a selfie. "Smile," he says.

Skye smiles the sort of smile that answers once and for all any lingering question about what kinds of films she stars in. Bruno, meanwhile, for reasons inscrutable and entirely his own, emerges from his hiding place and heads for the bedroom, taking the expedient route up and over the couch while using the two humans for traction.

Skye screams. Jackson swears.

Daffodil makes a little grunting sound and I feel a suspicious warm wetness where her bottom makes contact with my arm and my shirt. A whole new smell sensation follows.

"Your beast of a cat has mauled me!" Skye shrieks. "I'm bleeding! He's probably scarred me for life!"

I look her over. She's got a tiny little bead of blood on her forehead. Not exactly a career ender. Having experienced much worse myself I don't feel the need to be too sympathetic.

"In other news, I'm pretty sure Daffodil needs a diaper change." I make sure Skye can hear me above her own fussing about the cat.

She stares at me, like I've spoken in a foreign language, so I try again, enunciating loudly and clearly.

"You need to change your kid's diaper."

"I'm out," Skye says. "Of diapers. And formula. I spent all of my money to get here, expecting Rich to help. But now you say he's missing and maybe he killed somebody. And now my face has been ruined by your cat. What am I going to do?"

Her voice breaks.

If she was one of my brides having a pre-wedding melt-down, I'd know exactly what to do. But what do I know about babies? I am absolutely and completely out of my depth.

"Just to clarify, although I'm certain we've all guessed by now," Owen says. "You're looking for Rich because?"

"Duh!" Skye says. "He's Daffoldil's father. He didn't even tell me he was leaving LA. He just—I went to his apartment and all of his stuff was gone. And he wouldn't answer his phone and then—I wasn't about to let him ditch us like that so I followed him here."

"How did you know he was here?" I ask.

"What?" She stops mid-sob and glances up at me, tearstained and pretty, despite the tiny bead of blood on her forehead, and so very, very young.

"How did you know to come here?" I repeat.

"Um, he talked about you? All the time. Addy this, and Addy that. So when he vanished I knew if anybody knew where to find him, it would be you."

And there is the first lie I can really put my finger on. Skye has just made a huge strategic error. I know Dad and I know he hasn't been raving about his daughter.

"Seems like you might have called," I suggest. "Rather than driving all the way up here if you didn't have the money."

"How? I didn't have your phone number."

"And yet you had my address. My new address. The one that Dad didn't even know I'd be at when he left LA."

Sky tries the sobbing thing again, but this time it's a pretty feeble attempt.

"How did you find me, Skye?"

"Oh, fine." She abandons the tears-and-despair routine. "You want to know the truth? I'll tell you. That man is slippery as Daffodil in the bathtub. I knew that from day one, so I put an app on his phone so if he tried to skip out on me I could find him. It led me here."

"But he isn't here. Neither is his phone."

"Maybe he found the app and deleted it? This is the last place it showed me. And whenever I try to call I get some canned message about the wireless customer not available."

I know the message she's talking about. I've tried to call Dad and gotten the same thing. Why he came here in the first place is now perfectly clear. Any lingering hope that he really did come to spend time with me is now blown to smithereens, not enough of it left for a proper burial. Dad didn't want to pay child support. Or couldn't, if he really is broke. He knows I'm the only one in the family who would be gullible and soft enough to let him mooch off me. Then he saw an opportunity to put his hands on some money by exploiting yet another vulnerable woman, and he ran with it.

Whether or not he killed Johanna, he is guilty of a series of unforgiveable sins. Running out on Mom and me and Vic. Having sex with Skye, who may or may not be legal, and then running out on child support. Manipulating Johanna.

Meanwhile, Daffodil has had enough. She begins to cry again, a low, hopeless sobbing that goes straight to my heart.

"You really don't have any diapers? Or formula for her?"

"I hitchhiked up here and I'm totally stranded and I forgot Daffodil's bag in the guy's car so now I don't even have bottles if I did have formula. Could you maybe help me out a little?"

Skye begins weeping again, this time maybe for real, so that the rest of her words come out distorted and nearly incomprehensible. I've gotten pretty good at understanding crying talk, though, thanks to bridezilla meltdowns, and I catch the gist of it.

"And now Daffodil is going to starve to death, or else I'll have to give her up and some family will adopt her and I'll never see her again! What am I going to *do*?" She draws her knees up onto the sofa, buries her face in them, and weeps pitifully.

Jackson pats her shoulder in an attempt to be soothing and gives us a look that clearly says, "*Do* something."

"Maybe make another movie?" Owen suggests, apparently unmoved by her plight. "Sounds like those are popular."

"I can't, that's the problem! Don't you see? I couldn't work while I was pregnant. And now my body is ruined... And now my face because of that cat..."

"You're going to help her, right?" Jackson says, turning his attention to me. "I mean, Daffodil is your sister, right?"

"We don't know that," Owen says. "We only have Skye's word for it. And if you'll pardon me, that's not proof of anything."

"You're such a dick," Jackson says.

"It doesn't matter," I say. "Obviously we're going to help her in any case. We're not going to let Daffodil go hungry or put Skye out on the street, family or not."

The truth is, I have all the proof I need, right in front of my eyes. Daffodil looks exactly like pictures of Vic when he was this age.

Dad is evading responsibility, not only for Skye and the baby, but also for what happened to Johanna. At the very least, he knows something. I can no longer believe that him going missing at the same time as she got murdered is a coincidence. The two events are not random correlations, like American cheese consumption statistically matching attendance at a political rally or whatever.

Wherever he is, he's fully expecting I'll pick up the pieces and deal with the fallout of his mistakes. Well, if that's what he thinks, he's got another think coming.

"You and Daffodil can stay here for now," I say, decision made. "We're going to find Dad. He's going to take responsibility for his shit. And if Daffodil is really his, then you're both family. So. That's that. First things first, we really need diapers."

"I'll go buy supplies," Owen volunteers. "Jackson will come with me."

Jackson startles out of some reverie that I don't want to think about, but doesn't make even the smallest move to get up from his place beside Skye.

"What size of diapers? And what kind of formula? And is she eating solids yet?" Owen asks, all questions I would never have even thought of.

"Similac?" Sky says, although it sounds more like a question. "Last time, anyway. I buy whatever's cheapest. And she eats fruit and baby cereal and those baby veggies, too."

"Clothes and diaper size?" he asks.

"Huggies size 3, six months."

Well, there's the answer to how old Daffodil is. Six months.

I may not be a baby person, but I'm feeling protective toward this one. Fiercely. Pissed off equally at my deadbeat father and her incompetent mother.

"Hurry with the diapers," I say. "She's already leaking."

"Wrap a towel around her," Owen suggests. "We'll be back shortly."

"I'm staying here," Jackson says.

"You're not." This is a new side of Owen that I haven't seen before. His tone, his posture, his entire vibe very clearly convey the message Do. Not. Mess. With. Me. The effect on me is a sudden desire to drag him off somewhere private and take his clothes off. Mine too. Unfortunately we haven't even got to that third kiss yet, and the baby, the stripper, and the prickly adolescent are all definite deterrents.

Jackson sighs, but he gets up from the couch and follows Owen to the door. Just like that, they're gone, leaving me with a new baby sister and my father's baby mama, who shows absolutely no inclination to take responsibility for the current situation.

"Could I maybe have a shower?" Skye asks. "And do you have anything I could change into? I've been wearing these clothes for like, three days."

I remind myself that Skye is not much more than a child herself, take a deep breath, and decide to go along with her for now.

First, I take Owen's advice, grabbing a clean towel from the bathroom and wrapping the baby in it. Then, lugging her on one hip, I go into my room and use my free hand to dig out a pair of sweat pants and a button-up flannel shirt, both of which will be too big for Skye but warm and comfortable. God. We're going to have to get clothes for her too. Dad is not only missing and maybe guilty of murder, he's starting to be expensive.

"Here's something you can wear while we wash your clothes," I say, coming back out into the living room, but Skye has curled up on the couch and fallen fast asleep. She looks childlike and defenseless now that she's not radiating her overly sexy public persona, and my anger at Dad flares a little hotter.

I cover Skye with my cozy fleece throw. Daffodil starts to whimper again and I joggle her up and down, walking back and forth across the room. I'm sure the kid is hungry but I don't know what she might be capable of eating, or what might choke her or poison her or whatever.

She keeps fussing, escalating little by little into inconsolable wailing. Skye startles upright, and starts in on me. "What are you doing to her? Did you hurt her?"

"She's hungry and her diaper went south hours ago!" I retort. "Here. You hold her."

"I gotta pee." Skye disappears into the bathroom. The toilet flushes, and then the shower comes on. She is not a five minute shower kind of girl. Thirty minutes later, I hear the water turn off but she's still in there, doing whatever. Probably making use of my minimal makeup products. Daff is still crying and I want to call my mother for help and advice but I can't, because I am not going to be the one to tell her about Dad's latest indiscretion.

There's nobody else I can call. Vic would help out with the baby, but first he would yell at me for bringing a stranger into my condo. Britt would Google baby care tips, or ask her own mother, but she'd also tell Vic. Once again, I miss having

Carmen next door. Maybe she wouldn't have any brilliant ideas, but at least she'd be available for moral support.

After what feels like forty days and forty nights of pacing the floor with a crying baby, but is maybe an hour, tops, Owen buzzes at the door downstairs and I let him in. He and Jackson are both loaded down with shopping bags and two giant plastic bales of diapers.

Owen takes one look at my face and says, softly, "Here, I'll take her."

I hand over the towel-wrapped bundle of misery and he cuddles her against him, making little soothing sounds.

"Grab me a diaper, Addy, would you? And there's a changing pad and some clothes in those bags somewhere," he says.

"I got it." Jackson totally surprises me by helping instead of sulking on the couch. While I tear open the plastic on one of the mega packs of diapers, he dumps out the contents of the bags on the sofa, one by one, until he locates the changing pad.

Bruno slinks over, belly low to the ground, tail twitching. Obviously he's not at all sure about the intruders but curiosity is winning out. He leaps up on the couch and starts sniffing at the various items.

Owen spreads the changing pad out on the floor and gently lays Daffodil down on it. "You are totally a mess, little girl," he says. "But we've got you." He removes the toxic diaper and surveys the damage, which is much, much worse than just an excess bit of baby pee.

"Run some warm water in the kitchen sink, would you Addy?" he says. "This is beyond the power of baby wipes."

"But, that's where I wash dishes," I protest.

He gives me a look and I scoot into the kitchen and start

running water. Owen carries Daffodil over, all bundled up in the towel. He tests the water with a wrist. "Too hot. Run a little cold in there."

I comply. He tests it again, nods, and sits Daffodil down in the sink. She stops screaming and splashes in the water with her chubby little hands.

Jackson, without even being asked, brings over a baby sized washcloth and lays a fluffy towel on the counter.

"You could put the diaper in the trash and then take the whole thing out to the dumpster," Owen suggests.

Jackson shoots him a look of utter horror. "I'm not touching that. I'm not getting close to it. You've got some on you, Addy. Gross."

I follow his gaze to an ugly yellowish brown stain on my jeans and my shirt. There's more on my sleeve. He's right. It's disgusting.

"Don't look so happy about it," I mutter, planning to throw my clothes in the dumpster with the diaper. And the towel.

Jackson backs away, holding his nose, and plops down onto the couch.

"It's just a little baby poop," Owen says, laughing. "Not a national emergency."

"Do you have a secret love child you want to tell me about?" I ask, watching as he competently bathes Daffodil and wraps her in a fluffy towel, talking nonsense to her in a soft voice.

He laughs. "That was Leno's department. Watch and learn. You might have to do this yourself next time." In only moments she's dried, diapered, and dressed in an adorable little footie outfit with teddy bears all over it.

"Hold her for a minute," Owen says. "I'll fix a bottle."

I step backwards and shake my head. "I need to change my clothes. You just got her cleaned up."

He grins. "Hold her on your clean side."

"Give her to her mother."

"You and I both know you're going to have to step up," he says. "Come on Addy."

"Oh fine." I hold out my arms and he puts the baby in them. She grabs hold of my shirt and snuggles in.

"She likes you," Owen says.

She does seem to like me, but its Owen who has her full attention as he goes through the motions of measuring formula and water. When he holds out the bottle she reaches for it with a little pleading sound that does something funny to my heart.

"Hold the nipple where she can get her mouth on it," Owen says. "Keep the bottle at an angle so she's getting milk, not air."

Daffodil does most of this for herself. She grips the bottle with both hands and drinks hungrily, leaning back against me in total trust. Her eyes drift closed.

"You're amazing," I say, half to Owen, half to Daffodil, not sure which one of them has stolen the biggest piece of my heart.

"In case you're imagining I have a secret love nest filled with babies, the truth is that I dated a woman who had one," Owen says. "We were fairly serious, or at least I was."

"What happened?"

"Turned out she was mostly looking for free childcare so she could go out with another guy who had more money than me."

"Ouch."

He shrugs. "It happens. It was a long time ago." He reaches out and runs his fingers through my hair, then along the curve of my jaw.

"Addy, I need something to wear!" The bathroom door opens and Skye wafts out, wearing nothing but a cloud of steam. This is more education than Jackson needs, for sure, even though he's apparently already seen everything Skye has on offer. Owen, on the other hand, maybe has not and I'd have preferred to keep it that way.

"Oh, you're back," she says. She doesn't retreat to the bathroom or even look embarrassed. And why should she? If I had her body I'd probably wander around naked all the time. Pregnancy and childbirth are supposed to create stretchmarks and sagginess and ruin your body forever, at least according to my mother, but if this is the damaged version of Skye then life is even more unfair than I thought.

"Here." I pick up the clothes I'd dropped on a chair earlier and shove them at her, interposing my own imperfect body between her and Jackson, who I'm pretty sure is literally drooling by now.

She frowns and wrinkles her nose. "What is that smell?"

"That would be Daffodil poop. On account of the no diapers problem. Here. Get dressed."

She transfers her disgust to the clothes I'm holding out to her. "That's all you've got?"

"It's not like we're going out clubbing. Did you want my party dress? Never mind. Don't answer that."

She sighs, as if she's being coerced into cleaning toilets or scrubbing floors. "I guess this will do for now." She retreats into the bathroom to get dressed, but doesn't bother closing the door. I close it for her. Slam it, to be honest. This scares

Daffodil who startles violently, her big brown eyes opening wide. Her face scrunches up, ready to start wailing again.

"Hush, shhhh, it's okay." I jiggle her up and down. Her wide eyes search my face, and then I feel her relax as she grabs the bottle and brings it back to her mouth.

"Could you please hold her so I can get out of these toxic clothes?" I ask Owen.

"Of course. Come here, small person." He opens his arms and I hand over Daffodil, breathing in a combined smell of baby powder and aftershave and Owen that does something to my heart again.

It's too much for me. This intimacy of tending a baby. The softness in his eyes when he looks at her. The way his hands can be both strong and gentle, all at once. It's too good to be true. And anything too good to be true is, by definition, too good to be true. But my heart wants to believe otherwise.

It takes me a bit to find clothes, since most of them are still in boxes, but Skye is still in the bathroom when I'm done changing. Owen sits on the couch with Daffodil asleep in his lap. Bruno is curled up beside him, purring. Jackson occupies one of the armchairs, pretending to play with his phone but really keeping an eye on the bathroom door, probably hoping to catch Skye naked again.

I stand there, uncertain, not sure what to say.

"Jackson," Owen says. "Go out to the car and get the playpen, would you? And take that bag of trash to the dumpster while you're at it. All toxic goo is safely enclosed."

"Why me?"

"Because I asked you to."

"You just want to talk to Addy about me. Or make a move on Skye while I'm—"

"Now." Owen says. Not having ever really had a father, that particular tone and resonance of voice is not in my playlist but my body recognizes it all the same. Absolute authority. Testosterone and dominance. The promise of unpleasant consequences.

"You're not the boss of me," Jackson says, but he goes. He also slams the door behind him, but this time Daffodil doesn't flinch.

"This is not going well," Owen says, understatement of the century. "I'm meant to keep him out of trouble, not expose him to porn stars. Literally. In the flesh."

"You're doing better than either of his parents so far," I say, picking up Bruno so I can sit down with him in my lap. "At least you're making an effort. And you haven't killed anybody."

"Yet," he mutters, darkly. "I'm sorry, Addy. I have to keep Jackson with me, at least until court, and I can't bring him back here as long as Skye is here. So the painting—"

"Would have to wait, in any case. As long as she's here."

"What are you going to do?" he asks.

"Find Dad. Force him to take responsibility."

"Unless, of course, he's in jail."

"Right. Also that. Revised plan. Find Dad, figure out who killed Johanna, and then make him take responsibility. What's your plan? With Jackson?"

"Keep him away from Skye? The kid has been acting out. Unsurprising. He's pissed off and hurt and scared. The grandparents he's with can't handle him and you've met my mother. Which leaves me."

"Did you mean it about the group home?"

"I can't do that. Somebody needs to be responsible. And that is gonna be me."

"Of course! I'd help, only..."

"Your hands are kind of full right now. Literally."

We're both quiet for a minute, listening to Daffodil's even breathing.

"Addy..."

His voice is low, husky. I glance up from the baby to find his gorgeous gray eyes intent on mine. He reaches out and twirls a lock of my hair around his finger. "I know things are weird right now, but I hope..."

What he hopes, I'll never know for sure. The bathroom door opens and Skye flounces out. Dressed this time, but barely. My flannel shirt is unbuttoned to the middle of her chest and tied up at the bottom. The sweat pants ride low on her hips, apparently held up by a magic that might evaporate at any moment. Her hair is damp and wavy over her shoulders. She hasn't actually gotten into my makeup after all, but if anything she looks sexier and prettier without it.

"I guess this will do for now," she says. "When can we wash my clothes?"

Before I can answer that, the other door, left cracked when Jackson went out, opens, and he bangs his way in, wrestling a large, flat, cardboard rectangle and a half a dozen shopping bags that didn't make the first trip. "Maybe somebody could help me with this?" he snarks.

Owen is quick to his feet, handing me the baby and fending off Skye by handing her bags full of baby clothes and supplies. While she sorts through the goodies, he keeps Jackson busy assembling the play pen contained in the box.

"Daffodil can sleep in here," he says. "If you put her in the bed she might roll off. Same with the couch. And she can be in here when she's awake, too, if nobody has time to watch her since your place isn't exactly childproof."

I stare at him blankly. "She's not walking. Why would I need to childproof?"

"Never underestimate one of these little creatures. Is she crawling, Skye?"

"Kind of. Like a little inch worm. You know I don't have money to pay you for any of this."

"It's a gift."

Skye flings her arms around his neck. And clings. Owen's arms stay stiffly at his sides for a few seconds, but then they go around her, resting on her back just above her very shapely ass, which my baggy pants fail to disguise. She wriggles in a little closer, and my reaction is not, 'Aww, isn't that sweet.'

"I did it for Addy." Owen sounds like he's being strangled. My name has the effect of making Skye release him and he backs away.

Skye pouts, prettily.

"I helped," Jackson says, walking over. Before Skye can express any more appreciation, Owen puts an arm around his nephew's shoulders and steers him toward the door.

"We need to be going. Addy, I'll call you."

I shove Daffodil at Skye and walk Owen to the door. He leans down, his lips brushing my cheek, and whispers, "Be careful, will you?"

My heart, which is getting quite a workout today, gives an extra thump in my chest. I'm too busy re-adjusting my emotions to find an answer before the two of them are off down the hallway, and I'm left with my awkward and unwelcome company.

Skye lays Daffodil down in the playpen with a blanket,

then flops down on the couch. "Don't you have a TV or something?"

"I'm in the middle of moving, in case you couldn't tell. All these boxes? Those are the first sign."

She sighs and starts cruising TikTok on her phone.

I need to tell Vic and Britt what's going on, but obviously I can't call with Skye right here. So I take a pic of the sleeping baby, open a group text with both Vic and Britt and just send over the pictures without any commentary. I'm not above being entertained by a little shock reaction.

> Britt: Victor, is there something I should know?

> Vic: What do you mean?

> Addy: Meet Daffodil

> Vic: Who names a baby Daffodil? Especially that baby?

> Vic: I'm calling

> Addy: NO. Don't call. You'll wake her up

> Vic: And who is she, exactly?

> Addy: Daffodil. Skye is also here.

> Vic: And that would be?

> Addy: Dad's baby mama. Do a search for Skye and porn flicks and see what comes up.

> Vic: Tell me they're not at your condo

> Addy: Oh, absolutely here at the condo

> Vic: Why?

> Addy: Long story.

> Vic: You sure the kid is Richard's?

Britt: Are you kidding? If that baby isn't Vic's
kid, it's definitely his sib.

Vic snorts — I can't actually hear him, of course, but he's my
twin and I know his reactions.

Vic: all babies look alike

Now Britt is rolling her eyes. Again, I can't see her, but I
know her almost as well as I know my brother. She confirms
my guess with an eye roll emoji.

Britt:

Vic: DO NOT LEAVE THAT WOMAN ALONE
AT YOUR PLACE. You don't know what kind
of scam she's running.

CHAPTER 10

VIC HAS A POINT, but it's not like I can take Skye and Daffodil with me.

Ever After is no place for a baby. To be honest, it's no place for me, either. I've been in the building precisely once, despite living all of my life in Fox Valley. I've attended a few funerals, of course, but they were all held in churches.

Leno's body was the first and last I've come here to see, and that was only as support for Owen. As far as I'm concerned, I don't need to see another dead body ever again. Fortunately, Johanna's body isn't here. As for Ricky, the guy in charge of the funeral home, I don't exactly love hanging out with him, but at least he's not dead.

The two of us are faced off over the coffin Johanna picked out and paid for. It's middle of the road, as coffins go. Not a high-end ornately crafted affair made out of mahogany with genuine silver fittings, nor a plain oak box designed to serve its purpose but no more.

"I don't see the problem, Rick."

"The problem is that the medical examiner won't release the body for days. Weeks even, depending on how busy they are in Spokane."

"But she's already paid for it, right?"

"Well, yes, she did, but—"

"So why can't I sort of —you know—borrow it? Just for the party. I'll bring it back and you can put her in it whenever her body arrives."

"Not going to happen." Ricky, usually eager to please, is adamant.

"Why not, Rickster? Come on. Work with me here."

"Because this is a reputable establishment. Death has dignity. There are protocols. *Ever After* has a reputation to uphold. We do not rent out coffins for party decor."

"I'm not renting it. She already bought it. Besides, nobody will know. The coffin stays closed. You bring it over in the hearse, and then take it back when we're done."

"What if somebody opens it? Gets curious and sneaks a peak?"

"Can we put a wax figure in it? Of, I don't know, Dracula or something. I'm kidding, Rick. Don't look at me like that."

"Respect," Rick says. "For death and the dead and—"

"Seems to me respect for the dead would mean honoring her last wishes. What Johanna wanted—she told me this, Rick, as the deepest wish of her heart—was to have a Christmas party in her house, with her coffin as a centerpiece. Mind you, she wanted to be there and be in it, but given that's not possible—it's not possible, is it? We couldn't possibly sneak her out for a day and then give her back?"

"She was murdered. And I shouldn't even be talking to you, given that it's your dad that probably killed her and all."

"You know he wouldn't kill anybody."

"I don't know anything. I saw on the news how the police are looking for him. And now here you are, mocking the solemnity of death, just like you did with that frivolous bash you threw for Leno."

Ricky takes death seriously. I prefer to approach it lightly, if I can. Grandma Geneva once said, "None of us get out of here alive, Addy. It's not like we don't know that it's coming. Personally, I believe the most fabulous party ever is happening just the other side of our senses. Might as well join in."

Not that there's any point saying this to Rick, so I try another angle. "I guess I'll just have to see if I can buy a coffin somewhere. Spokane, I suppose. I can borrow a pickup truck from someone, drive up there, persuade somebody to sell me a coffin. Just a cheap one, of course. A theater prop, even. Nothing nice like this. I don't know what I'll do with it after, but it might be fun at Halloween."

Rick stares at me with growing horror. "But, people will think it came from here. That I was complicit."

"Can't be helped. I'm throwing this party, Rick. You can help me or not. Last call. I've got other things to do."

"Fine!" He flings both hands up in the air. "I'll bring the coffin over in the hearse. Christmas morning, right? What do you want to do when the ME releases the poor woman's body?"

"Bury her, Rick. Of course! She paid for a plot, right?"

"And who will be there for that? Just pop her in the ground, shall I? Like some Jane Doe without friends or family by dead of night?"

"I'll come. I'll bring people. All right?"

"It's not all right. But I'll do it."

"Thanks Ricky. Call me when you're on the way over so I can make sure the house is open and have some people to help you bring the coffin in."

He makes a sound I choose to interpret as agreement.

I PARK Jezebel on the street right in front of Johanna's house. Somebody has shoveled the sidewalk and the porch. There's no officer on duty and no crime scene tape, so they've already processed and released the scene. Maybe getting in will be as easy as asking for a key.

I call Chip's office but of course I don't get Chip, I get Charlene.

"I'll make sure he gets your message," she says, saccharine sweet, and it's obvious he will never know I called. I'll have to go to the office and barge in to make my request. Unless, of course, there's a key hidden under the doormat or under a rock in the back yard or something. Although, maybe a woman who never left the house didn't feel the need to leave a key.

I see the curtains twitching in the window of the house directly across the street, which stops me from peering in windows or going into the back yard. I'm being watched. Which reminds me that the neighbors might know something. The cops will have canvassed the neighborhood, of course, but Alex isn't going to tell me anything. Especially not about Dad.

But maybe the neighbors will, if I ask the right questions. Maybe they'll even tell me things they wouldn't think to tell Alex.

I call Britt, my usual partner in crime, but she balks at the idea.

"Let the cops do their job. What you should do is go home and make sure that Skye person hasn't already run off with all of your silverware."

"I don't have any silverware. My computer is password protected and encrypted, thanks to you. I've got nothing else worth stealing."

Which is true. Even more true is the fact that I'd much rather be out talking to strangers who may or may not want to kill me than trying to make small talk with Skye or being responsible for Daffodil, no matter how adorable she might be. Or, heaven forfend, unpacking boxes.

"I know what! We can go around and invite the neighbors to Johanna's party. And encourage them to gossip a little. I'll come get you."

"I think that would still be interfering with a murder investigation."

"Interfering is what I do best. Aren't you the least bit curious about how Johanna died? Don't you want to help me find Dad?"

"Not curious enough to get myself arrested. Or killed. What if one of the neighbors is the murderer?"

"Come on, Britt—"

"Not this time. Besides, I'm helping Mom get Christmas ready," she says.

I feel a little lost without Britt and think about my backup options. Vic is a hard no. Owen would have to drag Jackson along and that doesn't seem like a good idea. Fine. I'm all grown up. I can do this on my own.

I start with the immaculate bungalow across the street,

since the occupant already has me under observation. The sidewalk is shoveled. There's a lifelike manger scene on the front lawn, Mary and Joseph and the baby Jesus, plus a couple of sheep and a donkey.

Serena, the neighborhood spokesperson Britt and I met, opens the door. She's a substantial presence, and not just physically. Her dark brown eyes register a keen intelligence and I have no doubt she'll be three steps ahead of me on my best day, which today is definitely not.

"Serena, right? We met on Saturday." I give her my best smile, braced for the lecture about minding my own business.

But she looks me over, considers for a moment, then says, "I guess you might as well come in."

I follow her into a house where clutter would never dare to show itself. The carpet is vintage shag, perfectly vacuumed. The furniture is not new, but is well made and has obviously been cared for. A stand of thriving plants graces one side of the big window. The walls are lined with framed photos of people I'd guess to be children and grandchildren.

"This street is not what it once was," Serena says. "Hard to believe a woman could be killed like that, right in her own home."

"It's awful. I don't suppose you know how it happened?"

"I heard she was stabbed while she slept in her bed. They're saying it was that man you brought here. Your father. Did he really kill her?"

"The police do want to talk to Dad, but he's not a murderer," I say. The words are starting to sound like one of those auto responder emails. Or maybe an affirmation. If I repeat them enough times they will be true.

"Nobody wants to believe somebody related could do a

thing like that," Serena says. "I've got a grandson serving time. Never thought he was capable either, but seems like just about anybody will kill given the right set of circumstances."

She says this entirely without judgment, and it's tempting to let down my guard, but I suspect she's deliberately trying to connect. To make me feel comfortable so I'll open up. She wants intel as much as I do.

"The reason I'm here is because I'm looking for Dad," I say. "I want him to turn himself in so we can get to the bottom of who really killed Johanna. Wondering if you saw anything that might help?"

She shakes her head, slowly. "Nothing that is going to help, but plenty that makes him look guilty. I saw him and you go into the house. You left. The attorney and the notary left later. An hour, maybe an hour and a half? Never saw that man leave. But then, he came with you so it's not like there was a car parked on the street. He could have walked out the back alley any old time."

It's not what I wanted to hear at all. I want info that will either clear him or help me find him. Or both. This just makes him look guiltier.

"Now, what about Johanna's party?" Serena asks.

"You know about that?"

"We talked. We were friendly-like. When she first moved in she used to invite me over, or she'd pop into my house for a cup of coffee. First, she stopped going out. And then at some point she stopped letting people come in. But she'd call off and on, to ask a question or sometimes just to chat. Lonely, poor thing."

"Did she say anything to you about her will?"

"It's funny that you'd mention that. The day before the

emergency response people all came over here, and you and your friend, she called and asked me if I had a lawyer. Said she needed to make a will."

"Chip Fitzwilliam is your attorney?"

"Who's that, now? Is that the one she ended up with? I told her mine is in Spokane. Offered to call around and get recommendations, not that there are many options here in the Valley, but she said she couldn't wait and was going with some new guy that had room on his schedule."

"Did she tell you about the psychic?"

"Foolishness, that," Serena says. "When I heard she was dead I thought maybe she'd just scared herself to death, until the cops came around asking questions." She heaves herself up from her chair. "Well. This calls for coffee and consideration. I'll be right back."

When she walks through the door into the kitchen it's tempting to get up and snoop around her living room, but I need her to trust me. So I stay in my chair, trying not to twitch.

A few minutes later she returns, carrying a tray that holds two mugs of coffee, a sugar bowl and a little jug of cream, along with two slices of homemade coffee cake. The coffee smells like it was brewed a couple of hours ago and has been simmering away on the hot plate ever since. But burned coffee is a small price to pay for cake and information, and there's plenty of cream and sugar to doctor it up.

I take a bite of cake, which is buttery and moist and flavorful, and then wash it down with coffee that could clear a blocked drain.

"Can you tell me what the cops said, when they asked about my father? Are they the ones that told you she was stabbed?"

"No, they wouldn't tell me a thing. Just that they were looking for your father as a person of interest. Asking what I heard or saw. I made up the stabbing out of my own imagination, I'll admit. Figured if she was shot, I'd have heard something. Old Ralph thinks she was strangled, but that's just his imagination. It's what he'd do, if he was going to kill a woman. Hands around her throat, up close and personal, watching the life run out."

I shiver at the image her words bring up and make a note to add Ralph to the top of my suspect list.

"About Johanna's party," I say. "Will the neighbors come, do you think?"

"Every last one of them. They've all been dying to see what's behind those closed doors for years. Now that it's a crime scene? You can bet your sweet behind they'll be there."

"Did she tell you about giving the house away at the party?"

"She did not. What kind of harebrained idea is that she came up with? How would you even do that? The house will belong to whoever she gave it to in her will. Even if you could talk them around that's gonna take some time, what with probate and all. What is it, honey? You haven't finished your cake. Something on your mind?"

There is, of course, a lot on my mind. One of those things is deciding whether or not to tell her about Dad and the house. She gives me another searching look and the whole story comes spilling out of me.

She shakes her head. "That attorney doesn't sound like he's much good. Should have talked her out of that one. Still, I tell you this. Everybody will come out just to see the crime scene. If you're actually giving away the crime scene? They'll pack themselves in there like sardines. You sure you're ready for that?"

"I'm sure. And I'd better get a move on. I need to get into the house and get it ready for the party. I don't suppose you know if Johanna hid a key somewhere?"

Serena heaves herself out of her chair and returns to the kitchen. I hear a drawer open and close, and when she comes back she's holding a green plastic keychain, one of those generic things you can buy in bulk. Three keys are on the ring. "Front door and back, and the garden shed. If your father owns the house, I guess it should be okay for you to go in. Especially since I know Johanna wanted that party. Word of advice. The neighbors are all on high alert right now. If you don't want somebody calling the cops, park a couple of blocks away, come up by the back alley and in through the back yard."

"How did you come by the keys?"

"She gave them to me after that psychic told her she was going to die, and made me promise to look in if I didn't hear from her every day. She said she wanted to be sure she wouldn't lie there dead for weeks with nobody the wiser until the smell got so bad you could whiff it from the street. And she was worried about Nat finding her."

"Who is Nat?"

"Neighborhood kid who feeds her birds. Nat's kind of obsessed with birds. He woulda done it for free but she paid him. Paid him to shovel the snow, too."

"Could I talk to him, do you think?"

Serena laughs. "If Angel's home, no. She's downright fierce about protecting her little brother. Their mother got murdered a couple of years back, never was a father in the picture. They live in that gray house down on the corner, the one with the giant bird sculpture out front."

"I can't thank you enough. I'd better go see how much of a mess the crime scene investigators left behind."

"You need any help, you let me know. And if you want a little help solving her murder, I'm here for that too." Serena grins. "Don't you be looking at me like that. I know who you are. You didn't just plan a party for that Leno Masterson, you solved his murder too."

"I'll need all the help I can get," I tell her, reluctantly relinquishing my now empty plate as she reaches for it, and then setting my half empty mug on the tray with greater enthusiasm. "That cake was stellar."

"I'll make one for Johanna's party." She walks me to the door and as I navigate first the slippery porch and then the sidewalk, I don't need to look back to know she's watching me through her living room window.

I look down the street to the gray house on the corner where the kid who feeds the birds and shovels the snow lives. But then I see a man standing in the window of the shabby ranch style to the right of Johanna's and decide to talk to him first.

He unabashedly watches me cross the street and opens the door before I can knock.

"What do you want?" It's Ralph, minus the Santa hat. His head is bald and shiny and his house stinks of stale cigarette smoke and beer and dirty laundry.

I flash my brightest smile. "We're putting together a Christmas party at Johanna's, and I wanted to personally invite you."

"She's dead," he says. "In case you haven't heard."

"I heard. Before she died, she hired me to plan an after-death Christmas party in her house and invite all of the neighbors."

He glares at me, as if personally affronted by this news. "Why in blazes would she want a thing like that?"

I take a step back. Some people underestimate the elderly; not me. I figure they've got a whole lifetime of things to be pissed about and a whole lot less to lose.

"Why would you have a party in her house?" Ralph is warming up into a rant. Arms waving. Spittle flying. I take another step back.

"Johanna didn't even like people! Have some respect! Her body's not even in the grave! You can't have the whole neighborhood traipsing through there. Most likely stealing things."

"It's what she wanted," I say, soothingly. "It's not that she didn't like people, she was just phobic about going outside. I'm a party planner, Mr..."

"I ask you this. How did she know she was going to be strangled?" he asks. "So that she'd need to make a will and plan that party in the first place? Something smells fishy to me." He sniffs, nostrils pinched, as if maybe that something fishy is me.

I shiver, remembering what Serena said about Ralph earlier. Obviously, talking about the party isn't going to get me anywhere with him. Maybe his interest in murder will. I lower my voice. "I'm also... um, helping the police look for the killer."

"How do I know *you're* not the killer? Not a lot of people ever been in her house, and you are one of them. You and your friend and that other man who came here with you. I heard tell they're looking for him in connection with her murder. Maybe you were in it with him. Fine thing that would be, you prancing all over her house destroying evidence and whatnot while pretending to plan some party."

I manage to keep my voice level. "I thought maybe you'd like to help, is all. Since she was your neighbor."

"Get off my property before I call the cops and complain about you meddling." He slams the door shut and I hear the dead bolt shoot home.

I beat a hasty retreat, just in case he's got a loaded shotgun and decides to encourage me along in my departure.

CHAPTER 11

I TAKE Serena's advice and park Jezebel a couple of blocks away, then take the alley so I can enter the house through the back yard. I was smart enough to wear boots, not my tennis shoes, but they are short boots and the alley has not been plowed. Snow works its way down around my ankles, icy cold rivulets soaking my socks.

It's creepy in the alley. Nobody moving. Nothing but trash cans and fences and one lone crow, watching me from a leafless tree in somebody's backyard. A burst of common sense—deeply buried and rusty from long disuse—suggests that maybe I should turn around and walk away. In movies, alleys are where people get strangled and shot, abducted and raped. What if this is the path the killer took to get into Johanna's house? Obviously he—or she, because in my experience women can be every bit as dangerous as men—wouldn't just walk up to the front door, draw a gun, and go 'Bang, you're dead.' They'd sneak, so the neighbors wouldn't notice. Just like I'm sneaking now.

The gate to the back yard is closed, but not locked. Should it be locked?

Fear makes an appearance, partnering up with common sense. *Could be the murderer, come back to revisit the scene of the crime.*

"More likely the cops forgot to lock up when they left. Most of those guys can't find their ass with both hands," I say out loud, to bolster my courage. Still, my heart is on overdrive as I shove the gate open.

Somebody has cleared away the snow so that it opens easily. Footsteps have trampled all over the yard. Same cops who left the gate unlocked, probably. Looking for evidence.

A squirrel chatters a warning as I walk under a big tree on my way to the back door. Squirrels are always scolding but it does nothing to quell my uneasiness. If somebody nefarious has been here, there'd be no way to know. What if he, or she, is waiting inside the house? Ready to nab me when I walk in and then do away with me just like they did with Johanna?

Multiple sets of boots have trampled a path leading to French doors that offer entrance to what was once a wrap-around deck, and is now a luxurious, closed-in retreat. The entire space below an overhanging roof is walled in by glass, and I put my nose up close and peer inside.

Plants flourish everywhere, thriving in the light. A couple of hammock chairs are suspended from their own wooden frames. There's a window seat covered in cozy cushions. Three large bookshelves are full to overflowing. A low table offers the perfect place to set out drinks or snacks.

Other than black fingerprint powder marring the surface of the coffee table, everything looks normal and undisturbed. I open the doors, which are unlocked, and stop short. Two pairs of boots sit on a doormat in a puddle of melted snow. One pair is feminine but practical. The other pair is smaller. Kid sized.

Could be neighbors. Maybe that kid Johanna mentioned, Nat, came over to feed the birds, then figured he'd stick his nose in the house and have a little look around. What boy could resist the chance to investigate a crime scene? But then who do the other boots belong to? And why are the doors unlocked.

I stand there in the open doorway listening, thinking, knowing I should back away and call Alex, or maybe even 911. The house is quiet. What are the two of them doing in there? Maybe Nat is in danger, or maybe he's not here at all. Maybe the boots belong to looters. The thought of that sets my blood boiling.

Somebody murdered Johanna. Somebody else is not going to get away with stealing her belongings. I dig out my can of bear spray and close the doors behind me.

"Hello?" I call out. "Who's here?"

No answer.

I sniff at a tang of pleasant smelling smoke. Incense? Could something be on fire?

"Hello? My name is Addy Winters. I'm Johanna's executor. I'm coming in."

The only answer is a pathetic "*Meow,*" coming from somewhere in the house. Bagheera. The poor cat is probably starving.

"*Meow.*"

That settles it. I have to check on the cat. I leave my boots on, in case I need to make a run for it. The floor will need to be cleaned in any case; it's tracked with muddy footprints already, most likely from the cops and crime scene people. I'm not going to make things worse.

"Here, kitty kitty. Where are you?"

I try the first door that leads into the house, which turns out to open directly into the kitchen. And there I find the cat, a kid, a silver-haired woman, and the source of the smoke.

Bagheera, sitting in front of a full food dish, looks up at me, trills, and goes back to eating. A curl of smoke rises from a sage wand resting in an abalone shell on the kitchen counter. The boy and the woman sit side by side on stools at the breakfast bar with steaming mugs in front of them. The woman's is tea; I can tell because the tea bag is still in it. A third mug sits on the counter and I glance around, looking for another intruder.

"Indigo said you'd be coming," the kid says, "So we made you a cocoa. Do you like cocoa?"

The woman smiles and says nothing. Given the network of fine lines etched into her face and her age-spotted hands, she might be seventy, maybe even eighty. Older than my parents, younger than Grandma Geneva was when she died. Her hair is shoulder length, silver-gray. She's wearing a flowing caftan featuring swirls of teal and azure and violet over a pair of black leggings. Gemstone and silver bracelets circle both wrists, and a huge moonstone pendant hangs around her neck.

A small handgun rests on the counter beside her mug.

I stare at the gun, trying to calculate the odds of blinding her with the bear spray before she can shoot me. She says, calmly, "Your cocoa is getting cold. Have a seat."

Sitting does not sound like a good idea, even though my knees, which have gone wobbly, are at war with my feet, which want to run me right on out of there at speed. I also have the absolutely ridiculous thought that if this woman shoots me, it will make even more of a mess in Johanna's house, with blood and brains or whatever in addition to the fingerprint powder all over everything.

"I added extra sugar. And cream," the kid says, brown eyes shining with goodwill. "I gave Bagheera cream too."

He certainly doesn't look like he's under duress. No one is aiming the gun at him. The woman sits there, smiling slightly, like she's auditioning for the role of a senior citizen Mona Lisa.

"You're trespassing," I say.

"True. Technically. But Johanna doesn't mind." She sips her tea. No move toward the gun, lying between us on the counter.

Bear spray still in my right hand, out of sight below the counter between us, I pick up the mug of cocoa with my left and take a sip. "This is delicious, Nat. You are Nat, aren't you?"

"Of course I am," he says. "Am I trespassing too? I came over to feed the birds. I'm an or...thinologist. Or at least I will be. Angel says I have to get through school first and then go to college before I can be one, but I looked it up and it means somebody who studies birds and that's me now. Do you think I have to wait to be one 'til I'm grown up? Angel says it's pre...tentious to go around saying that. Do you think that's true?"

He doesn't give me time to answer. "Once you start feeding birds you have to keep on, did you know? Because you've tamed them. Like the rose in the *Little Prince* book. Sometimes they'll die if you don't keep feeding them. Sometimes Bagheera eats them. I'm sad when that happens. Angel says cats will be cats, and I suppose that's true, but I wish it wasn't."

"My cat likes to steal things from people," I tell him. "And eat mice."

"Mice are cute too," Nat says. "I like cats. I don't like that they are killers."

Bagheera meows, then leaps up on the counter and sniffs at Nat's cocoa. He puts his hand over the mug and shakes his head. "I don't think chocolate is good for cats."

"Death is not the huge catastrophe everybody thinks it is," the woman says. "A transition. Probably to something better."

"My Grandma Geneva said she thought there was some big party going on in the next dimension. She was excited to see what it was all about."

"Johanna wasn't ready, though," the woman says, calmly sipping.

My fingers tighten around my bear spray canister. "You're the psychic. The one who told Johanna she was going to die."

"And you're the person who plans parties for dead people. The one whose father is wanted for murder." She dunks the teabag up and down in her cup. "What is wrong with the food industry these days, do you think? When I was your age, tea tasted like tea. No flavor in this at all."

"You should have cocoa," Nat says. "We need to finish up the milk before it goes off. Wasting is bad, Angel says. She wouldn't like me being in the house. She didn't even want me to come over and feed the birds. But, I needed to... to *see*."

"I found him in the backyard when I arrived," Indigo says. "And then we both came in here to see how Johanna died.

Come here, kitty cat. You mustn't be on the counter." She picks up the cat, who does not resist, and settles him in her lap.

"You brought a kid in to view a murder scene?"

"Well, to be honest, I didn't want to break in and he had a key." She smiles, stroking Bagheera. "In any case, Johanna's death doesn't appear to have been violent. No blood stains anywhere."

"I was picturing all sorts of horror things," Nat says. "My mom was shot. I kept picturing Johanna lying in a pool of blood and I wanted to know how she died. I feel better, knowing it wasn't like that. Also, somebody needed to feed Bagheera. You won't tell Angel, will you? That I came into the house? She'll be so mad."

"I'll never tell," Indigo promises. Bagheera purrs and trills, butting his head against her breast. "Who is the sweetest pussy cat?" she croons, rubbing his chin.

This moment is surreal. The silver-haired, sweet-faced woman with her cup of tea, the cat purring in her lap, the kid chattering about birds, everything clean and sparkling and normal. Not a trace of fingerprint powder to be seen in the kitchen. No muddy footprints on the floor. All of it a cozy counterpoint to the fact of Johanna's murder, not to mention the handgun still sitting on the counter.

"We cleaned, before we made drinks," Nat volunteers, answering the question I haven't asked.

"Fingerprint powder doesn't just wipe up with a dish rag," I observe, sipping my cocoa. It really is deliciously creamy and sweet.

"Not my first crime scene, Addy, dear," Indigo says. "I came equipped with a cleaning kit."

I take a breath and deliberately dispel the illusion of safe and normal. "What are you really doing here?" I ask her.

"Cleaning the house," she says, in an tone of mild surprise. "Feeding the cat. Drinking inferior tea."

"You didn't come here from—from wherever you live—to clean up the kitchen and feed the cat. Or drink tea."

"Seattle, dear one. I saw that I would be needed. And so I came."

"You saw? Like a vision in a crystal ball, you mean?" I let skepticism drip heavily into my voice.

Indigo laughs. "Of course not. Don't be silly. A crystal ball isn't at all like turning on a security camera feed. In any case, the cards told me."

Misdirection. Normalizing actions that are not at all normal. These are classic Dad moves, familiar tools in the grifter's toolbox. *Don't look here, look over there.* How long has Indigo really been here? Did she need Nat's key to get in, or was that just a ruse? Has she cleaned up something besides fingerprint powder? Maybe she's the murderer, toying with me, blatantly sitting in the kitchen, petting Johanna's cat. I know she's hiding something. And there's the gun, sitting right there on the table. It's tiny and almost pretty. But it could still kill somebody.

And here I am, having a drink and a chat with her. And the kid. The kid should definitely not be here. He can't be older than twelve, despite the vocabulary.

"Do you think Angel might be missing you?" I ask. "Maybe it's time to go."

"Angel's at work. And I haven't finished my cocoa. Besides, I want to help."

"With what, exactly?"

"The party."

"What party?"

He rolls his eyes. "Johanna's Christmas party. Everybody knows about it."

"How? I only talked to Serena and Ralph before I came here."

"But Johanna asked you before she died, right?"

"How on earth does everybody know that?"

He flushes, dropping his gaze to the counter. "Johanna told me. And maybe I might have told Serena. And Ralph asked that woman who came with the lawyer what all the lawyering was about, and she told him Johanna wanted to give her house away at the party, and maybe Ralph told somebody."

I sigh. Gossip runs fast in a neighborhood, especially when there's death involved. And my attempt to get Nat off to safety has failed. I take another swallow of cocoa to buy some thinking time, and then I take the direct approach. I gesture at the gun. "Could you maybe put that thing away?"

"Do you not like guns?"

She picks up the weapon and I freeze with my mug halfway to my mouth, every brain and body cell focused on what is suddenly the most important object in the world. My imagination delivers five different scenarios within about five seconds: Nat shot and dead. Nat shot and wounded, me throwing my body protectively over his to save him. Both of us shot. Me spraying Indigo with bear spray and missing, maybe getting the cat. Me launching myself across the table and tackling Indigo, her chair going over backwards, her head smashed against the floor...

"You're right, of course," Indigo says. "I wasn't sure when you came in whether it would be you or somebody a little more sinister, so I had it ready just in case. Careless of me not to put it away. I'll just tuck it in my bag here, is that all right?" She stows the gun, a little carelessly, I think, as if it's a hairbrush or a tube of lipstick.

"Could you maybe also put the bag on the floor?"

"If that will make you happy." She dislodges the cat and grunts with effort as she lowers the bag.

"Tell me again why you're here?" I ask, getting to the point that is uppermost in my mind, now that the weapon is at least momentarily secured.

"People can't be allowed to just go around killing innocent and vulnerable people, can they? Obviously, I'm here to help bring Johanna's killer to justice. And to help with your party."

"Forgive me if I'm skeptical. You've broken into her house and—"

"I didn't break in. Nat unlocked the door for me."

"So you say. How do I know you hadn't already been in the house? How do we know you're not the one who killed her?" There, I've said it. I brace myself, ready to blast her with bear spray if she reaches for her bag.

"There now, that feels better, doesn't it, to get that off your chest?" She beams at me, as if I've said something flattering rather than accusing her of murder. "Honesty is so refreshing."

"Really? I'm not sure that you've said one truthful word to me."

"You are not a very trusting individual are you? If we're going to work together you'll need to—"

"We're not going to work together!" Some extra decibels—okay, a lot of them—have found their way into my voice. Bagheera lays his ears back and swears at me, tail twitching. Nat has shrunk into himself, his face tight with worry, clutching his mug with both hands. It's me he's looking at askance, though. Not Indigo. Which I suppose is fair since I'm the one who is shouting.

"Hush now, you're fine," Indigo says. My first thought is that she's reassuring Nat, but then she adds, "If you would please remove your claws from my flesh?" She caresses and soothes and cuddles the cat as if he's just been through some sort of major trauma. Which I suppose maybe he has, given Johanna's death. He probably knows who the murderer is, but it's not likely he'll tell us. A dog might growl and bark and maybe even bite the person who killed his mistress. A cat? Purrs and cuddles, so long as you feed him and cater to his whims.

I lower my voice. "Excuse me for saying this, Indigo, but if the cards told you Johanna was going to be murdered, why didn't you show up before she died instead of after? Maybe you could have stopped it."

Indigo sighs, the smile fading. "They didn't speak of murder, only of her death. Even if they had, I wouldn't have been able to stop it. When I was young I tried, a few times, to intervene in something that was going to happen. It always happened anyway. Once, I think more people died because I meddled. I've learned it's best to... step back, and let fate do what fate is going to do."

"Even if it's murder."

"Even then." She smiles, sadly this time. "I'm sure you're thinking about alerting the local authorities to my presence. That would be a big mistake."

She's right. That's exactly what I was thinking about doing. Just as soon as I can get Nat well away from her.

"Are you threatening me?" I ask.

"Oh no, dear. Not in the least. Just making sure you have all of the relevant information. I know you want to solve Johanna's murder. Clear your father's name, even, although I do sense some conflict around that. Is he innocent do you think?"

I stare at her, processing for a minute before I ask, "What do you know about my father?"

"He's wanted, honey. I saw it on the news. The police are looking for him. Now, as I was about to say, I have no doubt that you have personal connections with the local police. You'll tell them I broke into the house. That I threatened you with a gun. Enough to get me booked, at least overnight. If I'm in jail, you lose access to everything I know about Johanna. All of the things that she told me during our many sessions. How she came to inherit this house. Her childhood and the people in it. Who knows what else I know that might be relevant?"

"That's... blackmail."

Nat screws up his face and tilts his head to one side. "I thought blackmail was like... if she threatened to tell somebody a bad secret about you unless you did what she wanted. Mom used to say that if you do a thing, and another thing happens because you did it, it's not punishment, it's just consequences."

"There you have it," Indigo says, a spark of laughter in her eyes. "Or, if you prefer, think of it as the carrot and the stick. I help you catch Johanna's killer and plan her party. Or I don't." She shrugs. "Call them, dear, if you really think that's what you need to do. I'll tell them my story and we'll see what they say."

Her shoulders stoop, her back rounds into a hump. A tremble comes into her hands and her voice. "Officer, I didn't hear from Johanna and I was worried so I drove up to check on her. I see now that I shouldn't have entered but I was just so

worried. I had no idea she'd been... oh my goodness... killed."
Her voice breaks and big tears pour down her cheeks. She looks
ancient, frail, heartbroken.

The performance stops as abruptly as it began. She sits up
straight and flashes a smile at me, shedding at least twenty
years in the blink of an eye.

"Wow," Nat says, a little too admiringly. "That was good."

"No, Nat," I say, "it was devious. And a reminder to us both
that we can't trust a word she says."

"Oh, I wouldn't ever lie to Nat. Such a sweet boy." Indigo
beams like a proud grandmother. I notice that she hasn't said
she would never lie to me.

I get to my feet. "Well. This has been lovely, but it's time for
us all to go." By which I mean them, of course. I still want to
have a good look around the house.

"We need to clean up," Nat says. "Angel has a fit if I leave a
mess in the kitchen."

"Right you are, Natty." Indigo slides off her stool and
carries her mug to the sink. "Do you want to wash or dry?
Addy, why don't you take a quick look around the house and
then make a plan for the party? If you want to be ready by
Christmas Day we've got a lot of work to do."

"I don't think there's a *we*," I protest.

"Oh, of course there is! I wouldn't think of letting you try to
do all of this work alone."

"I have people who will help me."

"Nonsense. This close to Christmas? If they were going to
help they'd be with you now. Plus, I can talk while we clean
and decorate, and tell you all about Johanna."

The woman is unshakeable. Maybe a good thing to keep
her close, so I can keep an eye on her. But I need to get back to

the condo and put eyes on Skye. And Daffodil. Run intervention with Debbie the HOAR.

"Where is your car, Indigo? And where are you staying?"

"Oh, I parked a couple of blocks away," Indigo says. "The neighbors are bound to be curious. Johanna said the woman across the way keeps a sharp lookout. Just put those mugs back in the cupboard, would you Nat? And I'll wipe down the table."

"Where are you staying?" I ask, again.

She turns to look at me, blue eyes wide. "Oh, goodness, honey. You're worried that I'm planning to stay here! No, no. The energy in this house is too thick and stagnant for me. Cloying. I can barely breathe. I've done a brief clearing with the sage, but it's not nearly enough. I have a reservation at the *Fox Valley Inn*."

"What about Bagheera?" Nat asks.

"We'll be in every day, Nat, getting ready for the party. We'll make sure he's fed."

"But he can't be here with a bunch of people going in and out, can he? What if he runs away? And what about after that, when you give the house away?"

Indigo lifts her hands in the air. "I'm sorry, child. I have a cat already. She would not approve at all, I'm afraid, of inviting in another. Besides, I won't be going back home until after the party."

"Addy?"

"I too have a cat." *And a porn star, and a baby.* Bringing home another cat would be insanity.

Nat looks like he's about to cry.

"Johanna said he wasn't even her cat. She thought maybe he had another family. They might be worried about him, now that we've been keeping him locked up."

"I don't see any posters about a missing cat," Nat says.

"Why don't you take him," I suggest. "Then he'll still be in the neighborhood and can go back to his other family if he has one."

"I don't think he does. And he eats *birds*."

"Well, he might eat birds at my house too."

"But not my birds. Not Johanna's birds. Not the ones I feed and am responsible for. Besides, Angel would have a fit."

Bruno will also have a fit. But obviously, I'm the designated cat adopter in this situation. I sigh. "We'll have to get a cat carrier. He can stay here tonight, and I'll bring mine tomorrow."

"Johanna has one," Nat volunteers.

"Why would she have a cat carrier if she never went anywhere?" It seems like a logical question but Nat looks at me like he suspects I'm dimwitted.

"He had to go to the vet. You know, for his shots and a checkup. She got Serena to take him, but she'd put him in the carrier first so he'd be all ready to go. Come on, let's look in the garage."

"What makes you think it's in the garage? Have you been in there before?"

"Where else would she keep it? Come on."

I follow him out the kitchen door into the enclosed patio, and from there through another door into the garage.

"Whoa." Nat comes to a dead halt, staring at the nondescript, dark blue four-door sedan parked dead center.

"What's the matter, Nat? You okay?"

The kid has gone white as a sheet. "Johanna didn't drive. Do you think it could be the murderer's car?"

"No chance," I say, as if that idea hadn't flashed through

my own head. "The police and the crime scene people have all been here, remember? Pretty sure they would have noticed if the murderer left their car behind."

"But Johanna never ever went anywhere. Why would she have a car? What if..." He stops. Swallows hard. Gathers his courage and whispers, "What if there's, like, blood or something in the trunk?"

It's my turn to swallow. The 'or something' that could be in the trunk is... Dad. If somebody decided to kill him and wanted to hide the evidence for a day or two, what better place to stash him than in the trunk of a car that nobody drives? Especially if it was done after the crime scene was released. Or what if Dad's in there, still alive but injured and about to expire at any moment? Just because I feel a little murderous rage toward him doesn't mean I'm actually okay with letting him die a slow and wretched death.

"I guess we'd better look," I say, but I don't move. Neither does Nat. We both stand there staring as if the trunk is Pandora's box and opening it is going to unleash a series of plagues upon us all.

My lungs seem to have forgotten about breathing. My heart is hammering like a crazed thing and my hands are trembling as I open the driver's side door and look for the release button for the trunk. It takes way too long to find it, and when I finally do I wish I hadn't. When I walk around to the back of the car Nat follows behind me, and I hear him suck in a breath as I slowly open the trunk.

Both of us stand there staring down at a jack, a set of flares, a random plastic twist tie, and some bits of lint and fuzz. That's it. No evidence of violence or murder or death.

"There, you see?" I say, as if I've opened the trunk only for

Nat's benefit, and not to calm the fear unleashed by my own overactive imagination.

"Let's check inside."

Again, nothing of interest. The interior is pristine. Nothing on the floors or under the seats. The console is empty. The glovebox holds a maintenance manual, a map of Washington state, registration in Johanna's name, current and up to date, and receipts from Les Schwab for a complete set of tires, purchased in June of 2007.

"Here we go, Nat, it was her car. It makes sense, right? I mean she used to leave the house, so she would have needed a car back then. Looks like she bought new tires, even, but way back eighteen years ago."

"Why?" Nat asks. Color has returned to his face, but he still looks worried. "I mean, not why would she buy tires. Why would she stop leaving the house like that? And when she did stop, why not sell the car?"

I've been wondering the same thing. It's unsettling to think that one day Johanna drove into the garage, turned off the engine, and walked into the house for the last time. Did she know then that she would never drive the car again? Did she ever come out here and sit in it, daydreaming about opening that garage door and venturing back out into the world?

I imagine that moment so vividly I can hear the clicking of the cooling engine and a whiff of exhaust. But still, I can't wrap my mind around any moment where I'd know I wasn't ever going to step outside again.

"I dunno, Nat," I say. "But anxiety disorders don't always make sense."

"Maybe it wasn't anxiety," he says. "Maybe she was right to

be scared of something out there, and then it came in and got her anyway."

I feel like there's some comforting thing I should say to that to make his world safe again, but if his mother has really been murdered, then what security could I possibly provide? The best way for me to help Nat is to make sure the murderer gets locked away. Time to get back to work.

"Where do you think that carrier might be?" I ask. We start looking around the shelves, all neatly organized. I've barely had a chance to do any snooping at all before Nat calls out, "Here it is! I'll help you get him in."

As it turns out, Bagheera is not interested in getting inside the carrier and all three of us are frazzled and bleeding by the time the mission is accomplished.

"Remember to take food for him," Nat says, anxiously. "And his dishes."

"I've got cat food," I tell him.

"But it will be different than what he's used to. Staying with strangers is scary. He should at least have that."

Nat is close to tears and I find myself wondering what happened after his mother's death. Was there a spell of foster care in there before he was allowed to go back home and live with his sister?

So I go around the house with Nat, collecting Bagheera's bowls, his food, both wet and dry, a pillow from the closed-in patio that will smell familiar.

"Now," Indigo says. "It's time we get you home, young man."

"I'm find on my own."

"Nonsense. It's dark out and we've had a murder. We'll walk with you."

"I was thinking you might want to go check into your motel," I say.

She shakes her head. "No offense, but your little can of bear spray isn't really much by way of defense against a murderer."

Which is exactly what a devious murderer would say if she wanted to shoot us both out in the back alley instead of in the house. But she's already headed for the back door and by the time we catch up she's putting on her boots.

CHAPTER 12

NAT'S HOUSE is a ranch style home in need of some love. The sidewalk is shoveled, but the gray paint is faded and peeling. Someone has made an attempt to put a string of Christmas lights on the eaves, but one of the bulbs is burnt out and the whole thing is haphazard and uneven.

A bird-shaped robot towers over us at the boundary of yard and sidewalk. It looks futuristic and devastatingly apocalyptic, as if it once had life and predatory abilities, and is now immobilized but still sentient. And malevolent. Its eyes glow red. They look like they are capable of incinerating us with lasers.

"Halt. Who goes there?" it challenges in a rusty, robotic voice as we approach.

I stumble over my own feet and just barely save myself from falling into a snowbank.

"Isn't it awesome?" Nat enthuses. "Angel made it for me because of how much I love birds. Come on. You can meet her."

The front door opens.

The young woman standing there, backlit by the glow from indoors, reminds me of the bird. Even though her eyes are a dark brown, not red, they spark with anger. Her skin, which on another sort of woman might be a sun-kissed brown, seems to be internally lit by flame. I'd guess she's barely out of her teens. If this is Angel, she must be Nat's sister, far too young for the responsibility of a house and a kid brother.

"Where have you been? You're supposed to check in with me, remember?" she scolds Nat, before turning on me and Indigo. "Can I help you?"

It's clear that what she means by 'can I help you?' is 'please fuck off' only without the please.

"Hi, I'm Addison Winters. This is Indigo... um... just Indigo. We found Nat at Johanna's place and—"

"What the hell, Natty? That's a murder scene. I told you—"

"But the birds were hungry, Angel! The feeders were almost empty. And then I met Indigo and Addy came over and we were planning the party—"

"What are you even talking about?"

"Johanna Meyers had asked me to plan a party for her. On Christmas Day. In her house. I want to honor her wishes," I say.

Angel's eyes narrow. "I heard somebody shot her. How do I know it wasn't you? Nat, get in here."

Nat scampers up onto the porch and into the house. Angel tucks him behind her, protectively.

"We're not exactly the murderous type." I cross my fingers behind my back as I say it. I know I'm not a murderous type. I'm not so sure about Indigo. And I can't help glancing over my shoulder at the giant bird, half expecting it to swivel my direction, eye-lasers locked on us and set to kill.

"Did you make that bird robot?" Indigo asks. "It's fantastic!"

"My interpretation of the Thunderbird." Angel's expression softens. One slim hand shoves a heavy fall of raven black hair behind a well-shaped ear. "Obviously it's not traditional."

"I love it," Nat says. "It's the coolest ever. Can I help with the party, Angel? Please?"

"You'll stay away from that party. Bunch of morbid looky-loos, the neighbors. Always speculating. Johanna wanted to be left alone, what's so wrong about that?"

"I get that. She did. But she also wanted a party after her death. It sounds like Nat was close to her. Maybe—"

"You leave Nat out of this. Get off my porch before I call the cops."

She means it. From the look on her face, she'd be quite capable of shooting us first. I back away and the door slams shut. Angel's searing fury has burned holes in my reserves of optimism and left me feeling defeated and battle-weary.

"Lot of responsibility to carry for one so young," Indigo murmurs when we're back out on the street.

"That's what I was thinking."

"You carry a lot of responsibility also," Indigo says. "Running a business. Worrying about your father. Johanna. And I feel like there's something more..."

She's fishing, but I am not taking the bait.

After a long silence she says, "Listen. I can help you find your father."

"Yeah? And how would you help with that?"

"We can ask the universe. I can do that on my own, of course, but it will be more powerful if you are with me. Strong emotion helps to create the channel. And a spell is always stronger when cast by two."

"Like a witch spell, you mean?"

"If that's how you want to think of it."

"Yeah, I really don't have time for that." What I'm hoping is that she'll take a hint and leave. I'll lock the doors and choose to believe that she doesn't have a key or won't break in.

But she's not going anywhere. "Make time now to save time later," she says.

This sounds like something that might come from my mother, the irony of which is not lost on me. Mom is hard-core Bible-based old school Christian. Indigo is New Age free-thinking psychic. I'm not sure what I am or what I believe, but I'm more drawn to Indigo's philosophy than Mom's. I still hear Geneva talking in my head sometimes and it seems like a lot more than imagination. There was a moment at Leno's death party where I could have sworn I saw his ghost.

All of which, if I'm honest, makes me reluctant to go back into the house. When I open the door, the air feels thick, resistant to both my breath and to me, as if it wants to push me back outside.

"Simmer down, we're the good guys," Indigo says, as if she's admonishing some unquiet spirit.

"Is Johanna still here? Haunting us?" I'm not at all crazy about this idea, although it would mean she'd be present for her party after all.

"It's not Johanna, it's the house. And it's... not haunted, exactly," Indigo says. "There's just so much dark energy. From all the years she felt trapped here. And murder does disrupt the energy field dramatically, of course."

I let her enter first. If the house is in the mood for a sacrifice, then I'm willing to let it be Indigo.

She sniffs the air. Power of suggestion being what it is, I do the same. All I smell is books and plants, but Indigo says, "Definitely some hostility here. First thing, we open all the windows."

"You've got to be kidding. It's freezing out there."

"Who is the old woman here?" she teases. "Cleansing a house is not for the faint of heart."

"The plants will freeze."

"Not if we turn on these overhead warming lights." She flicks a switch and I immediately feel radiant warmth on the top of my head. "See? Just like at a hockey rink. Come on, let's do this."

I stay where I am, considering my options. I could be safe and warm in my condo, changing baby diapers while Skye lolls around on my couch looking sexy and reminding me how much of an absolute asshole Dad is.

Right. Freezing my ass off in a hostile house in the company of a possibly murderous psychic it is.

There are a lot of windows to open in the renovated deck area, not so many in the living room and kitchen. Cold clean air flows into the house as we go, and I begin to feel what Indigo is talking about, as if the house itself is breathing easier. Ridiculous, since houses don't breathe. Probably it's just me who is breathing easier. Still, when she heads up the stairs, I almost don't follow.

So far, I've seen no major signs of an investigation anywhere in the house. Certainly no blood or indication of violence. Which means Johanna was probably killed upstairs. I love mysteries and thrillers, both in books and on the screen, but I'm not excited about the real life experience of seeing bloodstains or brain matter or other fluids that belong inside the body anywhere outside the body, like on walls and floors.

On the other hand, this is an opportunity for Indigo to hide evidence or steal something, and it's up to me to watch her.

"Are you coming?" she calls, looking down from the top of the stairs.

Staircases in all of the houses of my acquaintance are properly hidden away inside surrounding walls. I feel oddly exposed and vulnerable as I start the ascent, as if the steps really are floating and likely to crash under my weight. Four steps up to a small landing. Then another fourteen, counted silently under my breath, one hand tight on a railing that doesn't feel strong enough to hold my weight.

The stairs open into a spacious wraparound loft, part library, part office, part AV center. Enough bookshelves and books to read steadily for years and never run out. An adjustable desk and a comfortable office chair in cushy brown leather. An enormous flatscreen TV in front of an overstuffed armchair. A door, closed, must lead to the bedroom.

Again, it's an airy, well-designed and beautiful space. There are no signs of blood, or even of a thorough crime scene investigation. No fingerprint powder. No disarray. Still, there's that odd sensation of the air being too thick, of darkness, even though none of the windows are shuttered and there's plenty of light.

"She always said that since she wasn't going out, the outside would have to come to her," Indigo says, looking around. "She has that big screen hooked up to her computer, so when we met she could see me 'large as life.' She's got surround sound in here, too, for listening to music or an immersive experience for watching movies. Speakers down-stairs too, I believe. And the books. Her friends lived in books, she said, so she couldn't bear to send them away once she'd read them. Well. Let's get the windows open, and then we'll look in the bedroom."

I help her open windows, my reluctance on that point now gone. The house feels grateful for the fresh air. Did Johanna never open the windows? Did her phobia of the outside world extend that far?

"Well, I guess we can't put it off," Indigo says, as if she's feeling the same dread of whatever lies beyond those closed doors as I am. We walk together, side by side. My heart is trying to beat its way out of my chest. I'm also shivering, although that could be because we've achieved sub-zero temperatures.

Indigo turns the knob and pushes the door gently open to reveal a large master suite, with a king-size bed, stripped bare. There are two sleek dressers, one long and low, the other tall and narrow, both with oval mirrors. A comfortable armchair, with a cozy fleece throw draped over one arm, sits next to a small bookshelf. A floor lamp stands directly behind it, perfectly situated for comfortable reading. A stack of books sits on a small round table in front of the chair.

Fingerprint powder is everywhere here, but there's no blood. No body fluids.

Most importantly, no dead body. Which is, of course, what I should have expected. Johanna was taken away before the crime scene was cleared. But even knowing that, a stubborn little part of my brain has been picturing her lying here in a pool of blood, open eyes gazing at me reproachfully. I wouldn't have been surprised by a pointing finger and a spectral voice accusing, "*You didn't save me. You should have stopped this.*"

"Breathe," Indigo says. She elbows me in the ribs to make sure I get the message and my breath whooshes out of my lungs and my breathing autopilot takes over again.

Even without blood, without a body, the imagined smell of death clogs my nostrils. I suddenly regret my cup of cocoa and make a dash to open the closest window. I stand there, hands braced on the frame, breathing in cold air until the wave of nausea passes.

Only then does it register that I'm looking directly into the house next door. Ralph's house. Not his bedroom, thank God, more of a mishmash between a den and an entertainment room. There's a computer desk and laptop, a battered and stained old recliner, and a big screen TV. An overflowing ashtray and a half a dozen beer cans clutter a coffee table, along with old newspapers and junk mail. And, surprisingly, a stack of books. Who would have taken old Ralph for a voracious reader?

"I'm guessing she died in the bed. There must have been a mattress cover," Indigo says, behind me. "They'll have taken that along with the bedding."

Her calm voice, along with the cold, clean air, steadies me enough to turn and look. I'd noticed the lack of bedding when I came in, but hadn't noticed that the mattress is bare, and pristine enough to be new.

"So she wasn't shot then," Indigo says. "She might have been bludgeoned or stabbed, I suppose. Most likely strangled."

"And you know this how? The spirits told you?"

"Logic, my dear Watson," she says. "A gunshot makes for a good deal of splatter. So does a bludgeoning. Even with a mattress pad, the blood would have soaked into the bed. It would be spattered on the floor or the walls."

"Doesn't a stabbing cause a lot of blood spatter too?"

"Usually. But if the knife is thrust into a vital place—the heart, say—and left there until it stops pumping, sometimes most of the bleeding is internal."

"You sure know a lot about murder for a psychic."

"I've helped in some police investigations."

"And what do your psychic powers tell you now?"

"That we need to check the balcony."

"Maybe that's less psychic powers and a whole lot of fingerprint powder on the door handle," I mutter.

Indigo laughs, the sound jarring. "Of course it's the fingerprint powder. Following guidance from beyond is a wonderful thing, but we are expected to use our own brains and sensory apparatus." She sets her bag down on the naked bed and starts rummaging around in it. I freeze, wondering if this is the moment she retrieves her gun and shoots me, but what she comes up with is a floral printed bandanna.

"Useful for many things," she says, using it to open the sliding door that leads to the balcony without getting powder all over her hands. "That's interesting."

"What is?" The balcony is empty. No chairs. No table. Not surprising if Johanna never went outside.

Indigo gestures at the railing. There's a couple of inches of snow along most of it, but there's a clear space at the center. Directly below is the roof that covers the closed-in deck. The snow on the roof is pristine and undisturbed.

"Somebody stood out here and leaned on this railing," Indigo says. "Maybe the killer."

"Or the cops. Somebody who wanted to get a look at the

yard. Or wondered whether somebody could have come up this way."

"Either way," Indigo says. "I'd wondered if the killer came or went via the balcony. It doesn't look like it. Leave the slider cracked. Let's check the bathroom."

A door opens into a full ensuite bath with separate tub and a spacious, tiled shower with a glass door. A rack in the shower holds shampoo and conditioner, face cleanser and body wash. Indigo and I are reflected in the well-lighted mirror that stretches the length of a generous countertop with two basins. Cosmetics are neatly arranged in a woven basket. Moisturizer, foundation, lipstick, mascara. No need to get elaborate when you never go anywhere. No towels hanging on the rack, no bath mat.

"Bet they took the towels and the mat for analysis," Indigo says. "Evidence."

I shudder, realizing this means evidence of Dad. His hair, his cells, his DNA. Same with the bedding. Those results won't be back yet, but his fingerprints will be all over everything. If he's been fingerprinted, and I'm pretty sure he has, then that match will confirm he's been here in her room. When the DNA comes back, it will incriminate him further. Add in motive and opportunity and it's hard even for me to believe he's innocent.

"Well then," Indigo says, briskly. "Nothing more to learn here. It's time to clear the energy in this house so we can close the windows before we freeze. Run downstairs and grab the sage from the kitchen, would you? Your legs are younger than mine."

Much as I don't want to leave her alone and unwatched, I've been raised to be considerate of my elders, even though I've never managed to be respectful, and I can't bring myself to tell her to go get her sage herself. I'm as quick as I can be, down the stairs and into the kitchen to scoop up the abalone shell and sage wand. On the way back, though, instead of running I pad up the stairs as silently as possible, like I'm sixteen again and coming home late. If she's up to something, maybe I can catch her in the act.

But she's not stealing anything or altering evidence. She's standing at the window that looks toward Ralph's house and doesn't turn when I tiptoe up to the door. Nothing in the room looks like it's been moved, but she's had plenty of time to sneak an item out of a drawer, or polish away a fingerprint, or get up to some other mischief.

"What do you think of the neighbor?" she asks, shattering my illusion that I've managed to observe her unaware.

"He's a grinch," I say, lightly. "Angry. Malcontented. Drinks too much. Smokes a lot."

"And apparently reads," she says, turning. "Good, thank you. Set the sage on her little table while I find the matches, please. Just a minute." She drops her bag on the reading chair and begins rummaging through it, muttering to herself. It's even bigger than the one I lug around, and apparently psychic ability doesn't help her find objects. It takes a minute before she unearths a little box of matches and a large feather.

"Here we go." Striking a match, she holds it to the end of the sage bundle until it catches, a thin spiral of pungent smoke rising into the air. She blows out the match and drops it into the abalone shell, then gently fans the smoke with the feather. "Repeat after me," she says. "I command all dark energy, bleakness, and despair..."

She pauses and looks at me, eyebrows raised. Obediently, I echo her words.

Indigo picks up the shell and the sage and begins moving through the room, fanning the feather through the smoke as she intones, "...and any non-benevolent beings present in this space to leave."

Again, she pauses and looks at me. It feels risky to start making demands of unseen forces or non-benevolent beings, but it's too late now; I'm already complicit. So I repeat, "And any non-benevolent beings present in this space to leave." Then I add, "Please. If you don't mind. Not that I hold ill will or..."

Indigo glares at me and my words trail away into silence. She says, her voice loud and authoritative, "I command all the negativity to empty this house to make room for positive light and energetic vibes."

She wafts the smoke toward the open balcony door. Then the open window. "You can close them now, Addison, please."

I slam the window shut, in case there really is something on the other side that wants to come back in, and lock it for good measure. Then I lower the blinds. I do the same with the slider to the balcony.

Indigo nods, then closes her eyes as she intones, "Now we invite in the good. May all the positive vibes of the magnificent universe that surrounds us fill this space with peace, love, and serenity."

Her eyes slit open and she looks at me, waiting until I echo her, this time with enthusiasm. I'm all about good vibes.

"Now, the rest of the house," she says. "Bring my bag, would you?"

I'd thought my bag was heavy. I don't know how a woman her age manages to lug this thing around. But I get it slung over my shoulder and follow after her, repeating the ritual in all the rooms, then closing and locking the windows as we go. I have to admit that when we're done the house does feel different. Maybe it's a placebo effect. Maybe we really have cleared out dark energy. Either way, it's easier to breathe and I don't feel like the house resents me.

We end up in the kitchen, the last window closed, the sage still smoking in its shell on the counter, as it was when I first came in, hours ago now, to find Indigo and Nat sipping their hot beverages and apparently waiting for me.

"Thanks for that," I say, surprising myself by meaning it. "But we do need to go now."

How much time has passed? It's dark outside, not that this tells me much because it gets dark at about 4 o'clock this time of year. But even that's too much time to leave Skye alone in my condo. And I need to be looking for Dad.

Indigo sits herself down on a stool at the counter, comfortably, as if she has no intention of leaving. "I was wondering," she says, "where was the last place you saw him?"

CHAPTER 13

For a long, disorienting moment I stand there in Johanna's kitchen, staring blankly at the sweet-faced, silver-haired, gun-toting woman who has apparently just plucked a thought right out of my head.

"I can help you find your father," she says. "But you'll need to work with me and stop holding back."

"How did you know he was missing?"

"Because I haven't seen on the news that he's been arrested. Unless you're hiding him?"

I sigh. "No. I have no idea where he is. The last time I saw him, he was here."

"Here? In the kitchen?"

"No. Here in the house. Sitting at the dining room table with Johanna's attorney and the Notary Public."

"That's where we'll start, then. Where your energy last intersected with his."

My stomach does one of those roll over anxiety moves and

I ask, "When you're talking about his energy—is it like when you're talking about Johanna's? Do you think he's dead? Maybe whoever killed Johanna killed him too."

"That doesn't make any sense, honey. If they left her body here, why would they drag away somebody bigger, heavier? Why risk being seen with the body?"

"They might have dragged him off at gunpoint. Kidnapped him. Killed him elsewhere. Buried him underground alive. Any number of things might have happened."

"Do you really think that's likely?" Indigo asks.

"No, it's much more likely that he's cashed the fifteen thousand dollar check he conned Johanna into writing, and is lounging around on a tropical island somewhere waiting to see if she does actually die so he can also cash in on the house and her estate," I admit. "But then, it's not exactly 'likely' that you would tell Johanna she's going to die and then she actually gets murdered, either. So if that can happen, then so can anything else, no matter how improbable it might be."

"Rather than guessing, let's consult the powers that be, shall we? See what they are willing to tell us. How about you fix me a cup of tea while I get set up? Use this." She scrounges in her bag again and pulls out a small glass jar of loose tea and a mesh ball on a thin silver chain.

"Are you going to read the leaves?" I ask.

"I was thinking I'd drink it," she says. "While we talk. You know, go over all of the places where your father might be. People he knows, that sort of thing."

"Oh." I feel unexpectedly disappointed. "I thought we were going to... you know... do some sort of psychic voodoo thing."

She laughs. "I thought you didn't believe in my psychic abilities."

"Desperation speaking," I say. But deep inside, I've always wondered about psychic phenomena. I mean, I've sort of had glimpses of both Geneva and Leno after they died. Maybe it's my imagination. Maybe it's something a little more. Part of me wants it to be true that we can connect with something beyond. Another part of me? Not so much.

"We will talk and consult the cards," Indigo says. "And we can cast a spell to call him back. You do know how to make a proper cup of tea?"

"Never drink it if I can help it. Maybe you should make it yourself." I've made tea for Britt and I know perfectly well how it's done. I just don't want Indigo wandering off and meddling while I do it. "I could make it with a tea bag."

She shudders dramatically. "Spirits forfend."

"You used the teabag before."

"That dear child needed to feel useful so I allowed him to make the tea. His mother was murdered, you know. Shot down in front of him. No wonder his sister is protective."

I watch her add tea to the little ball and pour not-quite-boiling water over it. Then she has to let it steep for precisely two minutes. Add a little milk from Johanna's fridge. A teaspoon of sugar. By the time she's done impatience feels like ants running all over my body.

"Deep breath, dear," she says. "Nothing is served by frantically dashing about. You're sure you don't want a cup of your own? I can fix you one."

"No! I do not want tea. I need to go home and check on the people in my condo and start unpacking. I need to prepare for Johanna's party. And I need to find my father so we can give away the house."

"You can't rush the powers that be, my dear. Everything

will unfold as it should. Would you be a dear girl and bring my bag? I don't want to spill my tea."

I hoist the bag up off the floor, wondering what else is in there. Some sort of cleaning supplies and a gun, that much I know. But it feels like I'm lugging a whole wall's worth of bricks. Fortunately it's not far to the dining room table and I hoist the bag up and drop it in front of Indigo. It thuds. Her tea cup wobbles and tea sloshes over into the saucer.

"Gently, child," she says. She takes a sip of tea, then sets it safely off to the side before getting to her feet so she can dig around in the bag. I watch her lay out objects with a growing sense of wonder that she's managed to cram everything in there.

The gun, which I look at askance, and a box of ammunition. A spray bottle full of some unidentified cleaning solution. A plastic bag stuffed with cleaning cloths. A roll of paper towels. Two more bundles of sage. A spare toothbrush. A white pillar candle. A jar that contains a crystalline substance that could be sugar for her tea or some sort of poison. A gemstone studded candle holder.

She sets the jar, the candle holder and the candle off to the side and packs everything else back into the bag, which she then lowers to the floor and slides under the table.

"Sit down, Addy. Across from me."

I do as she asks, looking across the table at the big windows and sliding door that open out into Johanna's enclosed porch, and beyond that to the big tree that dominates her snow- covered backyard.

"Do you have a picture of your father?" Indigo asks.

I laugh at the idea of me carrying a picture of Dad around with me, and then I feel sad about laughing. Britt's screensaver on her phone was taken at her college graduation. She and her father have their arms around each other. She's beaming, and he's looking down at her with obvious pride and love.

"Hang on, I'll find one." I search out his Instagram feed on my phone and slide it across the table to Indigo.

"Handsome man, your father."

I snort. "And he knows it."

"Does he go by Richard?"

"He refers to himself as Rich. Wishful thinking on his part."

"Rich it is. Put the phone away, now, Addy. Electronics will interfere with our psychic activity." She picks up a very sharp little knife and carves RICH into the candle, ribbons of wax curling around the blade. When she's done, she places the candle in the holder and slides it to the middle of the table, directly between us.

She opens the jar and passes it to me. "Pour a circle of salt around the candle."

Salt, then. Not poison. I do as she says. "What's the salt for?"

"A symbolic and energetic request to the powers that be to keep the object of our search safe," she says. "In this case... perhaps to protect us as well. There we go." She passes me the matches. "Light the candle."

"Why me?"

"You have the energetic connection to him. It will be more effective."

This is the time to get up from the table. Pick up my own bag and make a run for it. So what if this woman steals something from Johanna? So what if we never find Dad? It's not like he's ever been in my life anyway.

I select a match. Strike it against the side of the box and

then hold it to the candle wick. It catches, guttering for an instant and then burning clear and steady.

Indigo nods approvingly

"Picture your father in your mind. Particularly focus on the last time you saw him here in this room. What you saw. What you felt."

"Are you sure that's a good idea?"

"What's bothering you about it?"

"Not sure if it's wise to hold onto murderous rage while consulting supernatural powers. I'm pretty sure I saw a horror flick that started that way. It didn't go well."

"Nothing goes well in horror flicks, honey. That's the point of them. No harm is going to come to you."

"Some harm may come to *him*," I mutter.

"Thus the salt for protection."

"I don't think a little salt is going to protect him from *me*. If he's alive. If I find him."

"*When*. All will be well. Close your eyes, and focus."

Bagheera, utterly fed up with waiting us out in the carrier, yowls.

"Be patient," Indigo admonishes him. "Ignore him, Addy. He's not suffering."

I close my eyes. Call into my memory Dad sitting at the table right here with Johanna and Char and Chip Fitzwilliam. My anger and hurt and betrayal.

"That's the stuff," Indigo says. Then, in an eerie tone she continues, "We call on all benevolent powers of the universe for assistance in locating Richard Winters, safe and well."

A little shiver travels up my spine. Goosebumps pop out on my skin. This is as stupid as attending a séance or playing with a Ouija board. All things you should only do if you actually want to make contact with whatever lives beyond the pale.

A sudden draft sucks at my hair. I hear a door open.

My eyes fly open half in panic, half in amazement. Have we actually summoned Dad? Or his ghost?

But it's Ralph, the Mutant Santa next door neighbor, who is standing in the doorway that leads from the closed-in porch to the kitchen, apparently as surprised to see us as we are to see him.

"That's interesting," Indigo says. "Not precisely what we were expecting."

"Door was unlocked," he says. His eyes are moving now, taking in everything.

"Do you make a habit of just popping in?" Indigo asks. Her voice is calm but there's an undercurrent of something in it that reminds me she has a gun.

"And how did you know the door would be unlocked?" I challenge. The creepy vibe emanating from him is palpable. Maybe he's casing the joint for valuables, exactly what he accused me of doing.

Ralph shuffles his feet. Shoves his hands in his pockets, then removes them again. "This a séance? You calling up Johanna's spirit?"

"Can we help you with something?" Indigo asks.

His Adam's apple bobs in his skinny throat.

"I came for a, um, book," Ralph says. "Loaned her one. Never got it back."

"Never been in the house and we know she never went out, but you loaned her a book," I say. "Maybe what you're really after is a look at the crime scene. Or to steal something."

"We traded books," he says. "I told you that the first time

you came around, before she died. She'd leave that back door open. I'd set a book in there for her to read. She'd leave one for me. Sometimes we talked through the open window."

It's conceivable, but I'm skeptical. "Suppose you tell me what the book is, and I can return it to you."

"I know right where it is. I'll just fetch it myself."

He stomps across the floor, leaving wet boot prints and globs of melting snow in his wake. Indigo and I exchange glances, then we both follow him. I let her go first. I don't need to be sandwiched between my two top suspects.

Ralph looks back at us and growls, really he does, low in his throat, but keeps walking, leaving boot tracks as he goes. He pauses at the top of the staircase, his head swiveling around on his skinny neck. "Nice place she has here," he says. "Where was she killed? In there I bet." He heads straight for the bedroom.

"Blinds are closed, so of course I didn't see nothing. That man they're looking for closed 'em. You wouldn't want some-body watching you do the killing now, would you?"

"So you didn't see anything then," I say, reasonably calmly given that want I want to do is put my hands around his scrawny neck and squeeze.

"Told the cops what I saw and didn't see. No need to repeat it to you." He turns slowly around in the room, his eyes touching everything. He walks over to the bed and lays a hand on the mattress.

Indigo and I exchange a glance. Maybe she's thinking what I'm thinking, that some killers like to come back and revisit the scene of the crime. Wouldn't surprise me if Ralph was capable of murder. And now he's trying to make himself look innocent by claiming he's never been here before.

"You said you wanted your book," I remind him.

"Sure enough, and there it is right there," he says.

"And how do we know it's yours?" Indigo plants herself squarely in his way.

"You calling me a liar?"

Indigo, all sweet and non-threatening on the surface, doesn't back down. "I'm saying maybe you're a wee tiny bit mistaken."

If it comes to an altercation, my money's on her.

Since he hasn't yet gone for a concealed weapon or started swinging, I move in for a look at the book. A disbelieving laugh bursts out of me. "*The Women*? Come on. You're expecting us to believe that's yours?"

"Maybe I ought to be reading Zane Grey or that sort of thing, or maybe I'm too stupid to read at all. That it? I know that look on your face. Seen it before. Well, guess what, lady. I'm not stupid as you want to think. Besides, it's just a fuckin' book! Worth what, fifteen bucks brand new? You don't have any more right to this house than I do, you hypervigilant old biddy!"

"Humor the old biddy," Indigo says, holding out her hand for the book.

"Outa my way or I'll knock you off your feet."

She doesn't budge and it looks like he's going to run her over but at the last minute he swerves around her. She reaches for the book and he sweeps his arm up to hold it out of her reach. Something flutters out and lands on the floor. He's got too much steam up to notice, and I wait until he's out the door before bending to pick it up. A single sheet of computer paper, folded in thirds. Boring, as bookmarks go, but then I've been known to use whatever happens to be at hand, from grocery store receipts to bits of packaging. I stuff the paper in my pocket, then follow as Ralph stomps down the stairs, Indigo behind him.

"Well, that was interesting," she says, as he slams out of the front door high dudgeon.

"It was outright weird," I say. "What did he really want? Evidence tampering? Revisiting the scene of the crime? Stealing valuables?"

"Any and all of the above," she says, calmly. "But it didn't seem worth shooting him over. Well. I'm going to go check into my motel. What will you be up to this evening?"

"Changing diapers, probably." I sigh, thinking about the dinner and the kissing—definitely the kissing—that I might be engaged in with Owen right this minute if it weren't for Skye and Daffodil and Jackson and Johanna's murder and my missing father. If Indigo did a reading for me it would show that fate is conspiring against me.

"Do you want to meet for dinner?" she asks. "I could tell you what I know about Johanna. Help you plan your party."

I consider the possibility, then shake my head. "First, I really do need to check on my houseguests. And I want my brother and my friends to hear what you have to say. Could we meet for breakfast? Say, nine am at *Grounded*. It's right on main street, hard to miss. If that doesn't work out, I'll text you, if you'll give me your number."

"And the cat?"

I'd actually forgotten about the cat. He's been utterly silent, probably sulking. I grab his carrier and the bag with his food and bowls and follow Indigo out to her car. The carrier is heavy. The cat is howling. I didn't wear gloves, and my hands are freezing and half numb by the time we reach Indigo's car.

I watch her drive away, waiting until her tail lights vanish around a corner before slogging all the way back to Jezebel through what feels like ten miles of snow. She's all frosted up, of course, and it would be just like her to play dead after having been left alone all day in a strange place, but she starts up after only two tries, agrees to defrost the windows, and carries me safely all the way home.

We stop on the way for a bucket of chicken from Colonel Sanders, because even if there were food in the condo I am cold and hungry and tired and definitely not cooking. Especially not for Skye.

Turns out I didn't need to worry about her, she's sound asleep.

In my bed. Naked.

Seriously?

Well, at least it's easy to figure out what Dad sees in her.

Daffodil is in the playpen, sucking on the foot of a teddy bear. Bruno sits beside her in his best imitation of one of those Egyptian cat statues. He's about as successful in the pose as I would be doing an Egyptian princess imitation but he gets full points for effort. Bagheera, in the carrier, meows, and Bruno leaps out of the playpen to come and investigate the intruder.

Daffodil holds out her arms, not letting go of the bear, and makes a little gurgling sound, half sob, half hope. Her face is streaked with tears and snot but when I pick her up she clings to me with her free hand, nestling in with a little sigh.

My heart melts. She's my baby sister. And she is now high up on my list of responsibilities, because it's clear that while Skye might not be the worst mother in the world she's certainly not the best.

Daffodil drops the teddy bear and when I bend to pick it up I remember that Owen didn't buy any stuffed animals. Also, this isn't a kid's toy. It is—or was—white. Very plush. Very soft. There's a strand of pearls around its neck that is an exceptional replica of the real thing.

"Bruno, where did you get this?" I demand. I haven't let him out of the condo. The windows are closed.

Bruno ignores me, completely focused on Bagheera. Both of them are making those spine chilling unhappy cat noises that signal an impending altercation.

"Oh for heaven's sake you two. Nobody has time for your drama," I admonish. I carry Bagheera into my office and leave him in the carrier for now. "Just hang on a minute, Bruno. Daff first, and then I'll get you set up."

Thanks to Owen, with a little trial and error and some screaming from Daffodil I manage the diaper. I wash her dirty little face with a clean washcloth. And then, holding her on one hip, I manage to fix her a bottle. While she drinks it, I get Bruno some canned cat food and carry some into the office for Bagheera. I should have brought home his litter box; I can't keep him locked up in here without it. Oh well. The boys are just going to have to fight it out. So I leave the door open, ready to jump in and break up anything more than a spat.

Still carrying Daff, I drop onto my sofa with a couple of crispy fried drumsticks and a biscuit. Bruno, after growling and hissing at Bagheera, abandons the fray and comes to join us, his green eyes focused unblinkingly on Daffodil's face. He purrs, loudly, taking possession of the bear when Daffodil consents to let it go.

She falls asleep with the nipple still in her mouth, a little trail of milk and drool wandering down her cheek. I wipe it away with a corner of her blanket and lay her down in the playpen. Careful not to wake her, I cover her with a clean blanket, tossing the milk-soiled one into the laundry hamper. Bruno leaps into the playpen and curls up beside her.

Vaguely, I recall hearing some sort of story about cats smothering babies by lying over their faces. Or maybe it was stealing their breath. Myths, I decide. Nothing I'm prepared to worry about. I consider waking Skye and making her sleep on the couch so she can keep an eye on her kid. But I'm drowsy and it seems like a lot of work, so I lie down on the couch myself with a cushion and my favorite fleece throw.

Weary as I am, I send a text to Britt and Vic before I drift off to sleep.

Addy: Meet at Grounded tomorrow. 9 am.

Vic: To go over non-existent evidence that Richard is innocent?

Addy: About that...

Vic: Here we go 😒

Addy: I'm bringing Skye and Daffodil

Addy: And Indigo

Britt: The psychic? How did you even? 😵

Vic: OMG 🫠

Addy: Just be there

TUESDAY
DECEMBER 24

CHAPTER 14

I SLEEP SPORADICALLY. A cramp in my leg. A crick in my neck. My arm fallen asleep so that it feels like a heavy piece of rubber with no sensation. Every time I wake up I check on Daffodil. Is she still asleep? Is she warm enough, or maybe too warm? Is she still breathing? Is Bruno smothering her? Then, of course, I have to go look for Bagheera, who is still hiding behind boxes in my study. Visit the bathroom. Get a drink of water.

Morning happens with a vengeance at precisely six-oh-five am.

My phone rings.

Somebody knocks on my door.

Daffodil starts to cry.

Any one of these things would be more than enough to handle at this ridiculous hour, before coffee and after not enough sleep. The three things occurring simultaneously is enough to make me pull the blanket up over my head, hoping it will all magically go away.

The phone does stop ringing, but Daffodil keeps crying. Whoever is at the door keeps knocking.

I've slept in my clothes, so no need to get dressed. Whoever it is gets to talk to a bleary-eyed me with bedhead and yesterday's smeared makeup. Lucky them. I scoop up the baby and the purloined teddy bear, hoping it will soothe her. She dials back her wailing to hiccupy sobs, but Bruno meows pathetically to let me know that really the bear belongs to him and I should be carrying him, too.

"I'm coming, I'm coming, hold on," I try to shout, but it comes out as a croak. When I open the door, a bright flash of light burns into my eyeballs and leaves me seeing spots.

"Well, if that isn't perfect," an unfortunately familiar voice says. "You are the gift that keeps on giving."

"Lindy? What the hell are you doing here?"

"Following a story. What else would I be doing?"

I blink, still seeing floating spots, but between them I catch glimpses of the mega influencer, Lindy Lind.

"But FlatzandSharpz covers the music scene," I complain, feeling decidedly hard done by.

"And Richard Winters is an off Broadway star, and now he's wanted for questioning in a murder. I heard he was staying with you." She leans sideways to peer past me into the condo, as if Dad might be lounging around on the sofa while there's a manhunt going on.

"You heard wrong." I shove the door but it rebounds off of her body.

"Ow! Come on, Addy. We're pals, right? Plus, you owe me. Is that your kid?"

"I'm babysitting. Go away, Lindy."

"If you let me in, maybe I won't post that picture I just took."

"No, you'll post a worse one. I'm not stupid."

But she doesn't go anywhere, craning her neck to try to see farther into the condo. "Nice. I see you left the mural intact. You sure the kid isn't yours? I mean, you didn't look preggers last time I saw you but sometimes people of your build don't show right away. Oooh, was Leno the daddy?"

"She's not mine. If she were, I would have been giving birth around the time of Leno's party and I think my condition would have been obvious, despite my 'build.' Also, the baby is none of your business."

"It's my business, though," another voice says.

Oh, dear goddess. Debbie the HOAR is bee-lining toward us, impeccable in a skirt and jacket, hair drawn back in a smooth chignon. "I assume you've read the copy of the regulations I gave you?"

"Well, Debbie, I've actually been a little busy. But let me guess. You don't like babies."

"If you'd read the regulations you'd know... Oh, my God. That's my bear. You stole it from me?"

"Technically the cat did but—"

"Those are real pearls! It's not a toy for goodness sake." She snatches the bear away from Daffodil.

Daffodil screams. Bruno growls.

Of course this is the precise moment when Skye would materialize, wearing nothing but an oversized T-shirt she's apparently snagged from one of my unpacked boxes.

"What's going on?"

Daffodil, seeing her mother, amps up the crying program

170

and reaches out her arms, leaning across the room in a way that makes her unwieldy and hard to hold.

Debbie's face contracts, her nostrils pinched as if she's smelling a full diaper. Which, to be fair, is something I'm smelling too. "*If* you had read the guidelines, you'd know this is an adults-only community. We don't allow children, and we certainly don't allow babies. It shouldn't be necessary to tell you that you can't steal valuables from your neighbors."

"I told you that was Bruno," I say. "You should keep your doors closed, probably, so it doesn't happen again."

Her face turns an unhealthy shade of crimson. "This is what comes of certain people willing their property to inappropriate residents!" she sputters when she remembers how to breathe. "We need to update the bylines about who can inherit a condo."

"Oh, lighten up. Skye and Daff are staying with me for a couple of days. I'm not sure if you can legally keep me from having guests, but I'll consult with my attorney."

I'd had every intention of moving Skye and the baby into a motel, even if it meant mounting up credit card charges that I can't really afford, but I don't trust Skye to take proper care of my baby sister. Besides, Debbie rubs my fur all the wrong ways. Bruno is similarly unimpressed. He glares up at her, still growling. And then, as if they've had some sort of psychic meeting of the minds, Bagheera comes out to join him.

Debbie takes a step back, making a shooing gesture with her hands. "You have two of those things?"

She sneezes, explosively. Once. Twice. Three times.

"Bless you," I say.

Skye sashays over to the coffee table and brings back the package of tissues. "You've got a little something on your..."

she touches her own cheek in the place where, sure enough, a sheen of snot is visible on Debbie's face.

Lindy, never one to miss an opportunity, snaps a photo of Debbie wiping her nose. Then she gets one of Skye and the baby. And then she says, "Wait – I know you!"

Skye lights up. "You do? Have you seen my work?"

"I must have? Were you in a commercial or... Oh my GOD, is that Richard's baby? That's where I saw you. With Richard. There were pics on Star Struck! Addy, you absolutely have to let me in on this story."

"There is no story."

"But—"

"Out. Seriously. Both of you. Debbie, feel free to call my attorney. It's Chip Fitzwilliam. Lindy, please... go away."

Debbie is still in the hallway, but Lindy has edged across the threshold. I hip check her, using the hip not occupied by a baby. While she's off balance I give her a firm shove with my free hand. She stumbles backward and I slam the door, locking it the second it clicks into place.

Skye flops down on the couch. "Who was that chick? Not the HOA bitch, the other one."

"Lindy Lind," I say, bitterly. "Don't tell me you've never heard of FlatzandSharpz?"

She surges upright with a shriek of utter horror. "Oh my God. Lindy Lind saw me like this? She took a freaking picture!"

"She took a picture of me too, perhaps you noticed," I say.

"Well right, but you're you," Skye says, dismissively.

My phone rings. It's Britt, and I'm more than happy to turn my back on Skye and pick up.

"What were you thinking?" Britt asks.

"I'm gonna need a little clarification? I've been thinking a lot of things."

"Lindy Lind? You showed Lindy *the baby*?"

"I didn't know it was Lindy when I opened the door."

"You live in a gated community! How does this happen?"

"Exactly! I couldn't possibly have expected..." Reality begins to catch up with me. "Wait a minute. How did you know Lindy was here?"

"You don't know."

"Don't know what?"

"Look at Lindy's TikTok."

"Already?"

A wail of utter fury and grief coming from the couch indicates that Skye has already found the post in question. She stares at her phone in horror, one hand clutched in her hair.

"You know how she is," Britt says. "Are we still meeting?"

"Yes, we're still meeting."

"I can never show my face again," Skye says. "This is the end of my career. My life."

"You are showing your face again in about an hour. We're going to *Grounded*."

"I'm not going anywhere. Ever."

Again, I'm jolted by how young she is, remembering how every little social setback loomed like a life and death crisis when I was that age.

"Oh come on, it can't be that bad." I sit down beside her, aiming for being encouraging. She hits replay on the video. She's right. It's bad. Maybe not quite 'end of the world' bad, but pretty damn close. Not so much for her, in my opinion, but definitely for me.

Skye looks disheveled but sexy. I, on the other hand, look

like I've been out on a three day bender and am now homeless and in the throes of DTs. Daffodil, flailing in my arms, looks like she's trying to escape from a deranged person.

Lindy's video commentary doesn't help. "FlatzandSharpzers, do I have something special for you today or what? Did you see that pic?"

The photo is there to stay, with Lindy's talking face superimposed over the bottom corner.

"Recognize anyone? Of course you do! You're looking at Addison Winters—you may remember her as the party planner who put together that epic send off for Leno Masterson. She's also the daughter of Richard Winters who—you may or may not have heard—is wanted for murder! And the other woman you're looking at is Skye Warner. If she looks familiar, then you've been looking at naughty movies—shame on you. Or—*maybe* you saw her in the company of Richard Winters."

A new photo replaces the horror shot of me and Skye and Daffodil, but it's not an improvement. This one is of Dad and Skye on a dance floor. She's wearing a little scarlet dress that covers less of her body than my T-shirt. He's wearing a button up shirt with the sleeves rolled up and the top two buttons undone. He's flushed and disheveled and staring at Skye's abundant cleavage. You can practically see his tongue hanging out of his mouth.

"The question is—who does the baby belong to?" Lindy asks. "Is it Addison's? Possibly Leno Masterson's love child? Or is it Skye's—and Richard's—the unfortunate offspring of a porn star and a murderer? Stay tuned, FlatzandSharpzers. You know I'll have more for you soon."

"See?" Skye flings both arms up in the air dramatically. "What am I going to *dooooo*???"

"What *we* are going to do, is change Daffodil's diaper and feed her. Then we're getting dressed and going out."

"I told you, I'm not going anywhere."

"You are. We're having a council of war with Vic and Britt. We're going to find Richard and make him pay you child support. And do the right thing about Johanna's house. And answer for a few other little details while he's at it."

"I can't..."

"You can. You will. Pull yourself together."

"I... oh fine. But if I'm going out I need makeup and clothes. Where are my clothes? Did you wash them last night? You didn't, did you. You were out until all hours."

"I'm not your maid. Or your nanny, for that matter," I mutter, catching a whiff of rapidly ripening diaper.

"I suppose I can find something of yours that will work. I'm going to have a shower first."

"Hey," I call after her as she vanishes into the bathroom. "What about Daffodil?"

The door closes behind her. Daff looks up at me. I look down at her. I sigh. "Looks like it's just you and me, kid."

So while Skye showers, and then uses my makeup and rifles through my packing boxes for clothes, I change the baby and fix her a bottle. There's barely enough time even to wash my face and run a damp comb through my hair, which sucks, given the likelihood of another encounter with Lindy and the curious eyes I'm sure to encounter at *Grounded*.

I'm almost ready to go when a text rolls in from Owen:

> Owen: Hate to be the bearer of evil tidings, but I have evil tidings

> Addy: If you're talking about Lindy, you're too late to be the messenger

Owen: You haven't gone and had a secret baby with my brother have you?

Addy: You're very funny. Not.

Owen: How does she do it?

Addy: Let me guess: Jackson found the post

Owen: He did. Stalking Skye. Threatened to take his phone but I have no teeth and he knows it. Can we meet today? Sans Skye? I can ditch J. with his grandparents for an hour or two

Addy: After that post? Not leaving Skye alone anywhere. One day to find Dad & plan & execute Johanna's party.

Owen: I'd help but...

Addy: I know. Off to Grounded as soon as Skye settles her wardrobe malfunctions

Owen: ??

Addy: I'll explain later.

CHAPTER 15

WE'RE GOING to be late to the meeting at *Grounded*. Not my fault, to be clear. My suggestion that Skye wear baggy sweats and a ball-cap so she can fly under the radar is met with an eye roll and withering disdain.

"I'd rather show up naked," she snarks.

So while I get Daffodil changed and fed and dressed, Skye works her way through my entire wardrobe, making derogatory comments all the way. By the time we finally leave the condo, my bed is littered with clothes that Skye has deemed unworthy of her magnificence. She's finally settled on a dark blue suit jacket, open over a black camisole that displays enough cleavage to distract from the fact that that the suit jacket is too big for her. She's paired this with a pair of yoga pants and my leopard print heels.

When we get to *Grounded*, of course she leaves Daffodil to me. And she doesn't hold the door when she walks in first, so that I have to catch it with a shoulder to avoid it smacking into

Daffodil's head. No small feat, with the baby on one hip and my bag, always heavy and now loaded with baby items, hanging off my shoulder.

She pauses dramatically in the entrance, in a move identical to one of Dad's, giving all of the curious eyes time to notice and appreciate her. Momentum very nearly carries me, Daffodil, and the bag right into the back of her.

Britt and Vic are already settled at the wobbly table at the back, the one that nobody else wants but which is perfect for our meetings because it's out of the way and right under the speaker which makes it harder to be overheard. Indigo is already with them, damn it. I wanted to be here to facilitate the introduction and steer the conversation away from a couple of questionable topics. Vic, for example, does not need to know that I participated in an energetic house clearing and a psychic finding ceremony. I'll never hear the end of it.

Britt and Indigo already have their tea. Vic is working on a grande something or other, most likely drip coffee, black, because the man's tastebuds are set on bitter. All of them watch us walk in—Vic with clear suspicion, Britt with what looks alarmingly like baby fever, Indigo with an expression I can't decipher.

"Oh, she's beautiful!" Britt says, standing up and reaching for Daffodil. "Look at that hair! And those eyelashes! Can I hold her? I love babies."

I hand the baby over and she favors Britt with a toothless smile. The resulting sensation in my belly is definitely relief, not jealousy. Anybody else holding the baby means I won't have to.

I drop into an empty chair beside Indigo, careful not to rock the table, and take a good long swig of the drink they thoughtfully procured for me. It's half melted, the whipped cream dying the same slow death as snow at the end of February. Still. Sugar and caffeine are good for the soul.

Indigo glances up from the deck of cards she's shuffling, and I see at once, both by the expression on her face and the one card already laid out in the middle of the table, that we are not about to begin a game of poker.

I pick up the card, surveying the guy in armor riding a stylized horse and holding a big-ass gold cup. "What's up with the knight?"

"Put that back, Addy, please," Indigo says. "No, not that way. Upside down, as he was."

"We are asking the cards to find Richard, apparently," Vic says, not bothering to veil either his skepticism or his sarcasm.

In this case, I agree with his assessment of the situation, but I still adjust the card on the table to Indigo's specifications. "Since when is Dad a knight in shining armor?"

"The Knight of Cups reversed seems best suited to what I've been told of your father," Indio says, calmly, as if neither of us has been rude. "Self-centered. Irresponsible. Impulsive. Unreliable. A grifter and a very bad gambler and, from what your brother has said, most likely a narcissist."

"Also a cheater," Skye says, bitterly.

"Also that," Indigo agrees. "Addy, would you cut the deck please?"

She hands me the cards and despite my skepticism, I'm immediately disappointed that they feel exactly like oversized playing cards, and not at all like I hold the future in my hands.

Kathy, the world's best barista, hustles over. "What a gorgeous baby!" she says, not even noticing the sad state of my drink. "She looks exactly like Victor."

"Not mine, I swear," Vic says.

"Daff is Dad's love child, actually," I explain. "And this is Skye, Dad's...uh, Daffodil's mother."

"Oh no! And now with Rich missing, and what's happened to that poor woman! What can I get you, honey? It's on the house." Kathy beams a high wattage smile at Skye, who, despite the borrowed clothes, looks glamorous and undeniably sexy.

"I'll have one of whatever that is Addy is drinking, if it's not too much trouble?"

"No trouble at all," Kathy reassures her. "You must be so worried about Richard."

One perfect tear spills over and slips down Skye's cheek. "Addy's being so sweet about helping me, but I don't know what we're going to do if he's... if he doesn't..." Her lower lip wobbles. Another tear follows the first.

Her mascara doesn't even smudge and it's all I can do to keep from rolling my eyes. Instead I focus on the cards, splitting the deck roughly in half and setting it back on the table. Indigo shuffles one more time before laying out another card.

"Oooh, is this a finding reading?" Kathy asks. "I love tarot. Well, I better go get that drink for Skye. Be right back."

Off she goes, still failing to make an offer to make me a new one. I feel a tiny little hitch of jealousy but there's no time to nurture it, because Indigo is off and running with her reading.

The card she has just laid next to the knight depicts a figure lying face down in the dirt, impaled through the back by a bunch of swords.

"Oh my God!" Skye wails. "Does that mean he's dead?"

"This card is about Rich's emotional state," Indigo reassures her. "And the cards are always symbolic, so even the Death card doesn't necessarily mean death."

"Then he's suffering?" Skye looks more pleased than worried, and I don't blame her. A little suffering would be good for Dad about now.

Indigo lays down another card. "This one gives us information about who is with Rich at this time."

This one depicts a man and a woman, both of them naked. They're not embracing, and it looks like maybe they're separated by some clouds and a giant angel, bigger than either of them, with scarlet wings. None of that makes much sense to me, but the words THE LOVERS in capital letters is a clue.

"I thought you said he was suffering!" Skye huffs. "And now you're saying he's with some other woman?"

"I'm not saying anything," Indigo says, patiently. "We ask the cards to reveal information, and then we interpret it as best we—"

"So far, the cards are just arguing with themselves," Skye grumbles.

Kathy, who has returned with Skye's drink, sets it carefully down on the table and observes, "The Lovers reversed like that could suggest infidelity, but it can also mean moral dilemma, can't it?"

"Dad is not given to agonizing over morals. He doesn't really have any. And he's never been in sync with anybody because he's too wrapped up in himself. But he excels at infidelity so I bet it's that one," I say.

"This is more about who he is *with*," Indigo says. "That person's morals and relationships."

"Don't you look at me," Skye protests. "Just because I make

movies. He's not with me, obviously, because I'm staying with Addy. If I knew where he was I wouldn't be here."

Kathy pulls over a chair and has a seat. "I'm on break," she calls back over to the teenager behind the counter. He opens his mouth and then closes it again with a shrug. Kathy is a fixture. He's just here for a couple of months. She will do what she wants and he will also do what she wants. Those are the rules, even though they've never been written down.

Indigo lays down another card. Swords again, stuck into the earth this time, rather than into a person, but forming a sort of cage with a woman, bound and blindfolded, trapped inside.

"He's holding a woman captive?" Skye asks, skeptical. "That one doesn't really sound like him."

Even Indigo's patience appears to be fraying slightly but she keeps her voice level as she explains, "The cards are symbolic. This card represents Rich, not a woman, and it's the card that tells us of his physical location."

"Doesn't look like he's going far," Vic mutters.

"So you think *he's* a captive?" Skye asks. "A hostage maybe? Buried alive?" She sounds way too excited about this idea.

Indigo lays another card on the table. A mischievous looking dude in a red hat is in the act of sneaking off with an armful of swords, looking back over his shoulder.

"This is the card for trickery, dishonesty, basically somebody trying to get away with something," she says.

"Wherever he is and whatever he's up to, he'll make a good story of it later," Kathy observes, which is one thing we can all be sure of. If he's alive and survives.

"One more card for clarification." Indigo lays a card crosswise at the center, across the upside-down knight. "Well, that's helpful," she says, in a tone that indicates it's not helpful at all.

The clarification card is labeled The Moon which does at least clarify that the big yellow thing in the sky is, in fact, the moon and not the sun. A couple of dogs are howling at it. A lobster as big as the dogs, half in and half out of the sea, looks on.

"The Moon card means illusion," Indigo says. "Nothing is what it appears to be."

Britt has been silent throughout the reading. Now, she says, "With all due respect, not to diss the cards or your beliefs, but I don't see how this tells us anything at all."

"Are you kidding? It tells us that Rich is a bit trapped," Kathy says. "That he's taking refuge with somebody who has complicated emotions toward him—and who is maybe facing a moral dilemma. But that he's still scheming."

"If he's alive, he'll be scheming," Vic mutters. "Don't need the cards to tell us that." He turns to me, clearly wanting to move on from tarot cards. "Speaking of scheming. Besides using Lindy Lind to disseminate information via the internet, and Indigo to magic out Dad's whereabouts, what else is in the masterplan?"

"OMG, you got Lindy to film me *on purpose*?" Skye squeals, as if I've betrayed her into the hands of an enemy and she's about to be killed by firing squad. "How could you do that to the mother of your own baby sister!"

There's absolutely no point explaining that of the two of us, I came off much worse in Lindy's post than Skye did. I take another big gulp of my drink to fortify myself.

"I didn't mean on purpose on purpose," Vic says, warily.

"Who's the woman in the background on those posts?" Indigo queries. "The angry one."

"Some bitch who doesn't like babies," Skye says. "Debbie somebody or other. Can you imagine being mad because a baby is crying?"

I *can* actually imagine that, but there are more important things to worry about.

"So, Skye, let me get this all straight. You're a film star," Vic says. "And Richard knocked you up and doesn't want to pay for the baby."

"Or me," she says. "Obviously, pregnancy and childbirth kept me from work. So he owes me more than child support. Lost wages, cosmetic surgery, that sort of thing. If he doesn't start paying, I'm going to sue him."

"So it's not so much that you're worried about him, you're out to collect," Britt says. "Which is fair. Don't get me wrong."

"I love him," Skye says. "Really I do. I wasn't going to ask him for money, except for enough to support us, you know? But then he started in with this other woman so what was I supposed to do? Especially since I can't work anymore on account of Daffodil and the damage to my body."

"Somebody kill me now," I murmur, slumping back in my chair.

Britt, who has been busy on her phone, says, "'Mama on the Make' looks like it would be quite enlightening. Maybe pregnancy and childbirth haven't entirely kept you out of the business."

A touch of color rises to Skye's cheeks, but she lifts her chin and says, with unexpected dignity, "I've got to feed Daffodil somehow."

"Have we considered that maybe Daffodil isn't even Richard's kid?" Vic asks. "All we've got is your word for it."

Skye wilts, those ever-ready tears welling up in her eyes again. "I don't want to be a bother. Give me Daffodil. We'll go." She makes a pathetic, half-hearted effort to reach for the baby.

Britt cuddles Daffodil closer.

Vic, pretty much impervious to theatrics, is unmoved. "You could be running a scam. Pretty convenient to show up after he disappears, claiming the kid is his."

Britt says, "Don't be ridiculous, Victor. Daffodil looks exactly like your baby pictures."

"There are all sorts of cases of doppelgängers out there who are unrelated. Or maybe the kid is Richard's and Skye nabbed her from her real mother, seeing the opportunity—"

"Let me know when you're done with the insults," Skye snaps, in a voice I haven't heard from her yet but which I suspect reflects her real self. "I had DNA tests done. She's his and he's going to support her."

"Good luck with that," Vic says.

"We do need to find him," I remind everybody. "Today would be great, given as Johanna's party is tomorrow."

"You can't possibly think you're going to pull that off," Vic says. "Throw her a New Year's party, if party you must. But there's no possible way you can—"

"The party is tomorrow."

"And if you don't find Dad by then?"

"We'll find him eventually. We can still choose the house winner. It's not like they're going to expect to take immediate possession."

"Have any of you considered that if we do find Richard, we'll either need to turn him in or be charged with harboring a fugitive? He won't be much help with child support or party planning from jail."

That sobers all of us. I swirl the straw around in the melted mess that was once a macchiato, and take a sad sip. "I don't suppose any of you are available to help with decorating and setting up in the house for the party?"

"Me," Indigo says.

"Helping my folks get ready today," Britt says. "Sorry, Addy. I'd help if I could."

Vic drains his cup and sets it firmly on the table. "Sorry, Addles. Busy day at the *Raven*." Unlike Britt, he doesn't look remotely sorry. Plus, I know he's not that busy. He's the sole proprietor of *Raven Brews and Bites* and technically he's the manager, but it's Rosa who really runs everything.

"Don't look at me," Skye says. "I'll need to watch Daffodil."

Since she hasn't spent any time actually watching Daffodil since her arrival, this is the flimsiest excuse ever, but that's fine. I don't want her at Johanna's house. Of course, this raises the question of what I am going to do with her and who is going to watch Daffodil.

"Come on, Vic. Just for a bit? I've already arranged for Ricky to bring over a coffin. So all I need is—"

"A coffin." Vic interrupts. "Really?"

"Johanna wanted to be there," I say, innocently.

"But she won't be, will she? I assume there's going to be an autopsy and her body won't be released until after." His eyes narrow. "What are you really up to?"

"Throwing a party."

"Don't give me the innocent act. I know you."

Indigo grins, her Cheshire cat number, not the Mona Lisa, and proceeds to misquote Shakespeare: "The party's the thing wherein she'll catch the conscience of the king. Or in this case, whomever the actual killer is."

"You think the murderer will revisit the scene of the crime?" Britt queries.

"Or be conspicuous by their absence," Indigo says.

"Nobody can be conspicuously absent on Christmas Day," Vic protests. "People have families. Traditions. Parties that have been planned for months. Speaking of which, what are you thinking about telling Mom? She'll expect you to be at the house for Christmas dinner."

Vic's cell chimes and he checks the message, his face shifting from alarm to outright horror.

"Did they find him?" I gasp, my brain going directly to the worst possible outcome. "Is he dead?"

"It's worse. Mom's on her way over here."

"She's what? Why?"

"Apparently she came looking for me at the *Raven*. Rosa tried to cover for me but Mom said something about me probably being at *Grounded* with you and stormed out."

"I've been ignoring texts and calls from her all morning," I admit. "We've got to get out of here. Fast. She can't know about any of this." By which I mean Skye, Daffodil, Indigo, and the party.

"Too late. Somebody turned her on to Lindy's video." Vic scans the room with the sort of desperation that says he's considering flinging himself through a window. "Quick. At least stow those cards away before she gets here."

Too late. The door opens. Mom sees us immediately and heads in our direction with all the speed and certainty of a tornado headed for a trailer park.

"Lord have mercy," Britt whispers.

Everybody in *Grounded* knows Mom and probably they've also seen Lindy's posts because a hushed silence falls.

Skye utterly fails to read the room. "Who the hell is this?" she asks, in an imperious voice, as if she's a Queen and her throne room is being invaded by an uninvited commoner.

"This," Mom retorts, in an even more carrying voice, "is Richard's wife. The question is, who are *you*?"

"He's married?" Skye shrieks. "The bastard!"

"Was," I mutter. "*Was* married. Skye, meet my mother. Mom, meet Dad's new baby mama. And Daffodil. And also Indigo."

"Well, I never," she huffs, hands on hips, surveying Skye. "You're nothing but a baby yourself. Are you even legal? What in heaven's name is wrong with that man?" Her eyes travel to the cards on the table and she makes the sign of the cross, even though she is one-hundred-percent Protestant and not remotely Catholic adjacent. "Why are we trafficking with the agents of the devil?"

She glares at me, now, because obviously Victor would never sully himself with anything evil and everything is my fault.

"Rich is gone," Skye says, her lower lip trembling, perfect tears sliding down her cheeks. "We're all alone. And I don't know what to do. Indigo asked the cards to tell us where he is."

Mom huffs. "Somebody clear away these devil cards at once. Get me a chair, Victor. Brittany, hand me that baby. My goodness, she looks exactly like Vic did at that age. Daffodil, is it?"

All of us do exactly as she says, even Indigo, who silently collects her cards and returns them to a little velvet sack tied with a gold cord. Britt, wide-eyed, carries Daffodil over to

Mom, who settles into the chair Vic has brought for her. She smiles and coos and transforms utterly into a human I have never met.

"So what are we really doing about Richard?" Mom asks, looking up from the baby. "He didn't murder that woman. No man I married would ever dare to do such a thing."

"Mom..."

But she's already shifted her attention to Indigo. "Who are you, again?"

"Indigo," Indigo says.

Mom waves a hand, dismissively. "I caught your name, but not the connection. Skye's mother, perhaps? Grandmother?"

The grandmother snark is pushing the envelope, even for Mom. No way is Indigo Skye's grandma.

But Indigo smiles serenely, as if Mom has been polite and gracious. "While I would adore being grandmother to either of these lovely ladies, we've only met this morning."

Mom glares at her, waiting for her to explain herself.

Indigo sips tea and smiles gently back.

The battle of wills is setting my teeth on edge but I'm too curious to see who will break first to do anything about it.

Mom is the one who ends the silence, but she still doesn't ask outright what she's dying to know. "So you're here with Addy, then? One of her clients?"

"Not precisely," Indigo says.

"Oh, for crying out loud," Vic bursts out. "Mom. Indigo was the murdered woman's online psychic. She's here to..." His voice trails off as he realizes he doesn't have the intel to break the stalemate. "Why is she here, Addy?"

Indigo raises her eyebrows and I can see the laughter gathering in her eyes. She awaits my response with apparently every bit as much curiosity as everybody else at the table. I'm pretty sure she knows that I know that she hasn't told me the real reason she showed up at Johanna's house. Will I tell everybody that? I could. Or... I could use her presence to my advantage.

I take a thoughtful slurp of my now completely melted drink, then clasp my hands earnestly and say, "Indigo came in a spiritual capacity. After communing with Johanna's spirit, she is convinced that in order for Johanna to rest in peace, her last wish must be fulfilled. The party must take place."

All eyes at the table, including Daffodil's, are now focused on me. Vic's right eyebrow is slightly quirked, which means he is skeptical of either my words or my motivations. Britt, a total realist, but a polite one, is biting back remarks about ghosts and the afterlife and psychics in general. Daffodil would like a diaper change. Skye is annoyed that I've temporarily stepped into the limelight. Indigo is unmistakably amused. And Mom? She's not about to keep her thoughts to herself.

"There shall not be found among you anyone who burns his son or his daughter as an offering, anyone who practices divination or tells fortunes or interprets omens, or a sorcerer or a charmer or a medium or a necromancer or one who inquires of the dead, for whoever does these things is an abomination to the Lord," she quotes, in her King James voice. Then, more normally, "I'll thank you to leave my daughter alone and not seduce her into your evil ways."

Vic laughs. "You ought to have seen that coming, Addles."

He's right. I should have. And he should have foreseen what follows next.

Mom turns on him. "This is no laughing matter, Victor. Shame on you. I expect you to help keep your sister in line."

"Like that ever works."

"Were you aware that the same book of the Bible you are quoting is equally hard on adulterers and immorality? Shall we all stone Dad whenever we finally find him?" I ask.

Mom looks like she'd be totally capable of stoning Dad, and also Indigo, with possibly a non-fatal rock or two tossed at me and Vic for good measure. Somehow, Skye, despite the fact that she presumably was a party to the promiscuous sexual activity, doesn't deserve our fate. Fortunately, I'm used to being on the receiving end of Mom's disapproval and it doesn't faze me.

"Speaking of adulterers," I say. "Skye, you'd mentioned another woman. That Dad left you for somebody else. Can you tell me about her?"

"I don't even think about her," Skye says, with a sniff. "She doesn't exist for me."

"Maybe she knows where he is, though," Indigo suggests. "You do want to find him, don't you?"

"Sounds like Richard," Mom says. "I suppose it's surprising that Daffodil is the only out of wedlock baby to come from his philandering. At least the only one that we know of. Yet."

Skye stares at her in dawning horror. "You think there are *more?*"

"It couldn't hurt to contact this woman you've mentioned, Skye, and see if she knows anything," I say, thinking about that reversed Lovers card.

Skye looks at us all uncertainly. "I've never met her. I don't really know her name. I saw texts from her on his phone, is all."

"Maybe he wasn't actually boning her then," Vic says.

Mom covers Daffodil's ears. "Victor. There's a baby present."

I'm pretty sure Daffodil has heard words worse than

boning. Wouldn't be at all surprised if she's been present when there was boning happening, in fact, but I guess we don't need to contribute to her corruption.

"I did make note of her number. Just in case." Skye retrieves her phone from her tiny little handbag and consults it, as if it's an oracle. "Siri, look up Ugly Bitch and give me her number."

"Looking up the number for Ugly Bitch," Siri says. I tap the number into my own phone as Siri relays it.

Before I can call, Mom gets to her feet, still holding Daffodil. "Well. You are adults and the best I can do is pray for your immortal souls. But I can and will remove this innocent child from your midst. You too, young woman."

"Who, me?" Skye grasps her chair with both hands, possibly worried that Mom will actually initiate a stoning ceremony.

Mom, who has never ever once in living memory said *there-there* to me, reaches out and strokes Skye's hair. "There, there. Poor child. Don't be frightened. You come along with me until these two repent and come to their senses."

"But why?" Skye asks. A fair question. One we'd all like answers to, I suspect.

"You're family now," Mom says.

Daffodil begins fussing again, as if she understands the assignment and is helping out. "Where's your diaper bag?" Mom asks.

"I put a diaper in Addy's purse," Skye says.

This is a lie. I'm the one who put the diaper in my purse. Skye did nothing except co-opt my clothes.

"Wipes?" Mom asks. "Changing pad? Bottle?"

We look at her blankly.

"Obviously I have failed as a mother," she says. "Consorting with a sorceress. Turning to Devil cards. No idea how to care for a baby. Come, Skye." She cradles Daffodil as protectively as if she's rescuing her from a burning building while an assassin or two fire shots in her direction. "Please tell me you do at least have a car seat."

I feel like I'm six again, in trouble for neglecting my chores. Anything I say to my mother right now is going to come through in that same whiny voice. *It wasn't my fault. What do I know about babies?*

"The car seat is in my car. I'll get it for you." I start to get to my feet but Mom motions me back.

"You never lock your doors. You stay right here with this... this *sorceress*. Come along, Skye. I do believe I may still have a crib out in the garage. And I know I have some baby clothes that will fit perfectly. We'll put both of you in Addison's old bedroom. Oh, my goodness. Is Daffodil crawling? We'll need a baby gate, and some outlet protectors..."

Skye casts one look back over her shoulder at me as she is towed away, her expression hard to read, but I think it's a cry for help.

I wave and the door closes behind her.

CHAPTER 16

THOSE OF US who are alive and remain stare at each other across the table with the shocked expressions you see on survivors of an earthquake or a hurricane. We even look windblown, though that's likely the fault of the overactive heat vent right above our heads.

I shake it off and pull my copy of Johanna's will out of my bag. "Vic, since you're my company legal adviser, would you please tell me if this is legit?"

"What now?" he mutters.

I slap the will down in front of him. Britt leans in close so she can see.

"You can decline," Vic says, after he reads it through twice. "Let her attorney take care of the estate."

"Does Dad really get everything? I can't believe she'd make him her sole beneficiary."

"If he killed her he's barred from inheriting."

"You don't really think he did, do you?" I ask. "I mean, he's an asshole but...not a murderous one."

Vic gives me a long look. "It doesn't matter. I mean, of course it matters, but you need to say no to this no matter what."

I think about Johanna, her sadness and loneliness and her fear about dying. I think about her beautiful house and all of the love and attention she put into it. And then I think about cold-eyed estate sale professionals going through everything with an eye for nothing but profit.

"Would it hurt me to manage her estate?" I ask out loud. "I mean—the poor woman had such a sad life. And then she got murdered. It would be the right thing to do, don't you think?"

"No!" Victor says. "The right thing to do is let her lawyer handle it."

"You haven't met her lawyer, though. He's..." Words fail me. "I don't trust him."

"First thing we do, let's shoot all the lawyers," Indigo murmurs. "Shakespeare. Paraphrased. If the lawyer winds up dead, it wasn't me that killed him."

"If we could focus on this business with the will for a minute," Vic says. "I think—"

I interrupt him. "I wonder when she decided to make her will? I mean, did she already have one and get Chip Fitzwilliam to revise it? Or did she only make one because Indigo told her she was going to die?"

We all look at Indigo.

She looks calmly back at us. "I haven't any idea. Upon learning she was going to die she did not dramatically cry out, 'Dear God! And me without a will!'"

"What *did* she say?" Britt asks.

Indigo sobers and slowly shakes her head. "I gave her the interpretation of the cards. She sat there for a long moment, as if she hadn't heard me. Then she said, very softly, 'So that's it then.' She buried her face in her hands for a minute and when she looked up she told me she wanted to end the session. And that was it. The last time I saw her."

Vic picks up his cup and tries to drink, before remembering he's already finished his coffee. Britt fidgets. The silence grows, unsettled and heavy, full of things unspoken, and I know we're all feeling the awfulness of Johanna's dying without having really lived.

"Are we sure she didn't have family?" Vic asks. "This could be a revision of a previous will. If Fitzwilliam has an old one, maybe we could find out who was the previous beneficiary."

"Charlene would know. She stayed with the new firm when they bought the practice. And she notarized the deed for the house. Hey, Vic. I have an idea. Char likes you. Maybe you could—"

"No," Vic says. "Not getting involved. My advice? You'd let the attorney be the executor. But you won't. Because you want to dig through that poor woman's life. You're dying to know why she became a recluse. Find out if there's something in her house worth killing her over. Maybe get yourself killed in the process."

"I'm not going to get myself killed."

"Snooping around Leno's death got you half-scalped and run off the road on Suicide Corner. I don't know if you remember that part."

Britt, used to the two of us spatting and then making up again, sips calmly at her tea, then says to Indigo, "I find it difficult to believe you really predicted Johanna's' death."

"You have a logical mind," Indigo says. "To you I would say, as Hamlet said to Horatio, 'There are more things in heaven and earth than are dreamt of in your philosophy.'"

"I don't have a Shakespeare quote for this," Vic says, "so I'll say it directly. It makes much more sense that you predicted Johanna's death, murdered her, then hung around to collect the valuables, than that you predicted her death."

"Occam's Razor," Indigo says. "The simplest solution with the least assumptions. You have a flaw in your thinking though. It doesn't look to me like I'll be walking off with a single item from Johanna's estate."

"Maybe you thought she would make the will out in your favor. You being her only friend. Dad was the wild card you never expected."

"Then why am I still here?" Indigo asks.

"You're the psychic, you tell me." Vic shoves his chair back, gets up, and stomps out. I stare after him with my mouth open. He's the charming one. The polite one. I've never heard him go off like this before.

"He'll get over it, Addy," Britt says. "He's upset about Rich's baby more than anything and taking it out on you. Mom needs me today, so I'm off home, but I'll take a run at Char. Also, I've got the invites almost ready to go. I'll send the file over to Fox Valley Printers and call in a favor for a rush printing."

"Thanks, Britt. You're the best."

She gives me a quick hug and is out the door behind Victor, leaving me and Indigo alone at the table.

"So, how will we spring the trap?" Indigo asks, as if this is a logical and expected segue from the previous conversation. Also as if my brother hasn't outright accused her of fraud, murder, and grifting.

"The play's the thing, you mean? I'm not planning on putting on some sort of dramatic production at this party. There's no time to create a script, even if I wanted to."

"Well, of course not. But the whole point behind Hamlet's play-within-a-play was to recreate something that would trigger the murderer's guilt so they would reveal themselves. Don't look so blank, honey. Surely you had some sort of plan for ferreting out your killer at this party."

"I hadn't thought beyond getting people there and... I don't know... watching them to see what they do." This is only partly true. I have the glimmerings of a plan. I'm not about to share it with her, though. Vic's got a point, and I haven't ruled her out as the murderess.

"Have you considered that if your murderer is not one of the neighbors they won't get the invite and won't show up at the party?" she asks. "I do believe you're limiting the scope of the investigation. You have the perfect mass marketing vehicle at your disposal."

"Social media, you mean? I guess I do have an Instagram... ohhhh."

"Now you've got it," Indigo says. "Call her."

"I don't think that's a good idea."

"Oh, honestly," she says. "I'm disappointed. Here. I'll do it."

How she came by Lindy's number I don't know, but she's already dialing. Of course there's no answer, but she leaves a message. "I have intel about Johanna Meyers. Call me."

"Indigo. Think about this. We can't—"

Her phone rings back almost immediately. She answers with a fake accent that sounds like she's been born and raised in Boston followed by a year or two in Britain.

"Lindy, darling, I'm so glad you called right back. I've got to make this quick while Addy is out of the room. She wouldn't want me to tell you... Exactly. You know how she is. Mmm... yes,... I know, I know but she doesn't want me spilling the tea so please promise you won't tell her... no, they haven't located him yet, but... no, no, listen, darling. This is big. Addy is planning a party for Johanna, like she did for Leno Masterson. A Christmas party on Christmas Day, can you believe it? Here's the kicker. She's giving away Johanna's house as a party favor! No, no. Of course she's not telling the media. It's for the neighbors only... Can you imagine the chaos if everybody in and out of town knew what she was up to? People coming out of the woodwork just to get their hands on that poor woman's house... No, no, you can't tell everybody now! I thought you'd want to be there is all. I am absolutely not telling you who is calling... hello? Hello?"

She ends the call and smiles, Cheshire cat on steroids.

"What have you done?"

"Baited the trap."

"We don't have a trap. We barely have the house. We certainly don't have food and drinks or room for that many people. This isn't like summer, with overflow space on the lawn."

"It's quite a spacious house, really. No problem there that can't be overcome. And you are doing it drop-in, yes? They won't all come at once. Don't you want to find your father?"

"Of course but—"

"And bring Johanna's killer to justice?"

"Yes, but I don't—"

"We'd better get a move on. That party isn't going to plan itself. And the house needs decorating."

ON THE WAY to the house, I call Owen. When he answers, what comes out of my mouth is, "I need you," which wasn't what I meant to say at all.

"Words that go straight to a man's heart. I'm going to hazard a guess that you don't need me in the sense that life would come to a screeching halt without me. The moon fall from the sky, the waves cease to roll in from the sea..."

"I was sort of hoping you could help me with Johanna's party."

"You don't know how much I'd love to, Addy," he says, sounding only the tiniest bit sarcastic. "But I can't expose Jackson to—"

"Skye won't be there."

"What have you done with her? Left her alone at the condo? She'll steal all the silver."

He delivers the latter in his mother's snobby tones and I can't help laughing. "Had I any silver, she would be sure to steal it. As it is, my mother is the one whose cutlery is in danger."

Silence. Then, "I'm not sure I understand what you're telling me."

"Mom has inexplicably taken in mother and child as members of the family, to be nurtured and protected."

"Dear God."

"Amen. I'm on my way over to Johanna's house now. Indigo will be helping me. But I need somebody I can trust."

"And Indigo is?"

"Johanna's online psychic. She's in town."

Silence. "Is she...safe?"

"I think so."

"You don't sound exactly sure of that."

"I'm not sure of anything. Indigo could be the murderer. Vic is refusing to help and Britt is needed at home."

"So you'll be hanging out at the murder house with a charlatan who might be a killer."

"Something like that."

"And you want me to bring Jackson. To hang out in the murder house with a charlatan who might be a killer."

"I can pretty much promise you that she'll keep her clothes on and that Jackson hasn't seen her in a movie."

"Addy—"

"She's old enough to be Jackson's grandmother. Also, I was thinking Jackson could help Nat hand out party invites to the neighbors on the block, so he wouldn't technically be in the murder house hanging out with the killer."

"Is that that Addy chick?" Jackson's voice asks in the background. "Wait, is this about the party at the murder house? I am so in. Can I bring Tyson?"

"Do I want to know how he knows about this or why he's actually excited about something? Other than Skye, I mean," Owen says.

"I might have possibly leaked the news about the party to Lindy Lind."

"I have no words," Owen says. He means it, apparently, because the phone has gone dead. Which means I'm planning this party with Indigo and maybe Nat, if I'm lucky.

Maybe, for once in my life, I should abandon my crazy ideas and settle for doing what normal people do. I'm not sure what that even looks like, but I try to get a mental picture. Possibly, finishing up unpacking my condo and throwing a housewarming party, instead of trying to drag everybody I love into the chaos—and possible danger—of attempting find my father, pull off a party for a dead woman I don't even know in the house where she was murdered, and catch her killer. Having a real date with Owen. Buying gifts and enjoying Christmas. I could let Alex do his thing and trust that if Dad is innocent the legal system will clear him. Get to know my new baby sister, who is probably better off without Dad in her life anyway.

But.

Superimposed over all of that imagining of what normal might look like, I see Johanna's thin face and the mix of fear and resignation and despair in her eyes. She had this one crazy last wish, and I'm the person she entrusted it to. Besides, whether Dad murdered her or not, he still did serious harm. And that is my fault. I let him manipulate me and take advantage of her.

My apologies to the version of Addison Winters who could have enjoyed a normal, happy Christmas with her family, the one who might have fallen in love with Owen and had a Christmas romance, the one who opted to do what her family and friends want her to do for once—but I can't let Johanna's last wishes go unfulfilled, or her murderer go free. And I'm damn well not going to let Dad do to Daffodil what he's done to me and Vic.

So yes, I will be manipulating my nearest and dearest into helping me, because that's who I am and what I do. Vic will come around sooner or later. He always does. Britt will work her magic from home. And Owen... Well. A long distance romance or a Christmas fling? That I can handle. My track record for long term and committed is almost as bad as Dad's. It's probably a good thing if Owen is busy with Jackson and doesn't get involved, but I can't pretend that it doesn't hurt.

CHAPTER 17

I STOP by Nat and Angel's place before I go to Johanna's. Before I'm properly parked Nat dashes out the front door and over to Jezebel, completely underdressed for the weather in sneakers, jeans, and a T-shirt.

"Go get a jacket," I tell him. "You're gonna freeze." I'm sitting in Jezebel with the heater on full and I'm still shivering from the cold air flowing in through the open window.

"I'm not cold. Did you hear anything? About who killed Johanna?"

"Nothing yet. But. We are throwing her party tomorrow. You want to help?"

"You bet!"

"Angel will let you?"

"She's working today." His forehead creases. "Could we maybe not tell her?"

"I won't if you don't. But you know the neighbors will."

His face falls. Then he shrugs. "Worst she can do is yell at me, right? Too late to stop me."

An uneasy qualm about encouraging Nat to break the rules tries to present itself, but it's easily dismissed. It's not like we're dealing with an axe-wielding homicidal maniac. "Go get your jacket and some boots. I'll drive you. You can check on the birds while I get organized."

That last sets him scampering off to the house and he's back in two minutes wearing warm boots and a down jacket, with a dark green stocking cap pulled down over his ears.

"I'm ready!"

He chatters cheerfully all the way over to Johanna's. "Is Bagheera okay? You took him home, right?"

"I did. He's...adjusting."

As soon as I park the car Nat's out the door and running for the gate that leads into the yard. "Birds first!"

The house feels different than it did yesterday. The oppressive energy is gone, a testament to the fact that Indigo might be a little bit more of a real psychic than I want to admit. Now it feels lonely. A little bit sad, as if it misses Johanna.

"Don't worry, house," I say out loud. "We'll take care of you."

"What's that?" Indigo asks.

I startle, one hand flying to my chest to reassure my galloping heart. "God, you scared me. How did you get in?"

"Honey, everybody hides a key. Even a recluse. It was just a matter of finding it. I'm psychic, remember? Now, where do we start? I made tea. Cocoa for you and Nat. Come sit down and let's make a plan."

I follow her to the breakfast bar in the kitchen, wondering what else she's had time to do besides make drinks.

"Decorations and food, of course," she's saying. "More importantly, how do we keep eyes on all of the guests? Who are our suspects?"

She's done more than just make drinks, as it turns out. Two note pads and two pens are also laid out on the counter. I slide onto a stool and wrap both cold hands around the wonderfully warm mug of cocoa. Looks like Indigo has already started a list:

Things to Be Done:
Decorations (what, who how)
Food (what, from where)
Music
How to catch the killer

"Tell me what you're thinking," Indigo says, sitting down next to me with her cup of tea.

"We have to keep it simple. We're short on time and resources. And thanks to you getting Lindy Lind involved, we're going to have a lot more people here than just the neighbors on the block. We're going with a Christmas theme, so at least that's easy. For refreshments, we'll order from the bakery. We can get crackers and cheese and vegetable and dip platters from the *Raven*. The cook will complain about lack of planning but Rosa will make sure it happens. A couple of crockpots full of hot apple cider; that will also make the house smell amazing and we can do it ourselves. We need a Christmas tree and a few garlands and some lights. A wreath on the door. A way to manage the entries for the door prize and something to put them in."

"Any idea where to get the decorations from?" she asks.

"Maybe Johanna has more? We should have a look around." What I really want is a good snoop all through the house. In the closets, under Johanna's bed. All through the garage. To look for clues, to see what I can find out about her life.

"I love decorating," Nat says, opening the door into the kitchen that leads from the backyard via the enclosed patio. "Can I help?"

"You can! Come sit for a minute. Indigo made you cocoa."

I text Vic.

> Addy: Could I talk you into bringing over a tree?
>
> Vic: I told you I'm not getting involved
>
> Addy: It's just a tree. You can drop it and run.
>
> Vic: 🙄
>
> Addy: And the leftover decorations you didn't use for the tree at the Raven
>
> Vic: 😒
>
> Addy: 🎄🎁 Oh, and put in an order for some party platters for me? The veggie & dip one, and the cheese sampler?
>
> Addy: Thank you! You're the best!
>
> Vic: 😊

"Okay," I say. "Vic is coming over with a tree and some decorations, and I've ordered up the food from the *Raven*. I'll call in the order for the cookies and coffee. It's super late but I can call in favors and make it happen. I'm thinking, Indigo, if you would maybe start with cleaning up the rest of the fingerprint powder, since you know how to do that and have the supplies? Nat and I will look around for any decorations Johanna might have stored here."

"Wait. You're forgetting the most important thing," Indigo says.

"Which is?"

"Catching the killer. What about our play-within-a-play moment? Making the killer think we're on to him. Or her."

"I don't know what that would even look like," I say. "We don't know enough. We don't even know how Johanna died. Hamlet had his actors pour poison in the king's ear..."

Nat, who has walked in just in time to hear this, claps both hands over his ears and looks at us in dismay. "Somebody can kill you by putting poison in your *ears*? Like, you don't even have to swallow it? That's messed up!"

Indigo smiles and gently withdraws his hands from his ears. "That was an old, old story, Nat, all made up. I've never heard of anybody really being poisoned that way. I'm pretty sure you're safe."

Nat doesn't look too sure. I'm also suddenly feeling uneasy and creepy crawly. I've never even really thought about that way of dying. Somebody sneaking in through my window to strangle, shoot, or stab me? Yep. That's crossed my mind. But poison in my poor, vulnerable, undefended ear while I sleep?

I shudder, then push the sensation firmly away. There are much easier ways to kill somebody.

"We'll watch people's reactions to everything. Make a note of anybody acting weird. That sort of thing."

"It's a starting point. But a hidden camera would be good. Two, I think. One by the front door. One on the coffin. You are getting the coffin here, right?"

"Yes, to the coffin. But I don't think there's anywhere in Fox Valley where you're going to just walk in and buy a spy cam."

Indigo waves my words away with a casual gesture. "Not to worry. I always carry a couple with me. I'll set them up."

Of course you do, I think. *Don't all psychics travel with a kit for cleaning up crime scenes and a couple of spy cams?*

"Cool," Nat says. "Can I help?"

"Of course. But you must make sure not to tell anybody though, Natty. We don't want the word to get out."

"I won't tell," he says. "I'm good at secrets."

I leave the two of them to the cameras and am about to start my search of the house when the doorbell rings. Owen and Jackson are standing on the porch.

Owen looks exhausted. Dark circles under his eyes. New lines drawn in his forehead. Part of me wants to hug him. The other part, the part that was hurt by our last conversation, wins.

"Wasn't expecting to see you here," I say, blocking the door. "Did you need something?"

"I want to help with the murder party," Jackson says, pushing in past me. "Where did she die? Is there blood?" He stops when he sees Indigo and Nat. "Oh, hey. You're that bird nerd kid. What are you doing here?"

"Hey Jackson." Nat shrinks into himself, his eyes going wary.

I hadn't thought about the boys knowing each other, but of course they'd have to. Fox Valley only has one middle school. Jackson is older, but Nat is obviously a gifted kid, so no big surprise if he's a grade ahead. Also no surprise if this means he gets picked on by the cool kids, a state of affairs I have personal experience with, though not because I'm a brainiac.

"Nat feeds Johanna's birds. And he's helping with the party. Which is not a murder party." The thought that Jackson might be bullying Nat makes me furious, and my voice sounds a lot like Mom's did when she met Indigo, judgmental and downright frosty.

Indigo straightens up from where she's been concealing one of her cameras in a plant on the credenza in the entryway and turns to Jackson. "Young man, if you'd like to forget about your outrage for an hour or two, it will be waiting for you when you're ready."

He glares at her. She smiles sweetly back, then turns to Owen, looking him over from top to toe.

"So that's what Addy sees in you. I think I approve. Aren't you going to invite these gentlemen in, Addy?"

"I'm not at all sure they want to come in," I say, still all winter frost.

"Don't be silly, Addy. Of course they want to come in." Indigo closes the door behind them.

Jackson whistles. "Nice! Where do I enter to win the house?"

"You have to be of legal age to own a house. Or win one. Door prize or not," Owen says.

"If I win, I'll give it to you, Uncle Owen."

"I already own a house," Owen says.

"Whatever."

"You have to actually be at the party to enter," I tell him. "Actually, about that, I could use your help. Yours and Nat's."

Jackson immediately looks skeptical. "I am not going to be your coat check boy or dishwasher or whatever."

"Oh, I had something much more interesting in mind. How

are you with secrets? If I tell you something, can I trust you to keep it to yourself?"

"Depends," he says, but I see a glimmer of interest in his eyes.

"All right. Here's the thing. There's more going on with this party than meets the eye."

"Yeah, yeah. It's the murdered woman's last wish or something."

"Well, yes. But. It's also like a... sting operation. I need some people undercover. Hanging out, being normal, but watching all of the guests." I lower my voice to a conspiratorial tone. "It's possible the killer will show up at the party. If they do, maybe they'll do or say something that reveals their guilt."

Nat's eyes go wide. "You think one of the neighbors killed her?"

"We can't rule that out. What do you think? Are you two in?"

Nat nods, solemnly, accepting responsibility for the mission. Jackson still isn't willing to commit.

"Maybe," he says. "What would we have to do?"

"Well, today you'll hand out personal invitations to the neighbors on the block, and keep notes about anything unusual—"

"Are you crazy? It's cold out there," Jackson says.

"Cookies," Nat counters. "Every one of them will give us cookies. Except old Ralph, and I wouldn't eat anything he gave me anyway."

I hold up a finger. "And, tomorrow at the party, you two can be in charge of the door prize. Make sure all of our guests get entered."

"I guess," Jackson says. "Hey, can I see where she was killed?"

"Maybe after you hand out all the invites."

"I want to see it now."

Owen's eyes say everything. He's a volcano about to erupt and it won't be pretty.

Indigo pats his arm. "There, there. Johanna doesn't mind. She wanted people to come into the house. Maybe the boys can help solve the murder. Come into the kitchen and let me fix you a cup of tea."

Jackson is already heading for the stairs, Nat right behind him.

"No! I do not want tea! And I don't want Jackson involved in this." Owen fixes a stormy gray gaze on me. "I came over here hoping to make you see that this is a bad idea. And now you've totally undermined me with Jackson. Now if I tell him he can't do this he's going to fight me on everything, more than he already is."

His anger hits hard, but there's something else in his eyes. The same thing was in Jackson's, and earlier, in Nat's. All of them are dealing with the repercussions of murder. Nat's mother, Jackson's father, Owen's brother. All of them grieving. All of them angry, with an underlying fear of facing up to the broken bodies and any carnage left behind.

"Jackson's frightened, Owen," I say, softly. "Grieving. He needs to see where she died because whatever he's imagining is horrific. Don't worry, there's nothing to see."

Owen swallows and runs his free hand through his hair. His jaw is rock hard; a muscle jumps in his cheek. I want to put my arms around him and pat him, as if he's Daffodil. I can't imagine inheriting the responsibility for an angry and troubled teenager.

"I am in so far over my head, Addy," he says, in a softer voice. "I'm totally fucking this up. Maybe the group home would be better for him than me."

"Nonsense." Indigo pats him again. "The two of you need each other."

Footsteps on the stairs, and both boys come running back down.

"Nothing to see," Jackson grumbles. "Waste of steps."

"I'm glad she wasn't shot like my mom," Nat says. "You can't ever get the blood out."

CHAPTER 18

"Well!" Indigo claps her hands. "We need to get to work. If those invites aren't quite ready for the boys, I'd suggest we all do a little cleaning while we wait for that tree to arrive."

"House looks pretty clean to me," I say.

"Bathrooms need to be cleaned," Indigo says. "Surfaces dusted. Fingerprint powder cleaned up. If we all work on it, shouldn't take long."

"I'm not cleaning," Jackson protests.

"No, you are going to start getting set up for the door prize giveaway," Indigo says. "Owen, would you please clean the bathrooms? Addy, you can dust. I'll focus on anywhere there is still fingerprint powder. We'll mop the floor tonight on our way out. Sound good? Boys, come with me."

I stare after Indigo, not at all sure how I feel about her taking charge. Especially since it means everybody will be occupied with a project and there will be nobody watching her, but she's already leading the boys off to the dining room table.

"She's a force to be reckoned with," Owen says. "Jackson didn't even pretend to argue with her."

"You don't really have to clean bathrooms," I tell him.

"Are you kidding? I'm not about to disobey that woman's orders. Where is the bathroom? Where are my cleaning supplies?"

He's already moving, and I follow him, not sure myself where anything is since I haven't had a proper chance to explore. The first door he opens turns out to be a coat closet. There's a dead spider curled up on the floor, but it's otherwise empty. Johanna had no need for a coat. And she never had company. There's a whole row of hangers, empty, useless. This strikes me as sad, but Owen has already moved on and I run after him.

This time, the door he opens does lead into a half bath. Owen opens the cabinet under the sink, and comes out with a cleaning rag and a spray bottle of bathroom cleaner. "Everything I need is here," he says. "And look, there's a toilet brush. I'm in business."

His tone is light, but I haven't forgotten his words from earlier. Or that he hung up on me.

"Owen," I say.

"Hmmm?"

He turns toward me and I look up into his face, at a loss for words. "You're mad at me. Maybe you want to talk about that?'

"You are absolutely the most impossible woman I have ever met. It's hard enough with Jackson. You're not exactly helping."

"It's my super skill," I quip. "Making waves. Causing trouble."

"We should buy you a cape." His eyes focus on mine. His

breath catches in his throat. He's either still really angry or he's going to kiss me. Possibly both things are true.

The doorbell rings.

Indigo's voice drifts down the hallway. "Did you want me to get that?"

"Yes," I whisper, my eyes still locked with Owen's.

"It's your brother with the tree!" Indigo calls.

"Coming!" I call back, but I can't seem to move.

"Addy!" Nat arrives at the door. "Where do you want the tree?"

Owen turns away and starts spraying cleaning solution on the sink. I sigh and follow Nat across the living room to the front door, where Victor is standing on the mat in his snowy boots, holding a white cardboard box stamped with the *Fox Valley Printers* logo.

"Oh, you picked up the invites! And the tree! Santa better bring you something extra nice this year."

He snorts. "Santa has already gifted us both with a new sibling and a pornstar stepmother who is younger than we are. What more could we ask for? Where do you want this?"

"I'm thinking right over there." I gesture at a spot in the living room where the tree will be visible when people first walk in. "We'll need a stand."

"Already taken care of. Brought the extra decorations from the *Raven*, too." He looks at Nat, and at Jackson who has come over to see whether anything exciting is going on. "You boys can help me bring in the tree."

I hold the door for them while they lug in a nice bushy fir that's taller than Vic. Owen and Indigo both come over to help, because who can resist the allure of a tree? We get it into the stand and straight, with the requisite amount of arguing. Indigo adds water from a plastic jug.

"Can we decorate it?" Nat begs. "Please?"

Normally, I'd insist on doing it myself. Getting the decorations right is a top priority for any party. But I want to be free to do some snooping and to keep an eye on Indigo.

"Oh, all right. The two of you can do the tree. And then you'll take the invites around to the neighbors. Agreed?"

"Hey, I'll help with the tree but I'm still not cool with wading around in the snow and freezing my ass off," Jackson protests.

"It's part of your super sleuth assignment," I tell him. "Look for anybody that looks guilty. You've got a memo function on your phone, right? You can make voice notes about anything shady."

"Do you think that's safe? I mean, maybe the killer will try to poison us. Or take Nat hostage and I'll have to rescue him."

He sounds more excited about this idea than worried, so I figure he'll go along.

"And what are you going to be doing while we decorate the tree?" Vic asks, as if he thinks I'm wandering off for an afternoon at the spa followed by a mani-pedi and a fancy dinner out.

"I need to make some phone calls. Make sure all of the food is squared away."

Vic doesn't look convinced. I smile at him sweetly. "Going upstairs to use Johanna's desk."

He doesn't follow me, wonder of wonders, even though I'm sure he knows I'm bent on doing some snooping. I do have a business image to uphold so party requirements first. I call

Grounded and order carafes of coffee and hot water for tea. Then the bakery for a selection of cookies and brownies and other seasonal deliciousness. And then my usual florist to get a real wreath for the door and some poinsettias to help brighten up the inside, since Bagheera isn't here to poison himself by eating the leaves.

Everyone I talk to points out that it is the day before Christmas and rather late for orders, but they come around in the end.

And then the phone rings, caller ID flashing 'Ugly Bitch'.

I'd texted her earlier, but with absolutely no belief that she'd call back.

"If you find the bastard send him my way, would you?" a woman says, as soon as I answer.

"I was hoping you could tell me where he was hiding."

"If I did, he'd be minus a testicle or two. He needs to man up."

"Please don't tell me you're pregnant," I say. I'm not ready for another addition to the family.

She snorts. "Not likely. But I was abysmally stupid enough to lend him money. I suppose he's spent it on that Skye creature. The one who *is* actually pregnant."

"Skye stopped being pregnant about six months ago. Baby's name is Daffodil. And no. As far as I know, Dad has not spent the money on either of them."

"Figures. Well, if you see him, tell him I expect to be paid back," she says.

"Get in line. Word of advice, though. If he knows you're planning on collecting money, your chances of seeing him are nil."

"Well, you tell him this from me," she says. "Maybe I can't find him, but I can hire somebody who can."

"Will do. I'll tell him to look out for knee breaker hired by... sorry, what was your name again?"

There's a pause. Then, "If you don't know my name, how did you get my number?"

Damn. She's suspicious now and she's going to get all cagey.

"Skye grabbed your number from one of your texts. She's not very happy about you."

"She, what?" Her voice rises to a screech that makes me move the phone farther from my ear. "He told me he was through with her when he moved into my apartment!"

"He lies to everybody. Trust me. You are not the only one. And since you're not the only one, it would be helpful to have your name. Maybe where you live?"

"Just tell him I want my money." She hangs up.

Well, maybe Britt can work a miracle.

> Addy: If I give you a phone number do you think you could find who it belongs to?
>
> Britt: what kind of somebody?
>
> Addy: Skye referred to her as Ugly Bitch
>
> Britt: Oh, that somebody. Why don't you call her?
>
> Addy: I did
>
> Britt: And you didn't get her name?
>
> Addy: She was not exactly cooperative. Phone number looks like California area code. Maybe from LA?

Britt: Cell phones are hard. Buy it in one state
and then move across the country. Let me see
what I can do. I'll get back to you.

Addy: You're the bestest

I pull my notebook out of my bag and turn to my suspect
page, jotting U.B. down under Indigo and Ralph. Maybe this
woman was jealous enough to kill Johanna and make it look
like Dad did it. Maybe she's actually in town. Maybe Skye and
Daffodil are in danger. I should call Alex but I know how that
conversation would go so I don't bother.

Instead, since I'm sitting right here anyway, I go through
Johanna's desk. The crime scene people have taken her
computer, leaving the keyboard and the mouse and a couple of
connector cords behind. Other than that, the only thing on the
desk is a basket with a neat stack of mail. Phone bill. Electricity
bill. Internet bill. A bank statement.

I give it a quick glance, then squint my eyes and look again,
making sure I'm not adding any extra zeros. It still reads the
same: five-hundred thousand, two-hundred and fifty-seven
dollars and forty-three cents. There must be some mistake.
Surely she didn't will that kind of money to a total stranger.
But the date is current as of the end of November.

Well, hell. That could be reason enough to kill her. Would
that be enough money to make Dad cross the line? He could
have rationalized her death six ways from Sunday. She was
dying anyway. And she was entombed in this house. He could
have thought of it as a mercy killing. Or maybe there was a
previous will, and a previous beneficiary didn't know the will
had been changed. If somebody killed her for the money, and
she left the money to Dad, he really could be murdered and not

missing. And once he's out of the way, am I next on the murder list?

Focus, Addy. There's nothing else of interest in the paper inbox. A newspaper from last week. Nothing circled to indicate a secret message or something that sparked her interest. A couple of junk mail flyers. An invite from the Neptune Society to plan her funeral in advance. Well, that I already know she has done. No personal letters or cards, which would have been helpful.

Next, I sort through the drawers. Paper, pens, a notebook. I open the notebook with a catch of my breath. Maybe I'll find a record of secret meetings. A love affair. Memories of her childhood.

It's even better. There are notes on her sessions with Indigo, going back five years. On each page, a sketched layout of a tarot reading, each card labeled in capital letters. The last reading is dated the day she called and left me the voicemail that started this whole thing.

The Death card figures centrally. I also see The Devil. The Hanged Man. The Ten of Swords and The Tower and The Lovers reversed. Some of these are the same as in the reading Indigo did for Dad.

Beneath the drawing Johanna has written:

Indigo says I am to die. The news comes as no surprise, and no great shock. Perhaps I am numb, but I have been mostly numb for years, have I not? It's been a dying by inches. It's a surprise that I feel any resistance to the act of dying at all. Even that resistance is more of a small startlement. As if my plans to watch a movie had been deterred by a power outage or a network issue.

But now. Now, as I'm writing these words the feelings begin to surge. An ocean swell rising, rising under storm winds. I have not lived and now I am to die? By what means? I ask myself whether it can be staved off, forfended. Is it too late to breach these walls that hold me captive? To feel the sun on my face and see the untrammeled sky open above me... Perhaps even to love once more, to feel hands on my skin and seek comfort in the warmth of another?

No. It is too late for any of these things. But perhaps, perhaps... I can leave behind a memory. To leave some good feeling at my passing, make a tiny difference in the tenor of the world.

I feel Indigo's pronouncement to be true. It resonates in my bones. There is no time to play the victim, to weep for what has never been and it's always foolish to wish the past had been other than what it was. So then. Forward motion. I shall set my affairs in order. Perhaps Nat could take Bagheera? Or would he be happier staying here with the new resident of this house?

After that question, there is a short list:

> *Call that party planner*
> *Arrange to give away the house*
> *Find an attorney and make a will*

The rest of the pages in the journal are as empty as the years that should have been filled by Johanna's life. But there is one other thing of interest in the notebook: a thin stack of well-worn photos, tucked into the pocket of the back cover. These are the only clues to Johanna's past, and I lay them out on the desk and look them over carefully.

The photo on top, the one most worn around the edges, captures a man and two teenagers, girl and boy, in front of a house. It's spring or maybe summer; the grass is green, the trees are in leaf. There is nothing special about the house, a nondescript ranch style painted brown with cream trim, and flanked by carelessly tended juniper. The man leans against the side of a black pickup truck in the driveway, arms folded across his chest. Given the shape of his lips and the lines of tension in his body, I'm guessing the camera caught him right in the middle of a curse. Something that starts with an F and is followed by a U, I'd bet, given the position of his front teeth over his lower lip, the way his brows are drawn together, the stormy intensity of his gaze directed at the person behind the camera.

The girl's lips are turned down at the corners, eyebrows drawn together, one hand palm up in a gesture of contrition. She's in motion toward the angry man, her attention all on him. The boy, a little older, a little harder, has a hat jammed down over his head at an angle. Dark glasses cover his eyes but his face is turned toward the girl, his lips set in an ugly smirk.

I look at them for a long moment, wondering, begging them to tell me their secrets. The girl might be Johanna. The facial features are similar, and the hair and clothes fit with the late nineties, when she would have been a teen. Maybe there's some resemblance between her and the man, and also the boy, but nothing conclusive. Johanna has not helpfully written on the back the year or the place or the names of the people. Of course not. That would be too easy.

Indigo knew her better than anybody. Maybe she'll have some insights. I put the bills and the bank statement in my bag, then carry the journal downstairs. The boys are making progress hanging decorations on the tree, and I bite my tongue to keep from giving instructions about better places to put things and look for Indigo.

She's out in the closed-in porch with both Vic and Owen. She's cleaning up the fingerprint powder all over the door. Vic is dusting. Owen is washing windows.

Indigo turns when she hears me come in and gives me a searching look. "You've found something."

"Maybe? Some pictures. Could you take a look and see if any of them mean something to you?"

"Let's see," she says, plunking herself down on the window seat and holding out her hand. I sit beside her, surprised by how pleasantly warm it is in here with the radiant heat beaming down on us from above.

Owen and Vic stop what they're doing and drop heavily into chairs, as if they've been out in the fields harvesting hay or something instead of leisurely cleaning house for half an hour. I hand the photo to Indigo and she takes it gingerly by the edges, holding it up close to her eyes in a way that looks comfortingly like maybe she's at least properly near sighted, even if she's way too flexible for someone her age.

"Any idea who these people are?" I ask.

"The girl is Johanna, as for the others... I could guess, but I couldn't say for sure."

"But you're sure that's Johanna?"

"Oh, yes, dear. I looked up her online yearbook from when she was in high school. But I don't recognize the others. I don't remember seeing the boy's face in the yearbook, but that means nothing, really, as I wasn't looking for him. He might well have been there. And the man? You know... there is a family resemblance here between all three. Did you notice?"

"I did. But I thought I might be imagining it."

"Let me see," Vic says, and Indigo passes him the photo.

"She had a half brother," Indigo says, thoughtfully. "I suppose that could be him. She didn't really know him. Only met him once. He died years ago."

Vic passes back the photo.

I take another look, and something that has been nagging at me shakes itself loose. "I think I know who took the picture."

"So you're psychic now, too?" Vic asks.

"There's a photo of you and me and Dad with the exact same vibe," I remind him. "You know the one I mean."

Mom framed the shot and hung it on the living room wall, a twisted gesture of hostility, I've always thought. Certainly not a memory she's keeping alive for the love of it. It's still hanging there, showing us all caught out of time: Me conciliatory. Vic hostile. Dad angry.

I slide back into the memory.

It's the first time we've seen Dad since the divorce. Sunday. Post-church. We're sitting at the table eating pot roast and mashed potatoes, and all of a sudden Dad's at the door.

"What do you want?" Mom asks, blocking his attempt to enter.

"Please, Bethany, I want to see my children."

"Now you want to see them? What's it been—two years?"

"Beth."

"Your children don't want to see you."

I walk to the door, torn between anger at Dad for leaving, and the irrepressible hope that he actually cares about us. About me. My relationship with my mother is conflicted. Vic is her favorite child, and I'm full to the brim with smoldering resentment. I tell myself it's her fault that Dad left us. In case I've ever doubted it, this is proof!

Here he is, standing at the door, asking to see us.

And here is Mom, refusing to let him in.

"I want to see him," I say.

"That's my girl," Dad says. "Come out here and give me a hug."

Mom turns her back on him and faces me, still blocking the door. "Go to your room, Addison."

And in that instant I realize how much I've grown. I'm as tall as she is and am staring her directly in the eyes. I'm younger, stronger, and every bit as determined. Instead of caving in to her demands, I say, "If you won't let him in, I'm going out. Here, or through the back door. You can't block both."

"Victor," Mom says. No more than that one word, but we all know she expects him to stop me. My heart sinks down into my ratty sneakers. This is a defining test of loyalty. Vic has a clear choice—to align with our mother, or with me, his twin. Not with Dad, not that, ever.

"Let her talk to him," Vic says. "Better here than elsewhere."

A quiet warning, a reminder that if she pushes too far I could meet Dad elsewhere. Run away, even. Cause—heaven forfend— family drama.

"Oh, well then," Mom says. "Let's all go out, shall we? Let me get my camera so we can document the moment for posterity. God knows it's not likely to happen again."

"Bethy, baby. Don't be like that," Dad says, a feeble attempt at his legendary charm.

"Oh, come on, Rich," Mom says. "We all know you're more Halley's comet than Old Faithful. This is a once in a lifetime photo op..."

."Oh, *that* photo," Vic says, breaking me out of the memory. "I see what you're thinking. Johanna's mother took it."

"Or his, the brother's. What happened to Johanna's mother, Indigo? What happened to all of them?"

"Cancer took her mother. No aunts or uncles. Grandparents long dead."

"How did she come by this house?'

"It was her mother's. She grew up here."

"And no, there's not some big secret in the house worth killing her for," Vic says, correctly interpreting my thoughts. "No secret passageway. No treasure box hidden in the walls."

"You don't know that. We haven't had a chance to fully explore."

"If there was, then why would she want to give the house away to some random person who then might be killed by... whomever... knows about the secret and might kill again to get it?"

Even as he says it, though, his eyes turn toward Indigo. If anybody knows Johanna's secrets, it has to be her. And now here she is, inserted right in the middle of both my party and my investigation, with full access to the house.

"What was his name?" I ask.

"Whose?"

"The brother. The father. Both of them."

"Let me see if I can remember," Indigo closes her eyes and massages the back of her neck.

"You'll have kept notes," Vic says. "Like any good scammer."

"Or any good therapist," she counters.

"If you'd been an actual therapist, she wouldn't have spent

the last years of her life trapped in her own fears inside this house," Vic says.

"I did try to get her to talk to a therapist," Indigo replies, gravely. "She wouldn't do it. So yes, I did the best I could to help her deal with her anxiety and to interact with the world. Would you hand me my bag, Addy, please?"

"I'll get it." Owen retrieves the bag from a small table where Indigo left it. "God, what's in here, bricks?"

A gun is in there. Ammunition. Tarot cards. Who knows what other weapons she could be carrying around? Indigo smiles up at him like she's just an ordinary senior citizen. "Thank you, dear."

She roots around inside the bag and emerges with a small moleskin notebook. "Let's see, now." She licks her index finger and flips through the pages. "Here we are. Family notes. Mother, Angelica Marie Meyers, maiden name Walker. Died in 2003. Father, Walter Christopher Meyers. Brother, Christopher Gareth Cunningham. Both died when she was a young teenager, due to a tragic explosion. Natural gas. That's all I know; Johanna was there when it happened and she didn't like to talk about it. When I pressed her about her brother she said, 'I only saw him the one time. It's not like we were close'. Their father apparently never officially claimed him."

"I don't suppose we know the name of Christopher's mother?" I ask.

"Not a clue." Indigo beams at us all, as if she's just shared a secret that will bring world peace, rather than adding to the mystery of Johanna. "If that's all, children, we should get back to work, should we not? Times a-wasting!"

She's right, of course. We've still got a lot to do. I need to check on the boys and get them moving along. I want those invites out to the neighbors. But I want to know more about the family, so I send Britt another text.

> Addy: Hey, can you look for some intel on a Walter Christopher Meyers and a Christopher Cunningham? Walter was Johanna's and Christopher's father.

> Britt: Johanna had a brother?

> Addy: Apparently. He and her father died in some tragic accident

> Britt: I'm on it

> Addy: How's your dad?

> Britt: Sleeping. Christmas decorating done. Gifts wrapped. Oh, that cell number traces back to a woman named Deandra Delgado. Couldn't find anything else about her though.

Guilt, my ever faithful companion, makes its presence known. Unlike Britt, I haven't wrapped a single gift; I haven't even finished buying them. I still need something for Mom. And Owen. Do I need to get a gift for Jackson? What about Skye and Daffodil? Here I am again on a wild goose chase, neglecting the people I love in the process.

But those last words Johanna wrote in her notebook hold me steady. She's dead, her life cut tragically short. Everybody else is still alive. I can make it up to them next year. Also, I personally love receiving gifts after Christmas. Just when I think the fun and festivities are over and we're heading into the boring part of winter, somebody gives me a belated gift and it feels like Christmas all over again.

"Well, I'm going to get the boys headed out with the invites," I say. "And I think I'm going to run home and grab some decorations from Mom's garage. She's always got more stashed away than she needs."

"I'll go," Vic says.

"Don't be ridiculous. You have no idea what we need. What you can do is even out the decorations on the tree a bit after the boys are gone. I won't be long."

I can practically hear Vic's eyes rolling around in his skull as I walk away, but I'm used to it.

CHAPTER 19

THE BOYS ARE BORED with tree decorating and more than ready to move onto something else, although when I hand them the stack of invites Jackson does his best imitation of a prisoner being forced to work on a chain gang, barefoot, in forty-degree-below zero weather and waist-deep snow.

Nat, on the other hand, is all enthusiasm. "Everybody will have cookies," he says. "I'm hungry."

I watch them ring the doorbell at Serena's house while I start Jezebel. She coughs and sputters and suggests that perhaps we don't really need to go anywhere, but when I persist she gives in and allows herself to be started, backfiring loudly just as Serena opens her door. I wave as I put the car in gear and head off down the street. The plow trucks have been out, the roads are decent, and I arrive at Mom's house without any near-death experiences.

She meets me at the door, and I assume she's heard Jezebel's less than stealthy arrival. "What on earth are you doing here?" she asks, at a volume and projection level loud enough for half the neighborhood to hear.

"Um, visiting my mother?"

"Nonsense. When was the last time you stopped by just to visit?"

I have to admit she does have a point. Usually I come by either out of guilt, because it's been too long and she's called to let me know, or because I want something, or because I'm with Vic. It's not that I don't love her, but I've developed a low tolerance level for comments about my weight (too heavy), my wardrobe (too casual, too revealing, too flamboyant), my religious status (headed straight for hell), and my relationships (too single).

"Mom. It's Christmas. Plus, I wanted to check on Daffodil and Skye."

"This is not a good time," she says, as if I'm a door-to-door salesperson. She's avoiding my eyes. One hand rolls and unrolls the hem of her blouse. The other keeps smoothing hair that doesn't need to be smoothed.

None of this is normal for Mom. Something is up. Maybe Skye is holding her hostage, threatening her with a gun or a knife. We don't know Skye at all. We don't even know for sure that Daffodil is Dad's.

"I'm coming in," I say.

"Addy—"

I shove past her. Through the entry way, into the family room. I stand there, my eyes moving over the threadbare, well-worn carpet, the hand-crocheted afghan concealing the burned place on the old sofa where an early experiment with cigarettes went very wrong, the patched hole in the wall from the time we were wrestling and I kicked my foot right through the gyprock. School photos of me and Vic adorn the paneled walls, charting our growing up from Kindergarten all the way through high school graduation, me ever chubby, with varying hairstyles, braces, and unfortunate experiments with makeup; Vic always and ever adorable and picture-perfect. That framed photo of Vic and me and Dad.

All of the years of normal and ordinary are wiped out by the presence of Skye, sprawled on the sofa looking as if all we need is music and a sexy plumber to start recording a new porno. Daffodil, sitting in a playpen in the middle of the room where the coffee table is supposed to be, looks up at me out of wide brown eyes, sucking (and drooling) on one chubby fist.

Well, at least nobody is holding a gun to Mom's head or anything. Whether she's been brainwashed or hypnotized is another matter. If I showed up dressed like Skye I'd be sent to my room—well, a room, anyway, since I don't have one in this house anymore. But I'd be sent somewhere. Wrapped in a blanket if necessary. Forbidden to emerge until I put some proper clothes on.

Still, it's my faults Mom is focused on, not Skye's. "Really, Addy, it would be helpful if you call before coming over in the future. Daffodil could have been napping. Also, that sweater you're wearing. Do you really think... I mean, with that FlatzandSharpz person skulking around, perhaps you could wear something a little more... camera friendly?"

"Like Skye, you mean?" my mouth says, even though my brain knows so much better than to kick that little pile of festering drama. "A little more bare skin? A navel ring perhaps?"

Mom doesn't rise to the baited hook. She makes a move toward Dad's old recliner as if she's going to sit, and then veers toward the kitchen instead. "I'll be right back. Just need to check on something in the oven."

I sniff the air for the aroma of cookies or bread baking, or maybe something savory like a pot roast, but all my nostrils catch is a whiff of a vaguely familiar fragrance. Expensive. Masculine. I sniff again. My eyes follow the trajectory Mom almost took to Dad's recliner. An empty mug sits on the small end table beside it. The TV remote is also there. Mom drinks one cup of coffee in the morning. In the kitchen. And she never watches TV during the daytime.

Speaking of Mom, she bustles back from the kitchen, still shifty-eyed and unsettled. "I don't suppose you've come to help?" she asks.

"With?"

"Christmas dinner preparation. You do remember Christmas, don't you? It's Christmas Eve."

"Mom. About that... I'll be here for dinner but I'll be spending all day over at Johanna's house. We're having all of the neighbors come in—"

"Yes," she says stiffly. "I know. I know because Rachel saw it on Instabook or whatever that is and called to tell me. You could have had the decency to let me know yourself, I'd think. And I suppose you'll be dragging Victor away from me as well."

"We'll be here for dinner. Maybe Skye can help you get ready."

Skye gives me a look that makes it clear she doesn't plan to take her perfect body anywhere near a kitchen.

"I need to borrow the old decorations. Still in the garage, I assume."

Mom looks like I've dumped a bucket of ice water over her

head. Her mouth opens and closes. Her eyes go wide. Her face pales, then flushes crimson.

"I don't—they aren't there anymore," she says.

My mother never tells lies, not even the little white ones to spare feelings and avoid hurting people. Lying is on her list of unforgiveable sins. So she's very bad at it and it's obvious that she is lying now. She knows exactly where those ornaments are and she doesn't want me looking for them.

"Oh, I'm sure they're still there," I say, breezily. "Out in the garage. Up in the loft. I'm the one that carried them up the ladder."

"I—gave them away," Mom gasps, looking everywhere but at me. "To, um, Goodwill."

For a long moment I stand there staring at her, watching her trying and failing to meet my eyes. It would take something mighty big to make Mom lie.

Skye fidgets on the couch, twirling a strand of hair around her finger. Her eyes follow the volley of words from one speaker to the next, her lower lip caught between her teeth. She also looks guilty.

And that's when I remember where I know that fragrance from. It's Dad's cologne. Dad, who likes to sit in the recliner and drink coffee and watch TV.

"Wow, go Mom," I say. "This is so... not like you."

"It was only a little donation. I mean, we do try to declutter..."

"You know that's not what I meant."

She tries to block me on my way to the kitchen, but she's easy to avoid. As I'd suspected, there's not much going on food wise. Nothing in the oven. Nothing on the counter. But there are three plates in the sink. Three sets of silverware. Beer bottles in the trash can.

"I can't believe this!" I exclaim. "Do you know how worried we've all been? Not to mention the police. Alex stopped by my place looking for you, did you know that?"

"Addy, don't," she wails, as I open the door that leads to the garage. Mom's white Taurus is parked in its usual spot on the left. Dad's rental car is in the empty space on the right. Dad himself is nowhere to be seen, but I know he's in here.

"Dad!" I shout.

Silence. But it's a silence that feels like breath held, like the calm before the storm.

"I know you're up there."

I climb the ladder to the loft and sure enough, Dad is seated on an old beanbag chair behind the sheets of plywood Vic and I assembled as a makeshift clubhouse almost twenty years ago. Yogi he's not. He's sort of slouched with his back against the wall, knees drawn halfway up to his chest.

"I didn't do it," he says, first thing.

"Which thing? Sucker Johanna into signing her house over to you and giving you everything in her will? Steal fifteen thousand dollars in my name? Commit murder? Abandon a woman and a baby?"

Dad attempts to assume an air of wounded dignity, the effect of which is negated by his awkward position on the floor and me looking down on him. "Is that any way to talk to your father?"

"Is this any way to treat your children?" I retort. "You played me. You ran a scam on my client. Maybe you murdered her."

He scrubs both hands through hair that is already standing up on end. "You have to help me. I need you".

For once in my life, those three little words fall flat. "Save it for court. I'm calling Alex. Mom and Skye are both facing charges of harboring a fugitive, thanks to you. And your baby daughter—"

"That's exactly why you can't call. If you turn me in now, both your mother and Skye will be arrested. Then what happens to your baby sister? Are you going to take care of her?"

"You should have thought of that before you did what you did. If I don't call now, I'll be facing charges too."

"I'm being framed."

"So somebody else played on Johanna's vulnerability to steal her house and her money? And had sex with her?"

"You had sex with that woman?" Skye shrieks. "With that... that...dead woman?"

"She wasn't dead then, obviously," Dad says. "She was lonely. She thought she was dying. I gave her one happy night—"

"If that's what happy means, let me die miserable," I say. "At least Johanna didn't have a family for you to abandon."

Dad tries a different tactic. "I can't believe this happened just when we were going to have a chance to get to know each other."

"Let me translate that into English. What you mean to say is that you can't believe this happened while you were running away from your new family and planning to mooch off me. How do I know you would stop short of murder? Johanna was dying anyway, right? You were going to get the house anyway, right? Alex wouldn't tell me the details, but he claims to have a ton of forensic evidence."

For the first time since I've known him, Dad's carefully maintained façade totally breaks. His face goes sort of slack—his eyes droop, his lips turn downward. He basically wrinkles, like a shirt left too long in the dryer, and crumples back down into the beanbag chair he was in when I found him.

He rubs his palm across his forehead, over and over again. "Dear God, what have I done?"

It looks and sounds genuine. Naked and vulnerable rather than the usual self-conscious stagecraft. My heart turns upside down in my chest.

"Dad. You didn't actually..."

He drops his hands. "I don't know. I mean, I don't think I did."

"How can you not know if you killed someone?"

"I don't remember! I remember making love—"

"Bastard," Skye says.

"It's what he does," Mom says. "Trust me. Don't expect anything different."

"Could we maybe focus on the murdering part right now?" I call down to them both.

"Thank you," Dad says, possibly the most ridiculous words out of his mouth, since I am not even remotely defending him.

"Okay," I say. "So you remember taking sexual advantage of a vulnerable woman. Then what?"

"She wanted to," he objects. "She said it had been so long and she was going to die and she'd like to make love one more time before she died. Who was I to withhold that from her?"

A sound from down below that sounds like somebody vomiting is probably Skye. But it could be Mom, for all I know. I ignore it.

"Moving on. What happened next?"

"Nothing. I fell asleep. I never sleep like that; didn't even wake up to take a piss. Anyway, next thing I remember is patting the bed beside me. She wasn't there. The sheets were cold. She wasn't anywhere in the house. I walked through, looking for her, calling... It's not like she was going to go out and buy us breakfast or coffee, you know? She had to be there somewhere. So I assumed she'd be in her reading room, that closed-in deck. Her favorite place in the house. The door was cracked open and I went to close it and that's when I saw her. She was...she was hanging from the tree in the yard..."

"Wait, she died *outside*?"

This can't be right. I think about the bedroom, stripped down to the basics. Sheets and mattress, gone. Fingerprint powder everywhere. I stare at him in growing horror. "What did you *do*?"

"I... cut her down."

"Why didn't you call the police? What were you *thinking*?" Mom asks. Same tone of voice she uses on me when I do something she considers brainless.

"I *wasn't* thinking. How can you think at a time like that? She was... hanging there. Her neck looked so fragile with that rope around it, bruising it, her bare feet just skimming the snow... I couldn't leave her like that. And then after I cut her down, I couldn't let her lie there, she looked so cold. So I carried her into the house and I put her in bed..."

He makes a choking sort of noise and covers his face with both hands.

"God, Dad. At what point did you decide not to call the police?"

"I was thinking maybe she'd done it to herself, you know? Just decided to end things. But after I got her back to the bed I

239

started rethinking that. She'd never have gone outside for one thing. And there was nothing for her to... to stand on, to step off of, to be able to hang herself like that... I picked up the phone to call the police but then I just... didn't. I couldn't remember what happened and realized that all of the evidence led to it being me and I'd be suspect number one. It's always the last person to see the victim alive, isn't it?"

"Or the guy who had sex with her, got himself named in the will, and then ran off with the deed to her house."

"Exactly. I just... I panicked! I didn't want you to come in and find her like that, or worse, for nobody to find her for days. So I called 911 on her phone, didn't say anything, just left it there on the bed with her and I ran for it."

"Did you cash the check?"

"I needed the money."

"You're living off Mom. Somehow I doubt you're paying groceries and electricity."

He sighs. "The money was for Skye. For Daffodil."

"You didn't give us any money," Skye says. "You didn't even mention it."

"He's lying, Skye. It's what he does. If you haven't figured that out yet, now is the time." I turn back to Dad "I don't even want to know how you got Mom involved in this."

"I was thinking Daffodil deserves to actually have a father, unlike you and Vic, and if Rich was in prison he couldn't pay child support," Mom defends herself.

"He can't exactly do that if he's on the run, either, can he?"

"He can sell that woman's house and give Skye the money. Or give her the house, even. He can give her that fifteen thousand."

"You think I'm going to move to Fox Valley?" Skye squeals,

as if Mom's suggested she take up residence at the center of a swamp.

"Don't worry, Skye," I say, firmly, "you're not getting the house. It's going to be given away to somebody who comes to the party. The way Johanna intended. Dad is going to sign it over, just like he promised her he was going to do."

"He can't really do that from jail either, can he?" Mom asks.

"If he cashed the check, he needs to give Skye that money now. And then he needs to turn himself in. Pretty sure a lawyer can still get in to have him sign the legal docs while he's in jail."

"Don't have a lawyer," Dad says. "And I can't afford one."

"Then you'll have to make do with a court-appointed attorney."

His shoulders slump as he looks up at me in resigned disbelief. "You're really going to turn me in."

And this is when an idea pops up, waving its arms for my attention. It's an idea that isn't wrapped quite right, the sort of idea that could be walking quietly down the street with you one minute and start throwing glitter bombs—or hand grenades—at passersby the next. Vic would never entertain an idea like this for a fraction of a second. Me being me, I embrace it with open arms.

I smile at Dad. "You're going to turn *yourself* in. Only, not quite yet."

"I'm pretty sure I'm not," Dad says.

"Of course you are. You and Mom and Skye are going to do exactly as I say, or I promise you that I will call Alex and tell him Mom is harboring you. There's enough evidence against you to put you away for the rest of your life."

"Circumstantial."

"Yeah? What about your fingerprints all over the house and the rope she was hung with, your boot prints in the snow. You don't think they've got pictures of the tread pattern, measurements of your boot size? I bet those boots are somewhere in this house right now. And when the DNA comes back, they're going to find it all over her body and on her bed. Not to mention your fingerprints all over the crime scene. You, the last person to see her alive. Not to mention a killer motive. No jury is going to believe you didn't do it. You're not even sure you believe you didn't do it."

"What about Skye?" Dad asks. "She was—"

"Say a word and I'll ruin you," Skye says.

"Pretty sure I'm already ruined."

"Trust me, I can make it worse," she says. "Adjust the timeline of our relationship a little, for example. Maybe I wasn't eighteen when we got together..."

"You wouldn't do that."

"Try me."

"What about Skye?" I ask.

"Nothing," Dad says. "Never mind."

I look from one to the other and decide to let it go. Or at least to let them both think I have. "All right," I say. "Listen up. Here's what we're going to do."

WEDNESDAY
CHRISTMAS DAY

CHAPTER 20

CHRISTMAS DAY DAWNS BRIGHT, clear, and cold, with the thermometer hovering just below zero. Instead of a leisurely morning unwrapping gifts and eating all manner of treats at Mom's, I head straight for Johanna's house to put final touches on the preparations and to wait for Ricky to arrive with the coffin. My stomach is full of butterflies. I have plans and contingency plans and contingency plans for the contingency plans, but before the day properly begins a disaster happens that threatens to derail everything.

The house next door to Johanna's, Ralph's house, is a bustling crime scene. Yellow tape. Police vehicles. A crime scene van. I have a bad feeling that all of the activity is not due to evidence that Ralph is the murderer. That feeling intensifies when the coroner's car pulls up to the curb.

I slog through the snow at a pace between a trot and a shuffle and arrive at the car in time to open the door for Julie.

We're not exactly friends but we've never been enemies. It

was Vic, not me, who tried to charm information about Leno's death out of her. And it was Britt who hacked her computer for the details, which I'm pretty sure she doesn't know about. So I have no idea why she looks quite so hostile.

"Hey Jules. What's going on?"

She sidesteps with a question of her own. "What on earth are you doing here?"

"Big party today for Johanna Meyers. Seriously, Julie, what happened to Ralph?"

"Did they find your father yet?"

"Nope. Not yet." This is not a lie. I've found him. *They* have not. "You should come by the party later. If you're not still busy."

Julie's gaze shifts to Johanna's house. Her eyebrows draw together. She taps gloved fingers on the roof of her car. "That party is a bad idea. Especially in light of... Well. I think you should call it off."

"I'm guessing old Ralph didn't keel over from a heart attack," I say, speculatively, hoping she'll give me details.

"Geez, Addy, sharper than you look," she says, but then she laughs. "Stop fishing. No, his death was not due to natural causes. Also, no, I am not telling you anything. And another also... Seriously. You should stay out of Johanna's house until..."

She stops. I can guess what she's thinking. Ralph getting himself whacked a couple of days after Johanna, is not a coincidence. Maybe the crime scene people will want another go at Johanna's house.

Well, it's a little late for that. If there was any forgotten or overlooked evidence in there, it's all been cleaned up or packed away.

"Too late," I say, cheerfully, deciding that guilt would be counterproductive at this point. "Sorry, gotta go. Good luck with your crime scene."

She makes a little growly noise in her throat, like Bruno when Bagheera invaded his space. Or when I try to take a stolen object away from him. I fast-walk away. I don't want Alex to see me, because he really could stop Johanna's party.

I've got the house key on the ring with my car keys to keep it handy, so there's no need to dig around in my bag and I'm through the door in a heartbeat.

I flip on the lights and survey our handiwork. The entryway is decorated with garlands and lights and the credenza is set up with red and white candles and poinsettias. We've got a card table for people to write out their entries for the house, and I've got a festive cookie jar to put them in. Johanna's nativity set has been relocated from the mantlepiece to provide a centerpiece for the dining room table.

The tree lights are off, but the glass balls glimmer softly in the natural light. I'll get the apple cider simmering in the slow cooker in just a minute so that what wafts into the entryway will be apple and cinnamon and cloves, to me the quintessential fragrance of Christmas.

Slipping out of my boots and into the shoes I left here, I make my way through the house, running lists of still-to-do things through my head. Music. Making sure the food shows up and setting it out. Steering guests where I want them to go. Looking for signs of guilt. Getting Dad to turn himself in at the perfect moment.

What could go wrong?

Everything, obviously. Starting with Alex re-declaring this house as a crime scene and ending with Dad skipping town instead of following my instructions, with any number of unforeseen complications in between.

Exactly the sort of chaos I thrive on.

A brisk tapping at the door brings me out of my reverie. It's not Ricky, bright and early with the casket, but Indigo, her cheeks reddened with the cold, looking as fresh as if she's had a full eight hours of the most restful sleep ever. Which is a manifest injustice. We were both here until midnight, and she can't have slept in much longer than I did. And yet. Even though I'm at least thirty years younger, my brief mirror time this morning informed me that I look like I've escaped from prison and spent the night running through a forest while pursued by a pack of wolves. There are dark circles under my red-rimmed eyes. Lines in my face that I'm sure weren't there last week. Possibly a gray hair or two.

"What on earth is going on next door?" Indigo queries.

She looks innocent. She sounds innocent. She doesn't look remotely like a woman who might have murdered a grumpy old man in the wee hours of the morning while I was listening to two cats deciding whether or not to fight and trying to catch some sleep.

"Murder," I tell her, watching her reaction carefully. "You didn't see that coming?"

"I did not," she says, thoughtfully. "Foreknowledge is not a science. Even the weather forecast is often wrong and they have hard data to go on. Well. One thing at a time, I suppose. How did he die?"

"No idea. You sure you don't know anything?"

"Haven't got a clue," she says, cheerfully, setting her boots on the capacious doormat we purchased for this purpose. She hangs her coat in the closet. Rummages around in her bag for a pair of sneakers.

"Are you telling me you haven't snooped yet?" she asks.

I blink at her for a minute and then turn around and scurry up the stairs. She's right behind me, both of us arriving at the window that looks into Ralph's house short of breath. I'd thought maybe if we opened the blinds and cracked the window we'd be lucky enough to hear voices and catch a clue to what happened.

But the blinds are already open and I'm looking directly into the actual murder scene. Some things you can't unsee, and this is one of them. My skin goes cold and clammy. My stomach does a twist and dive thing like I'm on a rollercoaster. I press my hands over my mouth and swallow hard.

Indigo closes the blinds. "Well, that's one question answered. Come away, honey. I'll fix you a cup of tea."

For once in my life, tea sounds like it might be a good thing, and in any case I'm more than willing to get as far away from the window as possible.

Her hand is warm and steady, and I cling to it and let her lead me away and down the stairs as if I'm a frightened child.

"Ahhh," she says, as we reach the bottom of the stairs. "There he is."

Before I have time to ask who, the door from the closed-in deck to the kitchen opens and Dad comes in.

I run at him and try to shove him back out. "What the hell are you doing?"

"All part of the plan. Just like you said." He raises his eyebrows to signal his astonishment at my reaction.

"This is not the plan. You are hours early. You were supposed to—"

He waves his hand dismissively. "I'm improvising. This is better, don't you think? What's going on next door?"

"A murder investigation is going on next door. You can't be here yet! Nobody can see you until we're ready for your grand entrance. I gave you cue words and everything! And for the love of all things holy would you stop walking on this floor in your muddy boots? I just washed it!"

"You sound like your mother," he says. "You've gotten more like her as you've aged. You're going to have people in and out all day. You can't make everybody take off their shoes at the door. There will be footprints everywhere."

"Not your footprints. Not in this room. And not now. You have to go."

"Can't. Your mother dropped me off."

"Why? Why are you here already?"

He sighs. "Can you imagine being in a house with those two women? Jail would be better."

"Dad."

"Your mother caught me trying to lift the car keys. Yes, I was going to take her car and make a break for it. She said she was done being my aider and abettor. She made me get in the back seat of her car and hid me under a quilt. She drove me over and dropped me in the alley."

I close my eyes and suck in a breath and then end up holding it, pretty sure that if I release it words are going to also come out at full fishwife shrieking volume. My own fault, really. Of course none of them could be trusted to stick to the script.

"What's going on next door?" he asks again.

"The neighbor got killed last night."

"Dangerous neighborhood," Dad says. "Are you all right?"

I am not all right. At all. I'm having a hard time making breath go properly in and out of my lungs. My body is vibrating like the time I drank three back-to-back macchiatos, an overdose of caffeine and sugar that made me feel like one of those quivery little lap dogs that can never stop shaking.

If I'd made Dad turn himself in yesterday, he'd at least be off the hook for Ralph's murder. Now maybe he'll be suspected of that too. Which is my fault. Alex is so not going to be happy when he finds out what we've done. In his eyes, of course, it will be what *I've* done, since I could realistically be expected to know better. And if Alex or the crime scene people come over here to do any follow up on Johanna's house thanks to the murder next door and they find Dad here, we're all going to jail.

"Addy?"

I manage to get my lungs working again. I need to treat this like a glitch at a wedding and work through it one detail at a time. Right now, the first order of business is to get Dad out of sight. If nobody saw him, maybe we can still pull this off.

"Take your boots off. Go upstairs. Hide in Johanna's room. Lock the door. Take the boots with you."

"Why can't I leave my boots here?"

"Remember the bit about how the crime scene probably has pics of your footprints? All of those people are right next door! What if they come over here?"

"Well that explains everything," Indigo says, bustling in with a cup of tea. "Of course that's what the cards were trying to tell us with the upside down lovers. There you were, all along, with your ex-wife and the mother of your new baby. Uh, oh, there's the doorbell."

"Dad. For God's sake, go hide."

"I still don't see why I can't just stay here. Duck down behind the couch, maybe?"

"It's too risky. That will be Ricky at the door. You can't let him see you."

Dad still isn't moving. "Doesn't he have to abide by some sort of confidentiality clause? Like a priest. Or a lawyer."

"Pretty sure that is not the case."

The doorbell rings again.

"You should get that," Dad says, heading for the stairs. He's right. I should. Ricky doesn't need any excuses to change his mind.

I move slowly toward the door, giving Dad time to get out of sight. Praying that he'll follow directions. When I look back over my shoulder I can't see him anywhere.

"Finally," I say, flinging the door open. "I thought you weren't coming."

"Ummm," Owen says.

I blink, gazing up at him with my mouth open. "I thought you were Ricky."

His lips twitch. "As it turns out, I am not, in fact, your local purveyor of coffins and death. Did something happen to the neighbor?"

"He's late," I gasp. "Ricky, I mean. Ralph too, I guess. Late as in dead. Deceased. Murdered."

"Another murder? Next door?"

The murder is a big problem, obviously, but Owen is a bigger one in the moment. All I can think is that he can't come in. He can't know that Dad is here. So instead of saying something welcoming, I blurt out, "Why are you here?"

He blinks. "Thought I'd come give you a hand."

"We're good. Thanks for the offer, but it's all taken care of."

251

I start to close the door. In his face. Like he's a door-to-door salesman or a JW missionary, here to talk to me about my doomed immortal soul.

"Something I said? Garlic on my breath?" His expression is half hurt, half bewildered.

"It's just, um, not a good time." I shove at the door, but his body is wedged into the opening.

"I brought you a coffee."

He is, in fact, carrying what appears to be a perfect caramel macchiato in one hand. The fact that he knows me well enough and is thoughtful enough to bring me a big icy cup of caffeine and sugar on a freezing Christmas morning does something to both my insides and my knees, which were already wobbly and now threaten to drop me right there in the entryway.

"You are amazing," I say, gazing lustfully at alternately Owen and the coffee, while listening for Dad behind me. Did he go upstairs? Or maybe he's hiding behind the couch or a potted plant or even the tree.

I hear footsteps that do not belong to Indigo, and I grab Owen's face in both hands, draw it down toward me, and kiss him as if my life depends on it. Maybe it does. If he kisses me back, if he closes his eyes, if Dad has a grain of sense in his head, we can still—

"It's a little cold for canoodling with the door open," Dad says. "Owen, why don't you come in here before both of you turn into popsicles. And close that door, would you? Wouldn't do for the crime scene people to see me."

"Addy?" Owen queries.

I grab my coffee, and then his free hand, and tow him inside, slamming the door shut behind him.

"Want to fill me in?" His tone is formal and stiff. He's mad, and who could blame him?

"I will. I promise," I say, desperately. "Just not... I didn't want to put you in the position of, well, knowing."

"And now that I do?"

"Please. Owen. Don't call the cops. Dad is going to turn himself in."

"When?"

"Later?"

"No better time than the present," Owen says. "He could just walk right next door." His voice is twenty-below-zero and dropping. "I mean, I understand it might interfere with your party preparations but he is a wanted man."

"I didn't kill her," Dad says.

"Dad," I say. "Not helping. For the last time. Go upstairs and lock yourself in Johanna's room. Ricky will be here any minute. Owen, please. Don't make that call. I swear to you that Dad will turn himself in before this day is over. I just... need him for something first."

"For your party. To give away the house."

"No. Well, yes. But also to help me find the real killer. I'll tell you all about it, I promise. Leave now, so you're not part of it."

"I'm already part of it. I can't unsee him."

"Owen isn't going to tell anybody," Indigo says, gliding by all of us to the window. The blinds are closed, but there's a tiny gap in the curtains, perfect for peering out without being seen. "Lovely. Here's your hearse, Addison. And Owen can help us set up the coffin. Just put that phone away, Owen dear. You'll need both hands. Richard. Get upstairs right this minute."

All of us stand frozen in time for what seems like forever,

players unsure of their next lines in this bizarre story. But then Dad turns and practically scurries up the stairs, boots in hand. Owen puts his phone in his pocket.

"I can't believe you didn't tell me that you knew where your father was," Owen says. "I was worrying about you. About him. You said you thought he might have been kidnapped or killed. Here I was wasting my energy feeling bad for you all this time."

"Owen." I put my hand on his arm. It feels like stone. No give. No softness. His eyes are glacial

"Jackson is in the car," he says. "First he's exposed to Skye. Then a crime scene and a murder house. Now the actual murderer, knowingly harbored by supposedly law-abiding adults. And you want to make me a part of it."

"I don't want you to be a part of it. He just showed up like five minutes ago," I retort, defenses rising. "I seem to remember telling you to go away."

The doorbell rings and Indigo flings it wide open. It's Ricky, apparently still all tangled up about delivering an empty coffin. No hello, no Merry Christmas.

"I'll need help getting the coffin in the house," he says. And then turns his back and marches back to the hearse.

I slip on my boots and jacket, but the icy wind still blows right through me. My breath is visible, a frosty little cloud hanging in front of my face.

The door of Owen's car opens and Jackson gets out. "Is that a hearse? And a coffin? Cool. Can I see?"

"Get back in the car," Owen says. "We're leaving."

But Jackson is already watching Ricky unfold a wheeled contraption that reminds me of a stretcher, and he doesn't appear to have any intention of going anywhere.

"Give me a hand here," Ricky says, and Jackson helps him slide the coffin out and onto the wheels.

Owen glares at me.

"Trust me. I have a plan," I tell him.

"That's what I'm afraid of. You do know that all of the neighbors are watching. Probably the crime scene people, too."

"That's what I'm counting on. Hold up a minute there, Rickster. Please." I approach the coffin with slow, dragging steps, my head bowed. I rest one hand dramatically on the coffin and wipe away a couple of nonexistent tears.

Indigo, who has joined us, takes the moment next level.

Standing at the head of the coffin she spreads her arms wide and intones, loudly enough for anybody near a window to listen in, "Benevolent spirits of the universe, we commit unto your care the soul of this woman, known in this life and this body as Johanna Meyers. Dear soul, be free of this body. This world. As is it above, so it is below. Amen."

Then she turns to me and wipes imaginary tears from my cheeks. "Don't grieve for her, Addison. She is free now. No longer a captive in her failing body or in this house, no longer constrained by her fears and delusions. This is a time for celebration!"

Getting the coffin inside is delayed by Alex, who emerges from Ralph's house and charges through the snowy yard to loom over me, glowering. Steam puffs out of his nostrils with every breath and he reminds me of an angry bull in a cartoon. Which, of course, strikes me as funny and makes me smirk, which makes him even madder.

"What the hell do you think you're doing?" Alex demands.

There are many answers to this question. None of which

he's going to want to hear. "Um...," I say, to buy myself thinking time.

"Don't um me. I know you're throwing one of your after-death parties. What I don't know is why you're having a coffin delivered. Or how you have failed to notice that the house next door is now a crime scene."

"Gee, Alex, you *are* a brilliant detective! How did you ever deduce that I was planning a party for Johanna?"

"The Lindy Lind posts on FlatzandSharpz were a dead giveaway," he says.

"I didn't know you were a TikTok-er, Alex."

"The local news picked up the story. I know you think you're some kind of super sleuth after what happened with Leno—"

"I did kind of solve that case for you."

"What you did was almost get yourself killed, mess up evidence—"

"Alex, I'm kind of busy. Was there something you actually wanted? We need to get the coffin in the house. And finish getting ready for the party."

"We both know there's nobody in that coffin."

"Shhh. The neighbors will hear."

"Let me be clear. You can't have a party in that house today. Not with another murder right next door. Ricky, pack up your coffin and take it back where it came from."

"It's too late to cancel," I say. "People will be showing up any time now. They're always early for events like this."

"There *are* no events like this," he says. "And they'll just have to go away again."

"Sure, we'll just put a sign on the door that says PARTY CANCELLED. They'll mill around in disappointment. Try to look in the windows. Crowds of people, trampling all over Johanna's lawn. Spilling over next door to Ralph's to see what's going on. Gawking. Getting in the way. Corrupting evidence."

"So am I leaving then?" Ricky interrupts. "Loading the coffin back up?" He sounds hopeful for the first time since Johanna's death.

"Not so fast, Rick," I tell him, turning back to Alex. "Say the word, Detective."

He glares at me. From the way his jaw is moving I'm pretty sure he's grinding his teeth.

"Johanna's house has been cleared, right?" I ask. "I mean, it's not like you know of any connection to Ralph?"

"I'm not discussing the investigation," Alex growls.

I smile at him and lower my voice to a conspiratorial whisper. Alex is part of my plan and I need his cooperation. "Of course not. But, about that. I do have something to tell you that might be helpful."

"You've located your father?"

"His baby mama showed up. With baby. Her name is Skye. Not the baby, the mama. And we found a phone number for another one of his women."

"I don't suppose either one of them told you where he is," Alex says.

"They did not. But they might tell *you*." This is technically the truth. Skye didn't tell me anything. "Why don't you come over when you're through at Ralph's place? Skye will be here and you can talk to her yourself. If you call her, she might run off."

"She's evading law enforcement?" he asks. "A criminal type? Warrants for her arrest?"

"Porn star. Legal I think? But you never know what she might be hiding."

This is also true.

"Detective? Something you need to see," a deputy calls from Ralph's front porch.

"Coming," Alex calls back. Then he leans down close to me and says, "I know you Addy. You are up to something. You are hiding something. And when I find out what it is, so help me God I'll..."

"Me?" I ask, my hand on my heart. "Up to something? Hiding anything from you? I'm wounded that you'd think that of me."

I turn and get out of his reach before he decides to arrest me on some made up charge of tormenting an officer or some such. My mission is accomplished, at least for the moment. He's sure to pop into Johanna's later to talk to Skye.

"Well?" Ricky asks. "What's it going to be?"

"Oh, we're totally on with the party. Let's get this into the house, shall we?"

Jackson and I help lift the coffin and carry it up the steps. Indigo opens the door for us and I hold my breath, afraid Dad is going to be standing there watching, his curiosity having gotten the better of him. He's not in sight, and I breathe a silent prayer to all of the powers that be that he has decided to exhibit some common sense after all.

"Over by the Christmas tree," I direct, and we all proceed in a solemn procession, as if Johanna is, indeed, inside the casket. Once it's artistically situated near the tree where Johanna can be the center of attention and not miss out on any of the fun, I step back to survey the effect.

"I still can't believe I agreed to this spectacle," Ricky

complains. "You're making a parody out of what should be a solemn occasion with all of this theatrical rigmarole."

"I meant every word, young man," Indigo says. "Her soul is free. This is a joyous day."

"She was murdered," Ricky says. "I don't see anything joyous about it."

"And freed of her body in the process. Perhaps the murderer did her a favor."

A chill goes through me. I've never been able to think of a real motive for Indigo to kill Johanna, but a mercy killing fits. Like one of those doctors or nurses who decides sick people shouldn't suffer and starts putting them all out of their misery. Although, knowing what Dad told me, I can't imagine Indigo with the muscle strength to drag a terrified woman out into the yard and hang her. If Johanna had been shot, that would be another thing entirely.

"Well. I want no part of any of it," Ricky says, stiffly. "I'll be back to collect the coffin after the party."

He stalks away with great dignity, slamming the front door behind him.

"Don't let him get to you, honey," Indigo says, soothingly. "Most people have hang ups about death."

"I have hang-ups about death," Owen says. "And I'm opposed to anybody making that choice for anybody else."

"Oh, free will, of course and absolutely always," Indigo says.

What if she's a poisoner? Dad said he slept overly soundly. What if Indigo sedated them both, and then...

But that still doesn't work. She's still need to drag a somnolent woman out of bed, drag her downstairs, and hoist her up into the tree.

Jackson opens the coffin. "Cool," he says. "It's like Dracula. Can I be Dracula?" Before we can stop him, he climbs in and lies down on his back. Closes his eyes. Folds his hands across his chest. "Take a picture," he says.

"Absolutely not. Get out of there right this minute," Owen orders.

Indigo holds up her phone. "I've got you, kid. The two of you, stand around and look like you're mourners."

"No." Owen grits out between clenched teeth.

"Make it a video," Jackson says. "It will go viral on TikTok. You can zoom in close. I'll hold my breath and everything, just let me know when you're ready."

I'd been about to go along with the joke until he said that. Now I stop short. "You can't post anything. People need to believe Johanna is in that coffin. The two of you will ruin everything."

"Of course," she says. "Nobody's posting this now; we'll wait until after. Hey, we could close the lid and Jackson could push it slowly open, and sit up...that would be even better!"

She begins to lower the lid but Jackson holds up both arms to stop it. "No. Don't shut me in there. What if it locked?" There's a hint of panic in his voice.

"I don't think coffins lock automatically," I say. "Do they? If they do, Ricky didn't leave us a key."

"Don't you worry now," Indigo says. "They lock, but not automatically. As for the key, it's just a standard hex key, like you use for assembling do-it-yourself furniture. And there's enough oxygen in there to last for hours."

We all three stare at her. She smiles, the Cheshire cat version, inscrutable and smug.

"I don't want to know how you know that," Owen mutters.

"A long life provides many interesting opportunities to pick up bits and bites of info, don't you think? Well. I was going to get the cider simmering."

"I'm going to decorate the coffin. Jackson, could you bring over some of those wrapped gifts under the tree? We'll set them on the coffin. I'll grab the garland and lights."

The last thing we need is for the kid to go wandering upstairs and discover Dad; I need to keep him occupied. He's looking sullen and obstinate again, so I whisper, "Help with the party and I'll make sure Indigo shares those pics with you after."

"I heard that," Owen growls. "You're as bad as he is."

Jackson begins bringing over a stack of the books that Indigo and I wrapped up last night to create the illusion of gifts. I drag Owen with me to the garage where I've stashed the garland and lights for decorating the coffin. It's the perfect opportunity to steal a kiss but he won't even look at me. When we come back in, Indigo is humming to herself in the kitchen. Dad is still mercifully nowhere to be seen.

Jackson takes one end of the garland and I take the other, and we begin attaching it to the side of the coffin with double-sided tape while Owen uncoils the string of LED Christmas lights. As we work I dare to breathe again. Maybe, just maybe, we can still pull this off.

CHAPTER 21

WE'RE JUST FINISHING when the front door opens and Britt and Vic come in, together. She's carrying a coffee urn. Vic's loaded down with trays of snacks from the *Raven*—antipasto, veggies and dip. I knew Vic would show up for me; he always does. And I am genuinely delighted that Britt has made it after all.

Clambering to my feet I beam at them both, then do my best Vanna White gesture toward the decorated coffin. "What do you think?

"Well..." Britt says, eyeing the effect a little askance.

"If you were aiming for ghoulishly festive, you've hit the coffin nail on the head," Vic says. "A little bit Nightmare Before Christmas."

"I was thinking more just festive."

"I'm not sure you can do Christmas lights and greenery on a casket without it being a wee bit ghoulish," Britt says. "It might be a little over-the-top, don't you think?"

"Oh, it's definitely too over-the-top," Owen says. "But then, it's an Addy party. What would you expect?"

Indigo claps her hands, beaming. "Ghoulish and over-the-top is perfect. We want everybody a tiny bit off-center, don't we? So that the real murderer will more easily betray his or her guilt. Here, let me take those trays from you, Victor. Addy, relieve your friend of the coffee urn. After they bring in the rest of the goodies maybe we'll all take a quick break for tea. What do you think?"

Vic groans as if he's in mortal pain. "Addy. Tell me you're not really trying to create a trap for the murderer."

I smile, sweetly. "I'm not really trying to create a trap for the murderer."

"Hurry along now," Indigo says. "What good is it being the party planning team if you don't get first dibs on the goodies?"

"I could definitely do with some tea," Britt says. "I was up half the night doing... research."

"Honey, I know all about the research already, remember?" Indigo says. "You don't need to keep secrets from me. You'll have found something about Johanna's father and her brother."

"She has a brother?" Owen asks.

"Had," Britt says. "Tea, please. And I'll tell you all about it. Jackson, would you run out to the car and help Victor grab the rest of the stuff? I'm exhausted."

"You loved every minute of it," I tell her, as she slips off her boots and sets them neatly on the mat. "And I knew you couldn't stay away."

She laughs. "You know me too well. It was a rabbit hole. I forgot to go to bed, to be honest." She lowers her voice. "Any news about your father? And what's all the fuss next door?"

Lying to Britt is beyond my skill set. I want to protect her from the knowledge that the fugitive is probably eavesdropping upstairs, so I distract her instead. "The neighbor got murdered last night. Ralph. Remember the little guy in the Santa hat?"

"What?" she gasps. "So we're dealing with a serial killer? Maybe we should call this whole thing off, Addy. It could be dangerous."

"Too late. People are gonna show up. Besides, it would have to be a pretty deranged psychopath to start killing people with the cops and the crime scene people right next door. Or with this house full of people. Pretty sure we're safe."

She isn't convinced, I can tell, but also can't resist the allure of good hot tea when Indigo calls, "I've been keeping the kettle hot. I'll have tea ready for you in a jiffy."

"Jackson and I will help bring things in from the car," Owen says, heading for the door. For once, Jackson doesn't argue. Vic goes with them, and they make several trips, unloading food and drinks onto the dining room table and arranging them around Mary and Joseph and the baby Jesus.

My eyes keep traveling to the top of the stairs to see if Dad has succumbed to the aroma of coffee and food, but he stays out of sight, and when we're all gathered around the table with hot drinks and paper plates full of goodies, I say, "Okay, Britt. Tell us what you found out."

"Let me get out my notes."

She doesn't need notes, I'm pretty sure. Her capacious brain stores information like a squirrel stores nuts, and is much better at retrieval. But she likes to keep herself anchored in facts, and paper gives her that. In this case, she has both print-outs and handwritten notes.

Britt takes the chair at the head of the table and opens her folder. Before sharing anything she picks up her mug, inhales the fragrant steam and takes a sip. "Oh, wow. That is perfection." She offers Indigo a genuine smile, probably deciding that anybody capable of making perfect tea couldn't possibly be a murderer after all.

Indigo is at the foot of the table where she can keep an eye on everybody. I sit beside Britt with Owen on my other side. Victor and Jackson are across from us. Mary and Joseph and the wise men appear to be extraordinarily interested in our conversation. The angel not so much. If he had the gift of motion he'd be shaking his head.

Britt is rapturous over her perfect tea so I remind her to get a move on.

"Just spill the intel already," I say, impatient.

"Hold your horses." She takes another swallow, closes her eyes in appreciation, then sets the mug aside, glances at the paper, and launches in.

"All right. Johanna's father and mother were married in July of 1984 and Johanna was born a year later. Walter, her father, worked in real estate—he accumulated a lot of property and made a lot of money. This was his property and they lived here together when she was a child. Sometime in '95 he moved to Richland. A divorce followed a year later, and Johanna's mother retained this house."

"Let me guess. He was cheating on her," Owen says.

"To be fair, I think it's possible her mother could have been the one who cheated first," Indigo muses, sipping her tea. "Johanna mentioned coming home from school to find a man in the kitchen at some point before her father left."

"Marriage is a dangerous proposition," Owen says, with a

glance at me. Probably, I think bitterly, he's reminding himself that I am my father's daughter and not a good or safe love interest. Especially since I did kiss him to try to keep him from seeing Dad and he's smart enough to have figured out that's what I was doing.

"In any case," Britt goes on. "Walter apparently had a whole secret life while he was still married to Johanna's mother. He was seeing a woman in Richland, name of Rebecca Hollifield. He got her pregnant, and Christopher was born about a year before Johanna. Rebecca is now married to a Gordon Bentley. They live in Springfield, Illinois. I didn't find records of any other children."

"Johanna never mentioned Rebecca," Indigo says. "If they knew each other, I doubt that they knew each other well."

"Anything else on Christopher?" Vic asks.

Britt withdraws a sheet of paper from the folder and lays it on the table in front of me. "That's from a newspaper article in the Tri City Herald. Quick summary: there was a horrific explosion which was apparently caused by a natural gas leak. Johanna's father was killed instantly. Christopher was fifteen at the time. He was thrown clear but badly injured."

"But not killed?" I ask. "Johanna told Indigo he was dead."

"This is where I lost the trail," Britt says. "I have the news story from the local paper. Christopher was taken to Kadlec hospital by ambulance due to injuries from the explosion. The newspapers report him as being in critical condition. But after that I couldn't find him again. Before you ask, I'm not going to hack medical records systems."

"There has to be a death record, doesn't there?" Owen asks. "That's public info."

"You would think. But there isn't. Not under that name and

birthdate, anyway. There's a Christopher Cunningham who died in Kennewick in 2006 but his birthdate doesn't match."

"Maybe there was some sort of clerical error?" I ask. "A clerk was having a bad day and entered the wrong year?"

"It must happen," Owen muses. "At least, I mean, it could happen."

"We could talk to his mother," I say. "Maybe Johanna lied and Christopher's still alive."

"Why would she do that?" Indigo asks.

"Only one way to find out. Did you find her phone number, Britt?"

"Of course." She jots a name and number onto a sticky note, and hands it to me.

Vic sets his mug down with a little thud. "Come on, Addles. That's too far out there, even for you. I know what you're thinking, and the answer is no. What possible reason could a not-really-dead half sibling who Johanna only met once have to show up suddenly and murder her?"

"What I was really thinking," I lie, with as much dignity as I can muster, "is that if Johanna has a living relative then they should inherit her estate."

"Don't try to snow me," Vic says. "Admit it. You're thinking that a living relative might have a motive."

I look at him, making my eyes big and innocent, in the way I know annoys him the most. "I don't want Dad to inherit all of this, do you?"

"I thought we were giving the house away," Owen says. He looks like his head aches. I don't blame him.

"We are. But she willed everything else to Dad. I'd rather it went to her brother if he's actually still alive. Time to call Christopher's mother."

Nobody tries to stop me. A man's voice answers on the second ring. "Who is this?"

I can tell he's about two seconds away from hanging up. So instead of introducing myself or going into a long explanation I say, "Gordon? I need to speak with Rebecca. It's about Christopher."

"What about Chris?" he growls.

"My name is Addison Winters. I'm dealing with Johanna Meyers' estate and—"

"Johanna is dead?"

"Yes, I'm afraid so. I'm terribly sorry to be the bearer of the bad news."

"I didn't know her," he says.

"Well, as I was saying. I'm the executor of her estate. She didn't have any living relatives and I thought maybe Christopher—"

"What sort of mind games are you playing?" he demands. "You've got a lot of nerve trying to upset Becky with this."

"Johanna said he was...deceased, but I just wanted to— damn it." He's hung up on me.

"You can't be surprised by that," Vic says. "Some woman calls out of the blue inquiring about their dead son."

"Not *his* son," I say. "And I'm pretty sure if somebody called me out of the blue to let me know that somebody died and that somebody of my acquaintance—dead or alive, friend, family, or enemy—had an estate to inherit, I'd want to hear all about it. Just as soon as they convinced me that they weren't a Nigerian prince and that the whole thing wasn't a scam."

"It's near ten-thirty," Indigo says, shoving back her chair. "We need to clean up after ourselves and get all of the refreshments set out. Owen, Vic, and Britt, if you'd like to get started on that? And move the chairs into the garage, they'll only be in the way. I'm sure Addy has some last-minute details to take care of, so we'll leave her to it. Jackson, Nat should be here any minute. The two of you are still in charge of the door prize."

"Cool. How many times can I enter myself?"

Owen's gaze meets mine and then slides away as he gets to his feet. "I think we should go."

"Are you kidding?" Jackson protests. "I'm not losing out on my chance to maybe win us a house. Besides, this is the best murder mystery party ever."

"Your grandparents—"

"We did stockings this morning already. Grandpa doesn't even know if I'm there or not, anyway."

"Possibly not, but your grandmother does."

"Dinner's not until six, right? So we've got all day. We go back there, and I'll just be looking for trouble to get into with Blake."

"Nobody is going anywhere," Indigo says. "Here's Nat, now."

Sure enough, Nat pops in through the back way, flushed with cold, beaming from ear to ear. "I'm here to help! Angel's boyfriend is over and she didn't even notice I was leaving. Oooh, cookies. Can I have one?"

He doesn't wait for the affirmative on that, grabbing a giant molasses cookie from the platter and stuffing half of it in his mouth. "Is there still milk?" He goes to the kitchen and grabs the jug of milk from the fridge.

"Nat, you should really let your sister know where you are," I say, trying to be responsible.

"I left her a note. Can I help? What are we doing? Can I have coffee?"

"You can have cocoa, like Jackson." Indigo sets a mug on the table. "Sit down. Join the party."

"You and me are interrogating suspects," Jackson says. "Anybody who looks guilty. Of anything."

"Dear God," Owen mutters.

"Nobody is interrogating anybody," I say, firmly. "If you see anybody acting suspicious, you report that to me. Understood?"

"Sure thing!" Nat swallows the rest of his cookie and reaches for an apple turnover. "You sure you're going to have enough goodies for everybody?"

"Not if you and Jackson eat them all."

"You sure we can't interrogate people?" Jackson asks. "I've seen all the cop shows. I know how it's done. Nat can be the good cop. I'll be the bad cop."

"No interrogating! The two of you are key to this operation, but only if you stay cool and fly under the radar. There's a table set up in the entryway with slips of paper for the names and phone numbers and a couple of pens. And a snowman jar to put them in."

"I've got something better to put the names in," Indigo says.

She hefts her bag up onto the table and lifts out a large black jar, traced in gold. "Here we go."

It looks sort of like a gothic vase with a lid, but I'm pretty sure it's not meant for holding flowers.

"Is that..."

"An urn? Yes, dear. Somebody I knew was in this urn for a time. I scattered his ashes into the ocean, as per his request. And then I thought it was a useful item that I'd rather not throw away. So I washed it out... Really, don't look like that,

Britt. I ran it through the dishwasher. Perfectly clean and sterilized."

"And you just carry it around in your bag?" I ask.

"I had a feeling we might be needing it. I'd actually thought that perhaps if Johanna is cremated we could put her ashes in here. After we choose our winner for the house, of course."

"Cooool," Jackson says. "Too bad me and Nat didn't have, like, black tuxes or something."

"You and Nat will be fine in your everyday clothes," Owen says. "I really think that we should—"

"Owen, you'll be in charge of the music, of course," Indigo directs. "I don't suppose we could persuade you to make it live? You could stroll around with a guitar, singing carols."

I snort a laugh, I can't help myself. Owen on stage as a rockstar? That I can picture. I've already seen video evidence of him doing that very thing . But as the Christmas Carol Troubadour? Not so much.

"You could wear a Santa hat."

"Not funny," Owen growls.

I slap a hand over my mouth to hold back the giggles. He's already pissed off enough at me today, I don't need to make it worse.

"No?" Indigo says. "Well, that's what I expected but one can always hope. Make us a Christmas playlist and figure out how to run it through the speakers, would you?"

Owen gives me a tortured glance that clearly asks for rescue, but I just shrug, as if I too am helpless before Indigo's insistence, when in truth I think it's a brilliant idea. Of course, I've already made a playlist but Owen doesn't need to know that.

My phone rings. I motion everybody to silence and answer on speaker. "This is Addy."

"My husband said you'd called."

"Rebecca. Hi. Thanks for calling back."

"You know something about Chris? You've found him, then?"

"No. I was hoping you could fill me in. Did your husband tell you? That Johanna Meyers has died? I wanted to be sure that we found Chris if he was... um... alive, so he could inherit her estate."

There's a sharp intake of breath, followed by what sounds like a choked off sob.

"I'm sorry," I say. "The news about Johanna must come as a shock."

"I don't care about Johanna. It's not like I knew her, did I? Even Chris only met her one time. All I know is her father adored her, favored her. If it hadn't been for her maybe Chris wouldn't have..." A real sob, this time. A quavering breath.

"Listen, I'm sorry. I didn't mean to open old wounds."

"A missing child is a wound that never closes. How exactly do you think I can help you?"

"Wait, you said missing just now. Christopher isn't... um, dead?"

"Why does any of this matter to you?" Rebecca demands.

"Because if he's living, then Johanna's estate should go to him."

"Christopher vanished when he was seventeen. Ran away, we believe, but were never able to confirm that. Maybe he ran. Maybe somebody killed him. Truth is, I have no idea whether he's alive or dead but I persist in believing he's alive."

"So the police never found anything?"

"They were convinced he was a runaway, so they didn't look very hard. There was no evidence of foul play. He was so angry after the accident. At the world, at me. At his father for not claiming him officially. At Johanna, because she wasn't harmed in the explosion. He got addicted to opiates after the accident; he was in so much pain. He fell in with a bad crowd. There was some... legal trouble. And then, he was just gone."

"I'm so sorry, Rebecca. That must have been horrible for you."

Rebecca takes a quavery breath. "If you were to find him... you would let me know?"

I take a long breath of my own. "I think maybe I've already found him."

She doesn't hear me. She's already hung up.

But everybody else has heard, loud and clear.

Britt is already on her laptop, brow furrowed in concentration. "You're thinking Christopher has reinvented himself as Chip Fitzwilliam? I guess it could fit," she says. "Chip's scars could be from a gas explosion. But why? Why run away from home? Why change his name?"

"Why kill Johanna?" I add.

"Oh, come on," Vic says. "There's no reason to believe Christopher is Chip. Or that he killed anybody."

"Hear me out. Dad said he slept so soundly he never heard anything... and when he woke up he felt hungover—"

"Because he drank too much and was hungover?" Vic offers.

"Or, maybe he was drugged. Maybe they both were drugged. Char and the lawyer were the only people who could have done it. Pretty sure it wasn't Char."

"You really think the lawyer drugged your father and Johanna and then killed his own client?" Vic asks.

"Just consider the possibility. Johanna's long-lost half brother moves to town, sets himself up under false pretenses, insinuates himself into her life as an attorney."

"Come on," Vic says. "She wouldn't recognize her own brother?"

"She only saw him one time. They were both kids. Add in the name change and the scarring and the way people see what they expect to see, which means not seeing a dead person, and it's not at all surprising she didn't recognize him," Indigo says.

"How *did* he become her attorney, I wonder?" Britt mulls. "It would be a weird coincidence for her to just call him up and say, 'hey, I need to make a will.' I mean, yes, it's a small town but there are half-a-dozen others she could have chosen."

"I can answer that one," Indigo says. "After I told her the cards predicted her death, I suggested she make sure her affairs were in order. She said she didn't have an attorney. But then a flyer shows up in her mailbox advertising for a new law firm in town, and that's how she found him."

This is just a little too random and coincidental even for me.

"Johanna didn't plan on making a will, until you told her she was going to die," I say, slowly, my eyes on Indigo. "And then a flyer magically appears in her mailbox, which just happens to be for the law firm of her estranged and presumed dead stepbrother."

"It does all fit together neatly, doesn't it?" Indigo says. "Chip and I are in it together from the beginning. We know each other from somewhere, and he tells me his tale of woe and injustice and that he plans to get revenge and inherit all of Johanna's money. I agree with him that his quest is just and he agrees to cut me in on the profits. So then, I tell Johanna she's going to die, knowing that she'll want to update her will. Then Chip sends out the flyers, and bingo! He's in. He gets into her house and kills her, but only after she makes out the will to somebody else and makes you the executor, which guarantees that he gets nothing."

It does sound far-fetched when she spells it all out like that. But. She did break into the house. She was carrying a gun. There is ammo in her bag. Johanna wasn't shot, but Ralph was. And Indigo had plenty of opportunity to kill him.

"You know what is a wonderful thing?" Vic asks. "The police. You know, the way they can collect evidence. Interrogate people. Build a case."

"Where's the fun in that?" Indigo queries.

"You're as bad as Addy! This isn't supposed to be fun. People have been killed."

"And 'the police'"—I use my fingers to make air quotes around that phrase to make sure my own sarcasm doesn't go unnoticed—"are hyper focused on Dad. 'They'" (more air quotes) "aren't going to consider another suspect without serious evidence. Therefore, it's up to us to collect it."

"And you're going to do that how?" Vic asks. "Come on, Addy. Alex is reasonable... at least whenever you're not involved. I'll admit he lets his feelings around you and him get in the way. But if there's evidence, he'll pursue it."

I grin at him. "I'm just messing with you. Alex is part of the plan. He'll be over later and we'll tell him everything then."

CHAPTER 22

THE FIRST GUEST arrives at quarter to eleven. Jackson and Nat are on it, yanking the door open before the doorbell rings twice.

"Serena!" Nat crows. "You want to enter to win Johanna's house?"

"I sure do," she says. "Not that I need another house, but I could most certainly sell it and put that money into my retirement account. Just fill it in for me, Nat, would you? There's a dear boy. Shall I carry this coffee cake on into the kitchen?"

"We're setting out the eats and drinks on the dining table, if you'd like to take the dish there," I tell her. "Also, thank you! You didn't need to bring anything."

"Of course I did. I told you I would. Besides, you can call this a party if you want to, but it's still a funeral. I always bring something to a funeral."

"You can put that right here," Indigo calls, rearranging things on the table to make space for Serena's cake.

"And who might you be?" Serena demands, with as much authority as if this is her house and Indigo has walked in off the street. Which, technically, I guess she has.

Indigo tilts her head and smiles, the Mona Lisa number. "You're Serena, I'll bet. Johanna mentioned you often."

"Johanna didn't talk to people," Serena says.

"This is Indigo," I say, attempting to keep the peace. "She was Johanna's psychic and probably her only true confidante. She came to pay her respects and offered to help with the party."

"What good is a psychic who can't foresee a murder?" Serena says. "I'm sure I don't know what help it was to the poor woman to tell her she was going to die. If you hadn't, maybe she wouldn't have."

Indigo's smile fades as this shot goes home. "Foreknowledge unfortunately doesn't come with a guidebook."

"Yes, well. Easy to make excuses, isn't it," Serena says, rearranging the table to better spotlight her plate of coffee cake. My mouth waters and I reach out to snag a slice, but Serena slaps my hand. "That's for guests."

She's as bad as Mom.

As if that thought has summoned her, the doorbell rings. Jackson opens the door and Mom blows in, with Skye and Daffodil right behind her. She's carrying a tray of cookies. Because of course. As Serena says, bringing food to a funeral, even if it isn't a funeral, is what one does. These happen to be shortbread, which is my favorite.

"Victor," Mom says, catching sight of him in the kitchen. "Come and take this tray."

I roll my eyes. I'm already standing right in front of her, ready to help. But whatever.

"Victor," Skye coos, batting her eyes at Vic in a way that is wrong on every level. I mean, maybe he's not related to her by blood, but he is her baby's half-brother. Probably she's made movies with fathers and sons and brothers in them though, so it's not like that would bother her any.

Jackson stands by, alternately glaring at Vic and gazing at Skye in mute devotion. Nat is just as bad, although his expression is closer to fear than adoration. Neither of them says a word or makes a move to either get names for the drawing or take coats or carry anything.

Until Victor approaches. That jolts Jackson out of freeze mode and he runs an interception pattern, getting himself between Skye and my reluctantly approaching brother and going into helpfulness overdrive.

"Can I help you with your coat? Do you want to enter the drawing?" Jackson asks. "Did you know you could win this house? Then you'd live here in town instead of LA."

Nat continues to stand by, uncharacteristically quiet, hyper focused on Skye. He's pale and his hands are trembling. I can only hope to God that he hasn't also seen the videos.

"Why don't you hold the baby, Jackson?" Owen says, coming over to intercept. He takes Daffodil from Skye and deposits her in Jackson's arms before anybody has a chance to protest.

I hide a smile and turn to Mom. "I didn't know you were coming." A lie, but a little white one. From the minute she dropped Dad off, I knew she'd be back. She'll want to be here for the big moment when he turns himself in.

"My family all seems to be here, so it was either this or spend Christmas alone."

For once in my life I don't take the guilt bait. I pretend she's a bride gone ornery and smile calmly, staying out of dangerous territory. "Well, I'm so glad you did. Here, I'll take the cookies."

"Oh no, you don't." She holds the tray away from me, wiping her boots on the mat. "I know how you are with short-bread." Her gaze alights on Nat. "You, young man. Can you carry these into the kitchen without eating any?"

"Yes, Ma'am," Nat says, absently, his eyes still focused on Skye.

"Come and get them, then," Mom says, in a tone that suggests she's now wondering if he's a special needs child, a little slow on the uptake.

Nat jolts out of his reverie and approaches to grab the tray. "Good boy," Mom says. "You may have one. And bring one back for your friend."

"What about me?" I ask.

"Your dress is already a little snug, Addison. You might want to watch out for the Christmas goodies. I read where the average person gains ten pounds over the holiday season. Come here. I need to talk to you." She grabs my arm and tows me across the room. I glance back over my shoulder at Owen, who is keeping his eyes on Jackson and not even looking at me. Which is fair. I'm safer with Mom than Jackson is with Skye.

Probably. Though not by much.

She drags me behind the tree, then demands, "Where is he?" in a stage whisper that carries farther than her normal speaking voice.

Apparently she thinks the tree puts us in a cone of silence in addition to removing us from the direct line of sight. "Mom. Shhh. Please."

"Don't shush me. He's still here?"

"Of course he's here. You dropped him off yourself." I cross my fingers behind my back, hoping it's true. I haven't seen Dad since Ricky arrived. He could have easily snuck out the back door while we were all outside. Or out the bathroom window. Or over Johanna's balcony, even, if he did go to her room like I told him to.

"Mom. I need you to do the best acting job of your life. Can you just pretend you don't know that he came here? Everything depends on you."

"Don't you worry about your little production," she says, full Mom voice now. "All will go perfectly. I'll just oversee things with the food, make sure those boys aren't eating everything and it's all arranged properly. And then we'll make ourselves comfortable while we wait for him... for the... for the neighbors to arrive."

"What production?" Jackson asks, as we emerge from behind the tree. "Like a play? Or music? Is Owen really going to stroll around and sing?"

"No, Owen is not," Owen says.

"By production, we just mean this party," I say. "Owen, it's time to get the music started if you don't mind?"

"It's time to be long out of here," he says.

"I was thinking I'd just go make myself comfortable somewhere," Skye says, proceeding to do just that on the sofa in the living room, instead of following Mom over to the refreshment table. Jackson trails behind her like a puppy on a leash. And Owen, instead of going upstairs to pair his phone with Johanna's sound system, intercepts his nephew by taking the spot on the couch next to Skye.

She glances up at him through her lashes and rests a manicured hand on his arm. "Bethany tells me you're a musician! Are you sure you won't perform for us?"

Jackson, all scowls and frustrated hormones, stays standing in the middle of the room. I leave them to it, a little worried about the effect of Mom on the already volatile mix of Indigo and Serena. For good reason, it turns out.

"Perhaps you should consult your devil cards and see what they tell you about the placement of chips and dip relative to the baby Jesus and the nativity scene," Mom is saying, holding onto a container of dip the way Vic used to when we were playing a game of keep away with somebody's hat or mittens.

"I don't really feel that the nativity scene belongs on the refreshment table at all," Serena interjects. "Perhaps out in the entryway would be better? So people can be reminded when they first come in what the season is all about."

"You do know that Jesus was not actually born in December?" Indigo queries. "History scholars believe—"

"I don't want to hear your blasphemy," Mom says. "If he wasn't born in December why would we be celebrating Christmas now?"

"That had to do with the Catholic church co-opting existing pagan holidays in order to lure people into the fold," Indigo begins.

"Addy." Nat pads up behind me and tugs at my sleeve.

"Hmmm?"

I'm trying to think of a way to stop the epic explosion that is going to happen in a minute if I don't intervene.

Nat tugs at my sleeve again. "Addy!" I look down into a pair of worried brown eyes. "We need to talk," he whispers. "In private."

"It's not a good time, Natty. Maybe—"

"It's *important*," he insists.

"Can't you just tell me here?"

"And private."

It occurs to me that there really is no private place in this house, which is just too damned open-plan. There's the three older women duking it out by the dining room table. Dad hopefully in Johanna's room. Owen and Skye and Jackson in the sitting room. Things are only going to get more crowded. The only option is one of the bathrooms or Johanna's enclosed deck, and to get there we'd have to walk right past the dining room table which will raise all sorts of suspicions.

The doorbell rings, twice in quick succession.

Jackson makes no move toward it, intent on grabbing an opportunity to get closer to Skye. Nat stays where he is, looking up at me pleadingly, that worried look on his face.

"I'm sorry, Natty. Let's get the door real quick, shall we? And then we can step out on the porch and talk."

CHAPTER 23

LINDY LIND IS at the door. Her camera guy is with her, already recording.

"You're early. I said noon."

She "steps into the house like she owns it. "It's never really too early, is it? What happened next door?"

"The guy was murdered."

"For real?"

"If you go over there, the detective in charge will shut down everything. Including this party," I warn her. "He's not happy that we're still doing this as it is."

"Oh, all right, then. I'll snoop around later. Right now I want to get some shots of the house before all of the guests arrive," she says, but it's not the house she's looking at. She's practically salivating all over Vic, who has come over to see what fresh hell is happening now.

"Vic will be happy to show you around," I say, throwing him under the bus. I can't have her roaming freely all over the

283

house unsupervised. What if she discovers Dad before we're ready? I'm not cut out for jail. No macchiatos for one thing. Probably not much by way of coffee cake and shortbread either.

"Only downstairs though," I say. "The upstairs is off limits." I shiver and my stomach heaves again as I remember what I saw through Ralph's window. I have to be sure Lindy doesn't see that. Or the boys. Or anybody for that matter. Surely they've removed Ralph's body by now, but the blood and other body bits will still be splattered all over.

At this exact instant, instrumental music in full surround sound envelops us and a tenor voice queries, "Do you see what I see?" A quick glance over at the couch confirms that Owen has fled the battleground at Lindy's arrival, leaving Jackson to his fate with Skye.

"But people will want to see the upstairs, don't you think?" Lindy raises her voice to be heard above the music. "I mean, if they're going to win the house, they'll want to know what they're getting."

"Whoever wins can have a full tour after the fact."

"Oooh," Lindy says. "Was she killed upstairs? That's where the actual crime scene is, I bet. That's why you really don't want us up there."

It's a good reason, and one I should have thought of. Lindy sensationalizing the murder scene. Or at least what the cops believe is the murder scene. That we don't want. Or do we? The murderer might be set totally off balance wondering how Alex and the crime scene team got the place of death so wrong...

But no. Not with Dad possibly up there. Not with that view through the window.

"Later," I say, firmly. "If you want the exclusive breaking news I promised you, you'll do what I say."

"Oh, fine," she says. "Be that way. Come on then, Victor, let's get some pictures quick like so I can get a post out." She cuddles up next to him, vamping for the camera. "Let's do a little live, Jimmy. Are you ready?"

Jimmy, who has been fiddling with his phone, takes a step back, gets them in the viewfinder. "We are live on my signal."

Vic tries to pull away but Lindy clings to him like a burr, her smile never wavering.

Jimmy gives a thumbs up and Vic apparently decides he doesn't want thousands of viewers watching him struggle for his freedom and goes still. His jaw is hard as a rock and I'm pretty sure his fists are clenched and I know I'm going to pay for this later. But he'll forgive me eventually. He always does.

"FlatzandSharpzers," Lindy coos. "Do you know where I am? This house in the tiny town of Fox Valley was recently the scene of another horrific murder. Yes, that's right. Think twice about moving here! Only a few short months after rock star Leno Masterson was murdered, Johanna Meyers was killed. Here. In this very house. Addy Winters, intrepid party planner extraordinaire, is throwing another after-death extravaganza and guess what? You're invited! We know it's Christmas and you're with your family. We also know so many of you would love to take a break from family and pop in here to view the scene of the crime..."

She pauses here, grins mischievously, and then continues. "I didn't mean that. Of course I didn't. The crime scene itself it off limits but... are you ready for the big kicker? I already posted about this but in case you missed it earlier, the murder house is a door prize. So come on over, pay your respects to Johanna and make her dying wish to have her empty house filled with people come true. And while you're here, put your name in for the door prize. You might just be the winner!"

Jimmy taps the phone, presumably to end the live. "Totally rad work," he says. "Let's get some footage of the house and I'll edit and post that out in a bit."

Lindy still hasn't relinquished Vic but now that the camera isn't on him he extricates himself and turns on me.

"I can't believe that even you would think this was a good idea."

"Technically, it was Indigo's idea. Johanna wanted a house full of people. I'm making sure that happens. Just go with Lindy and keep her from looking for the actual crime scene, would you? Someone is at the door."

"I need to tell you something," Nat says. "About the woman with the baby."

Perfect. He's figured out Skye is a porn star, probably. We've corrupted an innocent. "I know, Natty," I tell him. "We'll talk about it later, okay? I promise. Can you get the door?"

He gives me a worried look, then does as I've asked.

A girl about his age bounces into the entry way, auburn hair in a thick braid, faded blue jeans, sweatshirt, keen blue eyes behind glasses. "Nat!" she crows. "Is the house *haunted*? Have you seen her *ghost*? Oooh, is that her *coffin*?"

Nat gives me a worried look over his shoulder as he follows the girl, who is making a beeline for the coffin. I should have anticipated ghost hunters. I didn't. At least so far it's only one.

Indigo swoops in. "Oh, don't look like that, honey," she says to me. "This is going to be a tumultuous and exciting time. But it will be fun. Just let go of control and trust the unfolding."

"The unfolding wasn't meant to involve quite this many complications."

"Of course it was." She pats me. "There, now. I'll get this next batch coming to the door and make sure they're entered and fed. You should talk to Nat."

She's already opening the door, this time to a group of people I recognize. Neighbors who were standing on the street the day Britt and I called 911.

How she knows I need to talk to Nat is one of those things I'm just beginning to accept. Maybe she really is psychic. But there's no time now because Aunt Rachel has just arrived, together with two other women from Mom's church group. They cluster together in the entryway, dressed in black, like a trio of witches only without the hats.

"We've come to pay our respects to the deceased," Aunt Rachel says, piously, raising her voice to be heard over a particularly obnoxious rendition of *Jingle Bells* that Owen has chosen, probably as revenge for making him the music guy.

Aunt Rachel clutches her well-worn Bible in one hand, her handbag in the other. Mrs. Markle bears her signature potluck dish, a horrible concoction of lime gelatin, cottage cheese, grated carrots and sliced grapes that once induced me to vomit all over everybody when I was six. Jeannie Goertzen has brought a casserole, which is likely delicious, but we're not set up for hot dishes. Also, it's unapologetically funeral food.

The music shifts to *Rocking Around the Christmas Tree* and the three of them exchange disapproving glances.

"Hardly decorous," Mrs. Markle says. "But of course, that's not surprising."

"What's surprising is that the three of you are here," I say.

"We felt the poor murdered woman deserved respect, so

we've come to give it to her," Aunt Rachel says, with a sniff. "Really, don't you think that music is—"

"Perfect for a Christmas party? Yes! Do come in. Let me take those dishes."

Jackson appears, suddenly and surprisingly. "Want to enter to win the house? Just write your name and phone number here."

"No, thank you," Aunt Rachel says, clasping her Bible against her breast and looking around as if she's wandered into a tavern or some other den of iniquity by mistake.

"Eats and drinks are in on the dining room table," Jackson says. "Here, let me take that for you so you can enter for the house." Jeannie Goertzen relinquishes her casserole but Mrs. Markle only clings more tightly to her Jell-O abomination. "I'll take it in myself. I will not be part of a tasteless scrambling after a poor dead woman's belongings. God rest her soul."

She heads for the dining room table without either removing her boots or even attempting to wipe them on the mat, tracking muddy water behind her.

"I'll enter," Jeannie says. She's always been the least uptight of the three. She even smiles at me before accepting a pen and writing down her name and phone number.

"Really, Jeannie," Aunt Rachel huffs. "It's indecorous."

"Relax a little," Jeannie says. "Jesus loved a good party, I've always thought. And it is Christmas."

Aunt Rachel opens her mouth to deliver some rousing message but is stopped by Mom entering the scene, carrying Daffodil.

"Oh my goodness," Aunt Rachel says, rushing over. "How are you holding up Bethany? You've not been taking my calls. All of this nonsense with Richard and a new woman. And this?

This is the baby? I suppose she's not to be blamed for her parents' sins but we will have to form a prayer circle, right away, to beseech the good Lord to intervene that she may not walk in the path of her parents."

I'm afraid she's going to drop to her knees and start beseeching the Lord on Daffodil's behalf right here and now. Lindy would have a heyday with that scenario. The doorbell drags me away again, and this time it's another neighbor, followed by a local news reporter who came over to check things out. The house is filling up with a mix of friends and neighbors and strangers—too many to let me keep eyes on everybody, so I need to trust that my crew is paying attention. I'm actually grateful for Indigo's spy cams and that Lindy is wandering around filming people randomly; she might just catch whatever we miss.

A thunderous knock at the door brings me running. That will be Alex.

But it's not Alex. It's Chip Fitzwilliam, attorney at law. Possibly not Chip Fitzwilliam at all, but Christopher, Johanna's brother.

My knees go a trifle wobbly, my heart kicks up a notch, this time not because of his piratical sexiness. He's furious. And his rage is locked, loaded, and focused in on me. I feel it like a physical blow.

"What the hell do you think you're doing?"

"If you only knew how many times I've been asked that question today. Did you want to come in?"

He comes in, all right. Before I have a chance to back up and get out of his way he's right up in my personal space, his eyes drilling into mine. He smells hot, in a brimstone and fury sort of way that makes me want to take a step back, then turn and make a run for it. But I don't give an inch. Never let an angry person see your fear.

"Did you want to enter for the house?"

"This is outrageous. I want it stopped."

"I told you I was throwing Johanna's party," I say. "And you knew that she wanted this. So what's the issue?"

"A few neighbors! That's one thing. But this? All over social media. All over the news. Random strangers coming over in the hopes they can win the murder house? It's like vultures picking at carrion. Johanna deserved better than this."

"Johanna deserved not to be murdered," I retort. "Also, the neighbors were equally curious and vultury. She didn't have any friends. You know that. Although... did you know she has a brother?" I watch his face carefully for a reaction, but he doesn't so much as blink.

"Her brother is dead," he says, dismissively.

I shrug. "Maybe. Maybe not."

Now there's a flicker of something in his eyes. A twitch of his lips. "What do you mean, maybe, maybe not?"

Curious eyes are turning in our direction. A few neighbors drift over to see what the excitement is all about.

He takes a deep breath and releases it slowly, the way I do when I'm trying not to react to Mom picking at my faults." Tell me about this brother. Johanna said he was dead."

"Not now. We can talk after the party. Maybe. If you promise not to yell at me."

His face reddens. I can see a vein on his forehead pulsing. But then he releases a long breath and offers the hint of a smile.

"I might possibly have overreacted. Forgive me?" He follows up the question with a hand on my shoulder. His eyes are fixed on mine, hot and hungry, but the heat is not quite so much anger and a little more... something else. I can't seem to either look away or move, even when his hand slides over my shoulder, down my arm, then comes to rest on the small of my back. I can feel the heat of it burning my skin through the fabric of my dress.

Somebody behind me makes a throat-clearing sound which startles me out of my trance and I swivel my head around to see Owen standing there. He's not looking at me, he's looking at Chip, and I have a suspicious niggling feeling that Chip knew he was there before he let his hand go wandering.

I pull away, resisting the urge to smooth my hair or moisten my lips. I can feel myself blushing as if I'm guilty of something other than being manhandled, and the awareness makes me blush even more.

Chip follows me, resting that hand possessively on the front of my waist now, just above the flare of my hip, an escalation in intimacy. I feel uneasy, vulnerable. In a weird state of slow motion I notice Owen notice Chip's hand. I notice Chip noticing him noticing.

"Chip," I croak, "this is Owen Masterson. My..."

All of a sudden I draw a blank. What is Owen to me, exactly? My friend? Something a little more than that, surely, but nothing I can claim. "My... Owen," I finish, lamely.

Owen smiles slightly, holding out his hand. "As Addy says, I'm her Owen."

For a long breath held I think Chip is going to ignore the outstretched hand. When he does finally release me so that he can shake, I half expect them to get into a contest of who can squeeze harder or some other masculine contest of strength and dominance. While I'm not going to deny a slight internal warmth at the idea that two men seem to be going all macho over me, it's also ridiculous and I'll have no part of it.

"I should check in on the food," I say, edging away while keeping an eye on both of them.

The door slams open without the warning of either knock or doorbell, and this time it really is Alex, looking thundery and grumbly and annoyed. I let out a sigh of relief. Alex is a known quantity, and his anger doesn't scare me. I've been annoying him since I was a kid, though of course he wasn't a cop then. Or my ex, with an axe to grind.

Alex sniffs, nostrils flaring, as if he can scent the testosterone in the room, right along with the apple cider. His eyes travel over me, Owen, and Chip, then take in the church ladies, the neighbors, the decorated coffin and everything else.

"You had to do this, didn't you?" he snaps. "If we did miss any evidence, we're sure not going to find it now."

"You did clear the crime scene," I remind him.

"Yes, well, I had no reason to believe that there was going to be a second murder right next door."

"You can't still think Dad is the killer. What connection could he possibly have to Ralph?"

"Wait just a minute," Alex eyes narrow. "How did you know the name of the deceased?"

We're attracting a lot of attention. All eyes are turned toward us. People are gravitating closer, hoping to hear better what we're saying.

I glance at Owen. He catches my telepathic message, fiddles with his phone, and the volume of the music sharply goes up, so anybody more than a couple of feet away won't hear anything. Of course, that means I can't hear anything either, and neither can Alex. He grabs my hand and drags me through the house, past the dining room table, and out into Johanna's porch sanctuary.

Chip follows us. So does Vic.

"This is police business," Alex says. "I only need Addy."

"I'm here as her legal representation," Vic says. "You did accuse her earlier of being some sort of accomplice. She's not going to talk to you without me present."

"Johanna's attorney," Chip says. "Making sure her interests are represented."

Alex looks like he's going to protest, but then decides this is not a hill he wants to die on. He ignores them both and turns his attention back to me.

"Tell me how you knew Ralph."

"I didn't *know* him. I mean, I met him. The neighbor, Serena, told me his name. Britt and I talked to him out on the street the first day we met Johanna. Not a pleasant man, but I don't go around killing the nasty people I meet."

"Did your father know him?"

"You'd have to ask him."

And that's when I remember Ralph and the book and the sheet of paper in my bag.

"What?" Alex demands.

"What do you mean what?"

"You look guilty as sin all of a sudden. I know you, Addy. Don't try to pretend there's nothing going on."

I'd rather not tell him, because now that I've remembered I realize I should have told him as soon as I knew Ralph was dead. Possibly before. There are so many things he's not going to be happy about I don't want to add this into the mix.

"Now," Alex demands, in his most annoying cop voice.

"Ralph came over here yesterday. Barged in without knocking and I think he was surprised that Indigo and I were here. Said he'd loaned Johanna a book and he wanted it back."

"A copy of *The Women* by any chance?"

"That's the one. How did you know?"

"Found it in the room where he was killed. Let me get this straight. Ralph comes over here and insists on retrieving a book—unlikely reading material for him, which by the way belongs not to him but Johanna—and that very night he's murdered, and you didn't think you might tell me about this?"

"I swear I forgot. There was a lot going on." For once in his life, Alex is one-hundred-percent right. I should have told him. And there are other things I need to tell him, like that Chip is actually Christopher, and that Dad is maybe hiding upstairs.

"Something fell out of the book. A paper with numbers and letters on it."

"You have got to be kidding me. I should arrest you right this minute."

"It didn't look like anything, Alex. And I was distracted. Just a minute and I'll find it for you."

"You realize you might have been the last person to see Ralph alive," Alex accuses, as I dig in my bag for the now elusive sheet of paper.

At this I bestir myself to muster some sort of defense. "Indigo was with me. And it was just a book, Alex. A paperback. I figured she was using the paper for a bookmark."

"You didn't think it was an odd choice of reading material for him?"

Alex is at his most annoying level of sanctimoniousness but he has a point.

"Well, I did, but—"

"But you think you're a detective now and that you're smarter than me, so you kept it to yourself."

"I didn't keep it to myself on purpose. It honestly just didn't seem important. Here we go."

I find the folded sheet of paper and hand it to him. "Hope this helps."

His face changes as he looks at it, in a way that makes me realize that the numbers and letters might actually mean something.

"What is it? Some sort of code?"

"My guess is it's a crypto key," Alex says. "Which could certainly be a motive for murder. For both of them. Any other small, insignificant detail you'd care to share?"

I shake my head no. Dad is not a small and insignificant detail, so technically I'm not lying.

Alex turns on Chip. "Did you know Ralph?"

"He was my client."

"You're as bad as she is," Alex thunders. "You're a common denominator. A link between two murder victims who lived next door to each other."

"Client-attorney privilege," Chip says. "There is nothing I can tell you."

"They're both dead," Alex says. "I can't imagine they'll bring a law suit."

"And you know as well as I do that confidentiality extends after death." Chip's face and voice give nothing away.

"I'd think you'd want to solve their murders," Alex presses. "If neither of them had anything to hide, you'd be more forthcoming."

Chip shrugs, allowing insolence into his voice. "Or maybe I just don't like your attitude and I'm choosing to be difficult. In any case, there's nothing I can tell you. But perhaps this young man has something to say."

We all follow Chip's gaze to where Nat is standing in the doorway, silently listening. His eyes widen as we all turn toward him, and he swallows, visibly, his face gone pale the way it did earlier when he'd said he needed to talk to me. I wait for Alex to blow up but his voice is surprising gentle as he says, "Nat. You're looking good. You and Angel doing all right?"

Nat nods. "We're good." But he looks like we're all about to be struck by a meteor or something.

"Glad to hear it. You let me know if you need anything all right?"

"Yes, sir."

"Good. Tell Angel merry Christmas for me, will you?" Alex smiles slightly, and I feel genuinely guilty all of a sudden. Alex can be a dick, and it's easy to forget that he actually is a cop and does good things in the community. Like, probably, investigating the murder of Nat and Angel's mother. And now, Johanna's. And Ralph's.

"Could I talk to you for a minute?" Nat says.

"Not just now," Alex says. "I'll come find you before I leave."

Nat opens his mouth but before any words come out the doors open and Lindy Lind and her camera guy are upon us.

CHAPTER 24

LINDY CROWS with delight and turns to face her camera guy, with our little huddle as a backdrop.

"FlatzandSharpzers! The police have arrived. And such a hunky detective at that. And what's this? Some sort of clandestine confab?" Keeping her face to the camera, she backs up until she's stopped by Alex's solid bulk. He puts out a hand to steady her and she leans into his arm as she turns so she's half facing him, half facing the camera.

"Detective, can you tell us where you are with the investigation? Have you located Richard Winters? Is he really the murderer? And is there a connection to the brand new murder next door?"

"Shut that thing off," Alex orders, flushing an unattractive shade of red.

"I have a right to film the police in action," Lindy says. "Do you have something to hide? Are you breaking rules, Detective? Because our viewers want to know everything!"

"Shut it off or I'll—"

"Make me? Break the camera, perhaps? FlatzandSharpzers, are we about to view police brutality live and online? I'm prepared to make that sacrifice for the sake of the truth, and for Johanna Meyers, a woman murdered right here in her own home."

"Oh for Christ's sake!" Alex shouts. "Addy. Do something!"

I shrug, indicating absolute helplessness. This is his fault for hyper focusing on Dad as the killer. If he'd done his job and been open to my suggestions there'd be no need for the dramatics.

"You may have a right to film the police," Chip says. "But you do not have a right to film the rest of us without consent. And I certainly do not consent."

"Oops," Lindy says, lowering the camera. "Too late. We were live. Mea Culpa and whatever. Who are you, anyway?"

"Chip Fitzwilliam, Attorney," he says. "Take down your post."

"I could do that," she says, eyeing him like he's a particularly delicious morsel in a buffet line. "But it would be counterproductive. Ten thousand people have seen it already, give or take. If I cut it, there will be questions. Like, what are you trying to hide? *Are* you hiding something? You look like you could be. Oh, please tell me you're hiding some delectable clue."

"Do you want to be sued? You're asking for it."

"Freedom of the press," she says, breezily. "Free speech. It's my constitutional right."

"If you think you are 'the press' you've got delusions of grandeur," he growls. "This influencer business has gone way over the top. It is not your constitutional right to film people in a private space—"

"Addy invited me."

"It's not Addy's space. And I never gave consent."

Realizing that it's my turn to step on stage I take a breath and do so. Literally.

"Chip, Alex, I apologize on Lindy's behalf. Come on, guys, it's Christmas. Chip, I think you'll see that there is a note on the door that states we are filming this event and by entering you are agreeing to the possibility that you will end up on camera—"

"That is not legally binding!"

"Perhaps you ought to go? I want to be able to share Johanna's party with the world. If you're not up for that—"

"I'll try to keep him out of the frame," Lindy says. "Or, you know, we could use the footage to make a short clip and get you more clients."

"I can get my own clients."

"Everybody can use more clients," Lindy says, dismissively. "All press is good press, right? Now, Skye is by the coffin waiting for me. We're going to do a little photo shoot with her."

"So help me, God," Alex mutters in my ear as we fall in line behind everybody else and proceed back into the main part of the house, "you are going to owe me for this."

"I'm helping you solve your murder. Be grateful."

I expect Skye to adopt the same pose as the hot babe in a bikini that hung on Vic's wall throughout his teenage years, only draped over the coffin instead of the hood of a candy apple red Lamborghini. But instead of the Lamborghini pose, she's snuggling a sleeping Daffodil in her arms. A ray of light from the window illuminates her hair like a halo. Boyz II Men are caroling "round yon virgin mother and child" through the speakers. But even with the baby in her arms and the musical prompt, Skye looks like anything but a virgin.

When she sees Alex, she stands up a little straighter, shifting Daffodil in her arms, the color fading from her face. She looks suddenly young and frightened and I remember that she's little more than a child herself, gone adrift in a big wide world.

"I assume you're Skye," Alex says. "Could we talk for a minute?"

"About what?"

"How about we go somewhere a little more private?"

"I'm not going anywhere with a cop." Her chin lifts in a show of defiance. "Anything you want to say to me you can say in front of everybody."

"I understand you might have some information that would be helpful. We can talk at the station if you'd prefer."

"I got nothing to say. Unless I'm under arrest. Are you going to handcuff me, Officer?"

"I'm looking for Richard Winters."

"Everybody is looking for Rich. He's a difficult man to find."

"You're saying you have no idea where we might find him? Has he been in contact?"

Mom creates a momentary distraction, choking on a slice of coffee cake. There's a flurry of activity all around her.

"Are you all right?"

"Should we Heimlich her?"

"I don't think you Heimlich if somebody is still coughing, do you?"

Mom waves everybody away, doubled over, tears

streaming while she continues to cough. And Alex waits until she's able to take a deep breath and stand up straight again, face red, eyes streaming, before turning back to Skye.

"Again and more directly. Do you know where Richard Winters is?"

"Reason I'm in town is I came looking for him," Skye evades. "Thought he might be at his daughter's place, but nope."

"So you followed him to Fox Valley. And to Addy's place."

"I was too late," she says, sadly. "Rich was already—" She stops, eyes narrowing. I follow her gaze. Thanks to a trick of the light, it seems to be Nat she's staring at, and he's staring back at her, the worry I'd seen on his face earlier now amplified into outright fear.

"And where are you planning to look for him next?" Alex asks.

"I have no idea where else to look. If only I'd come a day earlier, maybe I would have found him."

Uneasily, I realize she's shifted from evasion to an outright lie. Either she knows that Dad has flown the coop and will not be turning himself in, or she's distancing herself from any involvement with knowing his whereabouts.

Nat takes a huge breath. He's visibly trembling now. He crosses to Alex, and tugs on his arm.

Alex glances down at him and shakes his head in a way that means 'don't bother me now, I'm busy.'

"What is it, Nat?" Indigo moves up beside him and places a steadying hand on his shoulder. "It's all right. Tell the officer what you know."

"She's lying," Nat says. "Skye is."

"Listen, you little pipsqueak. You're going to regret making

301

up stories about me," Skye snaps. "Also, I changed my mind. Let's go talk somewhere private."

Alex ignores her. "You understand that lying to the police is a very bad idea, Nat?"

Nat nods. "Yes. That's why I need to tell you. I saw her, Skye, before Johanna was killed."

Skye scoffs. "You're going to listen to this kid? He's imagining things. Or making things up. Or he saw some other woman and now he wants to make her out to be me."

"Another woman who looks like you?" Alex queries, heavy on the doubt. "Go ahead, son."

Skye glares at Nat. He bites his lip and shuffles his feet. The volume of the music drops, thanks to Owen, who is managing sound production like a pro.

"I saw her on my way here to feed the birds, "Nat says. "She was walking down the sidewalk toward me. We passed each other. She got into a car and drove away."

"She was driving a car?" Alex asks.

"See?" Skye says. "He's making it up. I don't have a car. I hitchhiked. Addy can tell you that. The guy I caught a ride from dropped me at her condo and the security guard can confirm that. She's probably got his license plate number and everything."

"She was driving," Nat insists.

"Do you know what kind of car it was?" Alex asks.

Nat shrugs. "I'm not good at cars. It was a dark blue car. Four doors. I think. Like Johanna's."

Alex's eyes on Skye are cold and calculating. Cop eyes. No more sympathy. "What were you doing in the neighborhood before Johanna died?"

"I wasn't. The kid is making it all up. Maybe he needs more

attention or something, I don't know." She bats her eyelashes, makes her voice husky. "But you're really going to believe him over me? There's no proof of anything."

"There is, though," Nat says. "Angel's Thunderbird."

"See? He's crazy as well as attention seeking," Skye says. "I can't believe you're even listening to him."

Lindy, behind Alex's back, has her phone out and is recording again.

"The bird is a robot," Nat explains. "It has a motion sensor camera in it. Angel made it because I was scared after what happened to Mom, so we could watch for strange cars. I can check the feed."

He starts tapping on his phone. "I just need the day and the approximate time and... here. That's the car."

He hands the phone to Alex.

"He could be showing you any old car and saying it's mine," Skye says.

"Well, we can always check that license plate number and see who the car belongs to." Alex turns away and talks into his radio, his words lost in a sudden hubbub of voices.

Skye's lower lip trembles and two perfect tears spill over her cheeks. "It's because of my profession, isn't it? Just because I made some films, you're going to believe a messed up kid over me." Her eyes seek out mine, then Vic's, and finally Mom's, tear-filled and pleading. "I thought you all said you were my family."

Vic's expression is unyielding, Mom's uncertain.

I don't know what I'm feeling because my brain is too busy putting pieces together. Skye showing up at my place. Supposedly looking for Dad, but was she? Maybe what she was looking for was an alibi. Why would she kill Johanna? Jealousy, maybe. Or maybe Dad told her he was going to inherit money and she meant to come in for a piece of it.

A burst of static comes over Alex's radio and then a voice says, clearly, "217, car is registered to a Skye Warner, California. Status clear."

"You want to explain?" Alex asks her.

Skye's jaw juts out. Her face hardens. "So I have a car and I drove through the neighborhood. You going to arrest me for that?"

Alex considers. "I think I am. Skye Warner, you are under arrest for obstruction of an investigation." Probably conscious of the camera, he gives her the full Miranda warning, word for word before he even removes the handcuffs from his duty belt.

This isn't good. He's going to haul Skye off to jail. I need him to be here while Dad does his thing. If Dad is still here. I need to go look for him, but I also need to stay here and keep an eye on things.

Skye backs up against the coffin, holding Daffodil up like a shield. "You can't. I have a baby."

"Addy." Alex doesn't even look at me and my name is not a question, it's a command.

I reach for Daffodil but Skye clings to her so tightly that the baby wakes up and starts to cry.

"Just give her to me," I say. "You know we'll take good care of her."

"You'll have to tear her from my arms," Skye proclaims, a performance that would earn her an A in the over-the-top drama club. "You can't let him take me to jail, Addy. I've done nothing wrong."

"Just give me Daffodil. We'll sort it out later."

Her expression shifts into pure, spiteful mean girl. "If

you're going to arrest me, you need to arrest Addy. And Mrs. Winters. They are both harboring—"

A dramatic thump from inside the coffin cuts her off mid-sentence.

Another thump.

Everybody in the room freezes.

I know damn well that coffin was empty when we brought it in here. If something or somebody is in there it sure as hell isn't Johanna, but I don't exactly want this crowd to know that. I promised Ricky.

There's more thumping, and then a muffled, sepulchral voice calls out from inside the coffin. "Let me out of here, I can't breathe."

Chaos ensues.

Mom and her little circle of church ladies shriek and throw their arms around one another. Aunt Rachel begins reciting the Lord's prayer loudly and determinedly.

Skye stops wailing. Her eyes dart around the room, searching out an exit.

"She's going to make a run for it," I tell Alex, in a low voice more likely to be heard beneath all of the high-pitched exclamations all around us.

"Not going to get far," Alex says. "Stand by to grab the kid."

Owen moves up behind me. "How long has Rich been in the coffin?"

A burst of slightly hysterical laughter escapes me. "I have no idea."

"Everybody, please remain calm," Alex bellows into the crowd.

This has the opposite effect, everybody jostling for a good view.

Lindy is halfway up the floating staircase, filming.

Vic surprises me by approaching Skye. "Look. I don't know what's happening here but we'll get it sorted. Give me the baby. She doesn't need to be part of this."

Skye hesitates, then all of the fight goes out of her and she lets Vic take Daffodil. Tears are flowing now, maybe even real tears. She looks sad and scared and about sixteen years old.

"It will be okay," Vic says. "We'll get you an attorney."

Speaking of attorneys, I scan the crowd for Chip, but don't see him anywhere.

More thumping from the coffin, and Dad's voice again. "Let me out! I'm going to suffocate!"

"Where's the key?" Alex asks, as he snaps the handcuffs on Skye's wrists.

"I don't think it's locked," Indigo says. "We've got it all tied up with the lights and the garland. And the books we piled on it are heavy. Help me with this, Addy."

The two of us undo the decorations and move the wrapped up books. Indigo lifts the lid and Dad, disheveled and frantic, sits up gasping.

"Thank God. It was getting right stale in there."

"I need backup," Alex says into his radio. Then, "Richard Winters, you are under arrest for the murder of Johanna Meyers."

"Wait," Dad says. "I haven't turned myself in yet. That was the plan, to turn myself in."

"Oh?" Alex asks. "And whose bright idea was it to do that from the coffin?"

"Well, that was mine," he admits.

"Why would you do that?" I demand.

Dad evades my eyes. "I didn't want to miss out on all the

fun. I thought I could listen to everything from in here until it was time, instead of hiding upstairs. But then Skye locked me in."

"I did not lock you in! I didn't even know you were in there. Anytime you wanted to pound on the coffin somebody would have let you out."

"It's like the Halloween movie you did," Jackson says. "*The Coffin Consort*, right Skye? You did have a coffin key in that one. Do you still have it?"

"Obviously you never know when you're going to need a coffin key," Owen mutters.

"Stop!" Alex orders. I can hear the unspoken echo of 'or I'll shoot' hanging in the air, and am pretty sure that in the wilder parts of his soul there's an impulse to level us all. "What do you mean by 'until it was time?' If you were going to turn yourself in, why wouldn't you just do it and get it over with?"

Dad doesn't answer his question. His eyes scan the room and alight on Lindy, happily filming away from her vantage point.

"I want to make a public statement,"' he says.

"I want you to come out of that coffin so I can put cuffs on you," Alex counters.

"Not until I give my statement. Are you filming this? Okay, good. My name is Richard Winters," Dad proclaims, eyes on the camera. "I have been evading the police, as Harrison Ford did in *The Fugitive*, as Jean Valjean did in *Les Miserables*, as so many other innocent men have done before me, knowing they would not have the chance of a fair trial. But I cannot continue to drag others down with me, and it's possible that I know something that will contribute to bringing that poor woman's real murderer to justice, so I am happy to share all that I know with the authorities."

"All right, that's enough," Alex says. "Let's go."

"I'm not quite done," Dad says. "Johanna was a lonely woman. And, let's face it, she was an attractive woman."

Skye makes a growling sound in her throat.

"Johanna asked me to stay the night. I agreed. Who am I to turn down a woman in need?" He grins, but it's fleeting and his face goes somber. "Skye did come by. She was tracking my phone so she knew where I was. I don't know why she said she wasn't here until Monday... or that she didn't have a car..."

His eyes go wide and his gaze shifts from the camera to Skye. Color drains from his face. "Skye? You didn't... I thought I felt like I'd been roofied. I didn't drink enough to put me out that cold. Did you drug me and...dear God. Did you kill the poor woman? Why would you do that?"

Skye tries to run for it, but she's awkward and slow with her hands cuffed behind her and Alex grabs her before she can get far. For a brief instant she struggles, trying to bite and kick like a frightened animal.

"Don't make me tase you," Alex says, and she stops, tears pouring down her face. This time she's not crying pretty. These are real tears, and the torrent of words that comes out of her is broken by sobs and is only half comprehensible.

"I didn't kill her. And I didn't drug you, either. Maybe you shouldn't drink so much, ever think of that? The reason I said I wasn't here was because I had been in the house and my fingerprints are on stuff and I knew you'd try to put the blame on me after you killed her."

All eyes go back to Rich and he spreads his arms in a gesture of innocence.

"I only had a couple of drinks. And then we..." he glances sideways at Skye. "We, um, went to bed. When I woke up, Johanna wasn't in the bed beside me. I went looking for her. I felt ill, my brain wasn't working right.

"Johanna was nowhere in the house. The doors out into the backyard had been left open. Cold wind was blowing in, a powdering of snow. I looked out and that's when I saw her—"

"Stop there!" Alex roars.

Dad raises his voice. "That's when I saw her. Hanging from the tree where the bird feeder is. I couldn't leave her there, it seemed so wrong. So I cut her down and carried her back into the house and laid her in the bed. Covered her, so she wouldn't be so cold. I picked up the phone to call 911 and it was only then I realized that they'd think I did it..."

His voice is muffled now by Alex, who has left Skye and is leaning over him, grasping him by both arms.

"Come out of there now or I will lift you out bodily," he threatens.

"Oh, all right," Dad says. "You'll have to help me in any case. It's harder getting out of a coffin than you'd think. I'd appreciate a lift to be honest. Oh good, here's your backup. Give us a lift, Cyril, would you?"

"Yes, Sir, Mr. Winters," Cyril says.

There's some scrambling and scuffling, and then Dad is out of the coffin.

"Arrest him, would you?" Alex demands.

Cyril does not look happy about any of this this. He sat behind me in middle school social studies and used to pull my hair. He was friendly with Vic, has been to our house for pizza parties and ping pong. Also, I planned his wedding. Being a cop in a small town can get awkward. But he's still going to do his job.

"You're under arrest for the murder of Johanna Meyers. You have a right to remain silent—"

"Didn't you get married not long ago?" Dad interrupts. "I saw an announcement online. Gina or something? How is she?"

"Jenna." Cyril snaps on the handcuffs. "And she's great."

"Let me give you some advice, son. Be faithful to your wife. If I hadn't cheated on mine, I wouldn't be in this mess."

"You're in this mess because you're an asshole," Skye says. Mom looks like she agrees, with the sentiment if not the language.

"Enough. Let's go." Alex starts perp walking Skye toward the door, the crowd parting to let them through.

He pauses when they reach me. "If I had another pair of cuffs and another officer I'd be taking you in with us," he starts. "I can't believe you—"

Skye interrupts him as her gaze lands on Nat. "You'll pay for this, twerp."

Alex realizes he needs to keep moving, and with another glare at me, herds his prisoner toward the front door, Cyril right behind with Dad.

In their wake, a silence echoes, rapidly filled by voices talking about Dad and Skye and speculating as to how things really went down.

I'm about to turn around and comfort Nat when support comes from other quarters.

"That was so brave," the ghost hunter girl says. "Brave and smart. C'n I see a picture of the robot bird? I mean, how cool is that?"

"Sure thing." Nat whips out his phone and I smile a little and leave them to their conversation.

"That was interesting, don't you think?" Indigo appears at my elbow.

"Interesting, yes. Insane and chaotic, absolutely. Do you think it was Skye all the time?"

"I can't imagine that child pulling it off."

"I can imagine her killing any number of people."

"Well, yes. She's full of fury, poor child. What I can't imagine is her having the strength to drag Johanna out into the yard and hoist her up into the tree. They weighed about the same, so physics would also be against her. Johanna would have been panicked. It would have taken a good bit of strength to get her out of the house."

"Unless she really was drugged."

A sickening thought hits me in the solar plexus and steals my breath. What if Dad and Skye did this together?

Lindy zooms over. I can almost hear an electrical buzzing coming off of her skin. "People are leaving. Did you want to draw your winner?"

"Later. Let this die down."

She laughs. "Are you kidding? This won't die down for weeks. It would be good to have the drawing live, though, don't you think? So that nobody can accuse you of cheating? I mean, what if one of the winners is somebody you know and love? Or somebody you know and hate for that matter. Maybe you drop the winning name back into the kitty and draw again."

"She has a point." Vic has joined us. "You've already publicized this whole event. I assume Dad's little speech has already posted, Lindy?"

"Of course! And thank you for this, Addison. I owe you. My feed is blowing up. Everything has gone viral! You don't think that lawyer will really sue me, do you?"

"Chip? I don't know him. I hope not. If he sues you, he'll likely sue me while he's at it. Where has he got to, anyway?"

Lindy shrugs. "Haven't seen him."

"He's upstairs," Britt says, joining us. "I saw him going up just now and came to tell you."

"Damn it. Okay. I'll go see what he's doing. Can one of you check in on Serena? I don't see her either."

"I'll go with you," Owen says. "I don't trust that guy."

CHAPTER 25

CHIP IS in Johanna's room, next to her dresser. The top drawer is open. He's heard my footsteps and spins around, a pair of socks in one hand, a gun in the other.

"What are you doing?" I ask, as the world goes into slow motion. I'm aware of Owen beside me, but my eyes can't see anything but that gun. It looks enormous.

"Inventorying her belongings." Chip's voice sounds muted and distorted, like somebody talking underwater. "Seeing how much work it's going to be for you. I have experience with liquidating estates. I'd love to be of help."

"And that requires a weapon?" Owen asks.

My throat is too dry and tight for speech.

Chip looks at the gun like he's surprised he's holding it. "Oh, no. My God. Did you think I was going to shoot you? I found it. Here in her sock drawer." He illustrates his words by placing the gun in the drawer, and laying the pair of socks on top of it. "Too bad she didn't have it at her bedside where it

313

might have done her some good. Don't look at me like that. Obviously I don't know anything about guns or I wouldn't have been pointing it at you like that!"

He closes the drawer and turns back toward us. I can't breathe, and the sound of my racing heart is so loud I'm afraid Chip can hear it.

Owen steps forward and tucks me behind him. "Go, Addy. We'll meet you downstairs."

It's tempting to let him be my human shield but I can't do that.

"We're going to do the drawing for the house," I croak, moving off to the side. "Have you entered, Chip?"

"Conflict of interest."

It's all I can do to keep my eyes from Johanna's window. The one that is right across from Ralph's. I keep my gaze focused on Chip and force myself to walk toward him. One step. Two. Three. I dredge up a smile. "You'd be the perfect person to do the drawing. Except I told Lindy I'd let her film that and you're averse to the camera. Could I possibly persuade you otherwise?"

He moves forward to meet me, not stopping until he's well inside my personal space. We're not quite touching, but I can feel the heat of his body, way too close to mine.

And then one of his hands is on my waist, the other at the back of my neck. Next thing I know, he's kissing me. This is not romance. It's pure domination and anger and raw animal sensuality.

Owen's voice, dry and sarcastic, says behind me, "Nothing like a good murder scene to invoke passion, I've always thought. Whenever the two of you can come up for air, they're waiting for us downstairs."

"She's busy," Chip says, insolently. I try to pull away but he clamps me hard against him.

"Let me go."

He doesn't. His lips are on mine again, and my adrenaline switches gears from fear to fury. My right knee comes up, hard, a missile in search of a vulnerable target. There's a satisfying crunch. Chip releases me with a gasp, curling inward, both hands clutching between his legs. I step away. Smooth my hair. Wipe my mouth with the back of my hand and try to disguise the full-body trembling that has set in.

"That was surprisingly satisfying," Owen says. "Are you ready?"

"No."

"Do you want to call it off?"

"I'll do it. I'm coming. We should get the gun." I cross to the dresser, open the drawer, and slip my hand into one of Johanna's socks, using it like a glove before gingerly picking up the weapon.

Chip moans and gags and says something that is probably "bitch," but his voice is too strangled to make it out clearly.

"You got him good," Owen says. "I'm not sure whether to be impressed or terrified."

"I went to self-defense classes."

"I'll keep that in mind."

I smooth my hair again. "Do I look okay?"

"You mean, like a woman throwing a party and not one who was about to be ravished on the murder bed?" He won't look at me. His jaw is tight and hard. Can he possibly think I kissed Chip voluntarily?

"She wasn't murdered in the bed," I say. "Call 911 would you?"

"Now what?" he asks, after he makes the call and reports attempted assault.

"Well, either we induce panic by telling all of our guests that we think the murderer might be upstairs—"

"Wait," Owen says. "How did you make that leap?"

"Just trust me. I don't have time to explain it all right now."

Of course there's time, but I don't have any proof of anything and I'm pretty sure he won't believe me. We need to draw the door prize and then shoo everybody out before the cops show up.

"Come on," I say, heading for the stairs. "I figure we have five minutes before the cops get here. Maybe ten."

"What about the gun?" he asks.

He has a point. We can't just leave it lying around for Chip to grab. Owen takes it from me, checks it to make sure there's not a round in the chamber, and tucks it in the back of his jeans, pulling his shirt down to conceal it.

"What about fingerprints?" I protest.

"They'll have to rule mine out. Let's go."

All eyes are on us as we descend the stairs, like we're royalty or celebrity guests. My eyes pan over the gathering, registering details. Serena is arguing with Aunt Rachel. Britt and Vic are talking to Mom, who looks, not surprisingly, distraught but is holding it together for the sake of Daffodil, asleep on her shoulder. Indigo and Lindy stand together on the landing. Lindy is snapping photos. Indigo is holding the urn with the door prize entries.

"Oh, good, here you are," Lindy crows. "What were the two of you doing up there? Making out in the dead woman's room? Joking, I'm joking. Ha. Ha. Hey, are we going to draw the winner now? I was thinking, I'll stand here on the landing and

Addy, you can stand a couple of steps up and draw the name. That way everybody can see you and I can get a good angle. We'll broadcast live, so anybody who was here and had to go before we did this can be part of it. Don't you think? Does the winner have to actually be present?"

"No, anybody can be the winner. So long as they are twenty-one and a resident of the US and there's no other impediment to them owning property."

"Great! Just stay right there. Jimmy are we ready to go live?"

"Ready!"

Indigo hands me the urn, whispering as she does so, "Don't worry, honey. It's all coming out right in the end." Then she makes her way down the stairs to stand beside Vic. Owen stays behind me, and I know it's not because he wants to be on camera. He's making a point of staying between me and Chip.

"Before we go live—anybody have a problem being filmed? Showing up on social media? This is your chance to step out of the room," I say.

Nobody moves.

"All right then. Here we go."

Jimmy gives a thumbs up with his free hand.

"Who is going to win the house?" I chirp, engaged in perhaps the most demanding acting role of my life. "Shout holly jolly Christmas if you're set to go!"

"Holly jolly Christmas!" most of the room echoes.

I put my hand into the urn, swish it around in the folded pieces of paper, grasp one and pull it out. And sigh, dramatically.

"Well?" a woman in the crowd calls out. "Who is it?"

"Jackson Masterson," I read.

"Yes!" Jackson fist pumps and does a little victory dance.

"Wait up a minute!" somebody else says. "That's the kid that was entering people. How do we know he didn't cheat?"

"He's not old enough to win!" a man shouts.

The crowd is more intense than they would be over the usual gift basket door prize and I'm quick to pour oil over the troubled waters. "I agree. It's not a valid entry. I'll draw another—"

"No fair!" Jackson says.

I ignore him and draw another slip. "Jackson again. We'll try again, shall we?" I reach into the urn, shuffle around in the papers, and draw another.

This time I don't bother to read it out loud. "Jackson, for the love of God! How many times did you enter?"

He smirks. "I wanted to win."

Victor comes to my rescue a little late. "You're disqualified for cheating."

"Somebody else should draw the name," one of the neighbors calls out. "Somebody whose father didn't murder the woman who lived in this house."

This crowd is getting ugly. "That's a wonderful idea," I say. "What about you? Come on up here."

"What, no!" He turns his back as Jimmy points the phone in his direction. "Don't you be filming me."

"You were warned," Serena says. "Stop complaining. I'll do it."

She climbs up to stand beside me and shoves her hand into the urn. "Let's see." She stirs the papers around for what seems like a ridiculously long time, then pulls one out, unfolds it, and reads, "Owen Masterson."

"Wait, what?" Owen says, behind me. "I didn't—"

"FlatzandSharpzers, there you have it," Lindy sings out. The winner of the house is Owen Masterson, fair and square. He's of age and a US resident and is not a family member or employee of Next Level parties. Stay tuned—I'll be covering developments in the murder trial of our own modern day Bonnie and Clyde, Skye Warner and Richard Winters, and I think you can count on inside intel."

Lindy freezes in position, big smile on her face, until Jimmy gives her the signal that the broadcast has ended.

She turns to me. "Thanks for bringing me in on this. I owe you one. I'll see you at the courthouse. You will let me know when the arraignment hearing is, won't you?"

I have no idea how I am going to know when the arraignment hearing is but I mumble my agreement anyway. "Right. Yes. Sure. Thanks again."

Lindy hugs me, then signals Jimmy and the two of them make their way through the crowd that is migrating toward the door.

"Not cool," Jackson complains. "I won."

"You cheated," Owen says. "Get your coat and wait outside. Take Nat."

"What's happened?" Jackson has picked up on Owen's tension.

"For once in your life, just do as I tell you."

Jackson opens his mouth to argue, but apparently sees something in his uncle's face that changes his mind. He turns and heads straight for Nat. A moment of conversation, hand gestures, gazes directed at us, and then they've collected the girl and are out the door.

Vic reads my face and body language the way he always does, and makes his way over. "What happened?"

When I don't answer right away he says, "Owen?"

"Cops will be here any minute," Owen says.

"Again? Coming back for Addy and Mom? I can't believe you didn't turn Richard in right away, Addy. What were you thinking? Maybe Johanna's attorney will step in. I'm out of my league with this."

"Chip Fitzwilliam might not be the best choice in legal representation," I say.

"Where is he, anyway?" Vic asks. "Is he still here?"

"Johanna's bedroom."

"What's he doing up there?"

"He was, um, indisposed."

Vic takes another look at me, then turns to Owen. "What's happened?"

Which is when we hear the siren. Guests who are leaving form a bottleneck at the door, all in a hurry to see what's happening outside. Stragglers look out the window.

I figured Alex and Cyril would both still be busy, but I'm wrong. Alex is back. He takes one look at my face, and instead of being a dick he just asks, "Where is he?"

"Johanna's bedroom."

"You all right?" Alex asks me.

I nod.

He turns to the room, raises his voice to official crowd control volume. "Everybody clear the building now, please. Make it quick. The party is over."

"Why?" It's the same guy who was complaining earlier about me drawing names.

"Because I'm going to start making arrests if people aren't out of here in two minutes," Alex bellows. "Starting the count-down now."

The complainer is one of the first out the door. Others follow.

"What is going on?" Mom asks.

"I'll tell you later. Take Daffodil outside, and wait a minute, will you?"

She nods and heads out, towing a reluctant Aunt Rachel behind her.

Alex looks at me and Owen and Vic and Britt and Indigo and apparently recognizes we're not going anywhere.

"At least move away from the stairs. I'd rather there are no more dead bodies today, if you all might consider cooperating."

We obligingly retreat while Alex ascends the staircase, service weapon in hand, looking like every cop in every show I've ever watched who is clearing a house while looking for a bad guy. We huddle together over by the tree, listening for shouting or gunshots but all is silent.

"Do you think we should check on him?" I whisper. "Maybe Christopher was, like, hiding behind a door and cracked him over the head."

"Christopher?" Vic asks.

"Chip is Christopher, remember?" I say. "Johanna's brother. Keep up."

"What did he do to you?"

"Just a little involuntary kissing," I say, trying to sound light and casual. Because, really, that's all that happened. But it feels like a much bigger violation. I add, "Also murder. Although I can't prove that yet."

Vic rolls his eyes. "Explain that leap of logic, would you? How on earth did you go from assault to murder?"

"What's this about murder?" Alex asks, coming down the

stairs. "Your assailant is gone. Over the balcony and through the back yard, looks like. Are you sure you want to press charges, Addy? Gonna be honest, with him being an attorney and if it was just kissing, it's going to be hard to make it stick."

"He killed her, Alex. And Ralph too."

Alex sighs. "This isn't the time for imaginative leaps, Addy. I've got two very valid suspects in custody."

I turn to Owen. "Give him the gun."

"He held you at gunpoint?" Alex asks.

"Not exactly."

"Not in the mood for games," he warns.

"Me either."

"So tell me what happened."

"I went upstairs to look for him because he'd been missing for awhile. He was already on my suspect list, okay? And him roaming off to explore by himself upstairs felt odd. Anyway, Owen came with me. Chip—Christopher—was in Johanna's room, with his back to us, digging around in a dresser drawer. He spun around and pointed a gun at us. He said he found it in her drawer, and that we'd startled him."

"And then?"

"He put the gun in the drawer. And then he grabbed me..." I pause for a breath. "And he... he kissed me..."

"Thoroughly," Owen says, darkly. "Addy told him to let her go and struggled to get away but he just started kissing her again..."

"And then I kneed him in the groin," I finish. "Good and hard. He sort of crumpled up. I didn't think it was a good idea to leave the gun with him so we took it with us."

"And it's where now?" Alex asks.

"If you've got some gloves on you I could avoid putting any more prints on it," Owen says.

Alex looks at us both. Sighs. Says, "Just a minute. Don't move."

He goes out the door and when he comes back he's got gloves for himself and Owen and an evidence bag.

"You know, it's possible that he actually did find this in Johanna's drawer," Alex says as Owen hands it over.

"If you run it for prints and ballistics I guess you'll know whether it's the gun that killed Ralph or not," I tell him. "Pretty sure Johanna didn't shoot him. Can ghosts shoot guns? They wouldn't leave fingerprints if they did, would they?"

"There's no such thing as ghosts," Alex says.

"I do have to differ with you on that point," Indigo says. "But they don't generally go around shooting people and when they do they don't leave fingerprints."

Alex chooses to ignore this. "What I'd like to know," he says, "Is how you knew that Ralph was shot. We haven't released those details to anybody. Did a ghost tell your resident psychic about that?"

"No, I looked out the window in Johanna's room. Which looks right into Ralph's TV room and the crime scene people were in there, and Julie, and he was lying on the floor with part of his head missing. Also, for what it's worth, I locked that window the day after Johanna's murder and closed the blinds. They were open and it wasn't locked. If Ralph's window was also open..."

"You're saying you think that Ralph's attorney went upstairs in the home of his murdered client, opened the window, got Ralph, his other client, to open his window, and then shot him?" Alex starts out sarcastically, but by the time he's done he sounds like he might have convinced himself. "Shit. But why? Why would Chip Fitzwilliam kill either of them?"

"I don't know that for sure, but he's not really Chip Fitzwilliam. We don't think. We're pretty sure he's Christopher Cunningham, Johanna's stepbrother, who has been missing and presumed dead for years."

"Unbelievable," Alex says. "And you didn't tell me because?"

"Because I just confirmed he might still be alive when you came over. And he was standing right there and I didn't want to tell you in front of him, and then we had the Skye drama, and you weren't here to tell."

"And now, we have a whole group of people who know before I have a chance to look into it. I suppose I should be grateful that Lindy Lind person has gone." He stands up straight and puts on his cop face, fixing each of us with an authoritative gaze in turn. "You are not to say a word of any of this to anybody, do you understand?"

Everybody nods.

The door opens and Nat and Jackson come in, trailed by Mom and Serena and Aunt Rachel. "It's cold out there," Jackson says. "What's going on?"

"Nothing." Alex turns to Owen. "I suggest that you take your nephew home at once. Nat, I'll drive you to your place and you will stay there until further notice."

"Why?" Jackson asks.

"Because I said so," Alex says. "The rest of you... out of here ASAP, understood? Lock the doors and stay gone until I have a chance to actually do an investigation."

"Aye, aye Sir," I can't help saying, because even though he's doing his job and he's right to kick us out of here, I always go contrary when somebody gets authoritative.

He glares at me.

"I can't go quite yet," I tell him. "Ricky is coming back for the coffin. We need to put the food away."

"Well, hurry it up," he says. "I'll put out a search for Fitzwilliam in the meantime." He strides toward the door, then turns back to say, "Don't be stupid, Addy, for once in your life. You are not invincible. Nat. Let's go."

Alex ushers Nat out the door with a hand on his shoulder, leaving the rest of us caught in a freeze frame moment, which is broken by Jackson.

"Oh, man, what did we miss?"

"I'll tell you in the car," Owen says. His eyes find mine, intense, searching. "Listen to Alex, Addy, please," he says. "Don't do anything stupid. If you'd been hurt...or killed... I..." His breath snags on something in his throat. He bends his head and I think he's going to kiss me, but he turns abruptly, collects Jackson, and the two of them are gone.

Serena starts transferring cookies and pastries into storage bags. Vic rummages around in the kitchen drawers and locates a black trash bag. "Come on, Britt, let's catch the trash." He holds it open and she starts throwing leftovers and paper plates and cups into it.

Mom sinks down onto the sofa and eases Daffodil down beside her. "I'd forgotten how exhausting it is lugging a little one around," she says. And then, "Should we find an attorney for Richard, do you suppose? And for Skye? They are family."

Aunt Rachel is not about to either leave or pitch in and lend a hand when there's some juicy gossip to be had. She plops down in an armchair with a couple of shortbread cookies she snagged before Serena could bag them.

"I can't believe you actually harbored that woman in your home, Bethany," she says, nibbling away with apparently no qualms about ruining dinner. "It's a wonder you didn't wake up dead in your bed."

"She's such a sweet girl, really. I can't understand how she could have lied to us all."

"You do know what she does for a living?" Vic asks.

"Women do all sorts of things just in order to survive, don't they? I blame your father."

Given that Skye was doing what she was doing long before she met Dad, this seems unfair but I'm not in any mood to stick up for him.

"Addy, fetch me the diaper bag, will you?" Mom says.

I look at Daffodil, peacefully sleeping. "You're going to wake her up to change her diaper?"

"No, I want to have a look at Skye's cellphone. I saw her drop it in there earlier."

"How are you going to do that? She unlocks it with her face."

"It updated overnight and it wanted a password this morning. I happened to be looking over her shoulder while she entered it."

I hand her the bag. "And you memorized it? I'm impressed."

"Everybody knows you're not supposed to use 1234," Mom says. "So I guess she thought 0987 would be better." She taps the keys as she says it, and sure enough, the phone unlocks. Mom opens text messaging and right up front is a convo between Dad and Skye.

Rich: How did you find me?

Skye: Super sleuth skills?

Rich: You're tracking my phone.

Skye: What do you expect?

Rich: You wanted money. I'm getting it for you

Skye: Ha! You're lying. You're cheating on me

Rich: She says she's dying. I'm now in her will.

Skye: She looks pretty healthy to me.

Rich: I promise I'll take care of you. And Daff.

Skye: I'm thinking maybe I'll meet the family while I'm here. Addy first, right? She sounds like an easier mark than Victor or your wife

Rich: Skye, don't

Rich: Skye!!!

Skye: I'm at the Twilight Motel, Be here by 9 am or I'm going to Addy

Rich: Answer your damn phone! We need to talk.

"Well, that explains why she didn't come to my place when she first arrived in town," I say. "So where's her car? Maybe she's got an accomplice."

"Can I see?" Britt asks, and Mom hands over the phone.

"Uber," Britt says, a minute later. "She hired an Uber driver. He picked her up... let's see... in the Walmart parking lot." She hands the phone back to Mom and heads for the coat closet. I think she's leaving, but she retrieves her backpack and carries it over to the table, where she proceeds to set up her laptop.

"But why kill Ralph?" Indigo asks. "I see her being jealous of Johanna. Or wanting her dead so your father could inherit and split the money. But how does he fit in?"

I don't want to bother Alex right now, but I also don't want to keep information from him, so I send a text:

> Addy: FYI—Skye ubered to my place. Her car might be in the Walmart parking lot
>
> Alex: Have you gone home yet?
>
> Addy: Give me a minute. Also, you're welcome
>
> Alex: 🫤

Britt frowns at her laptop screen. "This can't be right."

"What?" Vic drops the dishrag he was using to wipe down the table and sits down beside her.

"I got to wondering about the other attorneys in Chip's firm. So I researched them."

"And?"

"They don't exist. Or at least, there are no board-certified attorneys in Washington state by those names."

"How is that possible? They've got a big-ass sign outside. Advertising flyers. Charlene was complaining about the extra hassle of working for three attorneys instead of one."

"Who is Charlene?" Indigo asks, plopping into a chair at the table and setting a plate of cookies rescued from Serena's storage bags in front of her. There are two of Mom's shortbread cookies on there, and I sit beside her and grab them both.

Greedy, yes, but I'm striking while the iron is hot. I may never get another chance.

"Char is Chip's front office manager," I say, with my mouth full.

"So call her up," Indigo says. "Ask her."

"She's certainly not going to talk to me. Let's just say we're not the best of friends."

"Me neither. She'd know you're the reason I'm asking." Britt dips a carrot stick into ranch dip, as far as she's ever going to fall into dietary decadence, and crunches away.

Vic sighs. "Give me her number. I assume you can find that, Britt?"

A minute later he's dialing. I stand right behind him to ensure I'll be able to hear. "Charlene, hey. It's Vic."

"What does Addy want now?"

"What *I* want," he says, "is to make sure you're safe. I'm a little worried about you, to be honest."

"Oh? And why would that be?" But her tone has shifted. She's listening. Which means she knows there might be good reason to worry.

"It's that attorney you're working for. There was a little incident with Addy, earlier. He seems volatile."

"Addy probably provoked him."

"Well, yes. She's good at that. She's provoked me often enough." He laughs, making a connection, turning Charlene into an ally. "You're not at the office, right? Given that it's Christmas and all. Are you at your folks' place?"

"Yes. What's this about, Victor?"

"We don't think Chip is who he says he is. And he has... had... a gun. I think maybe you shouldn't go home tonight, okay? Can you stay at your parents'?"

"You're scaring me."

"Don't want to scare you too much, just be careful. And if you see him or hear from him, let the cops know. Maybe we should warn the other partners in the firm?"

A long silence follows, and then Vic says, gently, "Are there actually other attorneys, Charlene?"

"He's trying to establish himself," she says, defensively. "He says it just looks more appealing to clients if he's part of a firm. What harm does it do?"

"Probably none," Vic agrees. "If that's all there is to it."

"I signed a NDA. I promised not to reveal that information. You'll get me fired. Or sued, or whatever."

Or dead, I think.

"I wouldn't worry about that. Just... stay where you are. Don't go home alone. Don't go to the office."

"All right." She sounds on the edge of tears, and for possibly the first time in my life I feel sorry for her.

"Thank you Victor. Merry Christmas."

"Merry Christmas, Char."

Vic hangs up and looks at us all soberly. "Not sure how much of that you heard, but there are, in fact, no partners. And now, I think we need to all clear out of here. Mom, I'll drive you and Daffodil. And we'll drop Britt off at her place. Everybody else, go home to your families."

"Or come on over and join us," Mom says. "Serena? You're welcome too, Indigo."

This invite is a Christmas miracle, even though Mom has no takers.

"Oh, I'm going to my daughter's place," Serena says. "But thank you. I do believe I'll head over there right now. Merry

Christmas, Addy. You'll be sure to let me know when this is all solved?"

"You bet." I give her a hug. "Thanks for everything."

She gets her coat from the closet and bustles out the door. Vic ushers Mom and Daffodil and Britt out to his car, coaxing Aunt Rachel along, which leaves me and Indigo.

CHAPTER 26

Indigo finishes her last bite of cookie. Wipes her mouth with the napkin. "You should have kicked him harder, Addy. When you had the chance. Are we really waiting around for that anxious young undertaker?"

"No. He's actually not coming back until tomorrow. I just wanted everybody to clear out."

"Which gives us another opportunity to snoop!"

"Well, that, and I thought maybe we should collect your cameras, in case Alex and the team decide they want another search. Also so we can look at footage. You will come to Mom's for dinner? And then you can come up to the condo for the night. We can review the camera feeds then. Besides, it might be safer."

"I believe I'm safer if I'm not too close to you. Maybe you should stay at your mother's."

"You think he's coming for me?"

"We know he doesn't have a problem eliminating loose

ends. Best to be prepared." She roots around in her bag and brings out her gun. She checks it, makes sure it's loaded, all of her moves smooth and practiced. "If you're going to involve yourself in any more murders, you should get yourself one of these," she says. "And go to the shooting range and learn to use it. Maybe a self-defense class while you're at it."

And then, because of course, she also pulls a holster out of her bag, buckles it around her hips, slides the gun into it, and then rearranges her floaty tunic over all.

"Now. Let's make sure all the doors and windows are locked. You take the upstairs."

I run up the stairs and start checking windows. When I open the door to Johanna's bedroom, Chip is coming in through the slider that leads out onto the balcony.

"We meet again," he says, with a sinister smile.

"Hello, Christopher. If you're looking for the gun, it's not here. Alex has it."

He shrugs. "Circumstantial. You saw me pick it up out of Johanna's drawer. Of course my prints would be on it. You know where they won't be found? On the trigger. Don't do that, Addy. You're not going anywhere."

I'd been backing up but I stop at his command. He's pointing a gun at me.

"Stupid of you to believe I wouldn't have another," he says. "And that I wouldn't come back for you. You know too much."

My ears are tuned, hopefully, for any sound from outside the room. Like, Indigo, warned by her supernatural abilities, on her way to rescue me. Or an approaching siren, if she's called 911. But I hear nothing other than my own harsh breathing. Maybe I can keep him talking and buy time for someone to rescue me. Feed his ego. Give him a chance to feel powerful and important before he eliminates me.

"I don't know nearly enough," I say. "I mean, it was very clever of you to shoot Ralph through this window. But I can't figure out why. Did it have to do with the book he borrowed?"

"Ralph was a meddler, like you. Couldn't leave well enough alone and he knew to much. Also like you."

"Alex knows who you are. You know you won't get away with this." My voice is wobbly and he smiles. I can tell that he likes my fear and I do my best to hide it.

"Oh, but I will. They can't prove anything," he says. "So what if they figure out that I'm Christopher? All the better. That way I can contest the will. They can't prove it was me that killed either Johanna or Ralph. If you hadn't still been here, snooping, you wouldn't have to die." He motions with the gun. "Downstairs."

"Why?"

"Do you ever just do anything without asking questions? Just walk down the stairs. Slowly."

I turn around and start walking. It's one of the hardest things I've ever had to do, knowing he's right behind me with that gun. That he could shoot me at any moment. And the only thing I can do to make it better is to keep him talking because somehow it seems impossible that he'll pull the trigger at the same time that words are coming out of his mouth.

"I talked to your mother," I tell him. "She misses you. Maybe, instead of shooting me, you could make a run for it. Go back there."

"My mother chose Gary over me. She wanted me to work for him, to spend the rest of my life in a run-down second-hand car lot. The man who beat me like it was his religion all through my childhood. I wanted to go live with my real father, ran away one summer to visit.

"But guess what? Dad loved his precious little angel Johanna. She was with him for the summer and he couldn't do enough for her. Anything she wanted he showered on her head. Me? I wasn't good enough for him. I asked him to let me live with him. His response? 'Get in the car, son, I'll drive you home.'

"And when he died, that little snot Johanna inherited everything. The house, all his money. Injury free. And what did she do with it? Holed herself up in her mother's house. All that money, and she barely touched it."

I pause at the bottom of the stairs, wondering if there's some way to get my hands on my bag. Bear spray against a gun is a long shot, but better than nothing.

"Keep moving," he says. "Go stand in front of the coffin."

I turn to face him. "Chip. Christopher. You don't have to—"

"Do it. Or I'll hurt you. You're going to die one way or another, but there's quick and painless, or there's me beating you up first and dragging you to the coffin by your hair. Your call."

I start walking, as slowly as I can get away with. Surely Indigo wouldn't just take off and abandon me to be murdered by this psychopath.

Unless she's in league with Christopher. Unless there's something in the house that she's after too.

"Is that what you did to Johanna?" I ask. "Beat her senseless so she wouldn't fight when you took her outside and hung her?"

I already know this isn't true because of what Dad saw, but I want to keep him talking.

He laughs. "I drugged her. Drugged them both, actually. Your father made such a fun and convenient patsy. It was all I could do to keep from laughing. Him thinking he was running the biggest scam of his life. And me, scamming him right out of his freedom."

"It all seems rather an elaborate way to get your hands on Johanna's money."

"That's just it!" I can hear the anger rising in his voice. "Why was it her money? He was my father too, every bit as much as he was hers. So why did she inherit everything? And why wouldn't she share it with me? You know what's really funny? I didn't actually plan this. Stop right there."

I stop as instructed. I'm standing in front of the coffin, a terrible, horrible understanding of what exactly he means to do sending a fresh wave of panic through me. The thought of being locked inside that coffin, even though I'm pretty sure I'm going to be dead and won't care anymore, makes my legs turn to jelly.

If I must die, maybe I can die bravely. I'm pretty sure the cameras are still recording. On the off chance that Indigo doesn't come back for them, maybe Alex will find them. Maybe at least they will know what Chip has done. Might as well get a full confession out of him if I can.

"So, what, you just ended up here in Fox Valley with no idea she was here? I find that hard to believe."

"Oh, I knew she was here. And I had every intention of getting my hands on the house and the property and the money. But I was content to wait. Contrary to what you're thinking, I'm not a murderer."

That makes me turn around. After all, he's going to shoot me anyway. Might as well be looking at him when it happens.

"Hate to break it to you, but you are a murderer, Christopher," I say, as bravely as I can. "You killed Johanna. You killed Ralph. And now you're planning on killing me."

"All of you made me do it," he says. "It's not like I've killed anybody before. I didn't torture animals or burn down houses."

"So this was all a coincidence? You being Johanna's attorney. Making her will. And then you just randomly decided to kill her?"

He shrugs. "Divine intervention. I knew she lived here. I send out those flyers specifically to people on this block. Ralph enlisted me to make him a will. That was a stroke of luck. He was one of the few people she actually communicated with, trading books. Poor bastard actually did like to read. I gave him a discount on his services in exchange for him referring neighbors my way. And then, she actually called. When she opened the door, she didn't recognize me. Didn't have a clue who I was."

"Maybe because she thought you were dead?"

He scoffs. "She knew I was alive. She didn't want me to have anything. That's the minute when I decided to kill her. I asked her, "What's the real reason you want to give the house away? You could come up with some other gimmick to get people here." And you know what she said? She said, 'I want to make sure my brother doesn't get his hands on it.' That, after all the pain I suffered. The scars I live with. 'I want to make sure my brother doesn't get his hands on it.' Can you believe that?"

"And her brother isn't going to get his hands on it," I say, "because she gave the house to Dad."

"Who is going to spend the rest of his life in prison. I did a good job of framing him to start with, and then he improved on my work."

"How did you pull that all off, anyway?"

"Brought over a celebratory bottle of champagne as a gift for completing the will. Popped the cork, poured myself a glass and doctored the bottle. Came back later to find Rich sleeping like a baby and Johanna in a perfect state of tractability. Of course, being outdoors, not to mention the cold and snow, woke her up nicely. Would have hated for her to miss out on the suffering."

I'd been wondering why he didn't just shoot her the way he did Ralph, but I get it now. Ralph's death was an execution, quick and clean. But Chip wanted revenge on Johanna. He wanted her to suffer a protracted and terrifying death. How much revenge is he going to want on me for kicking him? Maybe I can't fight him, or save myself, but I can try to minimize any pleasure he'll get from my death. I don't want him to get off on my fear.

"Champagne? Didn't Johanna think that was a trifle unusual for her attorney to want to celebrate her imminent death?" My voice only wobbles a tiny bit, although I'm sure he hears it.

He barks out a laugh. "A trifle judgmental for the woman who throws parties for dead people."

He has a point. And I can see why he thinks he'll get away with this. If I'm dead, he's the default executor. Also the long-lost brother. If there's no proof, even motive won't be enough to convict him. He doesn't know about the cameras, though. On the off chance that Indigo hasn't betrayed me, he's digging his own grave even as he's digging mine.

"Why kill Ralph?" I ask. "I know how you killed him, but

I'm trying to figure out why? If he witnessed the murder, you wouldn't have waited until today. Something to do with the crypto key, right?"

Christopher's jaw tightens. "What do you know about that?"

"It fell out of the book when he came over to fetch it. It wasn't his book. It was hers. But he wanted that book, specifically. You know what? I bet he did see something. He was blackmailing you. You left the crypto key in the book, and he came over to get it and lost it and you killed him anyway. Something like that?"

Christopher laughs. "You are not nearly as smart as you think you are," he scoffs. "You are right about the one thing. Ralph saw me in the back yard, tying the rope around the tree branch earlier in the day, so I wouldn't have to mess with it later. I would never have known he knew anything, but he got greedy. Instead of calling the cops, he called me after Johanna's murder, said he knew it was me and that he'd keep his mouth shut for fifty thousand.

"Obviously at that point he was always going to die, but the timing was bad. So I had some fun with him to keep him quiet for a bit. I told him I'd give him the money in crypto coin. That I'd leave the key in Johanna's copy of *The Women* and all he'd have to do is sneak into the house and get it. Poor bastard thought he was going to be rich. When I was here early this morning to take one more look at the place where Johanna died, he opened his window and berated me because I didn't put the key in the book after all. Told me he was going to turn me in. It was as good a time as any to shoot him."

"The cops have the key," I tell him. "They'll make the connection and figure out it was you."

He laughs again. "It wasn't even a real crypto key. I just made it up. Like I said, I was only buying time. The cops have a meaningless string of numbers and letters. Enough delaying tactics. Turn around and open the coffin. And then get in. No point getting blood all over my house."

"It's not your house. It belongs to Dad. It's going to be Owen's."

"Now!"

When I watch movies and the victim does whatever the guy with the gun tells her, I always think she's stupid to comply. Don't get in the car. Don't get in the coffin. He's gonna shoot you anyway. But the gun has a sort of hypnotic effect on me and I turn around and do as he says.

As soon as the lid lifts, Indigo sits up like she's spring loaded, the gun in her hand. Pointed directly at my heart.

The organ in question spasms and leaps. I'm struck by a sharp sense of betrayal. She was in on it. And now she's going to kill me.

"Duck," she says.

There's a sharp crack and a wet splat. Christopher gasps. I look up from where I've dropped to the floor. The gun falls in slow motion from his hand. His other hand presses against his chest. A red stain crimsons out, soaking his shirt. His mouth gapes open, his eyes wide in bewilderment.

He staggers back a pace, swaying on his feet. "You shot me."

"Get the gun, Addy," Indigo orders and I scrabble over to it on hands and knees.

Even as his legs give way and he sinks down to the ground he gasps, "Missed my heart. I'll deny everything I told you. You have no proof..."

"Everything is on camera dear," Indigo says. "Call 911, would you, Addy? And then help me get out of this coffin. Your father was right. It isn't as easy as it looks."

I call 911. And then I help Indigo out of the coffin. She kneels beside Christopher to assess the damage. "You'll live long enough to stand trial," she says, applying pressure to the wound. "At least I hope so. Johanna knew your father's death wasn't an accident, by the way. Which would certainly be another reason to kill her."

"You can't prove that either," he says, faintly.

"Possibly not. But I do make recordings of all of my client calls. And this one was special. I'm not sure what went wrong with your plan. Why you were still in the house when it blew up and she wasn't. But Johanna told me what you said, when they brought you out of the house. Before the paramedics took you away, and she ran over to you, in shock. She said you were burned and bleeding and half dead, and still, you whispered, 'It was supposed to be you.'"

He shakes his head, weakly, a denial. His eyes flutter closed.

"Don't you die on us," Indigo says. "Don't you dare."

I hear the siren and run for the door, guiding the ambulance crew through the house to where Chip is sprawled on the floor. He's pale as death and there's way too much blood but apparently he's still breathing. As the flurry of life saving activity commences Indigo looks up at me and smiles. "Don't you worry, honey. He'll live. There is absolutely a judge and jury in his future. The cards told me and the cards never lie."

TUESDAY
DECEMBER 31

CHAPTER 27

INDIGO WAS RIGHT ABOUT CHIP, aka Christopher. He's still in the hospital, recovering well, but there's a guard outside his door. Just a few more days, and off to jail he goes. No charges have been filed against Indigo, given that the shooting was in self-defense and definitely saved my life. Dad and Skye have both been released and yes, Dad has been staying in my condo for the last couple of days, but trust me. It's temporary.

We've all gathered at *Grounded* to sign over Johanna's house to Owen. There was some idle chat about doing this at the house in question, but nobody but Jackson, who maintains his enthusiasm for calling it 'the murder house,' wanted to do that. For me, in particular, it's the almost-*my*-murder house, and I haven't been able to bring myself to go back there, yet.

Indigo insists that she's scrubbed up all of the blood and any mess left behind by the ambulance crew and the cops, and has also smudged every single crevice and corner.

"Absolutely clean and clear and ready for new owners," she says.

"What did you have to go and do that for?" Jackson grumps. "My coffin video went viral. We could have made money if we kept it in there. Admission fees for ghost hunters and true crime lovers. And now you've gone and evicted all of the ghosts as well?"

You can't blame him. Besides the money making option, apparently he's got all sorts of girls wanting to meet him. Death and the trappings thereof are glamorous to a certain type of person. Owen isn't happy about any of it.

"We're not living in that house," he says, in a tone of voice that makes it clear this is not the first time they've had this conversation. "As soon as Addy gets the estate liquidators in to remove all of the furniture and Johanna's personal belongings, we'll put it up for sale."

"If you didn't want to keep it, why did you enter the drawing?" Mom asks, which would be a logical question if we didn't all know who actually entered Owen in the first place.

"For the last time, I did not enter Uncle Owen!" Jackson shouts, loud enough to turn the heads of all the other customers in our direction. He lowers his voice a little, though not nearly enough, as he continues. "I entered myself, in case you didn't notice. Repeatedly. I was banking on winning it. Why would I put his name in there?"

"Let's just get this transfer thing done so Char can go be with her family," I suggest, soothingly. "Dad signs first. Then Owen. Then Char does her notary thing and we're done." I shove the papers across the table toward Dad. When I sit back, I can see that all eyes at the table are on me. "What are you all looking at?"

"You had more access to the entry process than anybody," Skye says. "And all the reason in the world to want Owen to live here. There's obviously something going on between the two of you. Just admit it. You pulled some strings."

"No offense, Addy," Dad says, in the tone that always means some sort of offense is coming. "But you are maybe just a little insecure. Needy."

Nobody speaks up to contradict him.

"We all know Addison has daddy issues," Mom says, cuddling Daffodil. "Whose fault is that, I wonder?"

It's clear this attack on Dad is in no way a defense of me. She's just had more than enough of him, and now there is Daffodil to consider.

My eyes travel around the table and I can see that they all agree with Dad to varying degrees. And maybe they are partly right. I am a little insecure. But I am absolutely not needy. Stupid, yes. I did want a relationship with Dad, badly enough to trust him, a mistake I won't be making again. But I've never been a cheater.

"You all seriously think I'd cheat like that? Manipulate the system so Owen would move back to Fox Valley? Like he couldn't do that on his own if he wanted to? Owen? You think this too?"

"I don't think you're needy or insecure," he says. What he doesn't say is that he knows I would never try to manipulate him into living here by choosing his name for the house.

The truth is, I'm not sure I want him to live here. The idea of a distance relationship, with occasional hot sex and joint vacations sounds much more manageable than a long term, committed relationship. I'm not sure what that would even look like.

But I want Owen to want it. He usually seems to understand me almost as well as Victor does, but finds my faults endearing rather than annoying. The thought that he thinks I'd try to manipulate him into moving here is so bitter that even a swallow of my perfect caramel macchiato fails to sweeten it.

Indigo clears her throat. "I entered Owen for the drawing," she says, calmly. "You all owe Addy an apology. Also, Mr. Winters, I think it's important for you to understand that your daughter managing to hold an open space in her heart for a relationship with you is not neediness, but an act of courage you are incapable of even perceiving. Now. Let's complete this paperwork transaction, shall we?"

That does it. I'm grateful to Indigo for standing up for me, but it makes me feel like I'm back at school and a well-meaning teacher has told the kids to stop bullying me. Like I'm not capable and competent to stand up for myself. I very nearly shove my chair back and storm out in tears, even though I know it would escalate the drama. Indigo lays a gentle hand on my arm and for the briefest of flashes of insight, I see us all through her eyes.

Skye, a frightened and defiant child doing her best to find her way in a difficult world and care for a child of her own. Mom, worn out with responsibility but willing to take on both Skye and Daffodil and somehow dredge up love for them both. Dad, the boy who never grew up. Vic, trying to extricate himself from the legacy Dad left us and figure out what sort of man he really wants to be. Jackson, angry and frightened and bewildered by a life that so far has been anything but fair. Owen, torn between responsibility and his own dreams and goals and hopes. Britt, caught as always between loyalty to me and the way she feels about Vic.

All of them are my family. Imperfect, yes. But we've been through a lot together. Maybe they think I'm needy and insecure, but they love me anyway. Well, at least some of them do. I'll explain to Owen later, about me and long term relationships. It's a conversation we need to have. For now, everything is, if not exactly good, good enough.

I lift my macchiato in the air and say, loud and clear, "God bless us, every one."

Owen's gaze finds mine as he lifts his coffee cup and taps it against mine. "To a future with you in it," he says.

"To a future with you in it," I echo. It's Owen I'm talking to, but in my heart I include the others.

The bitterness I've been choking on has vanished. Owen and I will figure it out as we go. There are parties to plan, a baby sister to love, and, with any luck, plenty more mysteries to be solved.

ACKNOWLEDGMENTS

If you are reading this page, presumably you've also read the book. Thank you! This is a happy and satisfying thing for me as a writer, and hopefully for you as a reader, especially since this book acted at times as if it really didn't want to be written.

I owe a tremendous amount of gratitude to a great number of people and am horribly afraid that I'm going to miss thanking somebody here but hopefully I get it right.

Sandi (aka the magical Maddie Dawson) thank you for meeting me for our zoom writing dates. This kept me in my chair and my fingers on the keys even when I was in doubt up to my eyeballs and life chaos was swirling all around my ears. (Or, as the Viking would say, "I was up to my ass in alligators").

Huge thanks to Jennifer Moorman for always holding the positive vibe and believing in me and Addy and the book—your enthusiasm is infectious.

Pam Parisi—thank you for being the very first reader, and for the notes you sent while you were reading that set me to laughing and made me hope other readers would find the humor as well.

Heather Webb, my lovely and magical friend, thank you for the keen eye and fabulous insights and helping me keep the faith.

Trudy Morgan-Cole, huge appreciation for seeing all of

those pesky details my eyes were blind to. Also for being my very first ever writer friend, way back in the misty past.

Aimie Runyan, thank you for your ongoing support and your brilliant suggestions for the cover.

To cover designer Steven Novak, mega thanks for deciphering from my not clear comments what it was that I wanted and coming up with such a fun and captivating cover.

And to The Dream Team: thank you all for reading, commenting, reviewing, and otherwise supporting me and Addy on this journey.

Last of all, thank YOU reader, for embarking on this reading adventure. There would be no point in writing the books if you were not on the other end to read them.

ABOUT THE AUTHOR

Kerry Schafer (aka Kerry Anne King) is an Amazon Charts and Washington Post bestselling author. Known for her lyrical writing and memorable characters, Kerry weaves deep emotional insights, humor, and often a touch of magic into all of her tales. *A Party to Die For* is her fifteenth novel.

In addition to writing, Kerry co-hosts the One Happy Thing podcast with bestselling authors Jennifer Moorman and Maddie Dawson, and is the creator of Author Genie, which provides virtual assistant services to fellow authors.

Kerry lives in a small town in northeastern Washington with her real-life Viking and a crew of neurotic rescue animals whose favorite pastime is interrupting her writing.

Visit her at her website, www.allthingskerry.com.

instagram.com/all.things.kerry

facebook.com/kerry.schafer